IN MY POWER

POWER

A MURDER MYSTERY

by

R. S. DORIAN

Cover design by R. S. Dorian

ISBN   978-1-7353570-3-4

Published by Moonlight Alley Books
www.moonlightalleybooks.com

IN MY POWER

PROLOGUE

Rylen sat up in the bed, looking about the unfamiliar room and waiting for his memory to come back to him, but after half a minute, he had no idea where he was. The room was lit by a shallow light spilling in from the open door of a walk-in closet in the far corner. His eyes were the only thing that moved in the stillness, taking in the details of the room while his brain worked to recall how he had come to be there. They fell across the naked form of the woman who lay in the bed next to him. Her back was to him, and her bare torso rose and fell with the slow and unmistakable rhythm of the sound sleeper. He became aware of something else--he was naked as well. There was one thing the confused man was sure of as seconds crept into minutes: his memory would not be returning anytime soon.

Distantly wondering why he did not want to wake her, Rylen slid out of bed. He moved to his clothes that lay in a pile against the wall and dressed as silently as he could, the plush carpeting on the floor muffling his movements. What was the last thing he could remember? He had been at an event of some kind, but after that was a complete blank. He was putting on one of his finest suits, which had been carelessly piled in a heap like used hotel towels. But he was not in a hotel. He had stayed in too many to make any mistake, even if the walk-in closet and all too personal décor of the room had not furnished this information.

There was a four-by-six-foot painting on the wall across the room, mounted evenly between the door to the closet and a door out of the bedroom. It depicted a young, muscular man, kneeling naked with his hands bound behind his back. Standing in front of him was the flawless form of a woman in black heels with a garter belt and dark stockings, her head and shoulders cropped out of the top of the frame. She was holding a riding crop that touched the man under the chin, guiding his eyes up to a face left forever to the imagination. It was a masterwork. The gleam of the shoes, lacquered red fingernails, and even the nylons on the woman were exquisitely done. The enraptured look of the bound man was perfectly readable, even in profile. The bewildered Rylen had taken in its quality in an instant, despite the subtle lighting of the room. The gallery would never show art of that subject matter.

That was it; the memory hit him in a flash. He had been at a silent auction at the art gallery. That was where he met her, the woman in the bed. This was her home. It had to be. They connected immediately, and Rylen had found her captivating. Did he have too much to drink? Yes, that had to be it. He had one too many drinks, and she had invited him back to her place to have sex and sleep it off. Did they even have sex? He had been naked, but why could he remember nothing else? Not even her name was coming back to him. Was this enough for him to wake her and find out more about the missing hours? Perhaps, but there was another problem with his theory. Rylen never got drunk. He never had more than one.

A quick peek through the closed drapes showed him he was on the first floor of a house, and an expensive one, if the other homes he could see on the well-lit street were any indication. Good. He would not have far to go. Dressing as quickly and silently as he could, he took up his blazer, necktie, and shoes before making his way into the other room.

He found himself in a spacious, open-plan living room and dining area. It was tastefully and expensively furnished.

He put his wingtips down on the carpet and slipped them on, less worried about disturbing the sleeping woman from here. A lamp on a corner stand in the dining room provided what light he needed. Feeling his trouser pockets, to his relief, both his wallet and car keys were there. He crammed the necktie into the side pocket of his suit jacket, but halted in his movement to the front door, realizing that there was another obvious problem.

If he had been drugged and lost his memory, how likely was it he drove himself in the first place? He went to a bay window in the dining room and parted the drapes. He was in luck. The window looked out to the driveway, the dark form of his Cadillac visible thirty feet from where he stood. He unlocked the doors with his key fob to be certain. The car glowed to life.

Rylen turned and headed to the front door.

"I can make you some coffee before you leave," came a soft voice that froze him in his tracks. The woman was standing next to a lamp atop an end table beside the couch. She touched a switch on the base of the lamp and it bathed the room in a soft, yellow light, illuminating both the woman and the subtle smirk on her face. The question was not asked with a tone of concerned sincerity, but with a none-too-well-hidden sarcasm. She was naked except for black thigh-high stockings with a thick band of lace at the tops. Rylen noticed that a white satin robe lay over the arm of the couch. She raised an eyebrow questioningly and his eyes moved from the robe and back to hers. He held her gaze in awkward silence for a few seconds, waiting for her to become... what? Modest? Self-conscious? Whatever he had been expecting, she made no move to cover herself.

Snippets of what had transpired between them flashed back to him. They did have sex. Not just any sex, but the very best sex of his life, and for him, that was saying quite a lot. The reason he'd been so keen to leave without waking her became obvious now. There was another feeling that rose above the confusion that had taken hold of him when he saw her. This feeling was causing his heart to pound hard enough to cause the misaligned buttons on his shirt to move. Fear.

For some reason he had yet to figure out, he feared this woman, and he did not want her to know that he was completely ignorant of all that had happened between them. If she had slipped something into his drink, she would already know about his memory loss. If not, he would not place himself at an even greater disadvantage. He decided he would make his excuses and leave, then figure all of it out later.

"No," he said, hoping to pass off his unease as her having startled him. "I have to go and I didn't want to wake you."

"It's four o'clock in the morning," she answered, looking more amused than insulted or hurt.

"I need to be up early." He no longer cared how unconvincing he was. The flustered man gave up all pretense and turned for the door.

"You going to keep that as a memento?" she asked to his back.

He turned back sharply. "What?"

She pointed a finger toward his neck and tapped her own, so he would know exactly where she was pointing. Rylen raised his hand to feel a band of leather fastened around his neck which, until that very moment, he had not known was there. How had he gotten dressed and not noticed it before? His blazer still over one arm, he felt it with both hands and found the buckle. He removed it, his neck now cold the instant the air of the room touched it.

He found himself holding a thick collar of black leather, the inner side warm where it had rested against his skin for some time. The woman moved toward him with her hand out to receive it, but he tossed it to the couch, ignoring her and retreating from her advance. A thousand questions flooded his brain as he walked to the door, but he dared not ask a single one. He knew that one question would lead to others, and then he might never bring himself to leave.

"Your phone is on the table by the door," she called as he reached the door and opened it to the chilly morning air. He took his phone without pausing. "You have my number," he heard her say before he swung the door closed. Even that last statement, called in a voice that was loud enough to ensure he didn't miss it, was loaded with layers of meaning.

Safely behind the wheel of his car in her driveway, Rylen sat in silence, struggling to collect himself. He wanted to be away with all possible speed, but taking another minute to think would not make any difference. What had just happened? She must have drugged him. It was the only thing that made sense. They met at the gallery and came back here, to her home, where she drugged him and they had kinky sex until passing out. He wasn't entirely without memory. Glimpses of her riding him and his repeated orgasmic climax flickered through his brain. He grabbed onto the many fragments like random puzzle pieces. Soon he would have his memory back. Had he even used protection? He would have to get himself checked. All of these thoughts were secondary to the one that troubled him the most: why had he been so afraid of her?

When one wakes up naked in bed with a total stranger and has no memory of where he is or how he got there, he is sure to be shaken by the experience to some extent. Anyone would be. Could that be all it was? No. If he accepted so inadequate an explanation in an attempt to assuage his need to paint a complete picture, he would be cheating himself of the true answer. The fear he had felt with her was real, and it had not manifested from an awkward memory lapse. What had happened to him had not been voluntary... or had it been? The parts he was slowly recalling made him think he had been an eager participant. It was not a physical fear, but a psychological one that overtook him. She was no physical threat to him. At six foot three and well over 200 pounds, there was little chance of her overpowering him. Nor did she even try to appear threatening. In some way he could not fully understand, she had made of him a sexual tool.

That was the explanation for the fear. He had lost all control and had not been able to help himself. The easy and amused confidence of that woman was all the confirmation he needed.

She was aware of both her superior position and his total ignorance. Rylen was used to being the smartest person in the room and seldom had he ever been mistaken. In business, he could not afford to allow anyone to gain the upper hand from the other side of a negotiating table. This manic control carried into every aspect of his career and personal life as well. It was the reason he was so good at what he did. It was also the reason he had never taken a wife or had children, both being chaotic and unpredictable by nature.

The circles his superiors moved in were not the sort to tolerate legal entanglements of such a disreputable nature by one representing them. His position with the Foundation would be history if any of this were to get out, as it surely would if he ever chose to follow some legal action against her. His ego would never allow it, anyway. There was no way even his closest friends would ever know this had happened, so he certainly could not permit it to be made part of any public record. What could he even prove if he tried? He had nothing. He would find out who she was, then he would go about discovering how and why he woke up naked in her bed with a collar around his neck. What the hell was that thing for? What else did they do?

The drugs, if indeed any had been involved, had surely worn off. They must have. He knew his own mind, and he was back in full control of his faculties. There was no question of that. Primal instincts weren't something he thought himself above, but he was an intellectual whose mind never failed him when he listened to it. Whatever had happened to him, he was without all the facts, but once in possession of them, there would be a reckoning. He set the GPS to take him home and backed out of the driveway.

He was in the town of Lowell, not even an hour from his home in Boston. Good, Rylen thought. He would be home in time to avoid any real traffic. He drove onto Massachusetts State Route 3 and set the cruise control five miles over the speed limit. The last thing he needed was to get stopped by some underpaid cop with self-esteem issues. When his phone chimed with an incoming text message, he ignored it, but then grew curious. Who would be sending him a message at such an hour of the morning? His guard went up as soon as he saw it was a blocked number, but it was not even a written text message. It was a thumbnail image. Was it the woman whose home he had just left? If she was sexting him a photo, she was as crazy as everything else indicated. He tapped the thumbnail to bring up the image.

It was the image of a plant--or, to be more specific, a leaf. It was shiny and had serrated edges surrounding a delicate web of veins over its surface. Rylen felt a jolt of shock and recognition, yet it was just out of the reach of his comprehension. What was this? A call came in. Blocked number. He took it.

A woman's voice was talking to him. His mind registered only one word of the first sentence she spoke: *sleep*. A wave of exhaustion overtook him in an instant. He struggled for a second before his eyes closed. Blackness. Peace.

The last thing Rylen registered with his fading consciousness was the sound of his car leaving the smooth hum of the blacktop paving under the wheels. The car gave a lurch upward, and he felt like he was moving through air.

CHAPTER ONE

STUART AND THE GOOD DOCTOR

Stuart Hollister sat in his therapist's office, clenching and unclenching his right hand against the padded arm of his chair. Her office was small, but tastefully decorated. Entering from the hall, one stepped out of the sterile, corporate efficiency of the offices surrounding it and into a quiet pocket of domesticity that smelled of coffee and vanilla.

"How have you been sleeping?" asked Doctor Ella Pendelton.

He had been waiting for that to come up. "I don't like to sleep."

"Still having the nightmares?"

"No, they aren't nightmares. Not exactly," said Stuart with a sigh, removing his black-framed glasses and rubbing his eyes. "They're just intense dreams." Ella remained silent. "It isn't the sleep I hate, it's dreaming that I hate. I don't have any say in what I dream or any control of myself when I'm in one. Most of the time I'm not even myself and have no memory of who I am. When I sleep I dream. I hate to dream."

"Most people like to dream," Ella observed. "If the dreams aren't bad ones."

"I wouldn't sleep ever again if I could help it. When you're in a dream, it doesn't matter what kind of crazy shit is going on around you, it all makes sense at the time and... you know, you just go with it. Yet my consciousness is always tinctured with enough self-awareness to let me know that something weird is going on, but never enough for me to achieve lucidity. Then I wake up and think, *man, that was some crazy, fucked-up shit*, and I go on my way. That's why I hate to dream. It's like CS Lewis' silver chair, only in reverse. It's like going mad every night."

"Are your dreams never of an enjoyable nature?"

"No," he replied, a little too curtly.

"Have they ever been? Not even when you were..."

"No," he cut her off. "Least of all when I was a kid."

"And you still don't want to talk about that?"

"No, I don't. Like I said in our first session, I don't want to go digging through my childhood. It's in the past and has no bearing on the present. And it sure as hell has nothing to do with why I'm sitting in this chair," Stuart answered.

"No, you're here because you put two men in a hospital. One of them in critical condition. If he had died, you would have been up for manslaughter."

"They had the whole thing on video from the bar and it backed up my story. You didn't see the video, but you know the circumstances. It wasn't my fault," he told her. "One of those assholes slapped a woman I know, and I shoved him away from her. What was I supposed to do, buy him a drink for assaulting her? Then he and his friend attacked me."

"It was the second time in two months you ended up before the judge," Ella pointed out. "Want to talk about what happened at work?"

Stuart didn't. "I was working alone with a new guy--a contractor. We got to talking about our personal interests and when I told him I'm a full-contact fighter, he started to get cocky and took it as a personal challenge. The rest of the day, he just wouldn't leave it alone. He finally got to the point where he outright picked a fight with me. The guy was a crazy."

"Well, again, he got a trip to the ER with a broken nose and three fractured ribs... and you ended up in front of the judge."

"He didn't press charges, though. You know why? Because

he was fucking high at the time," said Stuart. "He was an outside contractor, so he didn't have to pass a drug screen. But I was put on a week of leave without pay. Which, now that I think about it, was a blessing in disguise."

"Meaning what?"

"The very first day I was out, this guy filling in for me had an accident. He fell down an open elevator shaft on the construction site and died. I probably would have been more careful, since he was right out of training, but who knows," Stuart said as something on Ella's desk caught his eye. He looked at it for a moment, ignoring Ella's expression of curiosity. "Can I see that?" he asked, pointing to a small piece of pottery that sat on the side of her desk nearest him. She nodded, giving the faintest smile as he took up the pottery and examined it with keen interest. Ella watched from her armchair opposite, taking a sip from her coffee as her patient turned the item over in his hands.

She never sat behind a desk when meeting with him. He liked that, but he also knew it was something one learned in counseling 101. Ella was not his first therapist, but she was the first he had to see by mandatory court order. Her chair was in front of his and they sat facing each other, but her desk was still within reach to his right. The piece was the size of a standard drinking mug and in a classic pot shape, broad at the top and tapering to the bottom. There were two rows of eight tiny loops protruding from the sides, like clay donuts had been stuck to the surface. They were perfectly spaced, one from another, and created tiny attached rings that were too small to pass a pencil through.

"My niece made that for me," said Ella at last, a slight tone of amusement at the strangeness of the item. "She wants me to try to guess what it is before I see her this weekend."

"How old is she?"

"Just turned eleven. Why such an interest?"

"This is a little small," he said absently.

"You're telling me you actually know what that is? I sure

don't. How can I look up something like that without knowing what it is in the first place?"

Stuart carefully placed it back on the desk. "She must be a precocious kid. It's a miniature model of a pithos."

"Which is...?"

"Pithoi were huge pieces of bronze age pottery used as shipping containers for wine, oil, grain, and the like. Ropes were strung through the loops on the surface to equally distribute the weight so they could be loaded onto boats with a crane. They were very hard to bake evenly and usually cracked, which was a problem for all pottery at the time, but these especially. That's where we get the word for someone genuine in our language."

"How's that?"

"Potters would sometimes repair a cracked piece with wax and glaze over it so an unsuspecting customer would never know he'd been cheated and sold a defective product. Until he put something hot into it and it leaked. The word *sincere* comes from the words *sine cera*, which means *without wax* in Latin."

"At least now I know what to tell her," Ella said to him with a smile.

"Sorry," said Stuart. "Not what we're here to talk about. I wanted to teach ancient history. I dropped out of grad school my second year. I couldn't handle it. That's why I became an elevator technician. Manual work tends to keep me... level. Found out at a young age that I'm more of a physical guy. Maybe the work we do chooses us after all."

"It really does make all the difference, you know." Stuart gave her a questioning look. "When you said that your past has nothing to do with why you're sitting in that chair and why you had to come to see me in the first place. But it does. If you took a trip of a thousand miles by traveling only one mile a day, that would be a thousand days in which you made a choice to travel that one mile. That's a thousand choices that placed you in the location where you would find yourself at the end of it. Could you then say the past had nothing to do with where you found yourself in that moment? Where you are now is the culmination of every choice and every day that you have lived up to the present. How can you say the past has no bearing on your present situation?"

"Doctor, I didn't choose any of these situations I found myself in."

"I believe you. But you need to admit that the way you handle a situation isn't always the best one. And that's one of the reasons I asked to take your case," said Ella. "I'm a lot easier to deal with than the city-sponsored support group."

Stuart had to admit it was true. Though he had never been to such a thing, he knew that whatever form of therapy the judge would demand could be far worse than seeing this beautiful, young doctor once a week. When his lawyer called and said he would not need to register or attend any meetings, as the judge had agreed to allow Doctor Pendelton to evaluate him at her own request, he knew it was a stroke of luck. She had chosen him from a stack of case files, although it was likely that his brother being a former patient of hers had more than a little to do with it.

"I appreciate your doing that," he told her. "I've been thinking about continuing to see you for my own reasons after our last session in two weeks."

"That's great. I'd be happy to take you on as a patient, Stuart. Of course it's up to the judge, but this is just a preliminary evaluation. She may require you to stay in therapy for a minimum period if I tell her I think it necessary, but if I say you intend to remain in therapy regardless, it'll carry a lot of weight with her."

"The thing is... the cost."

Ella smiled. "My rates are on a sliding scale. We can talk about that in a couple of weeks when your court evaluation is over."

Stuart thanked her and, as their time was up, said goodbye after setting an appointment for the following week.

When he left, Ella marked the appointment in the calendar on her laptop and removed her phone from the top drawer of her desk. She had a text message from Paxton that read, "Enjoy lunch with your friend. Looking forward to our night out, hon. For the record, I think you are a wonderfully brave woman." Ella smiled in a way that she would have suppressed had anyone else been in the room to see.

CHAPTER TWO

STUART GETS THE NEWS

"You ready to go? We're up," Lonnie asked Stuart, who was just finishing his warm up on the heavy bag. Lorenzo *Lonnie* Lopez was a relative newcomer to the gym, but he and Stuart had become frequent kickboxing sparring partners. Stuart strapped on his gloves and removed his glasses before getting into the ring.

Lonnie was a Cuban-American who had been a recreational boxer in the army. His background of classical boxing showed, as he favored punches more than a kickboxer should. His hands were lightning-fast and, at five foot ten, he had a reach advantage over Stuart as well. At a modest five foot eight and weighing one hundred eighty-five pounds, Stuart was solidly built, but rarely did anyone ever guess the physical strength he possessed when seeing him fully clothed. Three hundred pounds was an easy bench press for him, and a lifetime of Tae Kwan Do gave him the advantage of faster kicks with more power behind them.

They circled and exchanged punches, neither of them landing a clean hit until Lonnie feinted a front kick with his left leg and switched it to a right kick that caught Stuart in the chest, knocking him back into the ropes. "I've been saving that one," said Lonnie.

"It's only going to work once," said Stuart as he resumed his fighting stance. Lonnie had been working on his kick speed. He also had a habit of leading with his left and throwing his right hand over his opponent's guard. It made Stuart think of how ancient sword fighters would kill enemies carrying a shield by jumping and stabbing down over top of it. Lonnie's weakness was predictability. He widened his stance every time he was going to kick with his right leg, which he favored. Another round of blocks and strikes as Stuart watched for the high right kick. Third round. A series of quick jabs and Lonnie's stance widened as he put his left foot forward. Stuart dropped to the mat and swung a powerful reverse foot sweep that slammed into Lonnie's supporting leg as the high right kick came up. Lonnie's supporting leg flew out from under him and he crashed to the mat.

Lonnie lay there panting. "Conyo! You knew it was coming?"

"Afraid so," said Stuart, offering Lonnie his hand. Lonnie took it and stood.

"Go again?"

"Next time. I have to get to work."

The Thursday morning had been an early one for Stuart, but his recent insomnia generally made him an early riser. Back at home, he showered and changed for work. He ran his hand over his shaved head, lamenting the fact that he had started losing his hair in his twenties. He lost the fight against male pattern baldness and started shaving his head two years earlier. He grew the heavy goatee by way of compensation, as it was the same light shade of brown he liked putting a hairbrush through in the days of yore. However, it was his anxiety that really troubled him these days. His appointment with Doctor Pendelton had given him hope, and his workout with Lonnie gave him the release he needed to take the anxious edge off.

Ever since he was a child he had been troubled, but he had always managed to get by with very little therapy. With a scumbag of a father like the one he had grown up with, he had done well for himself, all things considered. Not so well as his older brother, perhaps, but he was happy with the work he did. It was only when he was in the throes of physical exertion at the gym or in a ring, trying to knock out a man attempting to do the same to him, that he managed to find relief from the emotional pressure. His job as an elevator technician engaged his mind, but still had enough of a physical and mechanical aspect to satisfy his particular needs. He was good at it, having brought his prodigious intellect to bare in learning his craft had made him among the best in the city. He ultimately decided he was not cut out for academics, but maybe he could go back and finish at some point. Many people with his background would have ended up in jail--or maybe even the psych ward.

If the good doc could help him with his legal issues, he would give therapy another try. He had everything to gain and not a lot to lose, except fines, community service, and probation. Jail was off the table, at least for the time being. If therapy helped, he would consider going back to grad school. He was only 32 and, with his solitary lifestyle and steady work habits, he had plenty of money saved. Anything was possible.

He touched at a sore area on his cheekbone where Lonnie landed a hook jab. It might bruise, but that did not worry him. Looks were never his strong suit; that winning hand had been dealt to his brother. When it came to intellect, his big brother had gotten a genius' helping of that side order as well. Stuart had hardly been cheated in that area, though. If the mental vice of anxiety had not held him back for so long, he could have finished his master's when he was twenty-four.

He did not understand why the vice on his head was tightening of late, but if he could sleep again without waking up more mentally exhausted than when he lay down, he could put some real effort into getting himself straightened out.

There was a knock at the door, pulling Stuart out of his contemplations. He hurried to the door, realizing that the person had already knocked twice, and opened it to find two policemen facing him. One was in full uniform and the other, in a plain suit, was the one who had been knocking.

"Yes?" asked Stuart after a second of imperceptible surprise.

The suit was a man of late middle years with thick, graying hair. He was the one upon whom Stuart decided to focus. "Are you Stuart Hollister?" asked the man.

"Yes. Is something wrong?"

"My name is Detective Connelly, and this is Officer Britano," he said with a politeness that Stuart had seldom experienced from law enforcement. The officer behind Connelly nodded in greeting, but said nothing. He could play football for the NFL and was definitely the backup to Connelly's lead. "May we come in? We have something to tell you."

Stuart stepped back to let them enter. After finding that he was alone, Connelly asked him to sit, and Stuart sat on the couch before the detective sat on the easy chair beside it. Britano remained standing. "I have some bad news for you, Mr. Hollister. Your brother, Rylen, was in a car accident early this morning."

"What?" said Stuart.

"I'm very sorry, son. He was killed instantly."

Stuart's world faded out. He was not sure how long it had been before he noticed the detective was still talking. He removed his glasses to find his face was wet. Tears? Stuart had not cried since he was a child. The two officers were still there, watching him silently.

"I'm sorry, what did you say?" Stuart asked quietly.

Detective James Connelly nodded. "It's alright. I asked if there are there any other family members."

Stuart shook his head. "No, just the two of us," he said numbly. "It's always been just the two of us."

The two officers exchanged looks at that, soon after which Connelly stood and Stuart realized there was nothing left for them to say. He stood as well. He wasn't sure what he agreed to, but it was something about going to the city morgue as soon as he was able. Something about personal affects and a certificate. He opened the door, and they exited.

As the two men were walking away, Stuart's mind sprang to life, and he said, "Wait!" The officers turned back to him. "How did it happen? I mean, was anyone else hurt?"

Connelly shook his head and said, "No, it was a one-car accident. It was very early and, as far as we can tell at this point, he fell asleep on the road. You have my card. If you have any other questions, please feel free to give me a call anytime."

He was indeed holding a business card that seemed to have appeared in his hand. "I will," he told them and watched them depart.

Stuart shut the door and stood there, blinking. Rylen was gone. He walked to the bookshelf where he kept a small chess board. He stared at it for a long time before he carefully picked it up and placed it on the dining room table. It was a game that he and Rylen had been playing for months. He picked up the black king and examined it. Stuart hated the black pieces. He could play chess like an expert, but only if he played from the white side of the board.

Memories of when he was eight came back to him. Two boys of eight and twelve were sitting in a darkened bedroom, the flashlight they shared lying on the bed between them. They didn't dare turn on the light in the room, as it could be seen from the other side of the door in the darkened hallway. If their father noticed it, both of them would have bruises for a week. The older of the two was teaching the younger one to play chess as a way to help quell the fear of their father returning home. The older boy always took the black side of the board that his little brother hated so much.

Stuart lay the black king down on the board and a second time, found his face was wet with tears. His glasses still lay on the couch, where he had removed them on the first occurrence. He went back to the bedroom and looked in the mirror for the second time that morning. There were two things he knew in that moment. Rylen was dead. The brother he loved, who had been everything he wanted to be but never could be, was dead, and he was truly alone. The second thing was that inexplicably, even miraculously, the vice on his head was gone.

CHAPTER THREE
LUNCH BETWEEN FRIENDS

"Would you like to watch a scene with me and my submissive?" asked Sophia Rubinstein, receiving a stunned look from Ella. The friends had been meeting every week at the bistro on Boylston Street for months. Rarely did Sophia fail to offer up some new surprise revelation or fascinating character trait. Ella first thought this was deliberate attention seeking, but she had mis-judged her new friend. The woman was, in fact, very open and immodest with her views, tastes, and inclinations, which inspired trust in others. She was in no way coarse or vulgarly explicit in casual company, as those who sought attention through shock value might be. She would only share information of that nature with one whom she trusted or considered a friend. It was through the trust and friendship that they had built that Ella came to learn what an extravagant character the woman genuinely was. When one was on intimate terms with her, she could discuss alternative sexual practices as casually as she might discuss the weather. She had the most unguarded, powerful presence of any woman Ella had ever known.

They met after a medical expo where Sophia had been the keynote speaker. As a neuroscience doctorate who had once been at the forefront of her field, Sophia had led a team of researchers who did groundbreaking work in pharmaceutical treatments for several neurological disorders including epilepsy. There were documented statements she had made in medical journals about working on treatments for specific neurological diseases that would be non-medicinal and non-invasive. However, they were quietly disregarded when she retired at age 41, citing personal issues.

"Would you like to?" Sophia asked, sipping her tea.

"Like to..."

"Would you like to watch a play scene with me and my submissive?" Sophia said again, unable to hold back a hint of a smile at Ella's discomfort. "You would be very welcome."

"You don't mean you want me to join you."

"No, I said *watch*. Only if you're interested. You always have so many questions, clearly you are curious."

Ella glanced at the nearest tables, hoping no one was overhearing their conversation. She was nonplussed. "Would the two of you have sex?"

"We do, but it depends on my mood at the time," Sophia replied. "But we won't have sex if it will bother you."

Ella thought for a second. This was wrong on so many levels. The offer was wrong. Her accepting would be wrong. Her wanting to accept was wrong. "Yes," she said at last. "I would like to. And no, sex doesn't bother me, but shouldn't you talk about it with your submissive first?"

"I will," Sophia answered, "but I already know he'll be fine with it." Sophia leaned to the side, noticing what Ella was wearing. "That suit is absolutely gorgeous on you, by the way."

In spite of her early retirement, the work Sophia had done and patents she had sold left her immensely wealthy. Ella often wondered about Sophia's net worth, but it was a rude question, and one she would never ask. At a women's fashion show they both attended, Ella had so admired a business suit on one of the models that Sophia later purchased it and had it delivered to Ella's home. It was already a perfectly fitting size eight, but it was delivered with a hand-written thank-you note from the designer herself, saying that she would make any desired adjustments free of charge. The jacket, skirt, and blouse had been priced at six thousand. Ella was flabbergasted when it arrived, but Sophia would not hear a word about her returning it, which in truth, Ella would have been loath to do.

When they first met at a private party following the expo, Ella found the woman herself as fascinating as the talk she gave. Ella was initially intimidated. Their host, a mutual friend, introduced them and Ella got to see the brilliant woman up close for the first time. She was five-foot-seven and, in her heels, taller than Ella, which was something to which Ella was not accustomed. Though Sophia was in her forties, her black hair showed not a hint of gray, but framed her beautiful face with layered wisps of ebony that fell past her shoulders. The eyes that looked out over high cheekbones were ice blue and betrayed the intelligence of the mind behind them.

"Have you had spectators before?" Ella asked.

"Yes, but not with Trent," Sophia answered. "I promise he will be on board, trust me."

"How can you be so sure if he's new to it? A man being dominated by a woman in private is one thing, but its happening in front of a complete stranger might change the dynamic."

Sophia shook her head. "It won't change a thing."

"Is he into having someone watch?"

"Not that we have discussed before."

"So you just know him that well?"

"We've only been together a few months, but I know the submissive male mind very well," Sophia replied.

Sophia's understanding of the human brain was profound, but her knowledge was from a biological perspective. Ella could not discern the scope of the woman's knowledge of the mind from a psychological standpoint.

What surprised Ella more than anything was how approachable and fun Sophia was from the moment they met. Her reputation as being an irreverent maverick was not undeserved, she found. When they were parting at the end of the evening, Ella asked in all sincerity if Sophia had ever received a nomination for a Nobel Prize. After all, the work she had done resulted in the development of a drug that improved the efficacy of treatment for epilepsy by fifteen percent. The woman smiled and answered, "No, but that's alright. I am a Jew; we have enough."

Sophia seemed impressed that a psychologist who specialized in hypnotherapy would be interested in a topic only peripherally related to her field of expertise. Once the two fell into conversation, they soon made plans to meet for lunch the following day. They became fast friends thereafter. Ella had learned early on that Sophia had a penchant for bondage and sadomasochistic practices in her personal relationships. Without wanting to seem prying, Ella had no end of questions on the subject. Sophia was pleased that Ella did not find the disclosure repulsive, as someone of a more prudish nature might have done. Ella had been to orgies in her college years and had romantic trysts with other women, but BDSM was something she had never been exposed to first-hand. She had counseled people who turned to it as a coping mechanism, and others who had been in it from the time they reached the age of consent. Sophia, however, was a BDSM lifestyle dominant and living it every day of her life. Ella wondered if she had been a little too exuberant in her curiosity.

Pausing to take a bite of her veal, Ella then said, "If you say he won't mind, I will have to take your word for it. You say you understand the submissive male mind, but I wonder if you underestimate the male ego."

Sophia favored her friend with a shake of her head. "I do not, in fact. I love the male ego. There's nothing more useless to a man or more useful to a woman."

Ella considered that for a second. "How do you figure that?"

Sophia said, "Because the only thing a man's ego is good for is fucking with his judgment. It makes him do things he doesn't want to do, just so he can prove things that aren't true to people who don't care."

Ella could not help a little laugh escaping at this. "That might be true of the stupid ones."

"All men are stupid if they're aroused enough. That little

fact is as old as the species. It's the ones you cannot seduce that you really need to watch out for."

"So you exploit the man's ego to manipulate the man?"

"Oh, not at all," said Sophia, taking a bite of her salad before going on, "or at least, not entirely. It could be done in that way, but most of the time a more subtle approach is all a woman needs. It's like tipping the first domino. Make some options so much more appealing and he will select them every time. Point him in the right direction and he manipulates himself." Sophia finished the last bite of her salad.

A thought occurred to Ella. "Then why is it that you use hypnosis?"

Sophia had mentioned using hypnosis with her submissives as a means of enhancing their experiences. She took a moment to consider her answer. "There are many reasons. It enhances the overall experience, which is a big bonus. But, if you fear that the control it affords is not consensual, I assure you it is entirely voluntary on his part--as it has always been with all of my submissives."

"I know some ways around that," said Ella. "But as a rule, you can't hypnotize someone against his or her will."

Sophia went still. "Of course you can."

Ella shook her head. "Yes, I know it can be done, but the ways I know of cannot be employed without given... preparations. I meant, it cannot be done without a level of cooperative awareness."

"How long have you been a clinical hypnotist?"

Ella considered. "About six and a half years."

"You see, that is the difference between our schools of training. Trancing an unsuspecting person is tantamount to force in your profession, so it isn't something taught in a classroom or clinical setting. The result is your thinking it is impossible."

"That doesn't mean that the psychology behind my method is not as sound," said Ella, growing less certain of her position.

"I have no doubt that it is, but there are keys to circumventing prohibitive safeguards."

"Such as?" Ella asked.

"Look around this restaurant," Sophia told her, gesturing around them, "take stock of as many people as you can. You can read people like no one else I have ever met. Do that now."

Ella nearly blushed at the compliment, but she glanced around discreetly. "What is it that I'm looking for?"

"Before we leave here, I will hypnotize one person in this restaurant without their knowing it," said Sophia, "and I want you to choose the person."

"Oh, no," Ella said, growing nervous, "we aren't doing that."

"Don't worry," Sophia said reassuringly, "I won't do anything to embarrass us. It's not likely anyone else will even notice."

"There are plenty of other ways to make your point." Ella knew that it was increasingly unlikely that she would talk Sophia away from this course. When the woman decided she was going to do something, the devil himself could not stand in her way.

"Well then," Sophia said, looking around at their fellow diners, "if you will not choose someone, I guess I will. And you will have to trust that I didn't arrange this ahead of time."

"Okay, I will pick someone," said Ella, reasoning that if her friend could not be dissuaded, then she could at least mitigate the attention by choosing someone whom she felt would be discreet. She thought it should not be someone in a group or, even worse, a couple. She spotted a young, blonde woman in a business suit. She was sitting alone, two tables away from their own. "The woman alone at the table over there," said Ella.

"I'll be right back," Sophia said, taking the napkin from her lap and moving to stand.

"You have at least five minutes before her appointment arrives," said Ella.

"How the hell..." Sophia began, but dismissed her own question with a dramatically humorous wave of her hand, which made Ella smile despite her unease.

Sophia walked to the woman's table as though she intended to pass by, but stopped and asked the woman a question. The woman looked up and smiled. She shook her head as she gave a reply Ella could not hear. Sophia then extended her hand to the woman, who shook it professionally. Sophia placed her free hand over the woman's wrist and leaned down to whisper something to her. Sophia was talking quickly, and the woman listened with intense interest. The woman nodded as if in answer to a question. Then Sophia, still holding the woman's wrist with her left hand, removed her right hand from their handshake and quickly brought it up to touch the woman in the middle of her forehead. The woman's eyes closed and Sophia let the woman's right hand fall into her lap. She lowered herself into a chair at the table. In seconds, the thing was done. Sophia was now sitting at the table and talking rapidly while the woman was nodding in silent confirmation. This lasted for a moment before the woman opened her eyes again, still in a state of trance, but in a trance that would be less obvious to others than it was to Ella.

All of this took no more than a minute before Sophia stood and continued on to the restroom. Ella sat watching the woman; she sat in a daze for a few seconds after Sophia's departure and then returned to herself, as though nothing had happened. She looked at her phone, talked to the waiter, sipped her water, and appeared entirely unaware that anything had transpired. It was daring and, although what Ella had just witnessed was a criminal act of assault, it was nothing short of remarkable.

Sophia soon returned to the table and took her seat across from Ella, who was left wordlessly blinking. The woman Sophia had hypnotized in a restaurant full of people never even looked in their direction. "So, about the play session," Sophia asked, "how is tomorrow for you?"

CHAPTER FOUR

A HOT DATE

"She did what?" Paxton asked Ella, interrupting her as she told him about what transpired during lunch with Sophia earlier that day.

Ella had to wait to answer as the waitress came to the table to refill their water glasses. "She hypnotized some woman, a total stranger, right there in the restaurant."

Paxton was having trouble processing this. He and Ella had been together for eight months and living together for three of them. Ever since she became friends with this Sophia person five or six months back, she always had some new and increasingly odd story or piece of information about her.

When Ella finished telling him about everything that happened at lunch that day, he asked if the woman was upset or if there was any aftermath. When learning that the woman didn't even seem aware that it had happened, Paxton stared at her in silence over his plate. "Don't you see anything wrong with what she did?"

"Of course it was wrong," Ella admitted. This made Paxton feel a good bit better until she followed it with, "But my god, was that ever amazing."

"Suppose that woman became incensed, what then?" he asked. "Could she get legal on someone for doing that?"

"No," Ella replied, but then considered it further. "Maybe," she said. "Okay, I don't know. And it was just a one-time thing to prove a point. But come on, Tee, you have to admit that was brilliant."

Ella was the only person Paxton allowed to call him by his first initial, as that was all he had. His parents could not decide on whether to name him *Tristan* or *Terrance*, so they named their only child *T. Paxton*. As a licensed architect, the initial caused him some problems early in his career. The fact that Ella used it on this occasion was a slip. She knew he did not like it and promised to break the habit, but it came out once in a while. He could not fault her. She had been calling him that for most of their relationship, before he decided two months earlier he would rather she call him *Paxton* like everyone else. He told her he was always on the fence about it because, though he didn't like anyone else calling him that, he liked her having a name that only she could use. The truth was that he never liked it, but never bothered to say anything. When he finally did admit to finding it annoying, he made up the story about being conflicted so she would not wonder why it had taken him so long to tell her. Otherwise, she would put the matter under her psychoanalytical microscope.

"I would think that, as a doctor, you might want to be a little more careful," he offered.

"Why? I'm not the one doing it, and if you ever met Sophia, you would know there isn't much anyone can do to talk her out of something."

"I look forward to meeting her. You'll have to invite her over for dinner."

"I have, several times, but it never seems to work out."

When the waitress returned, Paxton asked for the check and waited for her to depart before he said to Ella, "Well, it's time. You sure you want to do this?"

"Definitely," replied Ella. "It shouldn't be very busy up there on a Thursday, and it's a perfect night for it."

They stood to leave and Paxton realized Ella was wearing high-heel boots that he hadn't noticed when she entered the restaurant. He was six foot one, but when she wore heels like that, she was taller than he. As his hair and eyes were brown also, people could easily take them for brother and sister. But they were a couple and, as she was already five foot ten, he never warmed to the fact that she often wore five-inch heels. Yet it was something that she either didn't notice or chose to ignore. He decided not to mention it because she would automatically drop a clinical diagnosis that labeled him as insecure. However, as they were going to be walking a lot, he could take a chance. "You going to be okay to walk in those?" he asked, indicating her boots.

"I could walk all night in these," she answered as they made their way to the door.

Ella paused before the elevator, wondering to herself if doing this after dinner was the best idea. Paxton waited patiently for her to collect herself. "Listen," he said, taking both of her hands, "you don't have to do this if you don't want to."

"I want to," she assured him. "I just needed a second. I'm ready."

The couple soon found themselves walking around Boston's Skywalk Observatory, seven hundred feet above the street, the windows affording a three hundred and sixty degree view of the city in its full evening glow. After all, she was on the floor of a building like any other, albeit the top floor of a much higher one than most she ever entered--one with huge windows that made it impossible to forget the fact that she was so high up.

"You alright?" Paxton asked as she gripped his arm tightly. "Just say the word and we're out of here."

"I'm okay," she answered as they walked slowly. "I've been putting this off for a year, and now that I'm here, I am not going to run. Take it slow."

They gradually made their way around to see a magnificent view of Boston in every direction. Ella was determined not to embarrass Paxton by showing anything other than a collected calm, even though her heart had stopped the moment she saw the evening city below. The beauty of it gradually, little by little, overcame her fear. The experience of the transition made her lightheaded and exhilarated. It was truly wonderful, like falling from a great height and learning that she could fly.

After the second time around, Ella paused, fixating on the view out of the window. She let go of Paxton's arm and walked close to the glass. They were looking out of the north side. The glistening swath of Charles River reflected the glowing streak of Harvard Bridge on its surface. She wiped at a silent tear that slid down her cheek.

"I am so proud of you, honey." Ella had not noticed him at her side.

"I couldn't have done this alone," she answered.

"Of course you could have, but I'm glad I was with you when you did."

"Thank you," she whispered, hugging him tightly. She took this opportunity to speak quietly into his ear, lest passersby overhear, though no one was close. "I want to try some naughty things with you tonight," she said, sliding away from him to look him in the eye. "If you feel you can handle something new?"

Paton raised an eyebrow. "Oh, boy, I knew that was coming," he smiled.

Ella might have been more obvious than she intended. "And how's that?"

"Just the way you've been talking about your friend and the whole S&M thing she gets into. It's obvious you are really into it. You talk about it all the time."

"That transparent, huh? To be honest, yes, I find it exciting and right now, I am really fucking excited. So what do you think? Would you be up for a little bondage tonight?"

He contemplated this. "You really want to be tied up?" he asked, showing the first hint of actual curiosity on the topic.

This was an unexpected turn. "And what makes you assume that I want to be the one tied up? Maybe I like the idea of seeing you bound and helpless," she said, injecting enough levity into her tone to make it sound like a temptation.

"Wait, me? Are you serious?"

Ella opted for a long silence with a shrug, before breaking it with, "Would a little experimentation be so unwelcome? You might actually like it."

Paxton scoffed. "Not if it means playing the part of a victim. Honey, that just isn't me. It never has been and never will be."

Ella sighed. "Victim? No, you have it all wrong. It isn't about playing a victim, it's about... letting yourself go, giving control of yourself to someone else, and enjoying the experience."

"By being tied up? That definitely isn't me," he answered. "Look, I'm all about trying new things, but if I'm going to be honest in return, I don't like where this is going. I may not know anything about this friend of yours or this type of thing people do, but I don't get off on violence. When you get right down to it, that's what it is."

"Violence? And yet you were okay with doing it to me a minute ago?" she asked sharply.

"All I did was ask if that was what you wanted, I didn't say I was okay with it. I'm shocked by it, actually."

He was lying; she knew it. Worse, he was trying to hide behind a conversational technicality. "It's so much deeper and more complex than you think. It helps some people to establish rapport, trust, and understanding. Not to mention that it's pretty fucking exciting, too."

"And how well do you understand it?"

Ella wasn't sure if he was being obtuse or meant the question in earnest. Regardless, it stung a little. Here was something of a genuine interest to her, and he would not even discuss it. He was dismissing the idea out of hand, even though she felt it exciting and thought it might enhance their relationship. She had always thought Paxton more avant-garde than that; it was one of the things that first attracted her to him, and she knew that his only reluctance was his pride. Sophia was right. The man's ego was preventing him from even considering the notion of trying something because it might make him look weak, and he just wasn't willing to admit it. She weighed her answer. "I understand it a lot better than you do, but not as well as I want to."

"We better get going. We'll talk about it later," said Paxton, turning and leading the way to the exit.

"And I will know a lot more by this time tomorrow," she muttered to herself, too quietly for him to hear.

CHAPTER FIVE

MEET MY PET

Sophia paused inside the private elevator that would take the two of them up to her penthouse. She had already prepared Ella for what she was about to see on the drive, and Ella was not apprehensive in the least. Despite her professional interest in all aspects of human behavior, she was also personally interested. "There is one more thing," Sophia told her before turning the key in the elevator to unlock her floor, "don't bother to introduce yourself. You will be observing our interactions together and he will not modify his behavior."

"So I'm going to be the proverbial fly on the wall. You are sure he's fine with this?" Ella asked.

"You're the first to observe the two of us together, but yes, he is perfectly fine with it."

Ella shrugged. "I feel a touch voyeuristic."

"Good," Sophia smiled, turning the key and pressing the button for the penthouse. "Now you're getting it."

The elevator doors opened into a high-ceiling foyer. The first glimpse through the doors gave Ella a peek of a polished marble pillar stand under an abstract painting. She stepped out from the elevator behind Sophia and followed her through the foyer. Sophia's home was a 6200-square-foot penthouse condo on Boston's waterfront. Ella had been prepared for an impressive place, but was nonetheless taken aback by the opulence of Sophia's home. Everything was decorated in white and shades of cream. The white carpeting on the floor cushioned her steps as she followed Sophia into the vast central living space. The couches and seating were white leather, and all the other furniture was made of steel and glass. A glossy black grand piano, on a dais of black marble tile, gleamed in the daylight shining through glass doors to the terrace beyond. How had they ever managed to get a piano into this place? In spite of all its beauty, she could not immediately touch upon what it was that made this place lack the warmth of a home. The whole feel and atmosphere was more like that of a professional space. Then it hit her; there was no wood grain anywhere. The frames of the artwork on the walls were black metal, the tables and countertops were all glass--even the piano was finished with a black lacquer.

"Make yourself at home," said Sophia, walking behind a wet bar that Ella had not noticed before. "Something to drink?"

"No, thank you," Ella replied, still taking in the place. Spotting some framed photos on a side table, she was drawn to them, as they were the first element of personal character she had seen since she had stepped off the elevator. One was of Sophia with her arm around a girl in a black graduation gown. Another larger one was of the girl herself. She was fair-haired, but Ella could distinctly see a resemblance to Sophia in the lines of her facial features.

"Candice," said Sophia, her voice very close behind Ella, who had not heard her approach. "My daughter."

"She's striking," Ella said sincerely.

Sophia took a sip of her drink. "Yes. Yes, she was." Ella looked at her hostess. "She is the daughter I told you about, the one who passed away. The truth is, she took her own life last year. I haven't been able to put those away. A mother never forgets."

Ella shook her head sadly. "Oh, god, I'm so sorry. I had no idea."

"That's alright. You are welcome to look."

Ella knew Sophia had a daughter at one time and that the

girl had died, but it was the one topic on which Sophia was unwilling to volunteer details. Ella naturally never felt inclined to pry on this point. She assumed the girl had died at a young age, but this girl was in her mid-twenties. "She graduated from Harvard?"

Sophia smiled sadly at the photo and nodded. "I was on a corporate board then. I used my influence to get her a position in the company. She could have gone so far," she said with a sigh, as if bringing herself out of her reverie with an effort. "Come, I will summon Trent if you're ready."

"As ready I'm ever going to be," said Ella, returning the picture and moving to sit on the love seat.

Sophia touched an electronic pad on the glass coffee table and a melodic chime sounded that could be heard throughout the penthouse. She walked over and stood at the wet bar, sipping her drink in silence. After a moment, a young man entered the room and approached them. Ella did not recall in that moment what she had been expecting, but whatever she might have expected Trent to look like, he exceeded it. Ella would have put him at a maximum of 24 years old. He was shorter than Paxton, maybe five foot eleven, and was sculpted of marble. He was naked except for a pair of black boxer briefs and a plain black collar around his neck. It took Ella a moment to realize that aside from his thick, blond hair, Trent did not have a hair on him anywhere else. Whatever Trent was like on the inside, the outside assured a prosperous career as a model, if he was not one already.

He walked to Sophia and knelt in front of her, his eyes cast down at the floor. "Mistress," he said in a voice that was deeper than Ella felt suited him.

Sophia stared down at him and took her time finishing her drink. She placed the glass on the wet bar and ran her fingers through his hair. "I will be entertaining a guest this afternoon, pet."

"Yes, Mistress," Trent answered. "Would you like me to prepare a meal for you and your guest?"

"No. I need to release some stress. Go get the room ready and wait for me there."

"Yes, Mistress," said Trent before rising and going upstairs.

Sophia turned to Ella. "Isn't he lovely?" she said, as much to herself as to Ella, but without giving Ella time to answer. "Are you sure you wouldn't like a drink? I need to change for the session and it will take about 15 minutes. Please help yourself to anything you would like."

"Thank you," Ella replied as her hostess disappeared through a door at the far side of the penthouse.

After Ella made herself a vodka cranberry, and finished it, she soon found herself venturing out to the terrace. A long hesitation made her wonder if her success of the night before might have given her an overconfidence. Still, the view was calling her, so she slid open the glass door and crept out to the railing overlooking the harbor. She did not faint, but her heart beat quickly. She was doing something that would have been impossible a week before, and it mutated her fear into a joyous thrill as she stood at the handrail, taking in the view. She lost track of time and was still watching the boats when she heard Sophia's voice behind her say, "I love the view; it was what sold me on this place." Turning from the railing to the sliding door she had left open, Ella's mouth fell open as Sophia stepped out onto the terrace wearing a black lace body stocking and black stiletto pumps. She joined Ella at the railing and Ella instinctively looked around, forgetting they were on top of a high-rise building. Sophia smiled at the discomfort of her guest. "It's one of the benefits of being on the top floor," Sophia said, taking a deep breath as she gazed into the distance.

"You have the most beautiful home I have ever been in."

"Thank you," Sophia replied without turning away from the horizon.

"And yet you don't own a robe?" said Ella, deliberately inflecting the remark as a question, not wanting it to sound like criticism.

This time Sophia turned to meet her eye. "I do, but it is

hanging in the room upstairs, where we're going."

Ella had forgotten all about Trent. "Oh. Is he still waiting for us up..."

"The boy can wait," Sophia cut in sharply, taking on a regretful look at Ella's surprised expression. Sophia sighed and placed her hand on Ella's, by way of a tacit apology. The touch was lingering, soft, and gentle. Then she turned back to the harbor, leaving her hand atop Ella's on the handrail for another moment before removing it. "I guess he is, after all, only a boy," she said, her voice quiet and distant. Her eyes became wells of sadness.

Ella didn't wonder that a man of any age would find this woman attractive, especially for one in her middle years. The body stocking she wore left nothing to the imagination, and she was as muscular and firm as any fitness instructor half her age. Her nipples pressed against the stretched lace of the garment. Her ample breasts we perfect and if they were artificial, Ella could not tell for certain. Ella wondered for the first time how she got into such a thing, as it had long sleeves and came up over her shoulders to fit closely around her neck. Tilting her head slightly, she could see the upper portion of Sophia's back was bare. The black lace G-string she wore under the body stocking tied at the hips, creating a silk bow knot that was pressed flat by the taught lace.

As Ella preferred to see it, being a doctor of psychology didn't make her an expert of human nature, but a licensed student of it. She searched for motivations, be they hidden, obvious, or affected. When Sophia walked out onto the terrace and crossed the twenty feet or so to join her at the railing, there were countless things Ella perceived from her movement, her eyes, and her facial expression in those few seconds. Bravado might have caused her step to be overly bold, as though daring any insecurity to impinge upon her performance. Trepidation might have caused a slow, slightly hesitant step or darting eye, just discernible in spite of how effectively it was vanquished through force of will. Sophia exhibited none of these, but walked over and stood by her with a grace and poise any dancer would respect. She was fundamentally naked while standing at the handrail of her terrace atop a tall building, yet she had the same self-possession as one to whom all the world were invisible. It was on some level disquieting; on another, it was absolutely delightful.

All of this impressed itself upon Ella's mind in an instant and she was drawn back to the moment when the dominatrix said that it was time they head upstairs, turning to lead the way inside. Even more absorbing than the physical appearance and granite confidence of her friend was something Ella decided she would have to put out of her mind--the undeniably tantalizing thrill she had felt at Sophia's touch.

CHAPTER SIX

THE DARK ROOM

Ella entered the door behind Sophia, who motioned her to a black leather armchair in the corner. She seated herself quietly, trying to remain as unintrusive as possible while taking in the room. There was plain, charcoal gray carpeting on the floor and, though it did cushion her step, it was clearly of a more durable type. The room was roughly twenty feet square. The most immediately striking feature was that the walls were painted a satin black. The ceiling was white, with a metal ceiling fan light fixture at its center, and black privacy drapes covered two windows along one wall of the room. Ella suspected that these were rarely, if ever, opened. The wall opposite the draped window wall was hung with a dizzying array of implements of the BDSM lifestyle. Starting on one end were leather floggers, crops, canes, whips, and paddles. Beyond that were cuffs, chains, lengths of rope, gags, and hoods. One item that caught Ella's eye was a straitjacket and she could imagine a scenario in which that would come into use. Not all of the items were meant for restraint or to inflict pain; there were handled fox tails and floggers made of strips of soft fur and others of feathers.

In the center of the far wall opposite the door was a king-size bed, pulled out from the wall far enough for a person to walk behind it. The metal posts at the corners of the bed rose five feet above the mattress to support the metal frame that connected them. The most remarkable thing about this bed, however, were the sheets of black latex. When the women entered, Trent was applying a spray to them that gave them a gleaming wet sheen. Ella had no idea such things were even made.

With his standard preparations finished, Trent knelt, waiting at the foot of the bed and facing the door with his eyes cast down at the floor. He was naked except for his collar and the matching leather cuffs he now wore at his wrists and ankles. A chain leash was attached to his collar, the leather wrist strap touching the floor in front of him. Sophia walked past him to a bottle of champagne that chilled in an ice bucket on a side table near one of the windows, a tall glass flute beside it. She poured herself a drink and contemplated the chains that hung from the ceiling in pairs of two at different locations in the room. She put down her drink and went to the opposite wall, where she took her time in selecting the items she would need. She chose a crop with a broad leather head and a spacer bar, which was a plain black metal bar three feet in length with metal rings close to each of its ends. Carabiners clattered from the metal loops on the bar as Sophia took it from its place on the wall. She placed it on the floor under one of the pairs of chains that hung from the ceiling a short distance from where Trent was kneeling, a silent statue of subservience.

Sophia stood before him with the crop in her hand. "You cannot wait to please me, can you, pet?" she said to him.

"I cannot wait to please you, Mistress," came Trent's reply, his voice throaty with anticipation.

"Get up," she commanded. Trent stood. She took the leash that dangled from his neck and walked him to the chains over the spacer bar on the floor. "Spread," she ordered. He parted his feet the approximate length of the spacer bar and Sophia locked the carabiners on the bar to the steel loops of his ankle cuffs. She then rose and affixed his wrist band cuffs to the chains with a lock that hung on the ends. His hands were now secured over his head and his feet were locked into a permanent spread, his dick already fully hard.

Sophia paced back and forth behind him, gently tapping

his back and ass with the leather head of the springy crop. The taps were light, but so remarkably quick that it called to Ella's mind the nimble rapidity of a bongo player's hands upon the surface of a drum. She continued to tap as she spoke. "Listen closely, pet," she said, "since we went a little over your pain threshold and into your safe word last time, we're going to play a little game. Count to five." Trent did so. "Now, I'm going to give your skin a taste of my crop. You will give each stroke a number, one to five, one being what I am doing now. Five is the most pain you can tolerate and no more. If you say *six*, we are done here. Do you understand?"

"Completely, Mistress," he answered, daring a glance back over his shoulder.

"Good. Let me hear it." Sophia struck his ass cheek with the crop.

"Two," said Trent at once. She struck him again, this time much harder. "Four," he responded loudly.

For several minutes, the dominatrix and her submissive proceeded in this way, with her pacing and striking with controlled and precise intensity. Sophia never met Ella's eye directly through all of this, but a number of times during this display, Sophia would show a number of fingers behind her back with her free hand that only Ella could see. An instant later, her stroke with the crop would fall and every time, without exception, Trent's response matched the number of fingers she had held out. Twice did he go as high as five, and the power put into those hits was impressive. Ella looked for the man's immediate capitulation, but never once did he reach a count of six.

At last, Sophia stopped and exchanged the crop for a flexible leather paddle. "That was well done, pet," she said. "Tell me you belong to Mistress Sophia." The man repeated the phrase. She sauntered behind him, tapping the paddle on her palm. "Again," she said. The man obeyed. "Good. Now we are going to change things up a little. Each time you feel the lick of this paddle, that is what you are going to say. Understood?"

"Yes, Mistress," he dutifully answered. She tapped him on his ass with the paddle. "I belong to Mistress Sophia."

"Excellent," she said as she leaned in close behind him, "but here is the rub, pet. The less convincing you are, the harder the next stroke is going to be. If you are more fervent and sincere, the one after will not be harder than the last, but not any lighter either. Do you understand?" Trent nodded vigorously and answered in his given affirmative. She struck him lightly across the ass with the paddle.

"I belong to Mistress Sophia," said the man.

Sophia sighed. "Pathetic," she said before striking a sharp and painful blow.

"I belong to Mistress Sophia!" he shouted. She struck with the same intensity as promised. He repeated his mantra as she struck again and again.

She paused to grip his hair and tilt his head back so that she could speak directly behind his ear. "I don't know if you like this game or not, but personally, I'm loving it." She released him and went back to her task until Ella was sure the nearest neighbors were well aware to whom the man in the penthouse belonged.

At last, she tossed the paddle to the floor and released him from his bonds, unbuckling the wrist and ankle cuffs, leaving them attached to the chains and the spacer bar. Then, she embraced and kissed him passionately, in the manner more befitting a pair of lovers than a dominant and her submissive. Ella was curious at this and made a mental note to inquire about it when she had the chance. After the kiss was broken, they continued to stand, holding each other for a moment until separating.

"Kneel," Sophia told him; he knelt as he had been when the two women first entered the room, but this time facing the bed. She went to her glass and took a few sips of champagne. She took a shard of ice from the bucket and went to Trent, holding it before his lips. "Open," she commanded, and his mouth opened to receive the shard. She then took up his leash and put her left hand through the strap on the end, wrapping it around her hand twice. Her other hand slid under the crotch opening in her body stocking and tugged at the ties of her G-string before she pulled it off and dropped it on the floor. Sitting on the edge of the latex mattress, she then pulled on his leash, drawing him between her spread legs. When he could get no closer, she draped her legs over his shoulders and, gripping a fistful of his hair, she pulled his mouth into her crotch. Trent's tongue came out, dripping with cold, and he pressed it flat against her clit. Sophia moaned and lay back on the gleaming black latex. She was afloat on a glimmering black pool, looking as though she might plunge into it as she writhed. She still held the leash in one fist and Trent's corn silk strands in the other.

The man's powerful arms came up to wrap around the black lace thighs of his mistress and pull her hard against his tongue, which dripped profusely from the sliver of ice in his mouth. Sophia released his hair, but held firm to the leash. She stretched her free arm out over the black pool of ecstasy on which she drifted. Trent pulled harder, keeping his tongue pressed flat against her clit and moving his head up and down to brush the cold texture of his tongue into her, causing electric spasms of pleasure. Sophia moaned louder and began to thrash, but Trent was strong and held her fast, now lifting her hips clear off of the mattress with the rise and fall of his rhythm. She let out a cry and the waves washed over her. Trent ceased his motion at the crest of his lift and held her thighs tightly, lest she pull away, flicking her clit rapidly with his tongue to give her the last few spikes of rapture. At last, she could stand it no longer, at which point she patted the top of his head and he slowly lowered her waist back to the mattress, gently releasing her legs from his hold and drawing himself away from the bed as far as the leash would allow. He resumed his kneeling position.

Sophia drew herself onto the mattress and brought herself up into a sitting position, still catching her breath. "Go take a shower and go to class. I will want to talk with my guest in private this afternoon," she told him, crossing her legs.

"Yes, Mistress," he said before he bent and kissed the top of her foot. He then rose and left the room without so much as a glance in Ella's direction.

Sophia rose and retrieved a black silk robe from the room's private bath before returning to Ella, who stood at her approach. "Let's talk on the terrace," she said. Stepping out of her heels and leaving them on the spot, she took up the half glass of champagne and led the way out of the room in her stocking feet.

They went to the terrace and sat down under the light of the afternoon sun. Ella had many questions and was still formulating them as they sat down at a table on the terrace.

"Well?" Sophia asked, adjusting the sash of her robe. "What did you think? Was it all you hoped?"

"That and so much more," said Ella, which seemed to please her friend. "That was the most erotically beautiful thing I have ever seen. You do this all the time?"

"Not every day, if that's what you mean," Sophia smiled. "Trent stays here a couple days a week, as his class and work schedule permits."

"Why do you call him your pet?"

"Honorifics are defined by the roles we assume in the dynamic of our relationship."

"Is the term *pet* meant to be dehumanizing, as in denoting a lack of an emotional connection?"

"Not at all, though it might to some people. I care about Trent and he does about me. To some in the lifestyle, these qualities may sound diametrically opposed to the attitudes of a dominant to her submissive. However, doesn't a pet owner dote affectionately upon it? Might one not impose strict guidelines and boundaries that pets must follow, then reinforce them by rewarding obedience or punishing transgression?"

Ella had to admit she had a point. "How did you learn all of this?" she asked, not caring how basic she sounded.

"Dominatrices are like vampires; it takes one to make one," she answered, betraying her jest with a grin. "I can teach you, if you want to learn more," Sophia made the last sentence sound like a gentle offering.

Ella paused for only a heartbeat. "I think I would."

The two women talked until Trent passed in front of the open door, fully clothed with a backpack slung over one shoulder, on his way out of the penthouse. Soon after, Ella felt it was time that she took her leave as well. Sophia walked her guest to the elevator door. Ella had called an Uber and so declined Sophia's offer to have her driver take her home.

Ella thanked Sophia again and turned to leave, but paused at the elevator entrance and turned back. "And I'm not sure if such etiquette even applies here, but be sure to tell Trent I appreciate his agreeing to let me watch your scene today,"

Sophia was still sipping at the champagne flute, but the glass halted on its way to her lips as she favored Ella with a look of amused incredulity. "You really don't know, do you? I thought you had already figured it out by now."

"Figured it out?"

"My dear doctor," Sophia smiled, "I said Trent would be fine with it. And he was. Perfectly so. I didn't say he agreed to it. When I told him I would be entertaining a guest this afternoon, he assumed that guest had not yet arrived when he left us."

"What are you talking about?"

"Trent... he could neither see nor hear you. I hypnotized him and made him oblivious to the presence of any other person but me in my home today."

"What?" said Ella in disbelief. "He never saw me? The whole time?"

"That's right," Sophia said with a grin. "He thinks that he and I were alone upstairs. He truly has no idea that anyone else was ever here."

CHAPTER SEVEN

A MASSAGE AND A FLEECING

Lori Mercer rubbed the oil over the man's back as she talked. The lights in her room at the spa were turned down and the sound of ocean waves played faintly in the background. Her client, a player for the Boston Red Sox, groaned as she kneaded the muscles on either side of his spine with the tips of her fingers. She poured a generous amount of oil into her palm and rubbed it down the backs of his legs. She glanced at the clock. She started on the backs of his thighs and worked down to his calves.

"What are your plans for the off-season?" she asked, but received a reply that was too slurred to understand him. The clock told her ten minutes had elapsed. She reached into her pocket and changed the track on the playlist that piped over the Bluetooth speakers. The sound of ocean waves changed to that of soft Tibetan chimes. The man inhaled deeply at the sound and the touch of her hands on his back. She rubbed his shoulders for the second time that session. She said quietly, "Are you falling asleep on me?"

This time the man's voice was more distinct. "Yes," he answered.

"Good," said Lori, her voice gentle as she rubbed and worked the muscles in his back. "You know I love it when you sleep on my table. It means I'm doing a good job. And you love to sleep for me, don't you?"

"Yes."

"And what happens when you hear the chimes?" she asked, moving to his lower back.

"When I hear the chimes, I sleep and obey," came his automatic reply.

"Say that for me five times," she told him, "letting yourself fall ten times deeper with each repetition."

His voice was slow and heavy. "When I hear the chimes, I sleep and obey..." He repeated as instructed and with every repetition, his voice grew slower and less audible. At the fifth, she could barely hear him at all.

"That feels so good, doesn't it? No need to talk anymore, just give me a little nod." His head moved slightly. "That's why you always take such good care of me, isn't it? I always make you feel so good, and it makes you feel good to be so good to me in return. Isn't that true?" Again the man's head nodded. "Good boy. Now you sleep and dream about me until you hear the ocean waves, then you can awaken slowly. When you awaken, you will feel better than you have ever felt. You will remember nothing at all about the chimes or anything that we talked about. You fell asleep to the sound of ocean waves and dreamed about me. Everything else is even now disappearing from your memory and will be completely gone when you awaken. Sleep now. Sleep and dream."

Lori waited a few minutes before changing the audio track back to ocean waves and went to the sink to wash the oil from her hands. When she finished, her client was already sitting up on the table. "I fell asleep again?"

"You were all in tense knots," said Lori. "It's okay. This is one situation where your falling asleep on a girl is something of a compliment."

He looked at the clock. "I better get changed." He stood and wrapped himself in the towel. When he emerged from the changing room, he picked up the white envelope that lay on the counter and replaced it a moment later. "You give any thought to my offer to let me buy you dinner?" he asked.

Lori made a mock pout before she said, "And this was going so well."

He smiled before managing a wounded look. "Just asking if you had even thought about it."

"Since I already refused when you asked, I didn't need to give it any more thought," she replied. "I like having you as a client."

He spread his arms wide. "You could have all of me. And you can always get another client."

"My client relationships last longer," she answered. "And I have another one in ten minutes."

He nodded, taking the message. "See you next week?"

"Book on the way out and I'll be here."

Lori didn't bother to count the number of one-hundred-dollar bills he'd left behind in the envelope. She folded them into a packet that she slipped into her pocket before preparing for her next appointment.

CHAPTER EIGHT

A SHORT FUNERAL

The funeral service was held at a cathedral church where Rylen attended Mass. Working with a funeral home and making final arrangements was something Stuart had never prepared himself for. Death was expensive, but his savings would not suffer too badly. Rylen's house and everything else he owned went to Stuart, so he would be fine in the long run. Rylen had opted for cremation in his will and Stuart had to do everything from selecting the urn into which his ashes would be placed, to finding a photo that would be printed in large format to place on a tripod beside it. Stuart sat in the front row, tuning out the... what was he, anyway? A priest, deacon, or minister? Stuart didn't know the difference. Whoever he was or whatever his office, Stuart barely listened to what the man was saying about his brother. He talked as though he knew Rylen, and he probably did. Rylen had been coming to this church for years, though he was no more religious than Stuart. Stuart waited for the man to finish, privately thinking about how Rylen would have laughed at the display.

Only fifteen people were present--some were coworkers, some friends, none of them were anyone Stuart knew. Stuart had prepared himself to speak in front of a group of people. If he were to shut down, he would never forgive himself for it. All the same, he wished he were anywhere else at that moment. He realized that the priest, as he decided to think of him, had just introduced him.

Stuart stood and walked to the microphone. Why did he need to stand on a podium like he was addressing people in the balconies? The entire group in attendance wouldn't fill the first row on either side of the aisle, though some still sat in the second row so they were not pushed out to the ends. Maybe the podium wasn't such a bad thing after all, since he could now see everyone's faces. A blonde woman in the second row was the only one who looked in any way familiar. Stuart was sure she knew Rylen back in college. Why would she be at Rylen's funeral? Their relationship would have ended more than a decade back.

The tall, silver-haired man who introduced himself as Perry Tellerson tended to attract Stuart's attention more than anyone else. He was Rylen's boss and had the most commanding presence in the room. He was there with his wife and a young man who couldn't hide his muscular frame in a suit. Tellerson didn't introduce the man, but it wasn't necessary. The guy was too official and stiff to be anything but a bodyguard. Rylen's boss apparently thought himself too rich or important to let his security leave his side, even at a funeral.

It was then that Stuart spotted her. There was a woman in black, sitting at the very back of the church. The service was not over yet, so who had let her in? If she was here for the service, why did she sit in the very last row? The most striking thing about her was that she was wearing a hat with a black lace veil over her face. Who wore a veil to a funeral these days? She was leaning forward, her black, gloved hands resting on the row in front of her. She was holding a small book, presumably a bible, and she appeared to be in prayer. She was no more in prayer than he was, Stuart thought. The moment his eyes fell upon her, he knew that she was staring directly at him through that veil. He was certain of it.

All of this flashed through his mind in a few seconds, but he had been standing behind the microphone in silence for much too long already. "I know that many of you don't know me," he began, already feeling the need to improvise. "Well, none of you do, I guess." Some of his audience grinned at this, and he made a mental note to stick to his script. "Some of you might be surprised to find out that Rylen even had a brother. It was always that way, though. Even when we were kids, he was always the one to shine. Rylen would be upset with me if I ever tried to make him out to be a better person than he was. I know that because he once asked me outright why people always seem to deify the dead. It seems eerily relevant to me now, but at the time, I was surprised he even had to ask. I told him it's just bad form to put a spotlight on the wrong deeds or traits of any person. There's good and bad in everyone, and those who want to remember someone prefer to think of the good. I never minded the fact that I didn't shine as brightly as my older brother, because he was always there for me. When we were growing up, he was the father neither of us had. And when we grew up, he was the best friend I always needed. But he was always my brother. I might be a candle next to his torch, but if I'm able to find my own way now, it's because of the brother who led me for so long that I would even know how."

Stuart went back to his seat in the front row and, when nobody else wished to speak, the priest closed the service with a prayer and all stood. Stuart looked to the back of the church, but the veiled woman was gone.

Perry Tellerson shook Stuart's hand and told him to expect a phone call in the next few days to conclude the matter of Rylen's insurance. Stuart said that he would, but he was only half listening. He shook a few more hands before he met the eyes of the familiar blonde woman from the second row.

"Stuart?" she said, holding out her hand. Stuart nodded and shook it, not hiding the expression of trying to remember her name. "Krista Franklin. I knew Rylen in college."

It all came back to him in a flash. He had known her himself, at least for however long she and Rylen were together. They were seniors when he was a freshman, but he knew her well enough to recognize her after so long. "I remember you!" said

Stuart. "Thank you for coming. I'm so sorry, I didn't know that you and Rylen had kept in touch."

"We didn't," she replied without a hint of embarrassment. "I found out from social media. I hope you don't mind my coming."

He shook his head, though he was a little confused. "No, not at all. It's good to see you. What are you doing now?"

"I'm a nurse at Mercy Medical."

"I'm glad you came."

She gave him a red-eyed nod before saying, "I just wanted to say goodbye to a part of my past." She leaned forward and hugged him. "Take care of yourself."

She turned and walked up the aisle of the church. As soon as she stepped away from him, a man stepped forward and shook Stuart by the hand. He was one of Rylen's friends, whom Stuart had met for the first time before the service. Stuart tried to focus on the man before him, but he could not help glancing over to look at Krista walking up the aisle.

CHAPTER NINE

SPIDER

Spider sat at the table, drumming his fingers and waiting for his appointment to show. He was less concerned about this meeting than many of those in recent weeks. He had met this man the week before and charged him three hundred dollars to unlock the cell phone of his brother who had just been killed. The guy was on the level too, which was more than could be said for every client that came his way. It was easy money for him, not that he needed it. As a computer hacker, he was among the best, and discretion was his bread and butter. He knew hackers that would take a job and blackmail their clients for more money when it was done. That wasn't Spider's style, and he had a knack for keeping a secret. He had been hired by everyone, from people wanting to catch cheating spouses to those in the highest echelons of major corporations. Word got around. He was playing the long game and reliability, not to mention a healthy dose of caution, would keep him playing for a long time to come.

When he met Stuart and heard the story about his brother dying in a car crash, he assumed it was total bullshit. He didn't care. The guy had the cash in hand and Spider had the phone unlocked in minutes. He asked about the crash in a disinterested fashion, testing his client's thoroughness, and made a mental note of when and where it had happened. Later, after some simple investigation due to his own curiosity, Spider found that everything Stuart had told him was true. A man named Rylen Hollister had been killed in a car crash on the first of the month. Stuart, his brother, was his only surviving relative. The poor schmuck didn't even use a fake name. The job turned out to be honest work for once, and that was the only reason he was meeting the guy in person a second time.

There were many men sitting alone in the restaurant when Stuart last met him here, yet somehow Stuart walked straight to his table and introduced himself. Spider's physical appearance had evolved into the perfect cliché of the very thing he was. At six feet tall and thin as a rail, Spider knew he had spent far too many hours a week in front of a computer monitor. His unwashed, black hair and glasses only added to the effect. His two facial piercings and tattoo sleeves were the icing on the cake. He hated this, but by the time he was aware of it, he no longer cared to mitigate his cool geek persona.

He sipped his black coffee as he waited, his laptop case next to him on the seat of the booth, between himself and the wall. He would never meet a client in a place like this if there were any chance he was being hired to do anything more serious than unlock a phone. Still, what could Stuart want now? The thing that troubled Spider about it all was the timing. A guy loses his only living relative in a car crash and, just days later, he is hiring someone on the Dark Web to unlock his dead brother's phone? Had Rylen even been buried yet? Who does that? Bypassing a password without a hard reset was a simple issue. Resets and iTunes restores were risky. Something could get lost, which was why Stuart had come to him through their mutual Dark Web chat contact. Spider didn't ask what Stuart was hoping to find. Maybe he was looking for some photos for sentimental reasons, but Stuart certainly did not seem the sentimental type. More likely, he wanted what most people want when a sibling dies--to comb through the deceased person's shit and uncover all the dirty secrets he is no longer alive to keep. No doubt some insight would be coming soon, he thought as he watched Stuart enter the gas station restaurant.

Stuart walked over and sat down at the table without hesitation. "Hi."

Spider looked Stuart in the eye, hesitating for a second to realize that he had positively no idea what to make of this man. "You have it?" he asked, deciding to go straight to business.

Stuart pulled the phone from the pocket of his jacket and put it on the table between them. Spider picked it up and swiped to activate the phone. A photo of a leaf was already open. "That's it," said Stuart.

"This is what? What am I looking at?"

"That is the text message my brother got. I was wondering if you could trace it," Stuart told him, as though they had already discussed it.

"Trace an image?"

"The text message that contained the image. And the phone call that came in at the same time, but I can only assume they were the same person."

Spider sighed and put the phone on the table, already regretting taking this meeting. "Look," he said leaning back, "let's back up a second. The only reason I agreed to meet you without getting all the details was because you know a friend of mine and I know you told me the truth when we first met. Nobody ever does that. You said that there was some message on the phone I unlocked that you wanted me to trace. That implies you wanted me to track a phone number. This is a fucking jpeg of a leaf. What exactly do you want me to do with that?"

Stuart shook his head and held up a hand. "You're right. I'm sorry. I haven't been sleeping. Let me start over," he said before he asked the waitress to bring him some coffee and cream before continuing. "The night my brother died in the accident, he was driving home, ran off the road, and crashed into a tree. The highway patrol thinks he just fell asleep on the road, but here's the thing: he got a call from a blocked number and was texted this image from the same blocked number. I want to know whether it's possible to find out who that blocked number belongs to."

Spider rubbed his chin for a moment. Almost every single time something interesting came along in his line of work, it led to the disappointment of it being someone's paranoia. *Almost* every time. People had an innate tendency to find things that simply were not there. One minute would be all he needed to find the flaws in this guy's thinking. If his story held up, Spider decided he would look into it. If not, he would leave the restaurant and have nothing more to do with this crazy fool again. "Okay, your brother got a phone call from a blocked number and, at the same time, he's texted a photo of a leaf. And we can assume this was from the person he was on the phone with, since it was also blocked."

"Exactly. Can you find out where the call came from?"

Spider was not ready to agree to anything. "Hold on," he said, holding up his hand in a halting gesture. Normally he would not care why someone wanted the information he was paid to acquire. Stuart wanted him to find out who called his brother and he probably could, but he was curious as to what his client actually thought this was all about. He had learned that Stuart was an elevator tech, of all things. A decent and honest living, to be sure, but he was no corporate powerhouse. Spider was glad he had only charged him three hundred dollars. He would charge him more if he accepted this job, but the fee was outright laughable compared to what he would demand of a corporate slime-bag for the same service. If a job interested him enough, he was sometimes willing to do it for free, but Stuart did not need to know that. "What does that have to do with the accident? Maybe he got the call and the text and then fell asleep on the road, like the cops said. You said it was, what, four or five in the morning?"

"Yes, but he didn't just get the call on the drive home," said Stuart, pausing for emphasis. "He was on the call at the time of the crash. He wrecked the car while still on the fucking phone!"

"What? How do you know that?"

"The time of the call and the time of the accident aren't just close, but exactly the same. The system in his car notified emergency responders when his airbag deployed. I checked. It was during the call."

Spider had to admit that his interest was piqued, but there were still a couple ideal places for Occam's Razor to make a cut. "Instead of falling asleep, he was distracted. It happens all the time. He's talking, the person sends him a text, he looks at it too long and loses control of the car."

Stuart nodded. "That was what I thought too. That leaves us with the fact that the person on the other end of that call *knew* he was in an accident, yet no other calls were made to 911. The ambulance was there in 6 minutes."

Spider thought for a moment, already realizing the answer to his next question, but was thinking out loud at this point. "The caller was still connected and must have heard the crash. And they weren't disconnected when the crash occurred because..."

Stuart picked up the phone from the table and held it up, turning it back to front. "Because the phone wasn't damaged in the crash. There isn't a mark on it."

"So they heard the crash and hung up the phone later on. Were there any callbacks from a blocked number after that? Any in the days since?"

"Not a single one," said Stuart with a tone of finality. "Look at the length of the call. Eight fucking minutes."

Spider would have to verify all of this, but if this guy was right... "So the caller stayed on the phone listening to the police and EMTs talking? Then didn't bother to call back to see what had happened because they already knew. Fuck me... that's some cold-blooded shit," said Spider as he exhausted the last of his simplest explanations.

"Is it possible to find who that caller was?"

Spider nodded. "Yeah, probably. Five hundred." Stuart went to reach into his pocket, but Spider stayed him, holding out his hand. "We'll settle up later. This will take some time. You are one trusting shit, willing to pay up-front like that."

Stuart furrowed his brow. "I can't let you take it with you."

"Relax," said Spider, removing his laptop from the bag on

the seat beside him. "I can make a mirror duplicate of the phone to work from. But I have to tell you, even if I get the number the call came from, it might not be so easy to track it to an owner. It's more than likely a burner phone, which would make it tough to find your mysterious caller."

"There's something else," Stuart told him. "Rylen used his phone as his GPS. This may be nothing, but he was using it to get home that night. His home address was the last destination he routed."

"Meaning he was driving home from someplace he didn't know," finished Spider with a nod. "But that doesn't mean the place he was driving home from and the person he got the call from have got anything to do with each other."

"No, it doesn't," Stuart admitted. "Like I said, it may be nothing." He took a sip from his coffee before adding, "But if the person on that phone knew he crashed and did nothing... I'm sure as hell going to do everything I can to find them."

CHAPTER TEN
EMERGENCY MEETING

All nine members of the Tellerson Foundation were seated at the table, waiting for Perry to turn the conversation over to business. Perry Tellerson had been head of the Tellerson Foundation since he assumed the role five years before, and the Foundation was renamed accordingly. Since it was first established in 1978, this had always been the tradition with each successive person to hold the position. At fifty-one years old, with square features and steel gray hair, Perry was the epitome of a handsome, successful businessman. He could have had any public office he chose at a local and probably state level with the power at his disposal, but it was forbidden for any person in his position to hold a public office. Like all the other members of the board of trustees, he had earned his position and was appointed to the board by the vote of all its other members.

Though the Foundation had given millions to various charities over a period of years, it did not supply grants, and so the name itself was misleading. As a private entity, it functioned in the same way as a venture capitalist, but it assumed the rights to any patents obtained through any team, company, or individual it funded. The funding was more than generous, but that was not what made research teams who found themselves approached by the Foundation willing to sign the paperwork. The individuals would get all the credit for any product, drug, or technology they developed and gain all the recognition they deserved. However, they would also be given a large percentage of all earnings from the patent or would otherwise be offered an immediate buyout.

There was another side to the Foundation, of which only four of the board members were a part. These were the secret side dealings which the foursome exploited the Foundation's technological and financial resources to conduct.

The board members were seated at the conference table on the second floor of The Church, so named because it was indeed a renovated church, which to all outside appearances was just another office building. What few outside of the board members knew, was that this nondescript, two-story building at a remote twenty-five-acre site outside of Boston contained some of the most sophisticated security systems in the world, designed and installed by specialists in the Foundation's own proprietary technology. It housed data servers storing their technological research and development records. Many prototypes were secured at this location, where access could be restricted and any risks of sabotage, theft, and espionage were minimized.

The Church had gone black an hour before the meeting. *Blackout* was the term used for the strict protocol stipulating that all security personnel were restricted to the security building at the edge of the property, out of sight of The Church and its main access drive. All drone coverage and video monitoring inside the building and on the property was shut down for the duration. As this created an open door in their otherwise impenetrable security, making The Church vulnerable for a brief time window if anyone should learn how and when blackout protocol was implemented, only the head of the Foundation was permitted to enact it at any given time. This meeting was one of those times.

Among all the other matters this group would cover, there was one topic of an unprecedented nature--the sudden death of their trusted accountant, Rylen Hollister.

"As you all know," Perry began, "Rylen was killed in a car accident ten days ago. He's being replaced by one of two successors, both of whom have been with us for years and have done excellent work managing our overseas and domestic accounts. Each of you will be sent a full dossier on both and submit your choice to me by end of day tomorrow. If you have any questions or concerns, please direct them to Steve or the rest of the board as you feel appropriate. Any issues aside, one of the two candidates will be promoted to overseeing the accounts in a full capacity by the end of the week."

"Can you tell us about the accident?" asked Marcus Harrier of Great Britain, the only member of the board who was not an American. His soft voice and Oxford English accent were in sharp contrast to his imposing physical presence. At forty-three, his blond hair was streaked with silver and sat atop a six foot, five-inch figure.

Perry made a gesture to Steve McGuire, who had been responsible for handling all matters related to the incident. It was standard practice that a board member address matters of sufficient gravity personally, ensuring the sensitive information and materials the Foundation had in its possession were never exposed to the awareness of an outsider. He handled the gathering of full information, both public and not. "Between four thirty and five in the morning on the Thursday before last, he was driving home on Route 3," Steve began. "All indications are that he fell asleep while driving home and his car ran off of the road and crashed into a tree, killing him instantly. We have recovered his company phone and my contact tells me that the police notified his only family, a brother..."

"Just a moment," interrupted Marcus, "you said you recovered his company phone. What about his personal device?"

Perry answered, having anticipated this question. "Protocol does not dictate acquiring his personal property. His business phone was wiped remotely, but we still recovered the actual device within hours of the accident."

"The Foundation has its rivals," said Marcus. "Coupling that with the incident of espionage that took place last year, would acquiring his personal device not have been prudent?"

"As you say, it was over a year ago," said Perry. "That is exactly why all critical materials and data were moved to this location and there have been no breaches since. You don't seriously suspect Rylen of leaking information?"

"I would not go so far," said Marcus. "However, the fact that a key member of the Foundation dies in a way that could easily be orchestrated is worth investigating. Where was he driving home from at five in the morning? Where did he spend the night?"

Perry chuckled. "If you knew that man, you would be able to guess for yourself."

"His phone was provided with all the standard security measures as each of our own," Steve answered. "It cannot be tracked or hacked, not even by us."

"But we can gain a complete picture of all of his movements in the days leading up to his death with his personal device," said Marcus. "It may well be an accident and nothing more, but I would like to know all the same."

"Steve," said Perry, "Marcus is right; look into acquiring Rylen's personal phone and reconstructing his contacts and movements leading up to the accident." All at the table were in agreement.

"I hope you aren't easily embarrassed," said one of the others on the board. "Rylen was a notorious rake."

"We don't need to be invasive," said Perry. "Steve, when you have his phone, provide us with an outline of all activity in the seventy two hours before the accident. A transcript annotated with a contact description will be fine."

"Consider it done," Steve told them.

"See if his brother is willing to give us his phone if we promise it will be returned," Perry told him. "Rylen had only one family member, a younger brother, and the phone is in his possession by now. If it is still active..."

"It is," Steve interjected.

"When he sees the size of the check we are about to write

him, it will put him in a cooperative mood," Perry noted. "Speaking of that, have we contacted him yet?"

All employees of the Foundation were given a generous life insurance policy. For those who were employed at the higher levels in the Foundation, the benefits packages were far more substantial. "An agent has already called him and set up an appointment for Tuesday," Steve supplied.

"Excellent," said Perry. "We can ask him for the phone then."

Steve McGuire stayed behind in the boardroom after all the other members departed. "What do you think about getting Rylen's personal phone?"

"I know! God damn it," said Perry in reply. "You said it's still active. So you can track it."

Steve nodded. "His brother has it."

"Get it quietly," said Perry. "If there's anything on there that could point to what the other four of us have been doing, we can't risk his giving that phone to the wrong person."

"I'll get it before asking him for it. We can't let anyone else find out we never even made the request."

"Clean and quiet," Perry stressed. "I'm sure he isn't carrying it around with him, so that shouldn't be a problem."

"I already know who to call. You met Rylen's brother at the funeral. What is he like?"

Perry laughed. "He is the antithesis of Rylen in every way you can think of."

CHAPTER ELEVEN

MY BROTHER DIED

Stuart sat across from Ella, who made notes on a pad. Two weeks had passed since their last meeting. When she had called him about missing his appointment, he explained about losing his brother on the very day they last saw each other. Helping him to deal with his grief was part of her new agenda, especially as his sleeping problems were improving, according to him. His anger issues were evident, but he was no public danger in her opinion. She would say as much in his next court appointment. He spent some time giving Ella all the background he could on his brother and their childhood. "Thank you for not putting a box of tissues by my chair," he told her when he finished. "I would have questioned your skill as a therapist if you did that."

"They're close at hand."

Stuart's face remained stoic, but he tilted his head. "I didn't expect you to let me talk about this."

"No, what you expected was for me to give you a speech about the importance of allowing your own grief to play out, and how necessary it is as a part of recovery," she told him.

This time, Stuart didn't hide his look of surprise and something like admiration. "How did you know that?"

"You're a smart man, Stuart. And we're here to talk about whatever you need to work through."

"I can afford to pay you your standard rate now, by the way."

"Why is that?"

Stuart explained about the life insurance policy before bringing them back to the topic at hand. "Can you at least help me to understand why?" he asked. "Why am I sleeping now when I never could before? My anxiety is better too."

"Based on what you've been telling me," Ella said delicately, "Rylen was more than just an older brother, but something not unlike a father figure. Also, he was someone you tried very hard to live up to."

"He never wanted anything but what was good for me. And I was very proud of him for his success."

"No doubt you were," she replied, "but there are many ways we can try to live up to someone we idolize. We can do it through emulation, what they directly ask of us... and another way is to try to be what we think would make them the proudest."

"Which do you think I was doing?"

"What's more important is that you are not doing it anymore."

"Rylen was always there. We were there for each other. How the hell can I be cured of my anxiety by his death when I'm more miserable than I've ever been?" Stuart said, looking unsure of whether to continue. "It was always just us, you know... he was the one I always called when I couldn't deal. What am I supposed to do now?"

"There is a time to heal and recover and there is a time to move forward. Yes, I am working in the part about grieving now."

"Let's have the speech."

"It isn't a speech. There really is an answer to that."

"An answer to what?"

"An answer to what you should do now."

"I'll take it."

"Everybody faces loss, hardship, or adversity. How to handle it is a choice we all have to make. There are some people who are so afraid of getting burned that they will die in a fire rather than take a chance on running through a wall of flames to make it to safety. The other type is the firefighter who runs into a burning building to rescue somebody trapped inside. What kind of person would you want to be teamed up with when the shit hits the fan?" Ella paused as he seemed to be considering her words.

"You're saying I should stop feeling sorry for myself."

"Of course not. I'm saying you never had to worry about being the former because you always had someone there who was the latter. But now you have to be your own firefighter. You will be fine, Stuart, but only if you take the time to grieve and to heal. As to how you handle problems when your brother isn't there to help... ask yourself what he would do. You don't need your brother to be proud of you; be proud of yourself. When we look back at the worst times and situations in our lives, sometimes we're proud of the way we handled them and sometimes not. You are going to encounter a lot of those choices as you go through this process. Remember to ask yourself how you will handle it now. Be the person you would most want to have by your side in a time of crisis."

As their time had elapsed, he rose and said, "You work with the court, so do you get over to the police station over here very often?"

"The one right there on Cambridge? Sure, I'm there a lot."

"Do you know a Detective Connelly?"

"James Connelly? Yes, I know him. Why do you ask?"

"He delivered the news about the accident."

"That's odd. Didn't you say Rylen was driving on Route 3?"

"That's right."

"I would have thought that a little out of Connelly's district," Ella mused.

"Rylen lived in Newton. That might have something to do with it," said Stuart. "I have some questions about the accident and I'm hoping he'll take me seriously."

"What kind of questions?"

Stuart shook his head. "Nothing serious. I just wanted some

details."

Ella doubted his honesty. "Well, I like Connelly. If I had any problems, he is one of the first people I would go to there. He's a compassionate man, which is probably why he got the job of delivering the news. I think he'll help if he can."

"I hope so. When I called him this morning, he told me to stop by the station at eleven," said Stuart.

As Ella moved to the door, she said, "Again, I'm very sorry for your loss, Stuart. As I mentioned, I knew Rylen. He was a fascinating man."

"I had forgotten that. Can you tell me what he wanted to see you about? Surely it can't hurt to tell me now."

"It certainly can and no, I certainly cannot," Ella answered adamantly.

Ella could see he was deliberating. She expected him to make a further attempt at persuading her, but he said, "Until next week, then." He left without saying anything more.

CHAPTER TWELVE

MEET THE DETECTIVE

"This is your office?" Stuart asked as the detective pointed him to a chair on the other side of his desk. His desk sat behind a fabric panel partition wall that separated it from the rest of the open floor.

"Seniority has its perks," said Connelly as he took his seat.

Stuart leaned forward and examined a device on the detective's desk. "Is that a microcassette tape player?" he asked.

"Yeah, and it's the real deal. Go ahead and get your jokes out," the detective said with a gesture toward it.

"I wasn't going to make jokes; I just didn't know they still made those."

"You can still get them on Amazon or eBay for a fair price if you're lucky."

"You carry a smart phone, so why use that?"

"Because I like it. The department requires I carry the damn phone. But how I use it is my business. Sometimes, old school just fucking works," he said, leaning back in his chair. "Now, what can I do for you, Mr. Hollister?"

Stuart took a deep breath and pulled Rylen's phone from his jacket pocket. "I was wondering if you could tell me something," he began, handing the phone to Connelly. "On the night of the accident, my brother was on the phone with this person who has a blocked number. As you can see, the time stamp well overlaps the time of the accident. He also received a text message from the same blocked number that contained a JPEG file."

"A file of what?" asked Connelly, taking the phone and verifying the time.

"A leaf," Stuart answered. "The thing is, when I met you, you said it was assumed that my brother fell asleep on the road. But this shows he was on the phone at the time of the accident."

"I wasn't on the scene personally, but I know the officer with highway patrol who was," Connelly told him.

"Is he the one who found the phone?"

"Probably, but why the interest?"

"If it was a case of distracted driving instead of driver fatigue, I'd like to know. But if he was on the phone, who was he talking to, and why didn't that person call 911 when they heard the crash?"

Connelly rubbed the gray stubble on his chin. "Distracted driving kills more people every year than driver fatigue, but if you're looking for who he was talking to and why they didn't call anyone, Mr. Hollister, how do you expect us to help you with that? There's no crime here."

"I don't," said Stuart, wanting to derail this dismissal before it got firmly on track. "I just wanted to know if the call was still connected when the officer found the phone. Maybe it was, and maybe he talked to the person on the other end."

"I see," said Connelly, handing the phone back to Stuart. "I can already tell you that didn't happen."

"How can you be sure?" asked Stuart. "You said you weren't at the scene yourself."

"Because if that happened, it would have been reported by the officer."

Stuart had to resist the urge to roll his eyes, lest he antagonize the man. "He wouldn't have if he thought it irrelevant at the time. Detective, you have been on the force a long time, I'm sure. Would every officer report a detail he thought was insignificant?"

Connelly's hand again went to his chin. "Look, if that's all you want to know, we can find out easily enough. Come with me." The officer stood and led Stuart down a hall of offices until they came to a small room with the light off. He entered and shut the door behind Stuart as he flipped the switch on the wall. They were in a very small office that was empty, save for a clean desk with only a phone atop it. There were no chairs in the room.

"They have empty offices on the floor, but you get a fabric wall?" Stuart asked.

"Don't piss me off, kid," said Connelly as he walked around to the other side of the desk. He leaned on the desktop as he placed his mobile phone in the middle of it. It was already ringing on speaker phone.

"What's going on, Jim?" the voice answered with a tone of familiarity.

"Hey, Carl. Listen, I have a favor to ask. I have you on speaker and I'm standing here with the brother of the man in the accident you responded to a couple weeks ago on Route 3, on the morning of October first."

"What about it?" asked the man on the phone.

"Are you the one who bagged the contents of the car, specifically the phone of the driver?" Connelly asked.

"Yes, I did."

"His brother is here with me now. He has a question for you. You can speak freely," added Connelly, looking at Stuart with that same curious look that he had when he delivered the news. "He can handle anything you tell him."

"What do you want to know?" Carl asked.

Stuart leaned close to the phone on the desktop. "Hi, Officer, this is Stuart Hollister," he began. "I was wondering if you noticed whether a call was connected at the time you found my brother's phone in the car."

There was a telling pause on the phone before the officer answered. "It's odd that you should ask, but I did initially think there was a call connected when I found the phone on the floorboard."

Connelly raised his dark gray eyebrows as Stuart asked, "What did you do then?"

"As soon as I reached for the phone and looked at it, it was back on the home screen. I asked if anyone was there, but I could see that no call was connected."

"Really?" Connelly interrupted. "You didn't think that was kind of weird?"

"It was eerie," Carl said, "but I wasn't sure about it. I thought maybe I was mistaken. I couldn't check the phone later. It was already locked."

"Why was I told that my brother fell asleep behind the wheel?" Stuart asked.

"Mr. Hollister, your brother's car left the road and drove on grass for hundreds of feet before crashing into a tree. If he was awake at the time, he never hit the brake or even tried to steer back onto the road. There were no drugs or alcohol in his system or in the car. Is it possible that your brother committed suicide?"

Stuart considered this for no more than a second. "No, Rylen loved his life. We had just made plans the day before."

"Well," said the officer on the phone, "the only thing it can be is that he fell asleep. I must have been mistaken about the call, unless there's some way for a man to have a phone conversation and be asleep at the same time."

CHAPTER THIRTEEN

YOU SAVED MY ASS

Stuart crossed the cemetery and approached the chapel, but Spider was nowhere to be seen. Spider had chosen the spot well. There were not many people around a graveyard at this time of the morning. Upon spotting the white chapel, Stuart came within ten yards of its front steps when he heard voices coming from around the side of the building. As he got closer, he could make out the voices of two men arguing. One of them was Spider.

When Stuart walked around to the side of the chapel, he saw a concrete walkway that ran along the small stretch of grass between the chapel and a dense row of pines that screened it from the adjacent property. It made sense that the two men with Spider would bring him here to conduct whatever business involved one of them pinning Spider to the chapel wall by the front of his shirt. The one standing by was a large man wearing a New England Patriots jacket. He had his back to Stuart. The thinner man pinning Spider to the wall wore a sky-blue running suit. This man's hair was shoulder length, but had been slicked back into a permanent *just stepped out of the pool* look using products Stuart did not miss having need of. Spider was bleeding from a cut on his mouth.

"I was polite the last time," said the slick-haired man. He had a garish English accent that came from the back alleys of London. "That ship has sailed now."

None of the trio noticed Stuart until he was within twenty feet of them. Spider's head turned to see Stuart, and The Hair glanced his way until Patriots turned as well. "Get lost, man. We ain't giving you any money," said Patriots. He was definitely a Bostonian.

Stuart looked down at himself. He was wearing a baggy, gray pullover hoodie and navy-blue sweatpants with old sneakers. He had to concede that the man had made a reasonable assumption. Given his newfound wealth, he would have to do something about his wardrobe. "I'm here to see him," said Stuart, pointing at Spider. Patriots looked back at The Hair, who gave him a brief nod.

Patriots walked to Stuart. He was about six foot two and weighed two hundred eighty, as near as Stuart could gauge. He had a hulking way of moving and there was too much wobble in his upper body for much of his size to be muscle. He planted himself menacingly in front of Stuart and glared down at him. Stuart was sure he had done it to other men a hundred times before. "You a friend of his?" he asked, making it sound like a warning.

"No, I'm not his friend, so I'll let you finish your conversation. You were here first. I'm happy to wait," Stuart replied, with all the congenial calm one would use in conversation with a bank teller. Stuart leaned over to see past the big man to address The Hair. "But I do need him alive, if that's okay with you. Or I would appreciate it, I mean."

The Hair had a squinted, leering expression that made him look like he was smelling something horrible. Spider sighed and shook his head. "Get the fuck out of here! Run, you dumb..." Spider shouted, but The Hair gut-punched him and he fell to the ground in the fetal position, receiving a kick for good measure.

Stuart looked up at Patriots, whose face was a mask of confusion. His intimidation was failing spectacularly. He changed his expression. "Give me your wallet, motherfucker!"

Patriots must have decided that this was the best way to salvage his dignity. "Oh!" said Stuart with a look of honest surprise. "I thought you guys were drug dealers or some other higher class of criminals. I didn't know you were street punks, but then again, you thought I was a bum, so I guess neither of us is doing so..."

The man reached for Stuart's shoulder with his left hand while balling his right into a fist. He was not slow in doing this, but given the blink speed of Stuart's response, he might have posed to receive the thrusting upper cut that crashed under his jaw. With fists that had broken boards, bricks, and stacks of ceramic tile since his teens, their owner had knuckles of granite. The man's jaw snapped shut with a force that cracked the bone before his head snapped back hard enough for Stuart to hear his neck pop. He fell backwards to the ground. He would have his jaw wired shut and be in a neck brace for some time, but that was far better than leaving the guy a chance to pull a gun from under his jacket. Stuart was glad the man landed on the grass instead of the concrete walkway. Before he even lay still, Stuart was charging The Hair.

The remaining man stood over Spider, who lay on the grass against the wall, still curled up and trying to breathe. After seeing his friend felled, and that he was being rushed by the man who did it, The Hair stood his ground and sneered as he rushed to pull something from the back waistband under his jacket. The twenty feet between them was closed too quickly for the man to reach both hands behind his body, lift his jacket with one hand, and draw a weapon in time to use it. Halfway to his target, Stuart knew he would make it in time, but The Hair might be a faster draw than he would like. If he had time to get a gun in his hand, it might go off, even if he didn't have time to aim it. Stuart wasn't taking the chance and leaped into the air. He snapped a jumping sidekick to the sneering face. The Hair flew back into the stone wall of the chapel and fell to the grass above where Spider lay.

No gunshot. Stuart moved to kick the weapon out of reach of its owner. It wasn't a gun at all, but a large survival knife. Stuart stared at the thing on the ground, baffled as to what kind of international street thug carried a large survival knife around. He kicked it away, as the man had only struck the wall at an angle and was already struggling to sit up.

Stuart helped Spider to his feet. He could not run, but could walk with help. "Get your friend to the hospital," Stuart said loudly to The Hair. He and Spider slowly made their way down the walkway and out to the street.

CHAPTER FOURTEEN

YOU WANT A BEER

By the time Stuart and Spider reached the street, Spider was able to walk on his own. Keeping watch over their shoulders, they walked a few blocks, turning a corner at each and taking an alleyway to be sure they were not followed.

Spider stopped at the end of the alley and leaned his back to the brick wall. Stuart decided to give the man a break and stood watching until Spider said, "Hey, man, listen. I'm really sorry you got involved in that. But I got to say, I'm really glad you got involved in that."

"What did they want?" Stuart asked.

Spider shook his head. "We got business of our own. Look, there's a bar I know two blocks up. It's pretty early, but they're open. You want to get a beer?"

"A bar? At this time of the morning?"

"When you start as early as I do, this is happy hour."

Stuart agreed and two blocks later, they were sitting at a bar. Spider ordered a stout and when the bartender looked at Stuart, he hesitated a second and ordered the same.

In a moment, both men had mugs of coffee-colored beer in front of them. "That shit back there," Spider said, "I appreciate it, man. You could have just taken off."

"Yeah, but we weren't done with our business," Stuart replied, taking a sip of the beer and trying not to wince from the taste.

"You asked who they were. The British guy is named Mann. I never saw the other one before. Mann found out about my taking a job for one of his rivals and wanted me to help him with a credit card scheme he cooked up. It isn't a bad idea, but I refused--partly because he's a scumbag, partly because of that fucking hair, and partly because he's just too... street trash."

"Can't argue with your reasons," said Stuart, at which Spider shot him a sideways glance.

"He didn't accept them."

"How did he find you at the place where we were meeting? He just happened to drive by and see you in a cemetery, then jump out of the car with his buddy to get you to change your mind?"

Spider gulped the beer and wiped the foam from his lips. "No, when I was walking to meet you, this teenage shit kid I passed looked at me hard, like he knew me. I kept walking and didn't think anything about it. Nobody knows where I live, but they know my neighborhood. Mann must have had a couple of the locals keeping an eye out for me, promising to pay if they give him a call when they spot me. The punk must have followed me and told Mann where I was."

"Did I make things worse?"

Spider looked at his mug. "He really was going to stab me. It would have been worse if you hadn't... wait, what the fuck did you do, anyway?"

"You were there," said Stuart, forcing himself to take another sip of his beer.

"Yeah, well in case you didn't notice, I was kind of busy rolling on the ground getting the shit stomped out of me."

Stuart didn't want to go into details--at least not in a way that sounded like a braggart's bar tale. "When the big guy squared off on me, he looked back at the other guy, so I sucker punched him and charged Mann before he could pull out a gun or something. Knocked him into the wall. He was pulling out a knife, though."

Spider took another sip and then spoke over his beer

without looking at Stuart. "Why did you tell Mann to get his friend to a hospital?"

Stuart had forgotten about that part. Why was he so reluctant to tell Spider the truth? Somehow, saying he was a fifth degree black belt in Tae Kwon Do always sounded pretentious, and he never told anyone that if he could help it. "He fell backwards on the concrete. Hit his head. That can kill somebody. As we went to walk away, I saw he wasn't getting up. I think he needed a doctor."

Spider's mug was nearly empty when he took in Stuart's nearly full glass. "You drink like an old woman."

Stuart shrugged. "I can't help that. I hate beer."

Spider turned and stared at him for several seconds until Stuart, unable to ignore him any longer, turned to meet his eye. "You hate beer?" Spider asked.

"Yes, I do."

"Really?"

"Yeah, really. It's revolting. I don't see how anybody drinks this piss," Stuart replied, shaking his head in wonderment at the glass in front of him.

"Then why the actual fuck would you come here, sit down at the bar, and order a frigging beer?"

A good question, deserving an honest answer. "Because two guys going into a bar and having a beer is something normal people do. So when the chance came up, I thought I'd try it myself."

"What the hell is the matter with you?" Spider asked, looking at Stuart like he wasn't entirely sure the man was human.

"I thought we were having a moment."

"Yeah, sure." Spider turned back to the bar and drained the rest of his glass.

"I'm on the spectrum," said Stuart, taking yet another sip from his glass and wincing in disgust before putting it back down.

"Oh, fucking hell! Give me that," said the hacker in exasperation, sliding Stuart's glass in front of himself. In minutes, he had emptied that mug as well. "Come on," he said as he stood and dropped cash on the bar, "we can't talk here." Spider led the way, but he did not head to the main entrance where they came in. He walked around to the back of the bar, heading toward a fire exit in the corner.

When they passed through the fire exit, Stuart found that they were in a connecting space that was painted concrete block on all sides. It was about six feet by eight feet and was lit by a single light over one door to the right. The glowing exit sign under the sconce caused Stuart to realize it let out into the alley they had passed on the way in. Another door was straight across from the one they had exited. It was a plain, unmarked, steel door with a keyhole for a deadbolt lock. Spider went to this door and slipped a key into the lock. He pushed the door open to reveal a metal stairway going up. He beckoned Stuart to go up first so he could lock the door behind them. After they entered, he punched a security code into a keypad at the bottom of the stairs.

"What is this?" Stuart asked as he climbed.

"This is the reason nobody can find out where I live," Spider answered behind him. "Even the people who work in the bar just think I'm a regular. They don't know I live right upstairs."

CHAPTER FIFTEEN
I HAVE A NEW CLIENT

Ella stood at the island in the kitchen, sipping her coffee and tapping her tablet when Paxton entered. He wished her a good morning and poured a cup for himself. Inwardly, he was not sanguine about the conversation they were about to have, but he knew she would understand.

Paxton went to the other side of the island and leaned on it, facing her. "The good news is I have a new client. I'm only contracted for pre-design at the moment, but I'm pretty sure I'll get the job if they like what I come up with."

"Really? Who are they? How did you find them?" asked Ella.

"Brandon Holdshire of Holdshire Realty. And he found me. I was recommended by the owners of their parent company."

"What do they have you working on?"

"A 40,000 square foot mixed use, multi-story renovation."

"That's wonderful, sweetheart," said Ella. "You said that was the good news, meaning there's bad news?"

"Yeah, and... they want to apply for permits next month," he added sheepishly, "so they want to see schematic designs by the end of the week."

Ella smirked. "Seriously? We're supposed to leave for Maine tomorrow."

"I'm sorry, honey," he said. "I need a pre-design concept done and in their hands by Friday."

"If you must," said Ella. "Just as long as you understand that if I miss peak leaf season, it will be death to pay, mister."

"It's just one more day. We will be leaf peeping in Maine on Friday. Promise," Paxton answered.

"I guess I'm off tomorrow," said Ella.

"What will you do," asked Paxton before finishing with, "or do I even have to ask?"

Ella looked at him askance. "Does my friendship with Sophia bother you?"

"Not in the least," he said, though not entirely sure he meant it. "I am glad you have a friend you feel that close to, since..." He didn't finish. He met her not long after her childhood friend was killed, found strangled in her home. The killer was never caught. Maybe it was a mistake to even allude to it, but why not? It had been ten months, and he hated the idea of walking on eggshells about something that bothered her. A psychologist should know it unwise to keep things like that bottled up.

"You're right; I don't have a very healthy circle of friends and I do like her," Ella admitted.

"Even if she's into some really far-out shit."

Ella's expression was one he could not interpret. "I will see if she's doing anything tomorrow."

CHAPTER SIXTEEN

HOME SWEET LAIR

When Stuart reached the top of the stairs, he stopped to take in the space, nearly forgetting that Spider was on the stairs behind him. He took a few steps in to allow Spider to pass. He expected a hacker to live in a place that was a cross between a teenager's bedroom and a crack house. He found himself in a spacious loft apartment with exposed brick on the outer walls and hardwood floors. Area rugs defined the key areas of living, dining, and bedroom, with only the kitchen and bathroom having separate drywall partitions. It was sparsely but tastefully furnished, or perhaps it was merely the high ceilings and lack of walls that made the furniture pieces isolated clusters of comfort in a warehouse-sized apartment.

"Welcome to home-sweet-lair," said Spider, leading Stuart to the couches. "I would offer you a drink, but all I have is beer and water."

"Water is fine, thanks. How the hell do you afford a place like this in this part of Boston?"

Spider pulled a thumb drive from his pocket and tossed it to Stuart, who caught it and sat down on the edge of a recliner. "I do okay. That's everything," he said, pointing to the drive in Stuart's hands before he went to the kitchen, talking as he got another beer and a bottle of water from the fridge. "The owner of the building and I have a good arrangement. I help him out from time to time and he lets me stay here for a fraction of what he could get, but there's a catch. Most people don't want to live over a bar that plays live music three nights a week, so it isn't as great a deal as you might think. I don't care, I put on my headphones and drown it out." He paused and stared into the fridge in contemplation. "Why do people in movies always put a raw steak on a black eye?"

"Because it's cold and conforms to the shape of the eye, but people didn't know as much about bacteria when they first started doing..."

"It was a rhetorical question, man, Jesus!" He threw the refrigerator door shut and walked back to the couch, handing Stewart the bottle of water on his way.

"Some people would kill for this place," Stuart said, looking at the computer workstation with double monitors. It was more modest than he expected and not unlike most office setups, if slightly more upscale. He supposed it wasn't about the power of the machine so much as the brain behind it. Movies always made it seem like hackers had setups NASA would envy. Perhaps some do. Nonetheless, he had little doubt the computer was state-of-the art. "I always thought of a hacker as some guy who lives in his mother's basement."

"I'm not like most," said Spider as he sat down on the couch with his beer. "I never let a client know where I live, much less invite him inside."

"And I'm the exception because... ?"

"Because you saved me from getting stabbed today, for one thing," the hacker replied. "Make no mistake, that shit bag wasn't there to make me another offer." He took a sip of his third beer for the morning. "Also, I know you are who and what you say you are. That carries a lot of weight with me. I also know that an elevator repair guy doesn't make a lot of money, so consider us even."

Spider did not know about his brother's life insurance policy. Since it was a company life policy, it didn't have to go through probate--the Foundation cut Stuart a check for four million that very morning. If Spider did not know he was no longer a working man, there was no reason to disabuse him of the notion. "You were able to trace the number?" he asked hopefully.

"No, I wasn't. And that's what bothers me more than anything. Almost more than anything."

"What does that mean?"

"The reason I make so much money is that I'm very good at finding information that nobody else can find. If it's on a computer that's connected to the web, I will almost always find it." Stuart was inwardly embarrassed that it wasn't until that moment that Spider's name made sense, but he let the man continue. "You know how a car crash on TV makes the car explode like it's rigged with dynamite? That's because it is. You ever see a car do that in real life? Or the bomb that some lunatic in a movie builds always has a convenient digital display so everybody knows exactly when the bomb will go off."

"And?" asked Stuart, drinking from his bottle of water.

"Burner phones are the same way. Their being untraceable is only on TV. You go to a store and buy one, and that purchase was made at that location at that time, so it can be traced back to you. Your credit card paid for it. You can be tracked. Pay cash for it? Well, you're on camera buying that phone in the store. Pay some homeless guy on the street to go in and buy one for you? Guess what, you were at that store at that time. How would anyone know? Your cell phone tracks you wherever you go. So you leave your phone at home and go the homeless guy route. Your car's GPS puts you at the scene. What happens if you work your way around all the tracking and get the phone? How do you activate it? Credit card? You can't activate a burner without registering."

"I get the idea."

"Well, keep listening, because this is the good part," Spider said before a long preparatory swallow from his bottle. "The number that called your brother was a burner phone. That's all I can tell you because whoever activated it used a stolen credit card number they probably bought on the Dark Web.

The card was canceled within hours. Now, tracking all of that is easy if you're a government agency, but if you're one guy sitting behind a computer, the work is more herculean than you would believe, and certainly not something I'm going to do for five hundred dollars."

"How much?" Stuart asked, thinking this was a renegotiation of his fee.

"Keep your shirt on," Spider told him. "I could do all that and it would almost certainly be a dead end. Anybody smart enough to use a burner phone and pay for it with a stolen credit card is smart enough to know everything I just told you, use fake credentials, and get away with it. Or at least knows how to cover his ass. We know it was a burner with stolen info, so I stopped there and looked at that other little thing you mentioned about him using his phone as a GPS. I checked his last route and he spent the night at the home of a chick named *Lori Mercer*. She's in his phone under the name *Crystal*. Have you looked at the conversations?"

Stuart nodded. "I looked at all the text conversations he had over the last few weeks of his life. Nothing unexpected."

"The guy had a way with women, I'll say that much for him."

"I know."

"So, then, what you didn't see was any conversations between them. Which means he just got her phone number for the first time that night. Obviously, he wasn't in the habit of clearing his text messages, given everything else we found. Either way, I looked into her. Information wasn't hard to come by. She's pretty public about her lifestyle."

"What lifestyle?" Stuart asked.

Spider pointed to the thumb drive Stuart held in his hand. He chose that moment to pocket it. "It's all there, but I want you to promise me something before I tell you this."

"Tell me what?"

Spider rolled his eyes. "Promise me you'll listen and not jump to conclusions. Get it? Evidence is just that, evidence. It ain't proof of shit."

"Okay, let's have it," said Stuart.

"The woman that Rylen saw that night," he said, leaning forward to put the beer on the coffee table in front of him, "this Lori Mercer, she's one multi-talented woman. She's a massage therapist, does one day a week at a massage parlor. She's also a lifestyle and professional dominatrix who does the occasional demonstration at a dungeon in Salem called *The Cell*. Her specialty is hypnosis, which apparently is something of a rare combination. She doesn't hold any formal certification that I could find. She's smart, though. She has a master's in biochemistry, but she doesn't use it."

"Did you say she works in a dungeon?" asked Stuart.

"Still stuck on that, huh?" said Spider with a grin. "I had some fun with that one, too. But yeah, she's a dominatrix. A BDSM dungeon, not a medieval type, but I'm sure there's room for overlap."

"What does BDSM stand for?"

Spider looked at him curiously. "What exactly did you do in college, anyway?" Stuart ignored the question. "It stands for bondage, discipline, domination, submission, sadism, and masochism."

"That's six words for four letters. What did you think was going to send me over the edge?"

Spider looked at the floor for a second before saying, "Those are just side occupations. I'm sure they pay well and, if her social media is any indication, she enjoys both. A lot. She blogs about it all the time. Her main occupation is a tea shop she owns on Newbury. It's called *The Green Leaf*."

That was the connection between the woman Rylen saw that night and the mysterious phone call. Stuart was calm enough, but he was glad that he had put the thumb drive into his pocket or his clenched fist might have snapped it in two. "So she may have been the person who called him and distracted him while he was driving. He got into an accident, she hears it and doesn't do anything, but stays on the phone until after they're cutting his body out of the car," said Stuart, earning a stare from Spider that he chose not to notice as he followed his own logical reconstruction.

"That's the very thing I wanted to warn you about," said Spider, "you're already assuming it was her on the phone."

Stuart nodded. "You're right, we can't know that for sure, but if it was her then why didn't she do anything?"

Spider shook his head. "You're missing a couple points here. She already had his number, so why use a burner phone with the number blocked to call him after he just left her?"

"Unless she didn't want anybody to know it was her," Stuart proposed.

"Yeah, then text him a photo of a green leaf that's both the name and logo of a tea shop she owns?"

"That doesn't make sense. And what did you think I was going to do? Hunt her down and beat the crap out of her for not calling 911?"

"Did you miss the part about her being a hypnotist?" Spider asked. "Read the files on the drive. It is all there, but the cliff notes version is, she's really fucking good. She uses hypnosis in her BDSM shows. Naturally, there are those who think she's all bullshit, but more well-informed people--like me--say she's the real thing."

Stuart's mind was working. He took a deep breath and digested this last news before saying, "You think my brother was murdered by someone who hypnotized him to make him fall asleep behind the wheel of his car? That has to be the most insanely ridiculous thing I have ever heard."

"Whoa, hey, I know how it sounds," said Spider. "And I'm not drawing any conclusions. Read the files and decide for yourself, but don't do anything stupid. All you have is an untraceable call and a text of a leaf. You know they knew each other, but that's all. I can tell you that Rylen certainly knew her. He went to the dungeon where she would put on her demonstrations. He had been going there for months--I'm assuming whenever she was there. That much was easy enough to find out. He had never been at her house before that night, though. Pretty obvious since he needed GPS to get home. Another weird coincidence that he should die that same night."

"Very weird," Stuart said, now pacing the room. "There's something else I didn't think about until now. At Rylen's funeral, there was a woman sitting at the back of the church. She was in black and had a hat with a veil, so I never saw her face. I couldn't go ask who she was at that moment, but it was a closed service. Nobody should have been allowed in after the doors were closed. I asked about it afterward, but nobody saw a woman in a veil."

"And they wouldn't if she slipped them some money. Could you tell anything about her? Hair color, skin tone?"

"No, the hat and the veil kept me from seeing anything of her face," said Stuart. "She had black gloves on, too."

"Was she young, old, short, tall, fat, skinny--anything?" Stuart shook his head in dismay. "So it could have been a man in drag for all you know. Not too much we can do with that. We'll file that away for now." Spider stood up. "Except for the fact that it does point to a woman. Still pretty scant evidence. Swear to me you won't..."

"Do anything stupid!" said Stuart with more irritation than he intended. "I got it. What am I going to do? Go to the police? With a story like this? They'd laugh in my face. I'm going to go home and read." At that, Stuart removed his wallet.

Spider held up his hand. "It's on the house," he said. "Thanks again for today. I mean it. Thank you."

It was the first hint of the person behind the cynical attitude that Stuart had seen. He extended his hand and they shook before Stuart left. Their business was concluded, yet Stuart couldn't help thinking Spider's part in this drama was far from over.

CHAPTER SEVENTEEN

THEY TOOK THE PHONE

Returning from a morning workout, Stuart pulled into his driveway and went to his back door. As soon as he inserted his key into the lock, he knew something was wrong. The deadbolt lock turned too easily. It hadn't been locked at all. The doorknob also had a lock and Stuart gripped it firmly. Locked. Inserting the key, he slowly twisted the knob until the door opened. Entering cautiously through his kitchen, the home alarm pad on the wall chirped a countdown until he entered his pin and turned his attention to the rest of the house.

He would never leave home without setting the alarm and making sure the doors were locked. He always left and entered from the back door, as he had on this occasion. He had locked the deadbolt. He was certain of it. Since this door was in the driveway, anyone wanting to break in would choose the least conspicuous location. He examined the locks and there were no signs of scratches or stress; the door had not been forced, and the alarm had not been tripped.

Shutting the kitchen door behind him, he moved from room to room, stepping quietly in case someone was still in the house. To all appearances, nothing had been touched. He then did a more thorough check of each room, looking in closets and behind doors until he was satisfied that he was alone in the house. That was when it hit him. He went to the spare room that doubled as a guest room, though he never had guests. In this room he had only a sofa bed, a bookcase, and a desk where his computer was set up. He had left Rylen's phone on the desktop. It was gone. Stuart searched for it, but he knew he was wasting his time. It was kept in the same spot since the first day he got it, and one doesn't misplace something so important to him.

Stuart called Spider and explained everything. Spider tried to track the phone, but there was no signal. "This is some deep shit. Listen, don't worry; I still have a clone. There's something you need to do--what I would do, if I were you. Get in your car and go to The Green Leaf tea shop as fast as you can."

"What? Why?"

"It's after eleven. If Lori Mercer is there, you'll see if she recognizes you. Whoever took that phone knew that you had it and knew that it had important information. Worst of all, they're a professional. They didn't trip your alarm or damage your locks getting in. If she did it herself, she's one frigging piece of work, this chick. More likely, she had somebody else do it. If she's there and has been there for the last few hours, she will still know who you are. You would have to be one hell of an actor to hide it. If she doesn't know you, she may not be our suspect; she was probably just banging your brother."

"What if she knows me and freaks out? What about all that talk about not doing anything stupid?" asked Stuart.

"That still applies! More than ever. If she knows you, it will show, believe me. Just leave. You will have your answer and we will figure it out from there. The only thing that matters is what we can prove, and the last thing you need is to end up in jail. You're one screw up away from doing time, so leave. Call me as soon as you see her, no matter what happens."

"Okay, I'm going now." Stuart headed to the door.

"And one other thing," Spider added, "don't be so damn obvious about why you're there."

"What should I say?"

"It is a fucking tea shop--go in and buy some Earl Grey or some shit. But pay in cash!"

"Good point. I won't make a scene. She may be innocent in

all of this."

Spider laughed. "Not the word I would use to describe her."

CHAPTER EIGHTEEN

EARL GREY

The small wind chimes tinkled over the shop door as Stuart entered The Green Leaf. He was greeted by the scent of incense and spice. The interior was warm and welcoming, outfitted with dark wood paneling and fixtures to match. The interior decorations were a mixture of African, Asian, South American, and European, but done with such tasteful care that it had the desired effect of multiculturalism without gaudiness. There were plants strategically located throughout the shop, some in hanging pots and others growing in illuminated aquariums.

"I'll be right with you," said a woman from somewhere he could not see. There was no one behind the counter.

It dawned on Stuart that he had no idea what he was going to say. He wished he had given this more forethought. The matter was simple enough; he had to approach her and ask for some tea. "No hurry," Stuart replied to the disembodied voice at the back of the store. He walked up to the counter and, seconds later, Lori came from the back carrying an empty cardboard box.

Given Rylen's taste in women, Stuart expected her to be young and attractive; his expectations were accurate. He thought she could not be much above thirty. She stood about five-foot-six, and had an athletic build that was not hidden by the skinny jeans and store t-shirt she wore. Her skin was fair and her straight, honey-colored hair reached down to her mid torso. She had a button over her left breast that read, "YOU CAN DRINK AND DRIVE IF IT'S TEA." She smiled as she stepped behind the counter, dropping the empty box to the floor behind her. "What can I can I help you with?" she asked brightly.

Stuart knew at once that this woman was no killer. If she was, she had to be the most deceptive murderer in history. He immediately second-guessed himself, as he found it equally hard to believe she was some whip-cracking dominatrix. Could Spider have gotten his information wrong? It was unlikely, but Stuart had not yet had a chance to view the files on the thumb drive that was in his pocket at that very moment. She had met his eye without a hint of recognition. So much for that theory. Now he had to play it through. "Hi," he said congenially. He had hesitated a couple seconds too long, which gained him a puzzled smirk from her. What was it that Spider had told him to do? "I would like to buy some Earl Grey or some sh... or something like it."

"Earl Grey?" she asked, her face turning serious. "I need to ask you to leave now."

"What? Why is that?"

Lori laughed. "I'm kidding! God, I'm so sorry. I can be hard to get sometimes."

Stuart laughed in earnest. "Don't be. I'll be kicking myself later. I am now, actually. I was up all night, so I'm a little slow on the uptake." It was the first time he had actually laughed in weeks. Even before losing his brother, he had been so down that daily life had become a matter of autonomous repetition. Laughing at that moment felt strange and foreign to him. He felt worse for failing to know that she was joking. "Honestly, I asked for Earl Grey because it's the only tea I know. I thought it would make me sound cultured."

"No, just boring, maybe."

"Really?" asked Stuart. "Brits drink it all the time on television."

"We have some," she answered, stepping out from behind the counter and walking toward the back of the shop.

"I'm trying to kick the coffee habit. I was hoping you could recommend a gateway tea."

She halted and turned to him with a thoughtful smile. "Hey, that's pretty good. I'll have to remember to get that on a button. Let's try this: lightning round. Chocolate or vanilla?"

"Vanilla."

"Fruity or spicy?"

"Fruity."

"Dark or light?"

"Light."

"I think I have the thing for you," said Lori, going to a shelf and taking down a bag. "This is a white tea with orange peel and a little hibiscus to give it body. Want to try some?"

"You can do that?" asked Stuart.

"Of course," she said, going back to the counter and spooning some of the contents into a filter bag before dropping it into a cup she pulled from a brewing machine. She filled the cup with hot water and added a stir stick. "You have to let it steep for about a minute." She handed him the cup.

Stuart stirred his brew. "You didn't have to open a bag on my account."

"It's sold by weight," she told him. "Do you work at night? You said you haven't been sleeping."

Stuart shook his head and smelled the tea. "No, I've had trouble sleeping lately. Just stress. This smells delicious."

"Hope you like it. I'm Lori, by the way," she said, extending her hand.

"Stuart. Nice to meet you," he said, instantly regretting it.

"Nice to meet you, Stuart," she responded amiably, shaking his hand warmly and taking no notice of the name. It was not likely that Rylen would talk about his brother with a woman he was seeing, if that was indeed the case. Maybe she was his massage therapist. If she had been Rylen's dominatrix, there was a lot about his brother he did not know. Either way, it was too late for him to come up with a fake name. "What do you do?"

"I'm an elevator technician," he replied, realizing he was not cut out for deception of any kind. It then occurred to him that this was, in fact, a lie. He had quit his job and was now an unemployed millionaire. That idea would take some getting used to. He had managed to lie after all, "Basically, when buildings are going up, I install them. When elevators break down, I fix them."

"Maybe you *should* get the Earl Grey," said Lori with a wince and a shrug.

"Boring, huh? I would take offense if it wasn't true," he replied. "But if you went to step into an elevator and found you were plummeting down a twenty story shaft, it would seem pretty important then," he told her, recalling what had happened to one of his replacements.

"Does that happen?" she asked.

"Not if I show up to work sober."

"How's the tea?"

Stuart tasted it and genuinely liked the flavor. "It's very good," he said honestly. "I'll take some." He was glad that Spider had reminded him to bring cash. His name on the card was a dead giveaway, and he would not have thought of that himself.

Lori weighed out the contents of the bag and rang him out. She gave him his change and said, "You said you've been stressed and it's causing you to not sleep. Have you ever had a professional massage?"

Stuart's heart skipped a beat. "No, never. I try not to be too relaxed."

She furrowed her brow in puzzlement. "Why not?"

"It stresses me out."

Lori let out a little laugh that surprised him. She showed him a business card. "I'm also a massage therapist. I take Friday appointments and I work out of a salon in Chinatown. Give me a call if you would like to give it a try to help you unwind. It can do wonders for stress relief. That is, if you ever want to try going without it for a while."

"Thank you," Stuart said as she dropped the card in his bag. "I might do that," he smiled before leaving the store.

Back in his car, Stuart called Spider to tell him what had happened. Spider listened carefully without interruption until Stuart got to the point about giving her his real name. He intended to leave that part out, but Spider asked, "What name did you give her?"

"Stuart," he answered with a cringe.

"You used your real name, like you did with me?" Spider asked in disbelief.

"Yes, I did. Look, it was reflex. She shook my hand and I said my name without thinking. Then I said it was nice to meet her."

"Are you shitting me?"

"No, it kind of was."

"Oh, fucking hell. Dude, this woman was the last person to see your brother alive. Have you looked at that file I gave you yesterday?"

"No, I was going to do it this morning when I got back from the gym, but then my place was broken into."

"You still have the drive, though?"

"I put it on my key-chain after they took the phone. I didn't want to leave it at home."

"Good! Apparently locked doors and alarm systems aren't a problem for them. It sounds like she really didn't know you, but we can't be sure. At least whoever took the phone doesn't know about her yet, but that's only a matter of time. You have some heavy reading to do," Spider said. "Read it all. You don't know what might be useful to you later. Call me when you're done. See if you think she's all sugar and spice after you give that a gander."

CHAPTER NINETEEN

SPIDER SEEKS BUGS

Stuart had just arrived home when he got a call from Spider again. "Are you home?" Spider asked.

"Just got here."

"Have you turned on your computer yet?"

"Not yet. Why?"

"Don't say anything and don't use your laptop. This shit is worse than either of us thought. Stay there. I'm coming over."

"Okay, I'll be here." It was after Spider hung up that Stuart paused. He had never even given the man his address.

An hour later, Stuart opened the door and Spider walked past him carrying two laptop bags. "We have to talk, but before we do, your home is probably bugged. I want to check your house, your computer, and your phone before we talk about anything. You okay with that?"

Stuart was surprised, but Spider's attitude was one of deadly seriousness. All of his instincts told him to let Spider do what he needed. "Yes, I'm okay with it. What do you have to do?"

"Let's start with your computer," said Spider. Stuart showed him to his laptop in the spare room. Spider took an external drive from his bag and plugged it into the laptop before starting a system scan. Then he asked for Stuart's phone and plugged it into his own laptop to do the same thing. Stuart wasn't sure he liked the man's way of walking into his home and doing this with his personal equipment, but he was boring enough to not have anything to hide. He made a second mental note; he was now able to afford a few vices in addition to some fashion sense.

When Spider was done with the computer and the phone, he went from room to room waving a detection wand like Stuart had seen going through airport security. Where did one get all of this equipment? When Spider was finished he said, "I didn't find anything. We can talk now."

"Alright, let's do that."

Spider sat down on the couch in the living room. Stuart sat in the easy chair, thinking to himself that Detective Connelly was the very last person to sit in it. "Your brother's phone had monitoring software installed on it."

"Monitoring?"

"Spying software would be a better term," Spider answered. "It's the kind of software that, once installed on a phone, runs in the background. It's invisible and you never know it's there."

"If someone had that on there, why take the phone?" asked Stuart.

"Maybe to keep us from finding out about it. But the shit that was on that thing was custom. Think about that for a second. It wasn't commercial software that somebody bought and put on your brother's phone, it was written for private use. That was what had me spooked. Man, this is getting real. If they unlocked your doors, disabled your alarm, and left without leaving a trace, they could easily have left some cameras or listening devices in place."

Stuart considered that. "The software was custom, so you know what it did?"

"Everything," said Spider. "They heard everything you and I said to each other since we met. They know what I look like because it could turn the camera on. They were watching and listening to us in the restaurant. They could download all the data on the phone. Photos, messages, emails... they could hear every phone call. And they knew exactly where the phone was at any time."

"Any telling when it was installed?" Stuart asked.

"No, I have no way of knowing."

"Hold on a second: if that was on there at the time of the crash, why would someone call Rylen and send him a photo? They wouldn't have needed to stay on the phone all that time to be sure he'd crashed the car. Why stay on the call?"

Spider reflected. "The software works only one way. If the person who called was the same person who put the software on there, it was the only way they could talk to him or send him something."

Stuart stood and paced, thinking. "You say they were listening to us. So they know you made a duplicate of the phone. The software had to send that information somewhere, either another phone number or an IP address. Can you find them?"

Spider raised an eyebrow. "I already looked at that and the phone number that acted as a receiver was a burner phone that's been disconnected. And they covered their tracks. No credit card purchase. Like I told you before, it's no easy thing to make a burner untraceable--almost impossible now. They know what they're doing."

Stuart stopped pacing and turned to him. "But you have the number the software was set to use?" he asked. "Could you set up a phone with that number?"

Spider drummed his fingers on his knee. "Numbers get recycled when service stops, but they're usually out of service for ninety days. I might be able to hijack it. Why?" asked Spider. "I tried tracking it and it's gone dark. They've probably destroyed the phone by now."

"The person listening would know you're a hacker and anybody can track a phone with that app, so you would certainly be able to," Stuart said, pacing again. "Naturally, they would block it from being tracked. Since the software is custom and the person who broke in here was able to disable my alarm system, you would assume it's the same person because they both show such technical expertise. But what if the person who took the phone isn't the same person who put the spyware on it?"

"You mean that whoever took the phone doesn't know it's there," he said.

"If you can hijack that phone number, we should be able to spy on whoever came in here and stole it."

"Damn, you're starting to think like a hacker, dude," Spider said in admiration.

"How much?" Stuart asked.

"My fee?" Spider asked. "You're really fixated on this money thing."

"You already did me a solid on the research and the house scan," Stuart told him. "Helping you out with those assholes yesterday... doesn't mean you work for free now."

Spider rubbed his chin in. "Mrs. Chambers, my teacher from sixth grade--scariest person I've ever met. You kick her ass for me and I'll owe you for life."

"What? I can't hit a woman."

"Jesus, it was a fucking joke," Spider exclaimed. "Never mind. Look, whatever the hell is happening here is big, and it means your brother was either into some shit with some really dangerous people, or his death was not an accident. It's probably both."

Stuart nodded. "Taking the phone just tells us that this is important."

"Exactly. So listen, I underestimated the significance of the problem when you brought it to me. Then I cloned the phone and didn't know it had a custom monitoring program on it. I sure as hell didn't expect them to break into your house and steal it. I screwed up by not being careful enough, and whoever is behind this has been way ahead of me at every step. That shit stops now. That's why I came here; making sure there are no more leaks is step one to planning a strategy. This is the most interesting thing I've come across in years, so to be honest, I'm going to get to the bottom of it even if you aren't paying me. Hell, I wouldn't miss this for anything. So, are we good?"

Stuart nodded and extended his hand. "Yeah, we're good."

CHAPTER TWENTY
BRING HER IN

"And the good word is?" asked Perry Tellerson as he entered Steve McGuire's office. As the head of Technologies Research and Development, Steve's office was as much a computer lab as an executive suite.

Steve knew Perry was anticipating an easy solution, and it fell to him to deliver the bad news. "It isn't good at all," he answered, turning away from Rylen's phone that lay plugged in on the table in front of him. Steve explained what he had learned from Rylen's phone and where it was that Rylen spent his final night. Then he explained what he had learned about Lori Mercer and how she knew Rylen. "I already have someone looking into her. He'll have a preliminary dossier in a matter of hours."

Perry was quiet as he strolled to a table and picked up a small box of clear plastic, studying it. "A biochemist, a dominatrix, a hypnotist, and a tea enthusiast..." said Perry, contemplating. "I'm glad we kept an eye on his extracurricular activities, except now I wish we had kept an even closer one. So, in short, he meets this woman in that seedy S&M club he's been frequenting--then, for one reason or another, he meets her at an art gallery and gets her number before going home with her? Isn't that a little weird? I mean, if he was supposed to meet her that night, wouldn't he get her number beforehand? And if they met by chance or by some verbal invitation, why get her number before going to her home? Isn't that the sort of thing you'd do later?"

"They drove in separate cars," said Steve, "what if they needed to talk to each other on the drive? What if one of them had to stop for gas or take a piss? I don't know."

"Fair enough," Perry admitted. "Then he dies on the way home during a phone call that even we can't track," said Perry, returning the plastic box to the table and turning back to his colleague. "No, I'm not buying it."

"What are you thinking?"

"We don't have that many enemies; I'm thinking this is about the island resort. If anyone is after us, it's probably Curtis and his Jamaican contacts. They were way too eager to find out who Rylen was working for. We have to be sure. And we will need to get that from her. You know who to call."

"Isn't that a little extreme?" Steve asked. "This isn't some crackpot at a construction site on foreign soil. We're talking about the abduction of a US citizen in our own city."

Perry gave him an incredulous look. "You want to go home and find some men in your house holding your wife and son at gunpoint? Because that's the kind of people they are. So, if you think they're above hiring some slut to pump information out of our accountant and making his death look like an accident, think again. If they got to Rylen and found out who he really represents, they can get to either of us."

Steve leaned back in his chair and drummed his fingers on the table. "When we started out, we made all of these contacts and put these types of human assets at our disposal in case the day ever came that we needed to use them. Once we activate them and money is exchanged, there's no going back."

"Rylen's dead," said Perry flatly. "I think that day is pretty much fucking here. But let's consider: say it is some freak coincidence, which you and I know it isn't. We bring her in and question her. I can get James Anlo, the interrogator I told you about, to get what we need out of her. And if she had nothing to do with it, we let her go. She'll get over it."

"And if she was put up to it by the Jamaicans?"

"We'll let Doctor Anlo take care of her," Perry answered. "We'll fly her out to his boat and let him do what he does. My question to you is, can we afford to sit and wait?"

"No, we can't, thanks to you and your greed," Steve retorted, leering at Perry. "We could both be sleeping a lot easier if we'd given them what they asked for to begin with. Rylen would still be alive and you and I wouldn't be talking about kidnapping and murder!"

Perry raised an eyebrow over his glasses, and Steve knew what he was going to say. "You didn't voice any complaints when you got your cut. You had an equal say in the deal, and you agreed that their asking price was extortion. You didn't have any qualms about undercutting them when push came to shove."

"Are you sure you want do this?" asked Steve curtly. "I'll go along with it, but I want to know we're both clear that this is what we're going to do."

"If you have a better suggestion, now is a good time to come out with it," Perry replied, to which Steve shook his head. "We bring her in. We have Anlo question her."

"When?"

Perry considered. "Tonight. Does that give you enough time?"

"I'll make it happen." When Perry left, Steve turned back to the computer that Rylen's phone was plugged into. There was a section of highlighted code on the screen. Steve's eyebrows shot up and he grabbed the phone off of the table, only to find it hot to the touch. He dropped it and quickly checked the wireless dampening field device on another table. "Oh, shit," he mumbled to himself.

CHAPTER TWENTY-ONE

SHE IS GOING TO BE TAKEN

"We have to meet. Today!" said Spider as soon as Stuart answered the phone.

"What's going on?"

"Don't say anything else over the phone. How soon can you get here?"

"If it's that important, I can be there by two," Stuart replied.

"As soon as you can. I'll see you then," Spider answered and hung up.

As soon as Stuart arrived at Spider's apartment, Spider played the video he gathered from Rylen's phone. They were not able to see Perry Tellerson's face, but Stuart knew Perry's sonorous voice without question. They heard every word of the plan that Perry and Steve made to abduct Lori. He told Spider all he knew about the company and people Rylen worked for. Spider made a few quick notes.

"I called you as soon as I got this, but they plan to do it tonight," said Spider, "hence the urgency. Since he found the program on the phone, it was cut off immediately."

"First thing's first," said Stuart as he stood up from Spider's desk and paced. "Can he trace it back to us?"

"No," Spider answered, "and I'd try to look offended, but

I think you wouldn't get it. He won't even be able to tell for sure whether anyone was listening. As soon as he found the program, I disconnected the hijacked number. The program doesn't log transmission; it would defeat the purpose. No matter how good the guy is, he would have to go through the code and find out where the program was sending the data. Once he got the encrypted phone number, all he would have to do is ping it to find out if it's active. And what he found is that it was disconnected. He'll check the number and find it's been disconnected. He will have to assume nobody was listening."

"Will he still call off the abduction?"

"We can't know that."

"So what *do* we know?"

"We know a shit ton more than we did before," said Spider. "For starters, we know who they are and they don't know who we are. A good position to be in when the bad guys are killers. We also know that they didn't have anything to do with Rylen getting killed, and they don't know who did it either."

"Good point."

"I made notes of everything they said and it's a lot to look into," said Spider. "These Jamaicans they're talking about... sounds to me like they screwed over the wrong people on some resort deal outside the country and Rylen was the intermediary. Your brother's death has them scared. Is there anything else you can tell me about the Tellerson Foundation?"

"That's all I know. Not much that you won't learn from their home page. They sponsor tech startups and independents. I know they don't give grants. They own part of any technology developed by the people they hire, or even the companies they fund. They're a big outfit. The heads have to be making pretty good money. Hell, Perry wouldn't go to a funeral without a bodyguard."

"I don't know about that. The money they're making isn't exactly above board. Based on the conversation Perry had with that other guy, it sounds like a small group doing illicit business on the side. Your brother was in on it. Maybe Perry got a bodyguard after Rylen was killed," he speculated. "Maybe whoever killed your brother got the information they needed. They found out who Perry was and threatened or blackmailed him."

Stuart shook his head. "Too many *maybes* here. We can't act by going off on a tangent. We're trying to find out who killed my brother; the how and why is a secondary concern. Whoever killed Rylen, whether it was someone with a grudge against his employer or not, our best chance of finding them is about to get abducted."

"So?" said Spider. "Of finding *them*? Lori Mercer is no innocent victim. She may well be the killer herself. You seem to be forgetting that."

Stuart was not sure of his meaning. "I can't let them take her. I have to stop it."

Spider went to the couch, sitting down and putting his foot up on the coffee table as he stared at Stuart. "You have this real white-knight syndrome going for you, don't you? Let me ask you something: what do you mean when you say you have to stop it? I called you here to decide what to do, but I was thinking something more along the lines of putting a tracker on her and calling the police when they take her. The problem is, I don't have one."

"Really?" asked Stuart.

Spider was indignant. "No! I do not have a drawer full of spare phones and GPS tracking devices and, no, I can't get something like that in time. They said they're doing it tonight instead of looking for the best chance to take her. That tells me they aren't worried about means and opportunity. They must be pretty damned confident that whoever they're sending is going to get the job done."

"What if you did have a tracker, like my phone or something?" asked Stuart.

"You think professionals won't notice an extra phone in her pocket? Anyway, say I had a tracker. They're small and can be hidden on a person without them noticing it right away. I could run into her at her store and start a conversation. Whatever it would take to get close enough to plant it on her," he explained. "I can pick pockets like you wouldn't believe, so planting a chip is a snap."

"So what would happen if they took her without finding it?"

"They get arrested for kidnapping and whatever else they're into comes to light. Your brother's co-conspirators get locked up for a very long time. They're into embezzling or whatever and ready to commit kidnapping and murder, so I call that a big win. And get this, there are ways that video file could be used."

Stuart walked to the recliner opposite Spider and sank into it with a sigh. "Whatever they are guilty of, we know they didn't kill Rylen, though. Even if you did have a tracking device and used it, they might kill her before the police get there. Then we would never find out who *did* kill him."

"It's a moot point without any way of finding where they take her. If she does know anything, they seem pretty sure they'll get it out of her," said Spider.

"I got it. They already know the phone was bugged; we let them know somebody was listening. Send them a snippet of the video and say that if anything happens to Lori, it goes to the police. Shit, let's send it to the police anyway."

Spider chuckled. "You might think like a hacker, but you don't think like a criminal, and that's a good thing, bud. Think that through. I send them the video and hide my tracks. They will get spooked and call off the abduction. What will they do next? Eliminate any threat to themselves. They will dedicate all of their resources to tracking down whoever sent the message... and we know they have the means to make someone disappear."

"What if we tell them we're sending it to the police?" Stuart asked. "That would make them call off the attack on Lori and there would be no point in finding who did it after the damage is done."

"That ain't a bad one. And, out of all of our options, that would be my first pick," said Spider. "You have to realize that if we do that, and it was their enemies, these Jamaicans, who killed your brother, you'll never find out who did it. Perry and his buddy there might get investigated and go to jail eventually, but their enemies will disappear. If we can't find the person who had it in for your brother, at least we get to ass-fuck some really bad people."

"And if we don't do anything?"

Spider took his foot off the coffee table and leaned forward. "As I see it, we have two options. You have to be the one to decide how this plays out. And you need to decide fast because we're already running out of time, assuming they won't kidnap her right out of her own shop. It's a busy area, so it isn't likely. Anyway, I don't have any real skin in the game. You hired me to help you find your brother's killer, so where we go from here is up to you."

"I am open to suggestions," said Stuart.

"First choice is to do nothing. If Lori Mercer disappears, you know that these guys found out she was behind Rylen's death and they got rid of her for you. We let them go on about their crooked lives and we forget everything we saw. We go have a pint and move on. If, however, she's back in her tea shop and up to her whips and chains shit after tomorrow, you know she had nothing to do with it."

"Jesus!" Stuart huffed. "It would be messed up if she did it and worse if she didn't. Either way, that would make us no better than Tellerson."

"Chill, I'm just throwing spaghetti at the wall," said Spider. "I don't care for that one either. Our second choice, and my personal favorite, is to do what you came up with. Threaten them and go to the cops with the video. They won't be prosecuted for anything in the state of Massachusetts based on that, but the police will know they're into some organized crime shit and somebody will start looking into their business affairs. They'll certainly lose their jobs if everyone in the Foundation finds a copy of that video in their email one morning. I'm guessing there won't be any point to them retaliating. On the other hand, it doesn't help us get any closer to finding your brother's killer because we know *they* didn't do it and they want to find out who did, same as you."

Stuart took a deep breath and closed his eyes as he exhaled slowly. Spider watched him in silence. After many seconds had passed, Stuart opened his eyes and said, "I want to go with option number three."

"Glad you're still awake; it was starting to get creepy. And option number three is what?"

"Stop them from kidnapping her," Stuart replied, pulling out his phone.

"What are you doing?" said Spider, moving as though he was ready to snatch the phone from Stuart's hand.

"I'm going to ask her out on a date tonight."

CHAPTER TWENTY-TWO
A FOILED KIDNAPPING

Stuart sat in his truck with his phone in his hand, willing himself to press the call button, but unable to do so. Minutes were left before it was time for her to close the shop. He breathed a long, slow breath and pressed the button.

"Hey, are you here?" asked Lori, her voice sounding excited, which only sickened him with guilt.

"No, I was an idiot and took the interstate," he answered. "There's an accident and it's a parking lot. I don't know how much longer I'll be." He was amazed at how convincing he sounded.

"That's okay. I'll close up and wait for you here," she said.

He had prepared for this. "No, just head to the restaurant and I will meet you there. I may be a few minutes and I may be twenty, but I'll be there soon."

"Okay, see you soon," she answered.

Stuart watched the shop sign from his parking spot on the other side of the street. That was when it came; a white cleaning van drove up the street and passed his truck. The driver of the van touched the brake in front of the tea shop before driving on. Stuart's instincts told him there was no dismissing it as a coincidence. The van drove to the end of the block and turned the corner. He had no doubt that he had seen the people who were going to take her--or try to.

His brain was buzzing, just as it did when he pushed himself to muscle failure or when he was getting pounded in the ring. He was ready. In five minutes, the shop went dark. It was an unseasonably warm night for an October evening in Boston. Would she decide to walk to the restaurant? It was only five blocks, but he couldn't risk it. He was playing dice with her life and he hated it. He decided to follow her on foot.

She left the shop behind and walked down the sidewalk. She was half a block ahead when he crossed to her side of the street. He jogged to get closer, but not too close. He didn't know where she'd parked her car, but it was clear after the first block that she was going to walk to the restaurant. He came to within thirty feet behind her and then matched her walking pace. How close should he get? This was something he wasn't sure how to gauge. He had to stay close enough that he could be at her side in an instant. On the other hand, he needed to stay far enough away to give anyone trying to abduct her a false sense of security. If she turned and saw him, he would enter into a jog and pretend he was catching up with her.

Their side of the street would be a good opportunity--no people around and not many cars passing. If he walked with her, they would be prepared for him, or else look for another chance to take her when she was alone. There was nothing to do but follow this through. He had to look like a random pedestrian. As much as he hated handling the matter in this way, it was the only way he could keep her safe without divulging his secret.

She walked with a sauntering gait, looking at her phone as she went. She was wearing heels and the tap of her step reached him from her position ahead. She was wearing a short skirt and Stuart could make out the black seam of her stockings as she passed under a streetlight. Even at a distance on a darkened street, she was breathtaking. Was she dressed like that to go out on their date? She was dressed up for *him*. That was unbelievable. Had it not been for knowing she might be a killer, or that some killers were going to kidnap her, he never would have asked her out in the first place. Just how sick that was, he didn't want to ask himself. Asking her out on a date never would have occurred to him under normal circumstances; that was the saddest part. How many chances to be with someone had he lost because of his anxiety? In another life, he would be thrilled by his good fortune, but in this one, her saying yes to dinner was nothing more than a cruel joke of fate.

On the very next block, he knew he had made the right choice in following her, as the white cleaning van was driving up the street. It was driving too slowly for the street it was on. In fact, it was slowing even more at a gap in the row of parked cars. Whether he was right or wrong, Stuart was running before the van came to a stop. The door of the van slid open and two men in ski masks jumped out and closed the short distance between themselves and Lori. As Stuart ran to intercept Lori's two attackers, he noted a third behind the wheel of the van. He would not lose track of that one. Three men, then.

One of the two attackers who jumped from the van grabbed Lori from behind. He wrapped both arms around her torso, pinning her arms to her sides. She let out a stifled scream and struggled, but he lifted her from the ground and turned her to the second man who planted a stun gun to her chest. Stuart blindsided the man with the stun gun the second it touched Lori's torso. The ski mask made it hard to see exactly where on the face or head he was hitting the man. Stuart struck the center of the dark globe atop the man's shoulders with a straight left punch, putting everything he had into it. His fist connected with the man's skull and the hit sent a shock up his arm. This man was out of the fight. He spun backwards, the stun gun flying from his hand, and he landed face-down on the sidewalk.

The man holding Lori flung her effortlessly aside, and she landed on the pavement like a discarded puppet. The man swung a heavy fist that Stuart dodged easily, but he quickly stepped in and followed it with two more--one low punch to his abdomen and the second to the face. Stuart swung his left down to block the body punch and did a circular block with his right to stop the man's left that came at his face. He was too close for Stuart to kick, but his blocks threw the man's arms apart, creating an open cavity between them and exposing his opponent's chest for the split second Stuart needed to counter. He didn't waste it. He threw a straight punch to the man's sternum that forced him back a few steps and caused him to huff in pain, but not enough to do more than that. This was not a man who would be a one-punch knock down. His strength was tremendous, and he had a speed that men with that kind of strength could seldom boast of. The driver ran up in the seconds it took Stuart and the second man to exchange their first few swings, but Stuart had moved himself between Lori's prone form and her remaining attacker.

Instead of joining his comrade in the fight against Stuart, the driver shouted one word: "Abort!" The two men immediately lifted their fallen partner and returned to the van with remarkable efficiency, as though they had rehearsed the maneuver dozens of times. The door slid shut behind them and the van pulled away at speed.

Stuart was down at Lori's side the instant they were gone. "Lori!" he shouted. She was sitting up now. "Don't try to get up, I'll call an ambulance." She trembled, but made eye contact and shook her head. Stuart could not tell if it was the shock of the attack or the stun gun they used. He pulled his phone, but she slapped at his hand.

"No, I'm alright. I think," she said shakily.

"We have to get you to a hospital. He hit you with the stun gun." Immediately Stuart remembered that the stun gun had flown from the attacker's hand. Did they remember to pick it up? No, they'd left it on the ground where it landed. He would be taking that.

"He tried, but you hit him. It hurt, but it was getting thrown on the ground... took the wind out of me," she answered, panting.

"Did you hit your head?"

"No, I don't think so."

"Let me call 911."

"No!" she barked. "I'll be fine; just give me a minute."

"Then I'll at least take you to the hospital," said Stuart.

"What the hell was that?" she gasped.

"They were trying to kidnap you."

"You think?" she asked in a tone of disdain. "Help me up," she said, pulling off the one shoe she still wore, the other having come off in the struggle when the man lifted her. Stuart helped her to her feet and was surprised by how little help she needed. Both of her palms were scratched at the heels where she broke her fall with her hands. The stun gun hadn't made contact long enough to disable her. "I think I'm fine," she said, touching a knee she had scraped in the fall. The brush of her knee on the pavement tore through her stockings and scratched the skin, but she was fundamentally unharmed.

Stuart got her other shoe and handed it to her as she adjusted her clothing. "Are we really not going to call the police?" he asked.

"No, we're not," she said without looking at him as she took a few steps back and forth. Stuart got her phone from the sidewalk as she leaned against the brick wall silently for many minutes, in shock. Lori soon came to herself and brushed the sole of each foot before putting her heels back on. "I'm not feeling too keen on dinner anymore."

"Me either," he admitted.

"I sure as hell need a drink, though. Will you take me home? I can Uber to work tomorrow."

"Yes, of course," Stuart answered, holding out her phone. Lori took it and slipped the phone into the pocket of her jacket.

She stared at him for a moment and then silently wrapped her arms around his neck, embracing him tightly. Too tightly. His adrenaline rush didn't prevent him from returning the hug. "Thank you," she whispered, her lips pressed to his neck. He understood why she held him so tightly when he felt her twitch with the sobs that broke from her.

"It's alright. You're okay. They're gone," he said awkwardly, the mixed smell of her leather jacket, perfume, and shampoo making him heady.

Stuart inwardly cursed his Judas of a dick for betraying the effect she was having on him at a moment like that. He did, however, manage to keep it from making contact with her, saving himself that measure of embarrassment. She loosened her strangle hold and slowly pulled away, her face averted as she wiped at tears before noticing her scratched hands again. She pulled a small handbag out of the deep side pocket of her jacket and removed a small packet of tissues, using one to wipe the running makeup under her eyes. Stuart pretended not to notice, since she appeared embarrassed at his seeing her cry. How odd it was that they were both embarrassed by biological responses over which neither of them had any control. He remembered something and asked, "can I have one of those?" She pulled a tissue and handed it to him. He walked to the stun gun and used the tissue to pick it up from the sidewalk. He carefully placed it into the inner breast pocket of his jacket.

"What are you doing?" she asked.

"If you won't let me call the police, I will go myself tomorrow," he said, taking out his phone and making a note of the license plate and name of the cleaning company on the van. The van was either stolen or the company did not exist. At that moment, even he was unsure why he bothered. Appearances? If he planned on bringing her attackers to justice, this is what he would do. The problem was, he already knew who was behind it. What was the point of tracking down the dogs when he already knew who the owner was? Maybe the attackers getting caught would lead the police to take a close look at Perry Tellerson, but even as he considered it, Stuart knew that was a pipe dream. The best he could hope for was to remove these particular pawns from the board because if they were busy being questioned by the police, they couldn't try a second time.

"I don't want you to go at all," she told him firmly.

"But why?" he asked, confused. "Three men tried to kidnap you and you won't call the police!" She sighed and looked away. "Do you know who did this?"

"No," she said at once. "I really have no idea who would

want to kidnap me."

Stuart read her face. "You don't know who, but you have a pretty good idea why?"

"Maybe," she told him quietly. "Please, just take me home." He nodded and she took his arm. They walked back in the direction of her shop. "Listen, there's a lot you don't know about me. I make a lot of enemies in my line of work."

"I understand," said Stuart.

She cast a dubious expression at him. "You do?"

Stuart nodded. "Yes, I do. You're saying they work for Starbucks."

He was relieved that, given what she had been through, he had still managed to make her laugh.

CHAPTER TWENTY-THREE

TAKING LORI HOME

Stuart and Lori drove in silence for a few blocks before he said, "I don't know where we're going."

"Lowell," she answered.

Stuart headed for the interstate. They drove without talking for some time. At last, unable to take the silence any longer, Stuart asked, "Why do you think someone would want to abduct you?"

Lori was quiet for a moment before answering, as if unsure she wanted to answer at all. Finally, she said, "I am not just the owner of a tea shop." She was hesitant at the start, but spoke more freely as she went on. Stuart stayed quiet, hoping that if he were to provide enough silence, she would be the one to fill it. "Don't get me wrong, the shop does okay, but it's not all I do. I give massages on the side, but that has nothing to do with it. At least, not directly. I've done some bad things and have pissed off some bad people. Look, I don't know you and you don't know me. This isn't a confessional. It doesn't matter what the details are, I just can't go to the police without them wondering why it happened. They would start asking questions--questions I'm not ready to answer."

Stuart thought for a moment. Not only had she had just admitted that she was into something criminal, but it was something serious enough for her not to be surprised by a kidnapping attempt. He knew who was behind it and why, so he was ahead of her there. Could she have been behind his brother's death? He would never have believed it if she had played the innocent victim, ignorant of why anyone would want to hurt her. She was too smart to bother trying that ploy; anyone who was not guilty of something serious would have called the police immediately. However, it was clear she was not about to tell him anything incriminating. Why would she? Spider believed Lori was the most likely suspect, but Stuart had given her the benefit of the doubt. He felt like a complete fool for it in that moment.

"I don't blame you if you want to get away from me as fast as possible," Lori said into the awkward pause in the conversation.

Her comment made Stuart take notice of how long a time had passed without his saying anything. He still had an advantage. How could he use it to find out more? What would someone naturally say if he, in fact, knew nothing at all about her? "I don't know what you've gotten yourself into, but I won't go to the police. I promise."

Lori gave the hint of a smile, but Stuart could not tell if it was one of relief or triumph. "Thank you," she said.

"I'm not judging. And I would like a rain check on dinner."

"Are you sure about that?" she asked with a probing tone.

"Yes, I'm sure. Can we reschedule?"

She laughed unexpectedly. "You sure don't scare easily."

"I guess not," he responded, realizing he could stick to the truth and establish a trust. "Besides, it's probably better for me that you don't want to go to the police. I'm not so innocent either."

One of her penciled eyebrows raised at that. "Meaning...?"

He feigned reluctance for some seconds. "I'm on probation," he replied, "I was arrested for aggravated assault after getting into a fight in a bar this past Summer. My case came up in September and I was put on two years of probation."

"You got arrested? What about the other guy?"

"He got the same. The bar had it on video. He threw the first punch, but they said I contributed to the situation because I confronted him instead of walking away. And it was my second offense."

"What were you fighting over?" she asked, seeming very interested.

"I'm not much of a drinker, but sometimes I will go to this bar with the guys I contract with. This girl we know was hanging out at the bar. She works there. It was her night off and she was waiting for her friend's shift to end. This guy bought her a drink and later she didn't want to leave with him. He slapped her hard enough to knock her down." As soon as he said it, Stuart knew what was coming next.

"Quite the defender of women, aren't you?" she said, sounding kind rather than sarcastic, which made all the difference when she reached over and took his right hand off of the steering wheel. He let her take it. She held his hand in front of her and gently traced the pads of her fingers over the calluses on the back of his hand. Her slender, delicate fingers were exceedingly long, with a manicure of black nails sharpened to a point. He mentally berated himself for his own weakness, but the fact remained that she excited, enticed, and aroused him. Was it her physical beauty, her charm, her strength, her intelligence, or the fact that she had a secret side that was dark and hedonistic that made him want her so badly? He steeled himself and thought of Rylen, which dispelled her enchantment. His looks and social anxiety had seen to it that he had not had many relationships in his life, the longest of them having lasted a year. "Make a fist," she told him. He did so, and again she touched his knuckles with the tips of her fingers for an unnecessarily long time. "My god," she said, releasing his hand. He put his hand back on the wheel, a little self-conscious. "You work with your hands, so it's only natural that you would have rough palms. But you really are a fighter. Your knuckles are like pine knots."

"I've been slacking off on my moisturizing," he answered. She didn't laugh, and he hadn't expected her to, but he did not need to glance over at her to know she was staring at him. He let her continue to look at him in silent appraisal.

"I want to tell you something else. I'm a dominatrix," she said.

He didn't look in her direction, but could feel her eyes on him, measuring his reaction. Stuart was used to being subjected to the erroneous judgment of others. It came with his appearance and his social issues, but why the latter had dissipated since Rylen's death, he had yet to understand. He never took offense to people stereotyping him, or categorizing him into something that invariably made them feel superior. People generally thought he was about half as smart as he was, so in some ways it was an advantage. After revealing herself as a dominatrix, Lori was most likely expecting him to say something stupid. She no doubt got that a lot from those who judged her in the same way, but for different reasons. She was not going to have any of that on this occasion, though. "Lifestyle or professional?" he asked.

Her hesitation told him he had hit the mark. "Both," she answered. "That was a reassuringly informed question. Are you in the lifestyle?"

"No," he said frankly, there being no way that he could pull off the bluff. "I have always found it interesting." The statement was unintentionally true, especially after he learned that his brother frequented a dungeon, or that Rylen had such an interest in this woman.

"Interesting how?" she asked, her tone serious.

This was not the time to get cocky and overplay his hand. Since he really did find it interesting, he would go from there. "I spent my time on the Internet like a lot of guys, but honestly, I don't really know anything about it. I know enough to know there's a lot of bullshit out there."

"You are full of surprises," she remarked pensively. "I guess it's safe to say you won't be scared off by that either?"

"No, I won't."

When they reached her house in Lowell, Stuart had a feeling of dread. He pulled into the drive, knowing that this was the last place Rylen had ever visited. Would his unease show on his face?

"Come in for a drink?" Lori asked pleasantly.

"I had best not," he stammered.

"Just one drink. It's the least I could do."

"No, I need to get home. I'm a little shaken up after the fight."

"Your hand is steady as a rock," she smirked. "Are you really shaken or are you just trying to be a gentleman?"

"I would like to see you again," was all he could think of to say.

She faced forward. "Are you curious enough about the lifestyle to come and see me give a demonstration at my dungeon?" she asked at last. "I'm a hypnotist and am giving a talk about how hypnosis could be used in domination, submission, and BDSM play. If you really are curious, it'll be better than watching Internet videos. It's private, but I can add you to the list. Would it weird you out?"

This was something he had not expected. "You wouldn't mind? Because I think I would like that."

"So would I," she said cheerfully. "It's Saturday at eight. I'll text you the address." She then leaned to him and pulled him to her in an awkward embrace over the center armrest of his truck. She then placed one delicate hand to the side of his face. The rings on her thumb and forefinger were spots of coolness against the warmth of her palm. He could feel the rough area near her wrist that she scraped in the fall. Even her hand smelled of that accursed perfume that intoxicated him. He did not know why he closed his eyes in that instant and lost himself to the feel of her touch, but her lips were on his before he knew what was happening. "Thank you again for tonight," he heard her say before he opened his eyes to find her looking into them.

"It was nothing," he said, feeling ridiculous for having nothing better to say.

She looked aghast. "Saving my life was nothing?"

"No! Well, yes. I didn't mean it like that."

"I know!"

Stuart laughed politely, hating how easy it was to fool him. "You got me again."

"How is it that someone who knows how to be funny doesn't get it when other people are?" she asked, looking sincerely perplexed.

"Maybe you're not as funny as I am," he answered.

"See?" she said with a smirk. "We'll have to work on that," she added as she opened the door. "Text me with any questions. You're going to have a lot of them before Saturday night."

"I do have a question. You said in BDSM or domination..."

"Domination and submission, or DS for short. Usually written with a capital D and lower... never mind. What's your question?"

"Why do you use the word *play* in BDSM play?" What made him ask something so idiotic he didn't know, but he was biologically incapable of getting through an evening without saying something embarrassing. Nevertheless, he was genuinely curious.

Lori stood with her arm on the side of the truck and leaned in to look at him through the open door. "Don't let the word fool you into thinking we don't take it seriously. We use it in the sense of action, not in the sense that it's a game. You can engage in swordplay or gunplay, but if you aren't careful," she grinned in a way he did not altogether like, "either one could kill you. Goodnight, Stuart."

Stuart was still too stunned by her last statement to move, even after he watched her walk up the driveway to her front door and wave to him before she entered.

CHAPTER TWENTY-FOUR
WE FUCKED UP

Steve McGuire sat on the plush sofa in Perry Tellerson's office. He took several minutes to figure out how to open the blinds from the remote control pad cradled on its charging station on a side table. This was somewhat disconcerting, as Steve was a programmer who had started two tremendously successful software companies. Like many members of the Foundation, he was initially funded by them, but his being appointed to the board was the true turning point of his life.

When the blinds were open, he stood and walked to the full height windows and looked out over the city. The bare helipad on the edge of the rooftop awaited the helicopter that would return Perry from his meeting.

Steve had been a rising sun when he joined the Foundation in his early thirties. Now, at age fifty-eight, he had more of a kinship with the setting sun that poured a shadow over the city. When he looked back over the past, as he now looked out over the city, what sort of picture did his life paint? Was it one he would hang in his living room or one he would burn? He believed in the Foundation when he first joined them. He still did, for the most part, but since Perry had assumed his place at the head of the table, he had led the four of them down a dark criminal path. Now Rylen was dead and the four of them remained. The benefit of hindsight left Steve with a feeling that greed and self-interest benefited them at the expense of those who stood in their way. Perry had not deceived them; the wealth he promised had found its way into their hands many times over. They were making illicit deals that had made them richer than they ever expected. Where had it all gone so... evil? He had always been fully behind the decisions that their circle made. Until when? Until Sophia.

It was with her that it had all gone awry. She might have been angry, and she did threaten the rest of them, but they were supposed to protect their own. Nevertheless, the videos that Perry produced were convincing enough. She had to be voted out, not just out of their crime circle, but out of the foundation altogether. At the end of the day, only Marcus Harrier sided with her. Steve had made the right choice based on the information he had at the time, but it never sat well with him afterward. The question was, what could he ever do about it?

The helicopter landed, and Perry made his way across the deck. In a minute, the door opened and Perry came in. "Hello," he said in his animated way, shutting the door and moving to the liquor cabinet. "After five! Have a seat. Want a drink?"

"No, thanks," Steve answered, seating himself on the couch. Perry had been told that the abduction of Lori Mercer had been aborted by the team, but Steve had not yet told him the details. No doubt Perry was expecting to jettison the team again without delay.

"I hope you have some good news for me," said Perry, joining him by taking a second couch opposite.

"No," said Steve. "The news is terrible."

Perry raised his glass in a gesture that told Steve to continue. "Tell me."

"The team I sent to pick up Lori Mercer for questioning last night were thwarted in the act of capturing her."

"Thwarted? You said they aborted the attempt."

"They did, but after a man intervened and fended them off," said Steve, measuring out the bad news in small doses.

"Wait," said Perry, putting his drink on an end table and leaning forward, "*Fended* them off? Are you saying they tried to grab her off of the street?"

"Yes, that is what I'm saying. They were watching her and saw an opportunity when she was walking alone. When they tried to force her into the van..."

"What?" Perry interrupted. "Force her into a van? I said to bring her in so Anlo could question her about her relationship to Rylen, not kidnap her off of the street by forcing her into a van! You think we're the fucking mafia? Where did you hire these guys?"

"They're on our list of resources. We haven't had any need to use them before, but they're vetted professionals. All of them were Israeli Mossad."

"They couldn't just point a gun and say *get in the car*, or would that have been too easy? I said she was not to be harmed."

Steve nodded. "Yes, which is exactly why I ordered them not to bring a single gun with them. They might have had a reason to use it if things went south. I stand by that call, since things did go south and nobody got shot."

"How were they stopped by a bystander without anyone getting hurt?" asked Perry in confusion.

"I said nobody got shot; I didn't say nobody got hurt."

"What happened?" said Perry, rubbing his temples before leaning back and taking up his drink.

"The men saw their chance and took it on what they thought was a fairly deserted street. One would hold her and prevent her screaming and the other would stun her with a stun gun before they put her in the van. A third man stayed behind the wheel."

"A stun gun? They couldn't get her into the van without stunning her?"

"Who knows. While they were carrying this out, one of them was attacked from behind by a man they said came out of nowhere. Then, the one holding Mercer dropped her to defend himself. He fought with the civilian until Ari, the man behind the wheel and the head of the team, ordered for them to abort. They carried their fallen member into the van and took off."

"Carried?" Perry asked.

"The man went down as soon as he was hit."

"Mercer and the civilian?"

"Both are fine. According to them, he wasn't injured in the fight," said Steve, removing his phone from a pocket.

"Didn't you say these guys were Israeli special forces, all of them?"

"That's correct."

"And some guy on the street knocked out one and fought off another?"

"Not some guy on the street," Steve answered, handing his phone across the space between them. Perry put his drink on the end table and took Steve's phone to see a close-up photo of Stuart Hollister on the screen. "It was Stuart, Rylen's younger brother."

Perry stared at him, and the silence hung between them. "That can't be a coincidence. Are you sure?"

"When they told me the man was bald, late twenties or early thirties, bearded with glasses, it sounded too weird. On a hunch, I showed them that photo and they swore that he was the man. Dothan was the one Stuart fought with. He was demanding we do something about Stuart in retribution for their friend and team member."

"Demanding?" asked Perry sarcastically.

"He wanted us to authorize him to go after Stuart Hollister," Steve said. "Instead, I told him that his team has been delisted for service."

Perry handed the phone back. "Do Lori and Stuart know each other through Rylen?"

Steve shrugged. "Not that we know of. There were no chat conversations between Lori and Rylen."

"And you're sure they didn't hurt him and are lying to cover their own asses?" asked Perry, sipping twice from his drink.

"I checked. Stuart's fine. But Yosef, the Israeli he knocked out, died in the hospital."

"Died? What the hell did Stuart hit him with?"

"His fist," Steve answered, knowing how this would sound. "He fractured the man's skull when he punched him from the side. They called me from the van after the attack and said they couldn't revive him. I gave them orders to take him to our medical center on Broadway. Yosef was in a coma for 9 hours with no chance of recovery. His wife took him off of life support this morning. As far as the man's wife and anyone else knows, he fell off a ladder and hit his head while working second shift at his warehouse job."

"Hell of a punch Stuart has. Can he identify them?"

"They wore ski masks."

Perry rolled his eyes. "Of course they did. God, don't ever use those idiots again."

"Like I said, we won't be. And they weren't very happy about it."

Steve stayed quiet as Perry thought. People they contracted for work of this kind had no provable connections to them. Assets took their own risks. If they had found a less moronic way of taking the woman, this would not have happened. "Fucking ski masks..." Perry breathed quietly. "Cover the cost of the funeral," he said, still lost in thought.

"Already taking care of that. Anonymously, of course."

At last Perry said, "There's no way he knew her before. Mercer wasn't even at the funeral. How close could she have been to Rylen?"

"Unless she killed him. Or was involved somehow."

"You think she could have been solely responsible?"

"I'm not ruling it out. It happens. Crazy ex-girlfriend turns killer. You know what Rylen was like; maybe she killed him for her own reasons."

"How? Running him off the road? Tampering with his car? And then leave a clue pointing back to herself? I don't think so," said Perry, emptying the rest of his glass.

Steve mused aloud, "That's the problem with crazy, it never seems to make any sense."

Perry graced him with a smirk. "Obviously Stuart doesn't

think so either. He killed a man trying to protect her, though he doesn't know it. What about the police?"

"According to our contacts, no reports of the incident have been filed so far."

"Three men in masks try to wrestle a woman into a van and nobody calls the cops," said Perry. "The only time victims of a violent crime don't call the police is when they don't want any attention from the police themselves."

"Stuart has had a lot of run-ins with the law. Assault and battery, mostly. He's on probation and has to undergo a mandatory psych evaluation. Even if he was helping someone else, I can understand why he wouldn't want to talk to the police, but Lori Mercer is a question mark. Given the rumors our PI found out about her, maybe she figured her past is catching up with her."

"He had the phone long enough to go through it. Maybe he got suspicious for the same reasons we did. He saw the phone call and picture text and cross checked the time. He's following the same breadcrumbs. Fuck!" exclaimed Perry, pinching the bridge of his nose under his glasses. "This has to stop."

"What do you want to do?"

"Stuart Hollister. I want to bring him in," said Perry, contemplating. "Not like that!" he added when he took in Steve's stare. "The last thing we need is another botched black bag job. We're turning into Guantanamo."

Steve allowed himself a smile at that. "Where do you want to meet?"

"We'll meet here. And I'd like you present. The dampeners will handle his device, but it will present more of a united front."

"I would like to meet him, actually. How much will you tell him?"

"No more than I need to, which is to say whatever will get him to tell us about Miss Mercer. Any reason we can't fess up and give him his brother's phone back?"

Steve thought about the spyware he had found and disabled before he said, "No, we can give it back."

"Look, we know Rylen's crash wasn't just a car crash. He wasn't drunk or high. And we couldn't run tests for poisons or any other substances because Rylen was cremated before we knew it wasn't an accident. Now his brother knows it too. He's pretty clever if he got to her before we did; I met him at the funeral, so he knows me. I'll call him personally and set up a meeting. I'm sure we can trust him with a peek behind the curtain if it will help us find out whether Lori Mercer had anything to do with Rylen getting killed--and, if she did, then why she did it. He would want the truth, too."

"The way he handled the Israelis, maybe we should hire him instead."

CHAPTER TWENTY-FIVE

SPIDER HAS THE TOYS

Stuart and Lonnie sat in the cafe after a morning at the gym. Lonnie fought harder than he had before, and Stuart suspected that he was growing tired of losing in their kickboxing matches. Stuart fought harder too and ended the match with a spinning sidekick to the chest that took all the remaining fight out of his opponent. When they were done, Lonnie offered to buy Stuart lunch. He accepted. They soon found themselves sitting over plates of food at a nearby greasy spoon.

"Just saying, man," Lonnie told him over his lunch, "I haven't been beat up on like that since my big brother."

"You want me to go easy on you. I understand."

Lonnie paused in sprinkling salt over steak and eggs. "Oh, you had to go there, didn't you?" Stuart smiled, having made his point. Lonnie's Cuban/Boston accent became more pronounced at times, like he was making an effort to lose it. "You know, I never even asked you what you do for a living."

"I'm an elevator technician," Stuart told him. "Or at least I was. I just quit."

"Why?"

"It wasn't for me. I'll try something else."

"You going to be okay?"

"Yeah, I'll be alright for a while. What do you do?"

"I'm an electrician," said Lonnie. "Family business. I did two tours in Iraq and came back to Boston, just so I could figure out I wasn't cut out for civilian life. My father and brother were only too happy to train me to do something other than pull a trigger."

"Do you like it?"

"Electricity? It's honest work and it keeps my lights on." Stuart nodded as he took a bite of his fruit salad. "Why am I the only one who thinks that joke is funny?"

"That was a joke?"

"I'm glad I didn't go for a career in stand-up," Lonnie said as he stabbed a fork into his steak and eggs. "Anyway, an occasional electric shock helps with the PTSD."

"The breakers at my house have been tripping. Why don't you come out and have a look?"

Lonnie hesitated. "I really don't do residential."

"That's fine. If you can't handle it yourself, send your brother. I'd rather give the job to somebody I trust instead of somebody who will charge me a thousand dollars to change a fuse."

Lonnie shook his head. "None of us do. We only work on commercial properties."

"A family of electricians and none of you can work on a house?"

"Sorry, hombre."

Spider walked through the front door of Stuart's house. Spider sat on the couch and unpacked his laptop bag on the coffee table as Stuart shut the door and took the easy chair. "We have some planning to do, friend," Spider said, holding up a black box with an expression that Stuart could only interpret as unmitigated pride.

"This is an eyeball cam," he said, handing it to Stuart. Stuart examined the plastic ball camera. "The lens is floating and self-correcting. It has a long battery life and has wireless charging. It can rotate in a continuous 360-degree loop and can be set to a fixed position or to train in on motion. Also picks up audio. The video feed will be set to send any recording to your actual phone. So, no more uninvited guests while you're away from home."

"That's pretty sweet," said Stuart.

"That's just the cam. That ain't the cool bit. We're getting there. This," he said, holding up a black mobile phone that was like most standard models, including Stuart's own, "is my baby. I made an app that's already installed on this phone. I could install it on yours, but we need a device that won't lead anywhere if you get caught, or if she figures out what you did. With the app running, get this phone next to hers and it will hack into her device, no matter what type it is, and give us access to everything on it... contacts, message history, photos, emails... everything."

Stuart was doubtful. "How close does it need to be?"

"Touching, preferably, but within a foot is fine. Just set it down next to her purse or set your phone next to hers on the table. It will link with her device within fourteen seconds at most."

"That's some wickedly devious property you have there. This seems wrong, somehow."

Spider blinked in confusion. "We're dealing with some very wicked and devious people. But look, if you don't want to do this..."

"I do," Stuart cut in. "Thank you, I'm just not used to cloak and dagger."

"Says the guy who fought off three men hired by big-boss criminals. Anyway, if there's a way to find out if she had anything to do with Rylen, this is the best shot we have."

"Agreed, but if she's careful, she will have deleted any details off of her phone."

"Let me worry about that. You can retrieve deleted data. And Stuart," said Spider with a look of solemnity, "be careful. Don't let her fool you into lowering your guard. If she was put up to it, she's dangerous. If she was working alone, she's even more so."

"Let's hope she had nothing at all to do with it," Stuart said.

Spider gave him an enigmatic expression. "Yeah, let's hope."

CHAPTER TWENTY-SIX

A DUNGEON DEMO

Stuart found the building and parked his pickup in the lot across the street. The two-story brick building had a candy shop next door, which was how she said he would know he had the right place. There was a flagstone alley between the candy shop and the building next to it. It was closed off by a low iron gate, next to which stood a man dressed in black, looking at his phone. Stuart sent Lori a text message to let her know he had arrived. She replied a few seconds later, saying she would meet him at the gate.

He got out of his truck and locked it behind him, only to realize his heart was pounding. Was his anxiety making a reappearance or was it old-fashioned nerves? He crossed the street, filling his lungs with the chilly night air that smelled of saltwater and candy. He approached the man at the gate and said he was a friend of Lori's. He got a puzzled look before he recalled that *Crystal* was the name she used in these circles. A door opened at the far end of the dimly-lit alley, casting the brighter light of the interior onto the flagstones. Lori leaned out and shouted, "It's okay, Jake! He's with me!"

"Have a good night," Jake said to Stuart, opening the iron gate for him to enter.

Stuart walked up the gloomy alley, his eyes on Lori's shadow on the ground as she stood inside the light of the doorway. "Hurry up, it's cold out here," came her voice with

mock consternation as he neared the door. When he stepped
through the door, it was little wonder she was cold. Lori was
wearing a black leather corset with matching leather hot pants,
fishnet tights, and stiletto heels. When she shut the door, she
turned to him. "Well, well, look at you. I finally get to see you in
something other than workout clothes. Very nice."

Earlier that day, Stuart had asked her what he should wear,
and followed her advice to the letter. As he was not in the
lifestyle, she suggested he wear jeans and a tight black t-shirt.
When he asked, she said it was what she wanted to see him in.
The dungeon did not have a dress code. He was in the habit of
wearing over-sized clothing, and the tight t-shirt made him feel
naked without his jacket. He purchased the black leather jacket
that morning, wanting to have one without grease stains on the
sleeves. Lori drew close to him and put the palm of her hand on
his chest. "You look pretty incredible," he told her.

She smiled and drew her face to within a few inches of his.
In the five-inch heels she was wearing, she was inches taller
than he. She peered down at him, her palm still pressed to his
chest. She kissed him lightly, as not to smear the sheen on her
blood-red lips. The pounding of his heart was nothing he could
hide from her; he was certain she had placed her hand on his
chest for that very reason. "Follow me," she said.

She led the way down the hall, a couple of steps in front
of him. He inwardly chided himself for letting her physical
beauty get to him the way it did, but there was no denying the
attraction she stirred in him. He would need to keep reminding
himself that he was there for the data on her phone. Was that the
only reason he was there, to get information? He had accepted
her invitation before Spider thought to exploit the chance to get
her phone without her knowing it. No, that was not the only
reason. He would have accepted regardless. He was happiest
when he was in danger; he sought it out and lived for it. She
was dangerous. So, by her very nature, she possessed a macabre
attraction for him.

In that moment, he was not entirely sure that he was not in

one of the dreams he hated so much. In a matter of weeks he had lost his only brother, set out to find the killer, become a multi-millionaire, met a dominatrix, saved her from abduction by mercenaries, and was following that same woman to a dungeon to watch her demonstrate how to use hypnosis in BDSM play. How did an elevator technician with anxiety issues find himself in so bizarre a situation?

The ancient Samurai believed it should never take more than seven breaths to make a decision. He was not a Samurai, but he had a decision to make. Would he trust his instincts over the evidence and come to know this woman in the way that he would like? Or would he remain suspicious and guard himself against any threat she might pose, thereby denying himself any chance to be with the most remarkable woman he had ever met? Lori turned left down another hall and stopped by a set of metal double doors. By this time, his decision was made. She opened one door and gestured inside. He entered and she followed.

The dungeon was a large room, about forty feet square. One wall was brick and the other three were drywall painted to look like natural stone. The ceiling was black with multiple rows of track lighting. Numerous pieces of furniture, equipment racks, and devices--the use of which Stuart could not guess--had all been moved to sides of the room, creating an empty space in the center of the tile floor. A Victorian style armchair of red leather was placed in the center of the room. Twenty black metal folding chairs had been arranged in a semicircle around the ornate focal chair at the center of the room.

"I'll take your jacket," Lori said. "I'll hang it up in the changing room I use over there." Stuart slipped off his leather jacket and handed it to her. He continued pacing around the side of the room, fascinated by the equipment, when he noticed that he didn't hear the sound of stiletto heels on tile. He turned to see Lori staring at him, his jacket held in one hand.

"What's wrong?" he asked.

"Oh. My. God," she said, walking to him. She rubbed her free hand over his shoulder and down the side of his arm. "You look like a bodybuilder."

"I'm definitely not," Stuart said, feeling self-conscious. "I just work out a lot."

"Lift up your shirt."

"What?" asked Stuart.

"Lift up the front of your t-shirt," she repeated.

"Why do you want me to lift my shirt?"

She looked him in the eye. "Show me your fucking abs, now!" she demanded, managing to keep a perfectly imperious tone, but failing to keep a smile from curling the corners of her mouth. Stuart lifted the front of his shirt up to his chest. Lori waited. "Do it," she told him. He took a breath and flexed his abs as tight as he could. She traced her fingertips over the deep crevices.

"Can I tuck my shirt back in now, please?"

"Sure," Lori answered, putting her hand on his neck and looking him in the eye, emphasizing each word as she spoke. "You will never, ever, wear those loose, shitty, baggy-ass clothes around me again."

Stuart, shocked, could only nod. Lori turned and walked to the changing room to hang his jacket. "Wait a minute," Stuart said, increasing his volume as she entered the door of the changing room. "All my clothes are baggy!"

"Ever!" she shouted back from the dark interior.

Stuart dropped the conversation, such as it was, and continued pacing the edge of the dungeon. He recalled what he had read from the information Spider had collected on her. He learned that his estimate of her age was spot on; Lori Mercer was 31 years old, born and raised in New York City. Her parents were a Colombian immigrant father and Irish American mother. Mother deceased and the father's whereabouts unknown-- presumably no longer residing in the US. She took her mother's maiden name.

Lori was awarded a full scholarship to Cornell University and later moved to California, where she received her master's in biochemistry from UCLA. She then moved to Boston at age twenty-six. Spider annotated many of the details that he outlined, noting that she never actually used her degree. The rent on her tea shop space was five thousand a month and her lease was in good standing. Spider also noted the rent would be a bargain at twice that rate in that area. He then wrote that she did take out a loan for her graduate studies, but it was paid in full in two years. Her house had been refinanced in recent weeks. How she accomplished all of that was more than a little vague because her income from giving massages and the monthly sales from The Green Leaf were her only declared revenue streams, yet her annual taxes from the previous year showed a declared personal income of one hundred thirty thousand. Her personal tax filings were impeccable, so she wasn't worried about being audited. Stuart was astonished at the information that Spider was able to compile on this woman in so short a time. How had he gotten her tax records? Spider had chosen his name well; he could crawl through the web and get into any place he was not wanted.

"What is this?" he asked when she returned. He pointed to a large structure made of steel cross beams with a motorized pivot at its center.

"It is called a Saint Andrew's Cross," she answered. "After the demonstration, I'll explain what anything in this room is, if you like."

"I would like that. I think."

"But right now, I have a proposal for you," she said, walking to the chair in the middle of the room. "How would you like to be my volunteer for the demonstration tonight?"

CHAPTER TWENTY-SEVEN

STUART GOES UNDER

Stuart was not sure he had heard Lori correctly. "Your volunteer?" he asked.

"Yes. If you'd like to try it, I could hypnotize you for the demonstration tonight," said Lori.

Stuart rubbed his bristled chin. Was that why she had invited him? "I was just planning on watching," he said nervously.

"It's perfectly cool if you don't want to. I just thought I would see if you're up for it. We have twenty-six guests scheduled, so we can expect at least fifteen to show. Someone's always ready to volunteer, but in the event that no one does, Jake, the security guy you met at the gate, is my fall back volunteer."

A stab of jealousy shot through Stuart like an electric shock. The stupidity of that clawed at him, but he mentally suppressed it to keep his head clear. "I would, but you need to know, I may not be the best person for that."

"And why's that?" she asked.

"I sometimes have trouble with anxiety," he admitted, wondering if he should divulge that it had taken a vacation. "I have trouble sleeping because of it. Wouldn't that make it hard for me to be hypnotized?"

"Hypnosis isn't sleep. Think of it more like a visualization exercise. So I can assume you've never tried hypnosis before?" she asked, to which he shook his head in answer. "Have you ever been so wrapped up in your own thoughts while you were driving that you missed your exit on the highway? Or have you ever been so focused on something you were reading or watching on television that you didn't hear what someone was saying to you?"

"Yes, I have."

"Then you can be hypnotized."

Stuart was not convinced. "Even if I can be, I don't want to mess up your demonstration by being a crappy subject."

"Let's find out right now." Lori gestured to the leather armchair she leaned on.

He hesitantly sat in the chair, putting his arms on the soft leather rests. "Won't people start showing up soon? How long will this take?"

"They aren't allowed in until fifteen minutes before. Why do you think I had you come an hour early?" she replied. "We have plenty of time. And how long it will take... we'll know all we need to know in a few minutes. Can you see without your glasses?"

"Not as well I can see with them," Lori laughed and he decided to let her think he meant it as a joke. "Well enough, I guess. I can't read or drive without them. Even with them, I tend to have trouble in low lighting. With all the fights I keep finding myself in, maybe I should think about getting contacts."

"Keep them on, it's fine. We're just going to do a couple of quick tests." She had him place his feet together and face forward. She stood in front of him and held out her hand with the palm up. "Place one hand flat over mine and leave the other resting on the arm of the chair." When he did as she asked, she leaned forward and cupped his chin with her free hand, turning his face up slightly and leaning forward to look him in the eye. "Stare directly into my eyes and count backwards from ten to one." Stuart counted steadily aloud, never turning his gaze away from the soft hazel of her eyes. When he finished, she straightened and stepped back, withdrawing her hand from his. "Excellent."

"What was that?" he asked her. "I'm not hypnotized."

"Of course not. You said you can be anxious, so that was a suitability test. You don't show signs of anxiety. You're extremely focused, you aren't the least bit nervous, and unless you're on meds for it, you certainly don't have ADD."

"Lately, my anxiety has been kind of... quiet. I've never had ADD; you could tell all that?" he asked, but Lori ignored the question.

"Take off your glasses for this one." Stuart removed his glasses and hung them from the neck of his t-shirt.

"Now take your index finger and touch it to the center of your forehead," Lori said as she demonstrated on herself. He followed along. "Now close your eyes and imagine that while you touch your forehead, your eyes are glued shut. For as long as you touch your forehead, your eyes are glued and bonded together. Accept this idea completely." Stuart visualized this as clearly as he could, imagining that his eyes were in fact glued shut. He felt Lori's hand touch his left shoulder and her voice was close to his ear. "Just accept it. It's fine." Her hand left his shoulder and the sound of her heels on the floor told him she was standing in front of him again. "No matter how hard you try to open your eyes, the more impossible it becomes. You can try if you want, but you will now find that while you are touching your forehead, your eyes are glued, impossible to open."

Stuart tried to open his eyes, but managed only to raise his eyebrows, not his eyelids. It was unsettling, but he was also impressed and amused by it. "Yes, it's amazing when you first find how powerful it is. It's a lot of fun when you accept it and just go with it." Again, her hand touched his shoulder and she said into his ear, "Accept and go with it. It's fun." Her hand was removed from his shoulder and she was pacing in front of him. "Now, take your finger from your forehead and you will find that you can open your eyes normally."

Stuart lowered his hand to the arm of the chair and opened his eyes. "Holy... it really worked."

Lori nodded and smiled appreciatively. "Try some more?"

"Definitely," he responded.

"Normally, I would use a more rapid induction, but since we have time... Don't try to make sense of what I say, just listen as closely as you can. Each time I snap my fingers while I talk," she crisply snapped her fingers, "you take a deep breath and imagine yourself growing heavier, being pulled by *so sleepy* gravity down into the chair. Completely *focused on me* every word. Listening so closely to the *eyes so heavy* sound of my voice. Feels so good to *let yourself go* heavier and so relaxed as your *need to sleepy* mind goes completely empty..."

She paced back and forth in front of him like the pendulum of a clock, her steps tapping a slow, rhythmic pace on the tile. Her eyes never left his face as she paced. His eyes, however, never left the form of the woman in front of him, following her movements in rapt attention while she paced and spoke. She occasionally snapped her fingers as his cue to breathe deeply, and he felt himself growing impossibly heavy in the chair. Her words soon became a buzz in the background to the click of her heels and the infrequent snap of her fingers. He struggled to focus on her words and to keep his eyes open, but his eyelids felt like they had weights attached to them. He was no more able to move than a fly trapped in amber. The last word he heard clearly was the word, *sleep,* which was accompanied by the sound of a sharp finger snap.

"Three, two, one. Wake," said Lori, with a snap of her fingers. Stuart's eyes shot open. "Congratulations," she told him.

He stood and backed away from the chair. "For what?" he asked in confusion.

"For your first hypnosis experience," she said with a grin. "Turns out you are extremely good at going into trance."

Stuart hesitated, recalling her pacing in front of him and a feeling of heaviness overtaking his entire body, but he could recall nothing after that. "I don't remember a damn thing," he said. "What did we just do?"

"Helped you relax and release some of that anxiety you were telling me about," she answered. "How do you feel? Better?"

He did feel better. "I feel good," he told her. "To be honest, I feel great."

"Wonderful," she smiled. "I'll call you up first. Is it okay if I use your real name?"

"Sure."

"Have a seat. People are waiting to get in and it's time to open the doors."

Lori went to open the main doors to the dungeon and greeted the first attendees of the evening. Stuart sat in one of the metal folding chairs and tried to recall what happened while she had him in trance. He put his glasses on and instinctively reached for his phone before remembering that she had told him no phones were allowed in the dungeon. He had left it in the glove box of his truck. There was a clock on the wall that read seven forty-seven PM. He had pulled his truck into the parking lot across the street at a few minutes to seven. Oh, fuck, he thought. He had been in trance for more than half an hour and could not recall a single second. So much for being rid of his anxiety; he was going to have a heart attack. In spite of Spider's entreaties not to do anything stupid, he had done something very, very stupid. How well quick decision-making abilities served the Samurai in general, history did not record.

People entered and filled the chairs, but Stuart barely took notice of them. He decided he would have to leave as soon as the demonstration was over. He could claim he was not feeling well and leave as quickly as he could. When he did take notice of the attendees, he was relieved to find that less than half were in any kind of fetish attire, so he was less out of place in appearance than he had feared. They were a diverse group who ranged in age from twenties to fifties.

Lori greeted everyone and made a self-introduction before giving a short discussion of what hypnosis is and what it is not. Then she started talking about its applications in the BDSM lifestyle, but by this time Stuart had stopped listening--until he heard her say his name. She was looking at him. "Come have a seat," she told him. Stuart rose and resumed the chair he so regretted sitting in earlier. "All good?" she asked. He nodded in reply. She leaned down and whispered, "are you sure you're okay with this?"

"Yeah, I'm fine," he said, just loud enough for her to hear. "Go ahead."

"I had the opportunity to hypnotize my friend here before this demonstration, so I won't need to perform an induction like I will with some of you after this," she said, placing her hand on his left shoulder. "In his case, all I have to do tell him to *sleep!*" she said as she snapped her fingers a few inches away from the front of his glasses. The world went dark as relaxation washed over him. Stuart had the vague sense of his head slumping forward. Then he was awake again. "Bondage need not always involve some elaborate restraint, but when used properly, hypnosis makes any physical restraint unnecessary," said Lori. "Stuart, would you please stand?"

Stuart tried to stand, but could not budge from the chair. His arms were on the armrests and his feet were on the floor in front of him, but he was not able to get them to move. "I can't," he said. He felt much less silly at his own inability to get out of a chair in front of a group of people than he might have expected. It didn't bother him in the least. If anything, he was as entertained by it as the people watching. He had to wonder if his comfort was the product of the preconditioning she had given him.

"You look pretty strong," she said. "You sure you can't get out of the chair?"

He struggled, but could do nothing. "No, I really can't."

"So if you've been a bad boy, you would be in time out for a while," said Lori, "except you have been good, so..." She touched the center of his forehead. His limbs were freed and he stood up from the chair. "This is something that's great for travel and public play. And it's discreet, so no one will be any the wiser. How are you?"

"Never better," said Stuart. Lori motioned him back to the chair and he sat down again.

"Now, what if your submissive says something offensive or gets a little too mouthy for your taste?" Stuart had some vague inkling of what was coming. "In that case, we tell our sub to *hush.*" As she said the last word, she touched the tip of her finger to his lips. "How is that?" she asked him. Stuart tried to speak, but could not. He met Lori's eye. She waited expectantly. He tried to talk, but not even a murmur escaped his lips. He laughed in spite of himself. "But I enjoy your conversation." She snapped her fingers before his face and asked, "better?"

"Much," Stuart replied.

"Lovely," she answered. "Thank you, Stuart. Would someone else like to try?"

Stuart returned to his seat, and Lori selected a woman from the group of spectators. This woman she hypnotized in less than 20 seconds. This was the rapid induction she had talked about, but for reasons he was afraid to guess, she decided to forego in his case.

When Stuart read into the latter portion of her profile the night before, he found that the waters grew murkier when they covered her personal life. She had a website promoting her services as a professional dominatrix by the name of *Mistress Crystal Dark*. He privately thought the name was corny enough to be laughable. Her specialty was hypnosis, though where she received her training from was unknown. Spider noted that he believed she was self-taught, but may have received private instruction.

The dungeon itself was owned by a woman named Carol Benniga. Lori worked out of it and charged an unknown hourly rate for a private session. She performed demonstrations once or twice a month by invitation only. It was probably her way of drumming up new clients.

How had Rylen gotten mixed up in this? Was this how she made her income? When did she find the time? The Green Leaf was open five days a week, and she took massage appointments on Friday. She must have at least one part-time employee. Unlike her training in hypnosis and as a dominatrix, her license as a massage therapist was valid, and she completed the program two years after moving to Boston.

What sort of woman graduates from a school like Cornell, moves clear across the country to get her master's degree in biochemistry from UCLA, then moves back to the east coast to become a massage therapist and open a tea shop? Somewhere along the way, she gets into BDSM as a side profession and assumes her alter ego, Mistress Crystal Dark, a dominatrix who specializes in hypno-erotic fetishes. It was the most weird, wasteful, and contradictory resume he had ever heard of.

The rest of the demonstration was unlike anything Stuart had ever seen. Lori made the woman believe herself to be a man for a few minutes before returning her to herself. Then, she gave the woman a trigger word that, when used, brought the woman to full orgasm. Next she called up a male volunteer, a man of mid to late forties. She showed how compliance could be enhanced with trigger words, which could be used to reward with pleasure or punish with pain. After finishing with a third and fourth volunteer, Lori moved into a discussion on how hypnosis could be properly learned and utilized in a BDSM lifestyle scenario. She then closed with taking questions. When that was done, she thanked everyone for coming and they started making their way out. A couple of men stayed behind to talk with Lori. The three talked for some time until they finally departed as well.

Stuart kept to his chair until the last were gone and he was again alone in the dungeon with Lori. He stood and waited for her to close the doors behind Jake. "So," Lori said, "what did you think?"

There was no reason not to be completely honest on this point. "That was fantastic."

"You really think so?" she asked, seeming flattered.

"Yes, and I wonder if everyone here realized how fucking amazing that was," he told her.

"You never can tell how people will respond to it when they see it done for the first time."

Stuart shook his head in wonderment. "The average person can mistake something wondrous for something commonplace. That doesn't make it any the less brilliant, or you any less extraordinary."

Lori stared at him as though she were not sure she had heard him correctly. "You really are one bona fide sweetheart, aren't you?"

Unsure how to respond, Stuart said the only thing that he could think of. "Yes."

"Let me change. We'll go back to my house. You can cash in your raincheck for a drink."

Stuart remembered that he had a lie prepared. "Listen, you live in Lowell. It's a bit of a drive and I'm not feeling up to it."

She looked taken aback. "I thought we were going to hang out after this."

"I know. Sorry, I'm exhausted so I'm going to go home for the night."

Lori rested her hand on his left shoulder. "Be a sweetheart and follow me back to my place for a drink. It will be fun."

"Okay, sure, I would like that," he answered, and to his own surprise, he truly meant it.

"Great! Wait for me here. I'll go get changed and get your jacket." She walked to the changing room door.

CHAPTER TWENTY-EIGHT

INTO THE LIONESS' DEN

"Why use hypnosis at all?" Stuart asked Lori as they sat on the couch in her living room, sharing conversation over a glass of wine.

"Were you not paying attention tonight?" she asked playfully. "I thought I made a fan out of you already."

Until this point, he had mentally complimented himself on his self-possession. At an earlier time, he would not have been able to handle it. Maybe the Samurai knew what they were doing after all. Regardless of whether it was the decision to trust her, he managed to enter the house and sit down with Lori as though he were enjoying the company of any other woman. The thing was, Lori was not any other woman. He had a device in his jacket pocket that might help him find out if she was on the phone with his brother when he wrecked his car. Could hypnosis do that? After what he had witnessed at the dungeon, he was not as sure of her innocence as he had been. All of his instincts told him that he could trust her, but were these his mental or sexual instincts that he was listening to? How could it be mere coincidence that someone with so unique a set of abilities happened to be the last one to see his brother alive? "You did make a fan. It was amazing, but isn't it... dangerous? I mean, controlling people that way, can't it do harm or have some unexpected side effects?"

"Oh, that," said Lori, sipping her wine. "You can't be made

to do something you don't really want to do while you're hypnotized."

"Yes," Stuart answered, thinking of his conversations with Ella, "I've heard that somewhere."

"You heard right. If I hypnotized you, handed you a pair of scissors, and then told you to stab yourself in the leg, you wouldn't do it."

"Tonight at the dungeon, no matter how hard I tried to get out of the chair, I couldn't do it. You told me that I was paralyzed and I was. There was no way I was getting up."

"That's a hypnotic suggestion," said Lori with a grin. "If it was truly impossible to resist, we would call it something else. If I were to leave you there and the building caught on fire, you would get up and run with everyone else."

"So it worked because I wanted it to?" he asked her.

"Pretty much. People think hypnosis is something that is done *to* someone when it is actually done *with* someone. Massage and hypnosis are not so different."

It was an odd comparison. "How so?"

"Well," she explained, "you have to work with a hypnotist if you're going to go into a trance. You need to cooperate. I could chain someone down and give him a massage, but if he's struggling and fighting it the whole time, he will never get any benefit out of it. In massage, both parties need to work together for it to be productive. The same is true for hypnosis. Both the hypnotist and the subject need to work in tandem for the subject to achieve a trance state. The skill of the hypnotist is important, but the ability for the subject to enter a trance is important too. That's also a skill that can be developed, and something that some people are naturally better at than others. Like you. You're especially good at it."

He could see why such a woman would intrigue Rylen, but what was the nature of their relationship? If they had been close, did she even know he was dead? Maybe he was a client of hers; it would explain why she had not tried to contact him. It was possible that she knew, but not many people read the obituaries. Maybe they had common friends, but Lori didn't go to the funeral. A man as young, brilliant, and charismatic as Rylen having so few people show up at his funeral was wrong somehow. Most of them were work associates. What would she say if she found out he was Rylen's brother? He could never tell her, of course, but how did any of this get him any closer to finding out if Rylen was murdered? Spider's meaning now became clear to him; he had made Stuart promise not to do anything stupid. After reading all the information in the file, it was obvious that she had the skills and the opportunity to hypnotize Rylen and make him fall asleep on the road over a phone call, in spite of what she had just told him. If it could be done, she would be just the person to pull it off.

"So there's no way someone could be made to do something like commit a murder?" Stuart asked. The question fit squarely within the context of the conversation and matched the morbid curiosity someone might have. Still, Lori looked at him over her glass of wine in silence for more seconds than were warranted.

"An ordinary hypnotic trance can't make someone a murderer, unless that person already is one--or at least takes an enthusiastic view of it," she answered. "What you probably haven't heard is, even though you cannot be made to do something you don't want to do, you can be given a choice. And certain choices can be made to seem repulsive and others to seem irresistible."

Stuart considered this. "You're right, I didn't know that part. You said an *ordinary* hypnotic trance couldn't do that. So there's an extraordinary one?"

Lori nodded. "There are some extreme exceptions. Those involve using hypnosis in combination with drugs and forms of torture like brainwashing, physical abuse, sleep deprivation... nasty stuff like that done over a period of time. However, in domination and submission, a trance can be a wonderful experience when you give yourself to another. Hypnosis is just one of a thousand ways that you can do a power exchange in this lifestyle."

"Lifestyle," he said as though tasting the word, "and people build relationships on this?" he asked, having trouble imagining a relationship in which one party willingly submitted to the control of the other.

Lori laughed. "There are those of us who build their entire lives on it."

"But they're just pretending," he said, looking for affirmation in her face.

"You aren't pretending if you mean it, Stuart," was her only reply.

"If you're still in control when you're hypnotized, doesn't that just mean you're role-playing, like naughty nurse and dirty doctor?"

Lori shook her head. "Tell me this: what is the difference between reality and fantasy?"

"I think the difference is apparent."

"Except for when it isn't," she replied, "wherein lies the answer. The difference between the two is whatever allows you to tell them apart. Pretend two groups of people were going to reenact a battle from history, but both sides decide to use real weapons. Then they agree that they will not hold back, but genuinely try to kill each other. It isn't a game anymore, it's the real thing. If you can't tell the difference, then there isn't one. That is the beauty of hypnosis. It blurs the boundary between fantasy and reality."

"You said that the BDSM lifestyle is all about control and consent. If one consents to letting you control his mind, how can he ever rescind that consent once he's given it to you?"

"Bravo," said Lori, giving him a mock toast with her wineglass. "An excellent question, and not one many rookies in the lifestyle think to ask." Lori slid closer to him on the couch so that their legs touched. She slowly took the unfinished glass of wine from his hand, then placed both glasses on the coffee table.

"And the answer is?" he asked, not pulling away from her as all of his better judgment called for him to do.

"The answer is," she said, putting her hand on his chest and bringing her face closer, "beforehand, we agree on a length of time that he will be in my control. And then..."

"And then?" he asked, her lips inches from his.

"He just has to trust that I will return his free will to him when I am done with it," she finished, a smile tugging at her mouth. Lori pressed their lips together, the taste of wine on her breath mixed with the aroma of her perfume and the waxy scent of her lipstick. His hands instinctively roved over her back and he pulled her closer, feeling the corset she had been wearing earlier through the fabric of her t-shirt. She arched her back, pushing her chest into his as their lips opened and their tongues glided together. She leaned her head back, breaking the kiss, but pressing her body even more firmly into his. "Can I show you something else hypnosis can do?"

Stuart panted, his arms wrapped around her and his dick uncomfortably hard. "Show me," he said.

Lori's hand rubbed his shoulder, and their lips were together again. They shifted on the couch. He released her as she rose and straddled his lap. His hands wrapped around her again, this time touching the bare skin of her upper back over the corset. Startled, he gently pulled her away from him. Where she had been wearing skinny jeans and a t-shirt a second before, she was wearing only the corset, leather shorts, and fishnet tights she had on earlier that night at the dungeon. Somehow, she had frozen him in that instant and removed her clothes without his even being aware that any time had passed. "Surprise," she said, smiling at the wide-eyed confusion on his face.

"What the fu-"

"Did that just freak you out?" she asked.

"A little," he answered, looking down to her breasts. "Please do that again."

"We'll see," she said, taking his hands and standing. He stood as well. He raised his arms to allow Lori to pull his t-shirt over his head and throw it on the couch. Still holding one of his hands firmly, she used her free hand to stroke the pads of her fingers down his chest and over his abs. Stuart knew that he should feel a shred of shame at the pride he took in her pleased admiration. He was standing in the home of the woman with whom his brother had spent the last night of his life. Would this be his last night? He didn't believe Lori was a killer, but was he willing to stake his life on it? They were both half naked--he could do the smart thing and put a stop to it. He also knew that when a man like himself was half naked with a woman like her, wisdom did not usually stop it from going further. When she said, "Come," and tugged his hand to lead him to the bedroom, he let himself be led.

When Stuart entered the bedroom, his eyes fell over the massive bed and wrought iron headboard. The comforter had been turned down to expose sheets of black satin. It had no footboard, but two black chains snaked out from under the bed skirt at each corner and coiled on the carpet. A lamp on one of the lacquer nightstands illuminated the whole of the room with a dull light. Lori let go of his hand. She walked to the foot of the bed and turned to watch him taking in the room. As his eyes came upon the front wall opposite the bed. There, centered on the wall between the open door of a closet and the door from which he entered, was a large painting. It was that of a naked man, kneeling before a woman who held a riding crop, the tip of it touching his chin.

CHAPTER TWENTY-NINE

A NIGHT TO REMEMBER OR NOT

The painting arrested Stuart's attention. "Like it?" asked Lori, watching closely as he examined it closely.

"Yes, a little," he answered, "a lot, actually."

"I like it a lot too," she said as she went to the nightstand, opening and closing its small drawer. Then, slipping off her heels, she glided to his side.

"The woman makes me think of you," he said as she moved behind him and rested her chin on his shoulder, wrapping her arms around his waist.

"Funny," she said, whispering directly into his ear, "I was just thinking the man is very much like you."

"Me?" he said, twisting in her embrace so they faced each other. "That's not me at all."

Lori raised her eyebrows questioningly. "No?" she asked, a knowing gleam in her eye. "You say that because it isn't who you are right now and not who you were yesterday. But tomorrow, next week, next month... soon you're going to find that it is very much you, Stuart." She wrapped her arms around his neck and slowly turned, looking into his eyes with a mixture of lust and mischief. They turned around in a circle, slowly, as though she was leading a slow dance to music only she could hear. He inhaled slowly as they came to a stop. She took him into a passionate kiss before breaking away to say, "you asked me to do it again."

Stuart moved his hands over the small of her back, this time touching bare skin as he let one hand ride down over the curve of her hip, feeling nylon netting. "Shit, that's incredible. You're naked."

"Bright boy," she said with a smirk, "so are you." She stepped away from him; the air of the room was cold against his naked body. The rest of his clothes lay on the floor against the wall. He felt at his neck to find a thick leather collar had been affixed there. Stuart could only gape at this woman. She was not entirely naked. She remained in the crotchless fishnets she had worn under her outfit. For the first time in his capacious memory, words failed him. "Is that okay? I can remove it if it bothers you."

"What does this mean?" he asked, finding his voice again and touching the collar at his neck.

She stepped closer and gripped him by the wrist. "It means that you will do whatever the fuck I want until I'm satisfied." She raised his hand and pressed a condom into his palm, "Then maybe you'll get to be satisfied too."

He trusted that if he told her to get the thing off of his neck, she would do so. How could he know that? Was this role-play? He also knew what would make both of them far happier in that moment. Happiness? Knowing joy and pleasure again had become a forlorn hope since Rylen died.

"I can handle that," he told her.

She smiled approvingly, like he had passed a test, and said, "Then get that on." Stuart tore the condom from the pack and rolled it over the length of his shaft. "Can you also handle being tied up?" she asked, picking up one of the lengths of black chain from the floor.

"I don't want to be tied up," he answered. "I like to touch."

She let the chain rattle to the floor, making him realize that the chains, though thick and undoubtedly sturdy, were made of plastic. Lori moved to him and slowly removed his glasses. "We'll have to work on that," she said, stepping to the nightstand and placing his glasses at the base of the lamp. "And another thing," she added as she strode to his side. She gripped his cock in her fist as she slapped his ass sharply with her free hand. "Until I take this off," touching the collar at his neck, "you will address me as *ma'am*. Is that understood?"

His instinct was to be resistant, but she was right; he wanted this. He wanted *her*, very much in this way. He replied, "Yes, ma'am."

"You learn fast. Your next slip will get you a slap across the face, understand?"

There was no need for her to ask if he understood. She was testing him, to see if he found that disagreeable. He didn't, so he let her read the desire she sought on his face. "Yes, ma'am, I understand."

She retrieved a small plastic bottle from the other nightstand. She took Stuart's hand and squeezed a generous amount of the thick, clear liquid into his palm. She snapped the bottle closed and tossed it on the bed as Stuart rubbed the slickness over the sheer latex. "If you cum before I tell you to," she said, tugging at a small, metal ring on the front of the collar to bring his face closer to hers, a twinkle in her eye, "I will have no choice but to punish you."

"I won't, ma'am," he answered, warming to the fun of his role and banishing any awkward skepticism.

She sat on the edge of the bed and lay back invitingly. He stood between her knees and teased her clit with his tip, circling it for a moment to be rewarded by a moan from her. He put the head inside her, slowly easing in and out by degrees, giving the lube a chance to work as he pushed in and out with the half of his length. Lori had a different idea. She wrapped her legs around his waist and pulled him into her. He gasped at the sudden rush. "Fuck me hard," she said, loosening her legs and spreading her arms out to her sides.

Stuart obeyed her, but was still cautious, building into the force of his thrust, lifting her hips and pushing into hers. She responded, louder and more enraptured, while he--determined not to get carried away and hurt her in the throes of his own desire--continued the even build into a crescendo. At last, after a few minutes, she locked her legs around him and cried out as she thrashed against the mattress. Pulling him into her ever harder, she shook until the tension eased and her muscles slackened. Her legs released his torso, and he slowly slid out of her, causing her to let out a sigh and a spasm.

She put one foot on his chest and pushed herself fully onto the bed, breathing heavily and beckoning for him to join her. Stuart crawled onto the bed and lay beside her.

"You didn't cum, did you?" she asked, taking him in her hand and finding him firm.

"No, ma'am," he said with a smirk.

Lori smiled in return. "Good boy," she said approvingly, but Stuart was not sure if she said that in response to her finding he was still insanely hard or at his remembering to employ proper etiquette. "I'm not done with you yet," she said, rising up and crawling atop him. Straddling his hips, she rose up on her knees and guided his tip into position before lowering herself down and letting him slide up into the heat of her. Then, placing one hand against his chest, fingers splayed, she worked her hips back and forth, tightening herself around his shaft inside of her. He cupped her breasts with his hands, but she took his wrists and moved his hands down to her hips and held them there as she rose up and came down again. She did this several times, groaning in pleasure each time he reentered her. She released his wrists and increased her pace, one hand placed back to his chest, the other behind her, steadying herself as her legs pumped and she thrust faster, lost in herself.

She rose and fell like a bull rider, each rise pulling nearly the whole of his length out of her before thrusting him into her again. He kept his hands on the sides of her legs and could feel the muscular flex of her thighs through the silken netting stretched over them. She cast her gaze down to him, "do you want to cum?" she asked, arching her back and riding him even harder.

"Yes," he gasped, thrusting his hips up from the bed in time to her rising and falling against him. The nails of her one hand on his chest dug into his skin and she lashed out with the other, slapping him across the cheek without breaking the timing of her pace. Of all the times he had fought in a ring, no punch or kick had ever caught him so off-guard as that slap had. She had given him fair warning and he had agreed to the terms. Far from taking him out of their mutual passion, it increased his need. "Yes, ma'am," he breathed, not knowing how much longer he could forebear if she denied him.

"Are you ready cum for me?" she asked, grinning wickedly, toying with him.

"Yes, ma'am," he muttered.

"Cum!" she shouted between vocalizations. "Cum for me!"

He pulled her hips against his own as she still pushed against his hold rhythmically, but no longer sliding him out of her. He let the burning overtake him entirely and felt the energy pulsing out of him. He rode the wave of ecstasy for as long as it would carry him, until at last it deposited him, spent and listless, against the sheet. Lori stretched out her legs and collapsed atop him.

Stuart woke with a start, sitting up in the bed. The first thing he noticed was that he was naked, and so was the woman who slept next to him.

CHAPTER THIRTY

IN BED WITH THE ENEMY

Stuart sat still in the darkness. The dream he had been having faded, replaced by the memory of the ecstatic sex that caused him to pass out in the first place. Then, the gravity of everything he had done came back to him, full and fierce. He put his feet on the floor and sat on the side of the bed, not knowing whether he should leave or take this chance to copy her phone. Even if she had tried to look at his phone while he slept, he left his actual phone at home and carried the one Spider had given him. She couldn't unlock it, but then, what made him think she could not make him give her the code? She could make him do anything, it seemed. He could not even find it in himself to lie about how much that excited him, which worried him all the more. Perhaps he should just lie down and go back to sleep--to hell with everything and everyone.

He was struggling to reconcile himself with all the choices he had made the night before as he sat there in her bed. He felt for his glasses on the nightstand. Finding them on the corner, he checked the time. The red numbers of the clock glowed hot against the charcoal grays of the night. It was four fifty-one.

"What day is it?" Lori's voice asked in a whisper behind him.

"What?" said Stuart, startled by the strangeness of the question. She asked a second time, her voice still a dreaming whisper. She was half asleep and confused, probably wondering if she had to get up for work. He wasn't sure if she meant the day of the week or the date. "It's Friday," he told her absentmindedly, "October twenty-third." He spoke in the same hushed whisper, lest he disturb the ghosts of the countless men he was sure had been there before him.

"Stuart?" she asked, rising to her knees and drawing close behind him, putting her hands on both of his shoulders. "What is it?"

He waited a long time to answer. She unfastened the collar he still wore and let it fall to the floor beside the bed. "I have to go. I have an appointment this morning."

Her silent hesitation was telling. "I had a wonderful time last night," she said gently, rubbing one of her hands over his back. "Will I see you again?"

The question made him glance back at her over his shoulder. "I'm not running," he said, realizing how she had interpreted his distant demeanor and the vagueness of his reason for leaving at five in the morning. "I had the most amazing night last night. And I absolutely plan on seeing you again, if you're willing."

Lori rested a chin on his shoulder and whispered, "More than willing."

"I really do have an early appointment," he said, considering before he went on, "I'm seeing a therapist."

"There's nothing wrong with that," she told him, shifting away from him and putting her back to the metal headboard. He turned halfway to face her. "Do you want to talk about it?"

Stuart shook his head slowly, not sure if she could see the subtle gesture in the darkness. "Not really. I've been dealing with some stuff," he said, wondering if he should say more. He wanted to tell her everything, but he had made enough mistakes. "I lost someone close to me recently," he ventured.

"Oh, Stuart. I am so sorry, baby," she said with a sincerity and depth that crushed him.

"He... he was my best friend... and I don't have too many. I needed to talk to someone." He hoped he had managed to mask how touched he was by her... her caring? "I have an eight o'clock appointment and I would like to go home to shower and change first."

"Hey, if you ever want to talk to someone other than a therapist, I'm here, Stuart."

"Thanks," he answered, standing as Lori turned on the lamp for him to see well enough to get dressed.

As he pulled his clothes on from the pile on the floor, Lori remained quiet a moment before asking, "Did you really enjoy everything we did last night?"

He hesitated while pulling on his jeans and said, "Yes, more than I can tell you right now."

"Why don't you come by the dungeon tonight?"

Stuart looked for his t-shirt before recalling it was on the couch in the living room. "Tonight? What for?"

She stood up from the bed. "I'll block out an hour or two and we can have some play time. I'll show you some different things and we can see what you like."

"Can I let you know later?" It would be easier for him to refuse her when she wasn't naked in front of him.

"Sure," she answered, "I'll see you out."

When he got into his t-shirt and shoes, she walked him to the door. She took his face in her hands and kissed him warmly before getting his jacket from the closet by the door. "I'll text you later with the times the dungeon is available tonight. And Stuart?" He turned back to her as he stepped through the door. "Consider giving it a try. You were meant for this. I can tell."

"I'll let you know for sure before lunchtime," he answered, "I have a bitch of a day ahead of me."

"Text me when you make it home," she said before closing the door.

Back in his truck, he sat in the silent darkness for a minute, feeling the phone Spider gave him in the inside pocket of his jacket. He could not figure out if he even regretted never pairing it with Lori's phone like he was supposed to.

CHAPTER THIRTY-ONE

I MET SOMEONE DOCTOR

"Why does everything with psychologists revolve around sex?" asked Stuart, shaking his head.

"Psychology is the study of human nature," Ella answered, "and sexuality is a very powerful part of that. It underlies a larger portion of our psychological makeup than many people would like to admit."

"Like siding with a person you know is in the wrong because you're attracted to them?"

"That is one very small example, yes," she replied. "But it can also inspire you, both directly and indirectly. Ever compare the sculptures Michael Angelo did of men to those he did of women?"

A smile crept over Stuart's face. "Yes. The women were very masculine, like men with breasts that were tacked on as an afterthought."

"Exactly," smiled Ella. "His homosexuality drove him to sculpt and paint men with a care and passion he brought to no other subject matter. Empires fall, ids explode, great symphonies are written, and behind all of it is a single instinct that demands satisfaction."

"I've read that somewhere."

"Sherwin B. Nuland."

"He had a point. Without it, none of us would be here."

"Many of us wouldn't. The rest would be reading some

pretty dry literature."

"Why am I only learning about these desires now?" Stuart asked. "I've gone my whole life up to this point without wants or needs of this kind. If they are natural to me, why didn't I discover them sooner? I mean, could there be other things I don't know about myself? What if I'm really gay?"

"Do you have any homosexual desires?"

"No, I was being facetious," he said, holding up a hand, "but some of the things we did together... why would I like giving over control of myself to a woman in that way? It's a complete contradiction of what a man is supposed to be."

"And what is that, exactly?" Ella asked. "How do you know what a man should and should not be? Did you read it in a book? Did someone tell you that?" To this, Stuart could only shrug. "We get far too many of our fundamental perceptions from dubious sources like the media. They become generally accepted, but we are seldom taught to question societal expectations."

"How can I not know my own internal desires?" he asked. "That isn't the kind of shit that you just stumble into in your thirties."

"You were exposed to something new that you enjoyed. There's nothing wrong with that. And you would be surprised how many people do not start exploring their own desires until later in life, if they ever decide to pursue them at all. Fear and guilt fortified by a lifetime of conditioning are some of the hardest bonds to break."

Stuart rubbed his chin in contemplation. The image of what Ella would be like as a lover entered his mind, and he mentally berated himself for allowing that thought in. "What happens when my desires and my perception of myself are in conflict? How do I know which is the real me?"

"The real you? That is a tricky phrase," said Ella. "When the two disagree, either your perception of yourself is a facade and is false, or your perception of yourself is too limited and needs to evolve to include the new things that you're learning about yourself. They do not need to negate one another."

"So, what should I do?"

"Explore," Ella answered simply. "Repression and denial are never a recipe for any kind of happiness."

"What if it's just her?" he asked. "What if this is something I only want with her and has nothing to do with any latent desires of my own?"

Ella leaned back in her chair and looked at him candidly. "You're over-thinking it. There are almost never any easy answers in psychology, Stuart," she said to him, folding her hands in her lap, "but luckily, there is an easy answer to that question."

"And that is...?"

Ella smiled coyly. "Whatever you think about when you masturbate, that is what you really are."

CHAPTER THIRTY-TWO
A MEETING WITH THE ENEMY

Stuart rode the elevator to the top floor with less unease than he expected. He and Spider had discussed letting him carry some kind of listening device, but they both knew that was pointless. When Perry had called Stuart and arranged the meeting at his office, his first impulse was to refuse, but he was never one to waste an opportunity to stick his head into the lion's mouth. He was not a fool, however. They had chosen this location was because they were safest in their own territory. After discussing every possible contingency, he and Spider both agreed that whatever Perry wanted to talk about, it was worth the risk to find out.

The elevator reached the top floor and, when the doors opened, Perry's receptionist was standing there waiting to greet him. She smiled and said, "Mr. Hollister, I'm Sandy. Mr. Tellerson has asked me to show you in when you arrived."

"Elevator cams?" asked Stuart, following her as she led the way to Perry's office.

"Front desk where you signed in," she answered.

When Stuart entered the office, he was greeted by Perry himself on the other side of the door. "Stuart, I'm glad you accepted the invitation," he said, extending his hand. Stuart shook it reluctantly. Spider had warned him not to show animosity too early; he would be letting them know that he had heard their conversation over the spyware on Rylen's phone. "I hope you will understand that we want to make sure nothing we say here ever leaves this room. This is the head of our technologies division and a member of the Foundation board, Steve McGuire."

"With your permission, we would like to scan you for any listening or recording devices." Steve said as he approached Stuart; a nod of acknowledgment was all the introduction necessary. "Would you come this way?" he asked, gesturing to the seating area to the side of the office. Stuart followed him, noticing a wand scanner on the coffee table next to a rectangular case of clear plastic. It was the case that Steve picked up first. He opened the hinged lid and held out the open case to Stuart. "If you would put your phone in here, please," said Steve. "You can keep it on the table in front of you. It's soundproof and seals the phone off from any wireless signal."

Spider had prepared him for this, so Stuart offered no objection. He removed his phone from his back pocket and placed it into the plastic case Steve held. How could a clear plastic case block a wireless signal? Looking closely at the plastic it was made of, though clear, it had a fine diamond net pattern over the surface. Steve closed the case and a tiny green light came on over the clasp. "What now?" Stuart asked as Steve picked up the scanning wand.

"If you will hold out your arms at your sides, I will scan you for any other electronics. Are you wearing a watch?" Steve asked, to which Stuart answered that he was not. The long sleeve shirt and thin jacket he wore made it impossible to tell. When Steve was finished scanning every inch of Stuart's frame, he nodded to Perry who stood watching in silence.

"Can I offer you anything to drink?" Perry asked.

"No," Stuart answered.

Perry nodded. "You don't strike me as a drinker, but if you change your mind..." Perry left the statement unfinished as he walked to the couch and sat down. Stuart sat on the couch opposite Perry and Steve sat on the loveseat that faced the two ends. "First, I would like to put this more delicately, but since we are fairly sure you already know, I will just say it. We have strong reasons to believe that your brother's death was not an accident," said Perry, watching Stuart's face, but Stuart kept it a blank slate.

"Why would you think that?"

Perry sighed. "This is where I have to offer you my sincerest apologies," he said, nodding to Steve, who then reached into his inner suit pocket and removed a phone that Stuart recognized as Rylen's. Steve placed it on the coffee table in front of Stuart, who merely turned his eyes to it before turning them back up to Perry. "We were the ones who took it from you. We only did it because we believed his death was suspicious, the timing especially. We thought there might be some information that could help us find out. As you probably know yourself, that was very much the case."

"You could have just asked me for it."

Perry nodded. "Of course we could have, but we are a powerful organization and we have a lot of enemies. The work your brother did for us was critical. He was not only an invaluable asset to this company, but he was also someone I considered a personal friend. I would have preferred that you never know he was murdered. You have been through so much already; I would have spared you from knowing if I could. Asking for the phone would have raised questions."

"So to spare me from that, you broke into my home and stole it, rather than just asking to borrow it because it had some sensitive company information?" said Stuart, offended that this man believed him stupid enough to be fooled by such obvious bullshit.

"Would you have believed that?" Perry asked.

"Probably not," Stuart conceded, hoping the admission was not taken as an understanding between them.

"We would have returned it to you, but I thought this was a better way to get everything out in the open. And for the record, we hired the very best. They did not *break* into your home. They had strict instructions not to damage any property and to make sure nothing else in your home was touched," said Perry, the slightest hint of irritation seeping into his voice.

"So what did you learn?"

"Lori Mercer. How well do you know her?"

Stuart had prepared well enough to try feigning surprise. "It was you," he said. Perry nodded. "I know her well enough that I don't want her dead," he told him, leaning forward and taking Rylen's phone off the table. He examined it, as if to see if it had been damaged. The phone was off. It didn't matter since they had found the spyware.

As if reading his mind, Steve said, "The battery is dead, but all the information is there. We removed nothing. Not even the image you found."

"You're right," said Perry. "We were the ones who sent the men who tried to take her last Thursday night. But, please believe me when I say that a kidnapping was never our intention."

"It was my fault," said Steve. "The task was given to me and I hired some people through several intermediaries. Those men chose to handle it in a way we never intended."

"And what *were* they supposed to do?" said Stuart. "You hired some men you don't even know to do what? Ask her politely to join you for lunch so you could ask her if she committed murder?"

"You joke about inviting her to lunch, but the plan was actually to bring her to a restaurant I own and question her there," said Perry. "They were supposed to intimidate her, not use force. Once there, she would have been questioned but not harmed. If she wasn't frightened, there would be no point questioning her."

"And if she didn't answer your questions? What then? Or what if she said she actually killed Rylen? What would you do?"

"We aren't criminals." said Perry.

"Except for the two felonies you told me about just now," Stuart said, keeping his face and voice as devoid of expression as ever.

"Take the fact that we screwed this up so badly as evidence that we have no experience in matters of this kind," Perry said with visibly forced patience. "Also consider that you're sitting in my office and I'm telling you things that could put me and several members of my organization in jail. Your questions are valid, though. We would have let her go no matter what she said, but I had to know if she was complicit in Rylen's death. I made it personal and used the resources at my disposal to get the answers I wanted. I took Rylen's death very personally. But you have my word, if she had nothing to do with it, I will find some way to make it up to Miss Mercer."

"And if she did?"

"All I care about is who put her up to it. I have no interest in her personally," said Perry.

"What if she is solely responsible? What if she just killed him because she wanted to? Maybe they were dating and he cheated on her. What then?"

"Then we will gather whatever evidence we can and, if it is enough to be taken seriously, we will turn it over to the police. If not, there's nothing more that I can do. If the law can't prosecute her, I am done taking the law into my own hands. But in that case, we will both have our answers."

Stuart stared at Perry blankly. A newfound respect for the man was reshaping his initial opinion. Perry seemed absolutely genuine in every possible way. The way he was so sickeningly false in the beginning would lead anyone to believe that the guy was a lousy liar, fostering an unreliable sense of being able to see through him. Tell someone a few lies about irrelevant shit and lie badly so they will think that they can tell when you are lying. Then lie with all the sincerity of a newborn baby about the things that matter, and they are more likely to believe you. If Perry was a chess player, he was a damn good one. Unfortunately for Perry, Stuart actually *was* a good chess player, when he had the white pieces. No matter how sincere Perry appeared to be, Stuart only believed what appealed to his own sense of reason. A botched job, hired thugs going rogue, and all the rest of it was window dressing. If those men in ski masks had gotten Lori into that van, she would have died that same night. They clearly didn't know that he had heard them planning Lori's abduction. Therefore, the one thing he knew for certain was that these people were killers.

"I don't know Lori all that well," said Stuart, deciding that he should start sharing useless information, but it would have to be things they didn't already know if it would make them believe they had earned his trust. "I only met her after Rylen died."

"How did you find her?" Perry asked.

"I went through his messages and she was one of his contacts. She uses a nickname, as you know." They might be capable of finding out about any calls he had made on his own phone, he reasoned. He couldn't risk saying he called her. "Rylen told me he was seeing the owner of a tea shop on Newbury. He was really into her."

"How long were they seeing each other?" asked Steve.

Stuart gave them a false smile. "I can't say exactly, I just know it wasn't very long. Rylen changed women like he changed shirts. And I know it wasn't long because he only told me about her the last time I saw him, a few days before the accident."

"How did you meet her?" asked Perry. "She wasn't at the funeral."

Stuart considered asking Perry if he had noticed the veiled woman sitting at the back of the church, but decided to keep that to himself. If Perry hadn't noticed her, there was no need to clue him into the fact that there was a mystery woman there. "She didn't know he died. She didn't hear from him, so she didn't bother trying to call him either. She thought he ghosted on her. I went to the tea shop to introduce myself and tell her in person. I showed her the leaf photo and asked if she sent that to him. But she had no idea what it was. I thought it just a silly coincidence with the name of her shop, and I dismissed it after I met her."

"How did she take the news about Rylen being killed in the accident?"

His lie was already cast in stone; there was no backpedaling for him at this point. "She was upset, but like I said, they had only been together a short time. How heartbroken could she really be?"

"The million dollar question is, do you think she had anything to do with Rylen's death?"

"Not for a second," Stuart replied. "I asked her out to dinner so we could talk about it."

At this, the two men looked at each other. This time, it was Steve who took up the conversation. "You asked her out to dinner, suspecting she might have had something to do with your brother getting killed?"

"Of course not. You heard me; I didn't think she had anything to do with it. You wouldn't either if you met her. You can tell in thirty seconds she's no murderer," Stuart told them.

"And you're such a good judge of character? How many murderers do you know?" Steve asked him.

Stuart turned his gaze from one to the other of them. "I've been fighting my whole life," he said, then locking eyes with Perry Tellerson, "I know a killer when I see one."

The two men exchanged glances and Perry asked, "You don't find it odd that, within minutes of finding out a guy she was dating, however briefly, died in a car accident, she agrees to go out on a date with the man's brother?"

Stuart shook his head. "It wasn't a date. I asked if she would like to meet for dinner because she was at work and I just hit her with bad news. We didn't have time to talk there."

Steve again broke into the conversation. "Wait, you didn't seem very surprised when we told you we were behind Rylen's phone disappearing and the men who, I hate to even say it out loud, tried to kidnap Lori Mercer. How did you know it was us?"

Stuart was relieved that he and Spider had talked about this ahead of time. They didn't want the Foundation to know they had used the spyware on the phone, so they had prepared the most plausible explanation for this question. "I didn't until you called and invited me here. The phone led me to Lori; I knew whoever took it would be led to her too. Then she got attacked the night we were going out to dinner, so I knew the missing phone and the attack on her had to be connected. Your calling me for a meeting twenty-four hours after the abduction failed was enough for me to start putting it together. I met her in the shop around the time my house was broken into; so it certainly wasn't her."

Perry chuckled. "I told you we aren't criminals, but I should have said we're lousy ones. I'm just glad nobody was hurt."

"Somebody was hurt," said Stuart.

"They hurt her?" Steve asked.

"No. I hit one of them. The guys in the masks."

"Oh, that. Knocked him out with one punch, as I heard it," said Perry. "You left him a little uglier than he already was, but he's fine. You said you're a fighter. You must be a damn good one to take on three ex special forces fighters."

Stuart just shook his head. "I didn't. I hit one from behind and the other two carried him off."

Perry nodded. "You have my word that Lori Mercer has nothing more to worry about from us. You said she had nothing to do with Rylen getting killed. If that's good enough for Rylen's own brother, then it has to be good enough for me. You also have my word that I'll use all of our resources to trace that call."

"What do you think happened?" Stuart asked.

Perry looked at his technical specialist who answered by saying, "We don't know yet. He was called by a blocked number who stayed on the phone until the EMTs were trying to get him out of the car. It's possible that they used his phone to hack the onboard computer in his car and cause his steering to lock up. It could be done by using his phone as a relay and the text message to deliver the virus that allowed them to do it. He gets a call, then downloads the image, which is actually a virus that installs on download. It goes through the Bluetooth connection and they keep him on the phone long enough for them to connect to his car and cause him to lose control of his steering."

"Is that even possible?" Stuart asked.

Steve nodded. "Very possible, not that much of the general public is aware of it. I copied the data from Rylen's phone; I hope you don't mind. Keep it off until I'm sure that I'm wrong about all of this. I will call you and let you know as soon as I find out."

"And," said Perry, standing, "please let us know if you find out anything more."

"I will," said Stuart as he stood. He shook the hands of both men before retrieving his phone from the case on the table and leaving the office.

After Stuart left, Perry said, "Is even a word of what you just said to him a legitimate theory?"

"It could happen," said Steve. "It just isn't what happened. I already finished looking into that option, otherwise I wouldn't have given him the phone."

"Shit. You nearly had even me convinced. Why that whole show with the primitive tech when he came in here? His phone would no more work in here than it would on the moon."

"He had to know we would take precautions," said Steve. "Best to just keep him in the dark about what we have and are able to do."

"Then we're left with nothing," said Perry with a sigh. "Lori Mercer is our only real lead and, if someone wanted us to suspect her, she knows who it is even if she doesn't know she knows. I was hoping Stuart knew more than he realized and could help us find who wanted Rylen dead. I don't think he knows anything."

"Are you so ready to rule out the possibility that she killed him herself? With all the stuff we found out about her, murder isn't such a stretch."

Perry shook his head. "You're right, except that she's an opportunist. As far as we can tell, everything she has done to her victims has been about money. Rylen's accounts show no signs of his paying her a dime. No large cash withdrawals, no checks, no transfers, no expensive gifts. If she was in on it, she was paid by someone else."

"Do you think he'll tell her about all of this?" asked Steve.

"Doubtful, but what harm could it do if he does?"

Steve acknowledged the point with a nod. "What now?"

"We can consider this first mess cleared up. Now we pay Miss Mercer a visit."

"What for?"

"She isn't one to turn her nose up at a good old-fashioned bribe," Perry answered.

"We could have just started with that."

Perry leered at him. "If she killed Rylen, what good will a bribe do?" he said sharply. "Thanks to those fucking Israelis you hired, it's the best play we have. If anything happens to her now, there's one person in Boston who will know who's behind it. I don't want another mess to clean up. Stuart Hollister may be an unwitting adversary, but he's also one of the good guys."

"What does that make us?" Steve muttered.

"Hmmm? What does that mean?"

"If he's one of the good guys, you could have told him about Lori. We know what she does with men. Since Rylen died, Stuart has a lot more to lose financially. We should have warned him."

"You heard him," said Perry blithely. "It was just dinner. His personal relationships are his own business; he's a grown man. If she ends up turning him into her fucking bitch boy and cleans him out, it's none of our concern. Besides, the way he handled himself against the Israelis, he can take care of himself."

CHAPTER THIRTY-THREE

A NEEDED SESSION

When Stuart's phone rang just before noon, he took a long breath before answering. "Bad news," said Lori, "the dungeon is closed because of building renovations going on."

Stuart sighed, but whether in disappointment or relief, he was not sure. "That's alright," he told her, "maybe some other time."

"Hold on there, quickdraw," she said. "We can do it at my place."

"We can?"

"Does that surprise you?" she chuckled. "I'm a professional and lifestyle dominatrix; of course I have everything we need, just not as much as we would have at the dungeon. Just leave everything to me, sweetheart. You'll be in good hands."

"What time should I be there?" asked Stuart.

"By eight. I get home just before that, so I'll need some time to get ready, but it will give us a chance to talk beforehand." she told him.

When Stuart hung up, it occurred to him that they never even discussed whether he wanted to go through with it. Did he want to feel surrender to a woman who felt arousal at his pain? Why did that sound so sublimely erotic? Could this also be his chance to redeem himself for his failure to get the information from her phone? Double bonus. He would go. It would clear her as a suspect, and he could then tell her the truth. He cringed at the thought, but she would find out... eventually. The physical pain would be a release from the emotional. A part of him felt he desperately needed it.

He had not been off of the phone with Lori for more than ten minutes before receiving a call from Spider. He did not take it. A text from Spider came in a minute later asking what happened the night before. How to answer that? He sent a reply saying that he was fine and it went well. He was busy today but would get him all the information as soon as he could.

"I think I may have spoiled you already," said Lori when they sat down in her living room that night. They talked for some time about what they would do and what they would not. Then, they spoke of safe words and how this would only be an introduction. As Stuart was new, it would be milder and more explanatory. They would be establishing a base that they could build on if it was something he wanted to explore further. "There will not be any sex this time, either. I want you to experience a play session apart from the sexual connection we have already established."

"Meaning, you want to treat me like a professional client?" Stuart asked in confusion.

"Hardly," she answered. "We got involved on many levels at the same time, so I have done things with you that I would never do with any man or woman in a professional scenario. I want you to experience domination and submission alone. So, no sex tonight."

"I can handle that," said Stuart. "I think it's a good idea, in fact."

"You say that now," Lori said with a grin, "but you may feel different later. There's no shame in begging when I deny you, just know that going in. Submission can be very freeing, which is good. I know you've been dealing with a lot right now and a little catharsis couldn't do you any harm."

"Are you going to use hypnosis again?" he asked.

Lori considered this. "Is that a note of anticipation or apprehension? Would you like to be in trance when we do any of this?"

"No," he answered before adding, "well, not at first. Can we save it for last?"

She nodded with an approving look. "I think we're ready, unless you have any more questions before we start." Stuart shook his head. "Good. I need to get ready, so go take a shower while I prepare. Leave all of your clothes on the chair in the bedroom. Clean towels are on the shelf."

As soon as Stuart emerged from the bathroom, Lori entered from the living room. While he had been showering, she had changed into her dominatrix regalia of knee high leather boots, black leather miniskirt, black tights, and a corset. How did she manage to get into all of it in the time it took him to shower? On the bottom of the bed lay only the black collar, a pair of leather cuffs, a chain leash, and a single crop.

She fastened the leather collar securely around his neck, followed by her affixing a leather cuff to each of his wrists. "On your knees over here," she commanded. He complied, kneeling on the stretch of open carpet between the bottom of her bed and the wall where the painting hung. Perhaps she intended to recreate the scene in the painting. "Okay if I take these?" she asked, touching the sides of his glasses. He nodded and she put them on the nightstand. She then took the crop from the bed and tapped the middle of his back. "Back straight. Knees together. Hands folded behind your back. Chin up." She paced around him as she spoke, tapping each area of his body with the crop as she corrected his posture. "For the duration of the evening, I am Mistress Crystal Dark, so you will address me as *Mistress*. Is that understood?"

"Yes, Mistress," Stuart replied.

"Good boy," she said as she attached the chain leash to the collar. "Now stand up and follow me."

She led him by the leash to the living room, where two of her dining table chairs had been set side by side, less than a foot apart, in the center of the room. Upon a leather ottoman nearby, she had prepared an array of the implements she would need for all they had discussed. She detached the leash and instructed him to assume a kneeling position by placing one knee on each of the padded seats of the two chairs and using the backs to steady himself. The spacing of the chairs required his legs be spread. Two lengths of rope tied to the legs of the chairs were brought up and attached to each of his wrist cuffs. She then pulled each of the ropes taught, which pulled his arms down straight and slightly out to his sides. When his arms were thus secured into position, she tied a free length of rope around each of his ankles and secured them to the legs of the chairs on which each rested.

Lori stood in front of him, stroking his face affectionately in appreciation of her work. Reaching between the backs of the two chairs, she gripped his cock in her fist, smiling at finding it firm. "Now then," she said, taking up the crop again, "listen carefully. You will not silently endure. Since this is your first time, I want to hear from you repeatedly. So you will thank me as I cause you whatever sensations I please, to let me know you appreciate the efforts I am going to in training you. You with me so far?" she asked as she tapped each of his ass cheeks in turn with the crop.

"Thank you, Mistress," he said in response.

"Good. Now if anything is too intense for you, but you still want me to continue, you will say *please, Mistress* and I will lighten it up. If you cannot take any more and wish to stop altogether, you will say *I surrender, Mistress* and I will stop and untie you. Do you understand?"

"I understand, Mistress," he said.

Lori tapped his back lightly in various areas. "Repeat them back to me."

"Thank you, Mistress. Please, Mistress. I surrender, Mistress," he told her.

"Splendid," she said. "Those are the important ones, but do communicate anything else you feel moved to." Lori went to the ottoman and took up a black plastic case from which she removed a box with a coil of wires. She went to Stuart and placed it on the floor between the two chairs. He recognized it as a TENS unit. He knew a guy at the gym used one for physical therapy when recovering from a partial muscle tear. So this was the electro-play they had talked about. Taking his hard cock in her hand, she wrapped the cold electrodes over the length of it and turned a dial on the unit. A stinging but mild electrical current stabbed at his dick like tiny pinpricks. "There," she said, putting the unit on the floor between the chairs. "How's that?" she asked, stroking the side of his face.

"Thank you, Mistress," was his answer.

She smiled at this and retrieved her crop. She tapped the leather head over his back and ass. The pain was slight and Stuart intuited that this was only a warm-up. He was right. After a minute, the strikes became harder and the pain was biting. He held his posture and thanked her after every couple of strokes of the crop. Thoughts of everything that had happened tried to come to the front of his consciousness, but he forced it away with a mental effort. Had she done this with Rylen? He forced the question from his mind and stayed in the moment. He was with her in that moment; that was all that mattered. The impact stopped and he said, "That was wonderful, Mistress." He meant it.

"You're welcome, boy," said Lori. She took up what he would later learn was a rattan cane flogger, a handle to which several stalks of flexible bamboo were attached. She used this instrument in a similar manner, gently at the start and slowly increasing in intensity. The rattling sound of its impact over his back and ass was sharper, and the pain was intense. He felt as though he was harder than he had ever been in his life, and he knew what Lori had meant when she said he could beg without shame. He was hooked and he knew it. He wanted the pain. He needed it. More than anything else, he needed *her*.

He felt the fact that he was new was causing her to hold back. "Would you punish me harder, Mistress?"

"I know you like this, boy, but this is just a taste to get you started," she told him between raps of the bamboo cane. "You will learn to pace yourself. I will teach you." She crouched and turned up the power on the TENS unit, his throbbing cock stinging from the current. She then switched the bamboo cane for a large leather flogger. She deftly swung it in a crisscross fashion so that the tips barely grazed his skin. Soon, the flogger slapped against his back, lightly and steadily, the strikes moving up and down his back to cover the whole of it. Then they increased to full swings of the leather straps against his flesh.

"I can handle more, Mistress," said Stuart before the straps of the flogger splayed over his back. The pain was liberating. "More, please, Mistress." The flogger struck again, strong and biting, but still not with the intensity he hoped for. The physical exertion he had discovered as a means of controlling his anxiety as a boy had found a new permutation. He repeated his plea, but the flogger fell in controlled and measured strokes. Upon another repetition of his desire to progress, the impact rhythm was interrupted by a pause. Had she said something? "Please, Mistress."

"Stuart," said Lori, taking his chin between her thumb and forefinger, breaking his focus, "I said, *no!*"

"I can..."

"Quiet!" she shouted. "You get to decide what is too much, but *I* decide what is enough!"

Stuart panted, nearly choking on the ache of his need. "Thank you, Mistress," he uttered at last.

"Be still," she told him, turning off the TENS unit and returning both it and the flogger to the ottoman before releasing his wrist cuffs and untying the rope on his ankles. "Come on," she said, taking his hand as he stood shakily. Lori got him a glass of water and led him to the bedroom. She turned on the light to the bathroom and told him to splash cold water over his face. Stuart glanced at his back in the bathroom mirror. His back was a bloom of redness and raised marks. "It's alright. That will go away in a few days. There will be a little bruising."

"I'm no stranger to bruises," he said.

"I know, tough guy," she replied. She handed him a packaged toothbrush she took from a drawer.

"What about this?" asked Stuart, feeling for the buckle of the collar around his neck.

Lori stayed his hand with a touch. "That stays on until morning. House rules."

When they were done, they went to the bedroom and Stuart got into bed, watching as Lori pulled off her boots, skirt, and tights. When she took off her corset, he learned how she had gotten into it so quickly, as it fastened with clasps at the front. She pulled back the sheets and slid into bed, drawing him to her and guiding him to rest his face against her breasts. "I am sorry for..."

"Shhhh," she touched his lips gently with her fingertips. "It's perfectly natural."

"I wanted more," said Stuart. "I could have handled more."

"This was your first time," she answered. "You can afford to get swept up in the thrill of it. But it's up to me to guide you into it without going too far too soon. We'll talk all about it tomorrow. Sleep now."

"I feel drunk. Did you hypnotize me again?" he asked quietly into the darkness.

"No, you went into something similar to a trance all on your own. We call it sub-space."

CHAPTER THIRTY-FOUR

INDECENT PROPOSAL

Stuart awoke, but not with a shock as he was so accustomed to. His eyes opened, alert and instantly restless. He squinted at the clock, able to make out the time of a quarter after four, before rummaging for his glasses. Lori lay pressed to his back with her arm wrapped over him. When he slid out of bed, she stirred and rolled over without waking. He felt at his neck and removed the collar that had been such an arousal to him the night before, but which now felt like a noose.

A trip to the bathroom later, he slipped on his jeans and made his way out to the kitchen. Finding the cabinet where Lori kept her drinking glasses on the second try, he got a glass of water from the tap. He removed the phone Spider had given him from the inside pocket of his jacket that hung over one of the chairs at the dining table. He started the app on the phone and placed it on the table, close to Lori's purse. True to Spider's word, within twenty seconds, a notice popped up telling that a successful link had been established. He returned the phone to his inner jacket pocket. Then he went to the bay window and parted the drapes to look out to the dark street as he drank the glass of water.

The street was deathly quiet in the pre-dawn shadow. The street lamps were still lit, and a breeze swept dry leaves through the glow they cast on the sidewalk. The tableau was serene and haunting, which harmonized perfectly with his somber state of mind. Like the writings of Poe, great beauty can be found in the austere, which many appreciate, but few truly understand. What had he gotten himself into? Never in his life could he have imagined having so much. And yet, he was immersed in a Stygian pool of lust and danger from which he did not want to be extricated. It was entangling and emancipating.

"Another appointment this morning?" came Lori's sleepy voice from behind him.

He turned to see her naked outline on the other side of the table, illuminated by the glow of yellow light filtering in through the window. "Good morning. And no, I don't. I just couldn't sleep anymore."

"Are you working today?" she asked.

"No, I don't have to work," he replied, knowing she would interpret that as his having the day off, rather than his not having a job at all.

"What are you going to do today?"

He wasn't sure what to tell her, and he had no lie prepared. "I have some things I need to do."

Lori sighed and ran her fingers through her hair as she walked over and sat down at the table, taking the chair nearest the end. The gesture was so casual and so immensely sexy, but exactly why it was the latter, Stuart could not discern. He finished the water and sat in the chair at the end of the table so they shared a corner. "You know, if we're going to keep seeing each other, this whole early-riser, morning-person thing is going to have to go," she said.

The sound of that pleased him. What exactly did a woman like her see in him? He wasn't even close to being in her league. His league could get struck by lightning and she would never hear the thunderclap. "And are we?" he asked, receiving a quizzical look from her. "Going to keep doing this, I mean."

A puzzled expression played on her face. "We fell asleep before having our post-session chat, but I thought we would talk over breakfast. About whether we will keep seeing each other, I assumed we would, yes. You think I do this with everybody

I take a liking to? I never doubted that we would keep seeing each other," she said, waiting for a moment before following it with, "at least, not until this very minute."

"What? Why's that?"

"Stuart, this whole strong, silent type thing that you have going... I like it, I really do. You're whip smart, funny, brave, and you have a killer body, but this reluctant hesitance shit is getting old fast."

That came from out of the blue. Stuart considered before saying, "you're chiding me for being inexperienced?"

"I'm not talking about BDSM. You're just starting out, so I can give you all the latitude in the world on that." She leaned forward on the table. "A woman wants to be desired; that's especially true of a dominant one. I just asked you what you're doing today and you completely brushed me off. Answer me this: did you enjoy last night?"

He did not need to stop to consider this time. "Yes, very much so."

"Do you want more of it?"

"Yes, I do."

"Do you want me?" she said plainly. He hesitated on this last question. "Are you not sure, or what?"

"I was about to ask if you mean as a dominant, as a romantic partner, or a sexual partner, but it really doesn't matter because the answer is still the same to all three. Yes, I do."

"They why the fuck do I have to ask you!" she exclaimed.

"What do you expect, a sonnet?" he asked. "Are you looking for me to get down on one knee and express my adoration like some smitten schoolboy?"

She smirked. "For starters, yes, that would be nice."

"I've never been very good at that," he admitted, but it came out sounding like sarcasm. "Besides, don't you get enough of that from your clients?"

"I should expect less from a man in my personal life than I get from a paying client?" she said, her voice taking on a dark aspect. "All I'm asking is for you to be more open with me."

"Not what I mean," he said, showing a palm to defuse her rising anger. "I'm asking if you don't get tired of being pursued by men who will do anything you say without even knowing you? Like those two guys who stayed to talk to you after the demonstration at the dungeon. You could see their arousal coming off of them like heat. The younger guy would have licked your shoes if you had told him to."

"Tell me, why do you think I was dressed like that? You think I needed a corset and fishnets to give a hypnosis demonstration? It's sexually charged and it commands attention. A dominatrix is a sex worker, Stuart. You can't have any illusions about that. I wouldn't have half as many paying clients if I didn't look that part. In its own way, it's another form of manipulation."

"I'm just saying it wasn't about you personally. They don't even know you. Their compliance is their own fantasy; it's about themselves. So what real value is it to you if they offer you something they'll offer to any woman just because she *looks the part*? It's just business in their case; I get that. In my case, no, I will not get on one knee and talk about my feelings. I don't know you so well, myself. Doing something like that is an insult at worst and, at best, paying you a very poor compliment. At least if ever do, you'll know there is something real behind it." Stuart paused and considered what he had just said. If he was playing a role, he was managing to fool even himself.

Lori looked at him approvingly. "I never doubted that you have the eloquence for it, Stuart. I can't figure out why you're so passionate and warm when we touch, and at other times it feels like I have to fight you to get you close to me."

"Oh," he said heavily, "that... that's something else. Look, I've been going through a lot lately, but I'm working it out. It won't last much longer."

Lori leaned closer and put her hand on his arm. "I'm not saying I don't want to see each other again. Exactly the opposite, Stuart. I'm saying I want you to be my submissive."

CHAPTER THIRTY-FIVE

A WALK IN THE CITY

Stuart didn't drive home to Boston. Instead, he drove east to Salem. He parked his truck and soon found himself walking through the downtown streets of the Witch City. He loved seeing the historic buildings in the glint of morning. There was something magical about the city when it stirred in orange gold of first light. He walked and thought in an effort to understand where he had come to and where he was going.

She wanted him to be a submissive? *Her* submissive? How could she seriously ask that as if he even understood what it meant? Their experience of the night before had awakened something primal within him. When Julius Caesar crossed the Rubicon river that separated Cisalpine Gaul from the Italian Peninsula, he was committing a crime that made him an enemy of Rome and would bring about civil war. If Caesar had met Lori Mercer on the river bank, her flogger in one hand and riding crop in the other, he might have reconsidered trying to get his army across at all.

If he accepted her offer, would he then be molded to the tastes and desires of another? What would that be like? However poorly things worked out for Caesar, Stuart's personal Rubicon was already crossed. For him, there was no turning back.

Walking through Salem Common, a park in the heart of Salem's downtown area, he seated himself on a park bench. He was so lost in his own thoughts, he was surprised when a voice said, "Spare a dollar for some coffee, brother?"

There was a man with a blanket wrapped around him nearby on the pathway. Stuart paused and took a close look at the man. "Yeah, sure, buddy," said Stuart finally, reaching for his wallet when he stopped, recalling what he had in his wallet. "Wait, I don't have any small bills."

The man smiled knowingly. "Yeah, tell me something about that."

"I didn't mean it like that."

"It's alright. Is it okay if I join you? I don't smell bad or anything," he said congenially. Impressed by his pleasant manner, Stuart slid to the end of the bench. The man seated himself on the other end. "You look like you had a worse night than I had, if you don't mind me saying so."

After taking a moment to consider his answer, Stuart replied, "I spent the night with the most amazing woman I've ever met."

"If you are trying to make me feel like shit, it's working," the man replied.

"I wasn't," said Stuart before the man laughed. Stuart liked him immediately. He resembled a small version of the actor, Al Pacino.

"I am messing with you, son. It's all good. Happy for you."

"It isn't all good,"

"Why's that? Y'all fighting?"

"No, not at all. There is a chance she murdered my brother, but that was before I started sleeping with her. She doesn't know I am his brother, though. I will tell her everything once I can prove to my friend it wasn't her."

"Jesus Christ. You be sure and come find me. Let me know how that works out for you."

"It sounds worse than it is."

"Well, that's good, 'cause that sounds pretty damn bad," said the Al Pacino look alike.

"It's complicated."

"You ain't kidding, son. All I got to do is talk to myself and people think *I'm* crazy. You take the cake, boy."

"If you are trying to make me feel like shit, it's working," said Stuart. The man gave a surprised smile at having his own words used against him. "What is your name, mister?" Stuart asked.

The man's smile died away, his mirthful look shifting into one of curiosity. "The name's Lionel. Man, it's been a long time since anybody asked me that."

"Yeah, most people won't step outside of their bubbles," Stuart said, standing up. He reached into his pocket and pulled a bill from his wallet. "Enjoy the coffee," he said, handing it to the man.

"But I thought you said you only have... oh!" Lionel said as he took the bill Stuart offered him and looked at it.

"Did you get it?" Spider asked as soon as he answered Stuart's call.

"Yes, I got it," Stuart answered.

"Good! Where the hell have you been? You could have let me know that yesterday! We lost a whole day that I could have been going through her messages."

"I had a full day yesterday, but I did get it. And like I said in the text, I met with Tellerson too. Wait until you hear about that."

"Start the second app. That will let me download all the information and I can start going through it."

"When do you want me to bring the phone?"

"This afternoon. I will text you when I'm finished going through her contacts," said Spider. "If there is anything there to find, I'll find it."

CHAPTER THIRTY-SIX

PERRY GOES FOR TEA

The wind chimes over the door of the shop sounded and Lori looked up to see two men in suits standing in the entry. One of them walked swiftly to that back while the other stood in front of the door. The way they ignored her completely and yet moved through the shop with such purpose sent a streak of fear through her. They were making sure that she was alone. She was.

"What are you doing?" she asked loudly, trying to keep the fear from her voice. The man blocking the door just stared at her until the one checking the back room returned and nodded to him. The one standing in front of the door said something Lori could not hear, as though he were talking to himself.

Lori's survival instinct kicked in and she reached for a gun she kept hidden in her purse under the counter. As soon as her hand touched it, the man who had checked the back rooms had his hand on her shoulder.

"We are not here to hurt you. We just wanted to make sure the shop was empty. Our employer would like a private word." He reached under the counter and took the sub nose revolver she had been reaching for. The man at the front opened the door for a third man to enter.

"Miss Mercer," Perry Tellerson said, walking to her with his hand extended. "It is indeed a pleasure to meet you."

"Who are you?" Lori asked, ignoring his outstretched hand.

"We just need to have a little chat," said Perry, waving away the man who still had his arm on Lori's shoulder.

The man stepped away, holding up Lori's revolver to show Perry. "Not loaded," he said before putting it on the counter.

"Forgive me and my associates for frightening you, but I had to take some precautions before coming in here myself. I am probably one of the few men you have ever met who knows exactly how dangerous you are before it is too late for him to do anything about it."

"Who sent you?"

"Miss Mercer, please, do we really look like hired thugs?"

"What do you want to talk about?" Lori asked, her agitation growing.

"I am actually here to do you a favor," said Perry, reaching into his inner jacket pocket and pulling out a banded stack of one hundred-dollar bills, which he placed on the counter. Lori regarded the money and then turned to Perry. "Now that I have your attention, what can you tell me about Rylen Hollister?"

Lori's heart sank and she didn't bother to hide it from her face. "I have video monitoring."

Perry smiled. "No, Miss Mercer, you don't. Not since my men entered your shop. I am not about to waste time explaining it to you, but we are not being recorded by video, audio or anything else you might have. Look at your phone if you don't believe me," he said, gesturing to her phone on the counter.

Lori picked up her phone and looked at the home screen. The screen was dark. She tried to turn it on, but the power button did nothing. "What the fuck..." said Lori, looking at the screen on the cash register, which was also dark.

"Your devices are fine, I promise. As soon as we leave, everything will be back to normal. Nothing is damaged or will even need to be turned back on. It will be like we were never here. Think of us as walking dead zones for wireless electronics."

"That is impossible," said Lori, astounded.

"Yes, I get that a lot," Perry told her. "Now if you please, we have even less time than before."

The fact that he had brought cash to bribe her with, and that he bothered to assure her that her phone was undamaged, went far to quell her concerns about being murdered. "What about Rylen?" she asked.

"I am aware that you are friends with Stuart too. Did he tell you about our little meeting?"

Lori stared at him blankly, her head reeling as she tried to piece it together. "Stuart? What does he have to do with this?"

Lori could see a light dawn in Perry's eyes. "Stuart Hollister. He is Rylen's younger brother. Looks like I underestimated him. He had both of us fooled with his lies."

"What do you want to know?"

"I need you to be honest with me. I promise no harm will come to you either way, but I must know, did you kill Rylen Hollister?"

Lori had to think fast. Her life might very well depend on it. "I will tell you something, but you may not want them hearing this," said Lori, looking at Perry's men.

Perry looked at the man standing next to her. "Give us some space," he told him.

"Sir..." the man protested.

"Do it!" barked Perry. The man retreated and joined his companion by the door. "Now what do you have to tell me?" he asked.

"I can't take your money," said Lori, leaning close, "but I can tell you something I think you will be interested to know."

CHAPTER THIRTY-SEVEN
TIME TO CHOOSE SIDES

Perry Tellerson had barely finished the conference call with Steve and the two other members of the board that comprised their criminal faction when Steve McGuire entered his office. "We can't do this, Perry. It's wrong and we cannot go through with this."

Perry stood up from his desk and motioned for Steve to join him in the seating area. "I understand your feelings on this and I was conflicted myself, but the group has made its decision."

"You were conflicted? Then why did you vote to have Sophia killed?" Steve asked.

"I don't like this any more than you do," said Perry, removing two glasses and a bottle from his desk drawer and pouring a few ounces into each glass, "but I'm trying to save everything we have worked for. Something you seem to have forgotten about."

"That isn't what this is about and you know it."

Perry walked to Steve and handed him one glass. "I know that woman is a clear and present threat to all of us."

Steve scoffed. "Based on the word of that fucking whore with the tea shop!"

"No, based on the threats she made to take all of us down," said Perry. "That's not something Lori Mercer could have known about if it wasn't true. You are the only one who doesn't seem to be worried about the fact that she threatened us all. She has information that could get every single one of us put away. If she wanted to do that in retaliation for our removing her from the board, she could do it. Is it so hard to imagine her getting immunity for herself in exchange for her evidence and sworn testimony?"

"We were trying to find out what happened to Rylen. Even if she was telling the truth about Sophia, this still has nothing at all to do with that!"

"As he's dead and we're not. I would say this is a little more important, don't you think? We've all agreed."

"Not all of us," Steve said.

Perry nodded, taking a sip from his glass. "Pruett and Tallmeyer make it our three to your one."

"I cannot seriously believe this."

"Believe what you want. What are you going to do? Turn on the other three of us? Go warn her or something asinine like that?" said Perry angrily. "Go ahead, that's why I'm giving the asset priority one license. That way she won't have time to act on any warning... *someone* might give her."

Steve hurled the glass of scotch at the wall and it shattered in an explosion of shards, leaving a yellow stain. "Damn it!" shouted Perry. "That was some of my twenty-five-year-old scotch, you asshole."

"I'll release the asset if I have no other choice, but it will mean I'm out," Steve told him.

"You won't have to do anything! I'm seeing to it myself."

"I'm still capable of doing my job."

"No, you won't," said Perry adamantly. "I'll take care of it personally. I wouldn't want you to do anything you find unconscionable. Put the time to good use typing your letter of resignation, if you don't change your mind when you get back to your desk." Steve looked Perry in the eye until Perry said, "That means get the fuck out."

CHAPTER THIRTY-EIGHT

HOUSE CALL

Sophia opened the door and smiled warmly as Ella entered. She led her to the living room as an older man in a suit closed his briefcase on the coffee table. He took it and greeted Sophia's guest amiably.

"This is Mr. Aires, my attorney," Sophia told her.

"Sorry to interrupt," said Ella.

"We were just wrapping up some business," he answered as he took off his glasses and slid them into the inner pocket of his jacket.

"This is my friend, Doctor Ella Pendelton," said Sophia, with a motion to Ella.

Mr. Aires smiled and held out his hand to Ella. "Ah, Doctor Pendelton," he said as they shook, "you are very fortunate to have a friend like Doctor Rubinstein."

"Thank you, she means a great deal to me," Ella answered, causing Sophia to grin in a way Ella had rarely seen, which made her wonder if she had missed something.

"I will see you out," Sophia said to the attorney. "Please make yourself at home," she told Ella. Aires and Sophia walked to the elevator while engaging in some final private conversation. Ella sat down as she recalled the experience of her first visit to the penthouse. It was something that she would never forget. It made her look at both her chosen profession and her personal relationships in a completely different light.

Sophia soon returned and sat opposite her on the love seat. She was wearing a close fitting black skirt that came to her knees with a white silk blouse. She had on sheer black stockings and high heel pumps that she always wore, even in her own home with thick, pristine carpeting on the floor. Was it possible she slept in them? "I have something very serious I need to tell you, and it pains me a great deal."

"You can tell me anything," said Ella.

Sophia remained quiet for several seconds, tapping a manicured fingertip to her lips. She rose with the lithe grace that Ella never failed to admire, and walked slowly to her wet bar. After dropping a couple of ice cubes into the glass, she poured herself a drink. Sophia then asked Ella to join her at the dining room table. When Sophia sat down, she motioned Ella to a chair and took a deep breath before she began, "I used to be on the board of a company known as the Tellerson Foundation. It's a major corporation, but it's more than most people know. Some of the board members are corrupt and... I used to be one of them. I can't explain it all now, but four out of the nine board members today were in on it. All of them are very wealthy and powerful people."

"Are you telling me you used to be a white-collar criminal?" said Ella in disbelief.

"It was more than that. It started out as some land deals made abroad with the Foundation's money, which were extremely profitable. Later, we began to sell weapons designs to the foreign competitors of corporations we sold the patents to. Over time, as our wealth and power grew, we made deals with some dangerous foreign powers."

Ella's eyes widened and she asked, "Are you talking about terrorists?"

"No! Nothing like that." Sophia said as she put a hand on her friend's arm. "We backed out of two deals with foreign organizations we found had ties of that kind, and they would have had us all killed if they could have found out who we were. I personally saw to it that Perry would not be bringing any more deals like that to the table. Still, it became necessary for us to have certain types of people at our disposal as a measure of insurance."

Ella felt she had to stop her to ask, "Why would you even get into something like that? You could have written your own contract with any company you wanted."

Sophia gave Ella's arm a gentle squeeze. "I regret it all now, but we were making the kind of money only small countries could put forth. Look around. You would be mistaken to think I got the money to buy this place by the advances I made in medicine or through technical research. I could buy this building, Ella; our dealings made that possible. But that isn't important. What you need to know right now is that I have been marked for extermination."

Ella was sure she had mis-heard her. "Marked for...? You're not serious."

"Someone convinced them that I have been working with the FBI to help them build a case against the rest of them in exchange for immunity, which is ridiculous after a year! I still have one friend among them and Harrier was told about everything so that he could get a warning to me. Perry convinced them that I planning to expose the Tellerson Foundation and its corrupt board members. That's how he operates. Perry Tellerson has been at the Foundation's head for fewer years than most of the rest of us. He was the one who recruited us into making criminal investments."

"My god, I can't believe this," said Ella.

"I have a friend on the board, a man named Marcus Harrier. He's one of the good ones. I would have suggested bringing him in on the investment scheme, but he's the only member who isn't a US citizen. His being a foreign national would have made his inclusion on the first of our illicit endeavors complicated, so I never did. He's too much of a boy scout to go along with it, anyway. He's a good man and has been one of my dearest friends for two decades. One of the four members disagreed with the decision and went to Marcus with it, knowing he and

I have a history. They told him everything, which will also spell the end of their illegal dealings. Marcus could not tell me what evidence Perry used to convince the others, but it must have been *very* convincing. It was enough for them to give their consent to send one of their *assets*, as we called them, to kill me."

Instead of disbelieving her friend's story, Ella found she didn't doubt any of it. "What are you going to do?" she asked at last.

Sophia sat back, a contemplative expression on her face. "I'm going to do what any sane woman in my position would do."

"You're going to the police?"

"No, I am going to make them sorry they ever fucked with me," she said as though the answer should have been obvious.

"You have to leave!" said Ella. "Go away somewhere until you can contact whatever friend you have in that group and get them to try to stop this crazy..."

"It won't work," Sophia interrupted. "I know who Perry's sending after me. I used to be one of them, so I have the list of assets they hire for work of this kind. The contract was given to one of two people here in Boston that he would contact for a contract kill. He's a man named Christoph Koenig, a German immigrant. I don't know much about him except what he looks like and that he's highly trained. Where and how he got his training, I don't know, but he's damn good at his job. He's coming for me and I will not survive unless I know where and when, but not even Perry knows that. He leaves the details to the discretion of the person he gives the contract to. In my case, Christoph was given priority one license, which means kill as soon as possible and by any means necessary. That means doing it sooner is better than doing it discreetly, and the sooner it's done, the higher his pay. Perry is afraid I will prove that he provided false evidence against me. He can't afford to have me even see it coming. Unfortunately for him, one of the other three disagreed with the decision and passed a warning to Marcus Harrier."

Ella stood and walked around, trying to process all of this. "Paxton owns hand guns and knows how to use them," she said. "Even though he doesn't know you..."

"I can't bring you or anyone you love into this," Sophia said. "Paxton would get killed. If you think he would try to look out for someone he doesn't even know, he must be a good man. I'm sorry I always made some excuse when you tried to introduce us, but I never wanted to meet him."

"Never wanted to? Why not?"

"I was jealous."

This baffled Ella completely. "You were jealous of me? What a laugh."

"No," said Sophia, walking over to her and cautiously putting a hand on her arm, so lightly Ella could barely feel it, "of him. I was jealous of *him*," she said, moving her hand to Ella's cheek.

The two women stood looking at each other, Ella shocked into utter silence and the other trapped in what she could plainly see was a fearful hope. At last, Sophia leaned forward and touched their lips together with the gentleness of a light breeze. Ella did not move in, but neither could she pull away. Sophia kissed her more closely now, full and rich, her hand still touching Ella's cheek. This time Ella responded by returning it, her hand impulsively rising to rest in the small of Sophia's back, their mouths pressed together. Pausing for the space of a breath, Ella took the opportunity to take a step back, abashed and putting a space between them.

"I'm sorry, Ella. I didn't know if I would ever get another chance to do that. I'm sure he's a good guy, I just hope he's good enough for you," said Sophia in a tone one might use in delivering painful news.

Ella shook her head. "I don't even know what to say." Sophia snapped back to herself and walked to the living room. "What are you going to do?"

"You need to leave," Sophia said, pausing near the bar.

"Tell me what you are going to do," Ella repeated.

"I own a lot of real estate properties. One is a historic building in Salem that contains a BDSM dungeon. Luckily, the rest of the building is being renovated and the dungeon is closed. The upper floor is unoccupied. Just empty offices. I'm already set up in one of them, and it has video security. I'm going to go there and wait for my assassin to show up. I'm armed and it's the best plan I can think of. He will never come for me here, it's too secure. The dungeon is a different story. If he knows I'm alone in the building, he will do it there. Remember, I have hidden cameras there that only I know about."

"You're going to use yourself as bait? That's your plan?"

"Don't worry. I'm armed and I know my enemy. Also, he doesn't know the place like I do."

"Take some men with you," said Ella. "You have a driver, a bodyguard... what about Trent?"

Sophia chuckled. "Trent? He's a college kid, Ella. I would be bringing him to his death. Christoph will need to think I am vulnerable. I know what I'm talking about."

After a lot more remonstrating from Ella, Sophia finally prevailed upon her friend to leave.

Ella had driven all the way home, only to find herself unable to get out of the car. She sat behind the wheel with tears on her face. There were two possibilities: the first was that Sophia would be fine and all would be well. The second possibility was that she would not see her friend again on this side of the grave. That option pained her more than she could ever have imagined. Sophia cared for her in a way she never knew or even considered. Could she learn about it and lose her on the same day?

What could be done? She didn't even know where Sophia was. A dungeon, she had said. In Salem? How many could there be in a historic building being renovated?

Ella started the engine and backed out of her driveway.

CHAPTER THIRTY-NINE

HOW TO CATCH A KILLER

Sophia pulled her car into the private gravel lot behind the building and entered through the alley. She made her way to the second floor office with her bags and dropped them to the floor. How long would she be here? Activating the security cameras was her first priority. She could watch both entrances to the building as well as every room and hallway within. That done, she prepped her automatic pistol and the second gun she brought with her.

He would likely come at night, but in the meantime, the only other people who had access to the building were those using the dungeon and the construction crew. The former was put on hold because of the latter, and the latter were called off until further notice because of a false ownership dispute. It was possible that Lori might decide to use the dungeon anyway, but she was told it was closed. If she chose to ignore that and use the space, it would be her own peril to deal with. Would Christoph avoid collateral damage? Hit men do not walk into a building looking for a victim and shoot someone else, unless it were absolutely necessary. However, this particular killer was a professional and would not be surprised in that way. He would do his reconnaissance and not take action inside the building while others are moving about within.

A tone sounded and Sophia looked at the monitors. A man in a jogging suit had entered the door from the alley. Her eyes shot open before she took up both weapons and turned on the light in the office. She had meant to leave that door unlocked, but his showing up only minutes behind her still caught her off guard. He must have been following her. She stepped into the hallway and pulled the office door partly closed.

She quickly made her way to a janitor's closet she had prepared for this purpose. It had a steel door that opened out into the hall so it could not be kicked in. The three hinges would need to be cut off, and she counted on no killer having the tools or time to do that. She had chosen this location because it was at the opposite end of the hall from the office, a few steps away from the top of the stairs. His back would be to the door as he made his way down the hall to the office. She left the light in the closet off, but turned on the wireless monitor that would allow her to see the man's location in the hall outside the door. Barely had she turned it on before he was coming up the stairs, one hand poised inside his running jacket. He was looking for cameras, but they were hidden and she hoped he would not take the time to perform a thorough search.

He reached the top of the stairs and looked at the door to the janitor's closet. To Sophia's relief, he completely ignored it. He instead made his way down the hall to the office. This was her chance. Sophia had left the door unlocked so it would be silent when she opened it. She kept her eyes on the image of her assassin as her hand turned the knob. His gun was now in his hand as he moved slowly to the office door. In a few seconds, her window of opportunity would close and she would not get another chance. She opened the door and took aim at the back of the man in the hall. She fired.

There was a sharp, but subdued *crack*, like the sound of a ruler hitting a desktop. Sophia didn't wait to see where the dart from the gun struck her target. She shut and locked the door before she pressed herself into the corner to the side of it. She had aimed for the center of his back, but had no idea if she hit where she intended. A *thump* hit the door, and the knob rattled. The monitor showed that he was on the other side of the closet door, trying to open it. Sophia expected shots to be fired, either in an attempt to pierce the lock and open the door or to hit her through it, but neither happened. He was making his way down the stairs to the main hall. He held tightly to the handrail because he was already stumbling. In a second, he was out of the view of the camera. Sophia placed the tranquilizer gun on a shelf in the closet and pulled her Ruger .380 from the waistband of her skirt before opening the door.

She had to move fast, but not so fast that he could get off a shot. The dart was on the floor of the hallway, confirming that her shot had found its mark. She made her way down the stairs, aiming her gun as she went. She heard the front doors rattle and chanced a peek around the corner when she heard a soft shuffle followed by a muffled thud. He was lying face-down on the tile floor of the lobby, still moving, but barely managing to drag himself. Sophia approached, her gun aimed at his head, prepared to blow a hole through it if he twitched or reached under him. He was cunning, and she knew this might be a ruse to get her out of her place of safety. Having realized he had been injected with a drug that would knock him unconscious in seconds, he might well pretend to be out sooner than he was. As she got closer, she could see it was no possum ploy.

Both of the killer's hands were visible and his gun was missing. Had he returned it to the inside of his jacket? "Sophia?" came Ella's voice.

"Ella!" Sophia cried. "Get out of here! This is the killer they sent after me."

"Is he dead?"

"He's unconscious," Sophia answered, "or so I think." Seeing Ella made no move to depart, Sophia swiftly moved to the prone form of the man on the floor and swung the butt of her pistol against the back of his skull. He didn't flinch. "Now I'm sure," she said.

CHAPTER FORTY

A SECRET CONNECTION

Spider opened the door for Stuart and led him up the stairs to his apartment. "You aren't going to believe this one," Spider said as they both sat down. Stuart placed the eye cam and phone receiver on the coffee table.

"First, I have to say I went through Lori's phone and there isn't anything on there relating to Rylen. His name is never even mentioned in any of her messages and she hasn't cleared them. I saw that you talked to her yesterday, though. What was that about?"

"She called me to see if I got home okay," said Stuart. "The night at the dungeon was... impressive."

"I saw that it only lasted a minute or so. You can tell me about that, but first, I want to hear about your meeting with the mighty Tellerson. I checked him out; he's squeaky clean, it seems."

"He isn't," said Stuart, who went on to tell Spider everything that happened in the meeting with Perry Tellerson and Steve McGuire.

Spider listened intently until Stuart finished. "That's one brazen bastard to admit everything like that. It means he thinks he's untouchable."

"It could also mean that he actually is," said Stuart.

"So tell me what you learned about Lori."

Stuart's heart sank. All he was able to say in response was a muffled, "Hmm?"

"The demonstration at the dungeon? How you paired her phone?" asked Spider.

"Oh, that. Yes, so I went." Spider waited expectantly. "I have to say, she's pretty damn good."

Stuart knew his shifting behavior and lack of eye contact would make Spider ask, "What happened?"

He could not lie about what had transpired, since he could not keep secrets and expect Spider to continue to help him in finding his brother's killer. "I was one of her volunteers," Stuart admitted, not hiding his shame at this.

"What! You let her hypnotize you?" Spider asked in disbelief. Stuart nodded. "You got your proof of her ability first hand. At least it was in front of a group of people."

"Oh, yeah, it was," he said, then quickly adding, "except the half hour that we were alone together before everybody got there and then again later on at her house."

Spider buried his face in his hands. "You're fucking with me, right?"

"No."

"You went back to her house? Did you fucking sleep with her?"

"Yes, I did."

"What the hell?"

Stuart told him everything that happened from the moment he arrived at the dungeon to the moment he left Lori's house the next morning. Spider sighed and shook his head in disbelief, saying nothing for a long time. "You remember that talk we had when I repeatedly asked you not to do anything stupid?"

"Yes, I remember."

"Well, that was pretty fucking stupid."

"I didn't plan on it happening and I honestly don't think she did it. I'm not sure I ever really did. I just copied her phone so we could eliminate her as a suspect," explained Stuart. "It's done and over with. What do you want me to do?"

Spider gave a mirthless chuckle. "Damn, you see?" he said,

pointing at Stuart. "That shit right there! That is exactly what I am talking about. You just don't get it. You could be dead right now. You walked into a dangerous situation, handed your enemy a loaded gun, and painted a target on your chest."

"I do get it."

"No," said Spider, "I don't think you do." His expression changed. "Wait a second, where were you last night?" Stuart stayed quiet and let his silence speak for itself. "Oh, my fucking god. You were with her!" Stuart didn't answer. "Are you planning to see her again?"

Stuart hesitated. "No, I won't see her again," he answered, but the words sounded hollow, even to himself. Spider was right. The thought of never seeing Lori again saddened him in a way he hadn't expected.

A text message came in on Stuart's phone. He took up his phone and read, "STUART, STOP LOOKING FOR ANSWERS. YOUR BROTHER WAS A SERIAL RAPIST IN FOUR KNOWN CASES, BUT DOUBTLESS THERE WERE MORE, LIKELY MANY MORE. YOU WILL NEVER FIND THE ONE BEHIND HIS DEATH AND WILL GET YOURSELF KILLED TRYING. DO NOT TRUST LORI MERCER."

He handed the phone to Spider, who read it aloud. He looked at the sender, but found a hexadecimal string instead of a phone number, meaning the call had been sent via a computer or device with a software that encrypts the contact information instead of blocking it, all of which he explained to Stuart. "Jesus, we've gone down the rabbit hole on this one," said Spider. Stuart tried to reply to the message and ask the sender to identify himself, but it did not go through, just as Spider told him it wouldn't.

"Can you trace it?" asked Stuart.

"Oh, sure! Let me get on that," said Spider, taking in the look on his face. "That means no! What the fuck."

"It doesn't matter, I'm pretty sure I know who sent the message," Stuart told him. "Steve McGuire. The part telling me not to trust Lori gives it away."

"The man from the video? The one who was in the meeting with you and Tellerson? A little fucking late with that piece of advice, pal."

"Yeah, he's also on the Foundation board and head of the technology division. He has my information, and he's the only one besides you, me, and Perry Tellerson who knows I met her."

"*That* is the bit you're focusing on? The parts about getting killed or your brother being a serial rapist doesn't bother you at all?" Spider asked.

"It's a lie, obviously."

"For what purpose? Just saying, four cases sounds pretty specific."

"You aren't really going to believe anything these people say, are you? I knew my brother. It's complete bullshit."

Spider was silent for a long time. He ended his silence by saying, "I'm out, Stuart."

Stuart was not sure what he meant. "You're out?"

Spider nodded and stood. "Look, I think you're a good guy, and I'm really sorry about your brother, dude. But I can't help you with this anymore."

"I can't do this without you," said Stuart. "I can pay you. I have money now; Rylen was insured..."

"Stop!" said Spider, holding up his hand. "I know you have money now; I don't care about that."

"You knew about the policy?"

"I didn't have to know about it. I found out where Rylen lived and that his house and cars were all paid for; what more did I need to know? You were his only relative and you guys were tight. Everything he had would go to you, even if he didn't have a will. But of course the guy would have a will and an insurance policy! I'm not an idiot."

"Then let me pay you for your help."

"Use the head on your shoulders for a change and consider your position. She got to you. There is no, and I mean not *one single fucking way*, that this won't end badly. Just go. I was doing this because Rylen was murdered and I really do hate when the bad guy gets away with it. Then you kept me from getting stabbed, which definitely put you in my good graces. And it was the right thing to do. And I like a challenge. With all of that, I was willing to do this for nothing."

"None of that has changed," Stuart felt the need to point out.

"Except for the fact that you'll let this chick seduce you right into your own grave, you dumb shit!" said Spider, calming himself with a sigh. "Look, I've worked with a lot of dangerous people. It's part of what I do. That message is right; you'll get yourself killed. But you aren't only going to get yourself killed, you're going to get *me* killed. Whoever killed your brother is smart, resourceful, and well-connected. You have no idea what you said or didn't say to Lori that night. And I can't go up against the kind of people who have mercenaries in their contacts when the guy on my side is getting brain-fucked by our number one suspect. I'm sorry to have to say it, man, I really am, but you're on your own."

Stuart wanted to persuade him further, but instead he nodded and extended his hand. "Thanks for all your help."

Spider shook it. "Watch your back, man," he said, "and good luck." Stuart turned and left without another word.

CHAPTER FORTY-ONE

ENEMY MINE

Christoph opened his eyes. He was lying with his arms splayed and each limb securely bound. He tried to raise his head, but quickly learned that his neck was secured to some sort of metal table.

"Good morning, sunshine," said Sophia's voice from somewhere out of his range of vision. He could hear her heels on the tile floor, but she was not approaching the table. He struggled against his bonds but immediately knew it was a waste of energy.

The table on which he was lying was not a table at all, but a steel restraining device they used in places like this. The entire contraption was shaped like a giant X, to which a person's limbs may be bound. He had seen things like it in the clubs of Berlin when he was younger. Normally they stood upright, but this was of a sophisticated design that stood on a large wheeled base. The center of the cross was hinged in such a way that a bound person could be tilted back 90 degrees into a lying position. It had a center plate to support the person's weight with an additional beam through the center to support the back. It was to this center beam that his neck was secured. Leather straps at his wrists and ankles, as well as a heavy chain around his neck, affixed him to the steel contraption. The woman whom he had been sent to kill had even thought to wrap his arms to the frame with duct tape. If he could not bend his arm, he could not pull on his bonds in any way that gave him the slightest chance of freeing one of his hands.

"Where is your help?" Christoph asked at last, having taken in as much of his present predicament as his bonds would allow. He spoke with a Germanic accent, but one that was so faint, one would have to listen closely to detect it at all.

"Think you can stand?" Sophia asked, walking to his side so he could look up at her. "I can turn you upright now if you want." The assassin nodded and Sophia stepped back behind the table shortly before activating the motor by some means he could not see. The entire cross slowly rotated into an upright position, and all the man's weight shifted to the metal plates under each of his feet. "There now," said Sophia, walking back around the cross to be face-to-face with her would-be killer, "I'm sure that's better. And to answer your question, you'll be meeting my *help* very soon." Sophia walked over to a table and took up a black bladed folding knife that had been in an ankle holster on his leg. "And you know I had help because you know your quarry. It's not likely that a woman my size would have the physical strength to get a big man like you bound in that position all by herself. Are you gathering intelligence or was that actually supposed to impress me? How pathetic. Now tell me, where's your gun?" Christoph remained silent. "Oh, well, in due time."

Christoph's jacket was missing. He was wearing a black pullover sweatshirt and matching sweatpants. His clothes were an expensive brand and sufficiently loose-fitting for him to hide a silenced Heckler and Koch 9mm handgun and a knife sheath. Plain running shoes made him look like any athleisure wearer when he was out on the street. He stared defiantly into Sophia's eyes when she unfolded the knife and slowly stroked the point of it up the front of his sweatshirt. "So what's the plan?" he asked her. "If you wanted me dead, you had plenty of time."

"Yes, I did," said Sophia absently, as if thinking on other matters.

"So what is this? Are you going to torture me before you kill me? Isn't that what you do here? I'm not one of your perverted scum."

"*Perverted* is a very interesting choice of words, Mr. Koenig," grinned Sophia, taking the collar of his sweatshirt and pulling it taught until his neck strained against the chain. She used the knife to cut a clean slit down the front of his shirt, exposing his bare chest. "It can mean one whose sexual proclivities deviate from the conventional and boring," explained the woman, as if schooling a child. She traced the outlines of the assassin's chest muscles with the point of the knife, never breaking the skin. "Then, it can also mean one who has been corrupted, misdirected, or in some way led down a tangential path from his original direction. What if I told you that these will all apply to you before the day is out?"

Sophia withdrew the blade from his torso and he exhaled heavily. He was sure she had been about to stab him. "What good would it do to torture me before you kill me? You already know who I am and who sent me. I'm not so foolish as to think you will let me go. I know you are not so foolish as to think I will not still kill you if you do."

Sophia favored him with an amused glance. "Well, you're wrong." She bent over and cut the right cuff of his sweatpants, carefully working the blade upward through the fabric, slitting his right pant leg open from ankle to waist, talking meanwhile. "There are, in fact, three things that I promise you, Mr. Koenig. Do you mind if I call you Christoph? We will soon be on such familiar terms, anyway. Yes, that will do." She finished with the right leg and cut through the waistband and drawstring of his pants. Then she did the same with his left leg. "The first is that I am not going to kill you. The second is that you will be free to leave here tonight, completely unharmed." She then finished with his left leg and pulled his shredded pants away from his body, tossing them somewhere behind his line of sight.

Ella entered the room carrying a black laptop bag and a hard black carrying case. "All good, no prob..." she stopped, both in her speech and forward movement when she beheld

Sophia, knife in hand, standing before the almost naked man bound to the cross. Only his running shoes and black sport briefs remained, save the cut sweatshirt that hung open on either side of his torso.

"It is quite alright, doctor," said Sophia amiably, holding out her hand for the bag. "No harm done here."

Ella recovered herself, handing her the bag and case. Drawing the wheeled table close to their captive, Sophia placed both items atop it and donned latex gloves. She then took up the knife again and cut the sport briefs from the man and threw them away. Christoph never made a sound, though he now stood there, trapped, splayed, and entirely naked. "You are not really going to rub it on his penis and..." Ella began, but interrupted herself.

"Hmmm?" Sophia replied, turning to her questioningly.

"His dick. You aren't planning to smear it all over his genitals, are you?" Ella finished.

"Oh, not at all!" answered Sophia as she took up a small bottle of cloudy oil from the table. "That was because I wanted to," she said with a shrug.

Ella let out a small chuckle. Christoph was impressed. This woman was not a soldier and had never seen death or an interrogation, he was certain of that. Yet she still managed a laugh. "What is that?" asked Christoph, sounding menacing, but knowing his apprehension was evident in his voice.

Sophia poured a generous amount into her latex covered palm and rubbed it over his chest as she answered. "This is a special massage oil invented by a very brilliant friend of mine. It contains a drug called S-24, which is a derivative of Scopolamine. It is quite safe in this form, but still most effective."

"Effective at what?" he asked, not caring if his concern was clearly audible now.

"Making you more... agreeable," answered the woman with a calm amiability that he found truly unsettling. "It comes from South America, and this dose," she held up the bottle for him to see, "is just enough for a man your size. Fun fact: do you know who used Scopolamine in its raw form for interrogation experiments? Josef Mengele of The Third Reich, also known as the Angel of Death." Sophia paused to look Christoph in the eye. "You know, Mr. Koe... uh, Christoph, I would explain why that makes all of this an irony worthy of Shakespeare, but I have a feeling it would be lost on you."

Ella's sharp inhalation at that caused Sophia to turn, as though having forgotten that she was still standing there. "How long will it take?" Ella asked.

"The process itself will take an hour, but I will be done in about 10 minutes. You can wait for me upstairs if you want," Sophia answered, turning back to Christoph to rub the oil over the rest of his torso and legs.

Ella responded in a tone of indifference, "I'll wait."

"How are you mixed up in all of this?" asked Christoph, directing his question to Ella, who now watched from a ladder-back chair she drew up from elsewhere in the room. "I'm not here to hurt you." He was managing to remain calm. He did not struggle or curse, as he knew some prisoners in his situation might naturally do. He had been a soldier who was trained well enough to know when physical effort was useless. If he could keep them talking, he might find a way of turning them against one another.

"Oh, good lord," said Sophia sharply. "One more word to her and I will gag you. I have plenty of those on hand, make no mistake."

He turned his attention back to Sophia. "Does she know that she will also be marked for extermination for helping you?"

Sophia looked at Ella, who appeared less frightened than someone in her circumstances should. "No, you won't; that isn't how this works. They aren't the mafia. It's what he's trained to do. This is where he tries to get you to help him escape by turning you against me. He will trust that you know he is only here for me. He will promise you a reward and assure you that no harm will come to you if you turn on me, that he is a hired professional and only harms the target, blah, blah, blah." Sophia turned back to Christoph and said, "Listen, the massive sum of IQ points in this room is in no way improved by your puny contribution. You're no better than a child trying to deceive an adult with a magic trick they taught him."

Ella told Sophia, "I know he's lying."

"Oh, of course you do!" Sophia said, turning back to her. "This fool doesn't know who he's talking to."

"And he has a backup," said Ella. "Either a tracking device of some kind or a partner who will follow him. Might want to check his clothes."

Sophia smiled approvingly. "He did indeed! He carries what is known as a delayed tracer. We developed this one for our own assets. It activates if he doesn't reset it after a predetermined time; it's a fail-safe in case he gets captured or killed."

"I'm guessing it couldn't have gone off before you found it because he would have needed time to kill you and get away before resetting it..." Ella said, thinking aloud.

Sophia nodded. "You can be a little scary sometimes, and honestly, it's something of a turn on. It was in his left sneaker; I cut it out with the knife and stepped on it. How on earth did you know that?"

"I didn't. I was fishing and reading his facial reactions," Ella answered.

"It might be cruel to tell him this room was proofed against tech of any kind getting a wireless signal in or out, including that which was developed by our trustees."

"Oh, and he doesn't mind what you're doing even though it might kill him." It was not a question, but a statement of fact.

"Oh? You mean he isn't the consummate professional?"

In answer, Ella merely pointed to Christoph. Sophia turned and looked at her captive in confusion, before noticing he was fully erect. "Oh, I see," she said. "It seems the man who kills women shares the same weakness for them... how interesting."

"It's fear," said Ella.

"I know. It must be deliciously mortifying for him, regardless. Anyway, before you walked in, I was explaining to

Christoph here that he isn't going to be harmed and will be free to leave tonight."

"He will?" asked Ella, now wearing a look of surprise herself.

"Oh, absolutely. I am using the conquered foe to augment my own strength," said Sophia, rubbing the last of the bottle of oil over the man's body as she spoke. "I don't suppose they teach *The Art of War* in assassin college, hmm?" She leaned close to him, pointed to his erection and asked in a tone of sarcastic confidentiality, "I bet you wouldn't mind if I did something about that, would you?"

Christoph leered at her and said, "You plan to make me an ally? You really are mad. I will do you a kindness and tell you it will never work."

"You let me worry about that," answered Sophia, pulling off the latex gloves and opening the laptop bag.

"The third... thing?" asked Christoph, the drug in the oil already starting to have its subtle effect.

"What was that?" asked Sophia, not turning to look at him as she unwound cables for a silver VR headset she took from the case.

"You said you make three promises. I would not be killed and I would leave unharmed tonight. What was the third?"

Sophia turned her ice blue stare on him. "I promise that when you leave here, you will love me more than life itself."

No words the woman might have said could have caused more terror in the killer. He distantly felt fear stab at his heart, but the sensation faded as he slowly descended into indifference.

CHAPTER FORTY-TWO
GOODBYE FOREVER AGAIN

Ella stood by as Sophia tapped at her laptop. She desperately wanted to ask Sophia what she was doing, but felt it just wasn't the time.

"Christoph, where's your gun?" asked Sophia, not looking at him.

"I hid it inside the casing of a drinking fountain in the lobby," he answered.

"Why did you do that?"

"I had been shot with a drugged dart and would pass out soon. Even if I were to shoot you, I would then be an unconscious murderer. I could not even fire my weapon. It had become a liability. My priority shifted to saving myself. I had to rid myself of the gun and make it out to the street where someone would call an ambulance. I would be a man found unconscious. If I had a silenced gun on my person, it would be another matter. So I hid the gun inside the building and tried to get out to the street. The front doors are locked from the inside."

Smart, Sophia thought as she said, "It is a violation of fire codes, I know, but we're closed for construction so I think it's okay."

Sophia took up a virtual reality headset with a metallic gray finish and instructed Christoph to let her put the rig on him. When she finished preparing Christoph in the headset, she gave him a series of video and audio tests to make sure it was working properly. She then set the program in motion on the laptop, telling him not to resist it, but to follow all instructions given in the audio track exactly. She motioned for Ella to follow, leaving the room and shutting the door behind them.

Sophia searched the drinking fountain in the lobby and found Christoph's gun inside the metal casing. Then, she and Ella went upstairs to the office after making certain all building entrances were locked.

The office was a large room with only an old wooden desk and a new desktop computer set up atop it. There were eight flat screen monitors covering one of the walls. They were all turned on and Ella could see they were camera feeds from the dungeon, as well as various locations both inside and outside the building. Two were for the dungeon alone. Christoph made for a peculiar sight, being a naked man wearing a VR headset while bound on a Saint Andrew's Cross. There was a brown leather couch in the room that was obviously new and a half-size fridge in the corner.

"I apologize for the state of this place; I am planning to renovate the whole building," Sophia said. "Are you sure you aren't too freaked out by all of this?" she asked, placing Christoph's silenced 9mm and knife on the desk.

"No, I'm not," she said at last.

"Good." Sophia rushed forward and threw her arms around Ella's neck. Ella let out a little squeak of surprise that was cut off by Sophia's lips pressing into hers. She returned the embrace, and this time, kissed with a longing and abandon. "You were willing to face a killer to save me, you crazy bitch," she told her with their faces inches apart, her arms still wrapped around Ella's neck.

"Yes, I did," said Ella, considering it for the first time. "We make a good team."

"You just don't know." Sophia pulled her into another kiss that lasted for some moments before slowly parting. Sophia became a few inches shorter, as she had taken off her heels and had been standing on her toes. She was still in the same clothes she had on at the penthouse.

"Is that what one wears to catch a killer?" Ella asked.

Sophia smirked. "The bastard didn't even give me time to change. I planned on being here for a while." She pointed to a large duffel bag by the door to the bathroom. "The plan was to turn some music on and wait behind the closet door on the other end of the hall. I was going to tranq him in the back when he opened the office door. I had only just arrived and got the monitors turned on when I saw him opening the back door. I got my tranquilizer gun, and stuck my Ruger in my waistband. I hid in the closet and shot him as I planned. He made it down to the lobby before the drug started to have an effect."

After getting clothes from the duffel bag and changing into yoga pants, a t-shirt, and sneakers, she saw Ella watching Christoph on the monitors. "Is that a VR rig? What's that doing to him?" she asked.

Sophia sat down on the couch before answering. "That is a prototype design of a project I developed. *Tungsten* is the working name I gave it at the lab, and it stuck. It's something I was working on to help treat therapy patients. It was meant to help with a number of things like phobias, PTSD, and accelerated learning, but we discovered it could be used for something too dangerous to let anyone else know about. It uses a series of lasers to send extremely fast color impulses directly against the retina that can induce a trance in seconds and plant a suggestion in minutes. It worked too well."

"How do you mean?" asked Ella, pulling herself away from the monitors and sitting down on the other side of the couch.

"You know how brainwashing works, yes?" Sophia asked. "Well, the ideas that a person is forced to adopt--through whatever means of torture or psychological coercion are employed--create physical connections in the brain that, when reinforced over time, become their own. It can be used positively as with positive affirmations, or negatively, as in the case of brainwashing. That device is now giving our friend down there the equivalent of a year of brainwashing in the course of an hour. There wasn't any need for the building of mental connections and conditioning; it literally reprograms the subject's brain. After all, the brain is a bio-computer which can be reprogrammed like any other. You just have to know the right coding language to do that."

"How long does it last?"

"Permanent, unless it's replaced with something else."

Ella stared at her friend for many seconds before looking at the monitors again. "My god, Sophia," she said, turning back to her, "that's horrible."

Sophia frowned and nodded grimly. "I know. It has terrible potential, which is why I never used it. Well, not outside of the initial tests we did on volunteers. Its effects were terrifying. It worked so well that I had to call a stop to the tests because of my concerns for the volunteers. None of them were harmed in any way," she added quickly, "but it was obvious very early on that we could make anyone believe or do anything. So, I called a secret meeting with the two lead techs I was working with and offered them a payoff to keep their mouths shut about what we had found. They agreed with no persuasion at all. They were probably thinking the same thing, but were afraid that all of their work would be for naught. The money I offered them allayed any concerns they had on that account. We falsified our results to the Foundation, making the project look like a failure, and I took the only prototypes and software backups. I couldn't be more relieved I did that because Perry would have it now."

"Why call it that? What does a heavy metal have to do with anything?"

Sophia smiled lightly, as if recalling a private joke. "The shell, the outer casing on the initial prototype, was produced by an actual manufacturer of VR equipment. The plastic casing could be made in a few different colors of plastic. The matte silver color was called *Tungsten* and I liked it, so that was the project code name I gave the device itself. *Buttercream* was another color option. I'm glad I didn't go with that."

Ella cracked a smile. "What was that stuff you rubbed all

over him? Was that really Devil's Breath in the oil?"

"No, it isn't Scopolamine, but something much, much bet... more reliable. It's safe, more potent, and leaves no aftereffects. It was necessary to use that to get his compliance for the first few Tungsten cycles. It can be injected or imbibed, but I didn't had a syringe solution prepared yet, and I wasn't about to try to get him to drink something. If I put him into the Tungsten, he could shake his head to throw it off, or resist it by closing his eyes or not following the audio suggestions that are being fed through the headphones. The S-24 insured he would do everything he was told in the audio track and cooperate fully for the critical first three cycles, which last about 10 minutes."

"Does that thing have anything to do with how you were planning to treat a disease like epilepsy without medication?" Ella asked.

"No, that was something else entirely, which failed miserably, I'm sorry to admit, but it did free us up to work on this project," said Sophia, watching as Ella looked back at the monitors. "You're not really worried about me turning that murderous bastard over to our side?"

"*Our* side?" said Ella.

"Like you said, we make a great team."

"What happens when it's done?"

Sophia rubbed her hands together thoughtfully. "I will have to see what his orders were, but most likely..."

Ella's eyes widened in realization. "You're going to send him after Perry!"

Sophia put her hand on Ella's knee. "I won't lie, I would do that in a heartbeat, but that won't get me out of this. You don't know the people I'm up against. I'm in so deep a hole right now that I may never dig myself out again. And I'm not going to have you risk your life any longer. There's nothing more you can do, anyway. If I'm still alive tomorrow, I'll be home free."

Ella grew worried. "What are you saying?"

"I am saying that you should go home and wait to hear from me. If you haven't heard from me by midnight, I'm probably..."

"No!" said Ella, taking Sophia's hand. "What more has to happen?"

"A lot," Sophia answered. "Remember, I still have a friend on the inside. Marcus is going to try to prove what Perry did and that whatever bullshit evidence Perry put forth against me is, well, bullshit. I need to stay alive long enough for him to do that. While Perry is focused on me, Marcus is on his way here to do just that. Either way, Perry and his crime ring are finished."

"How sure are you that you can trust him?" asked Ella. "Isn't is possible that he's playing you and working for Perry? What better way for Perry to keep tabs on you than for him to provide you with a false advocate that reports back to him?"

Sophia gave Ella a smirk. "You're really good at this, hon. Are you sure you weren't cut out to be a spy?" Ella chuckled lightly. "Well, you can relax. He and I go way back. I met him when we were both undergrads and I was taking a couple of semesters at Oxford. We were friends before either of us ever heard of the Foundation. The name always changes when a new chairman takes over, but the Foundation has been around a long time. I was the one who sponsored his entry into it. That's how it works; you gain entry to the board by being sponsored by an existing member before the others vote on you. Anyway, yes, I can trust him."

Both women were quiet for a moment. Then Ella said, "I don't think I can say goodbye forever twice in the same day."

In answer, Sophia moved closer and pulled Ella to her, kissing her again before saying, "As much as I would like to suggest we make use of this sofa bed we are sitting on, I need to contact him and find out if I'm going to be alive for another day."

"I think that might take priority," Ella smiled.

CHAPTER FORTY-THREE

AGENT RODRIGUEZ

Stuart opened the door after checking the peephole to see Lonnie on his stoop. Checking who it was had become a recent habit, given the situation he was in. "Lonnie? How did you know where I live?"

"Hi, Stuart," he said, not answering the question. "Listen, can we talk for a bit?"

"I'm about to head to the gym," Stuart said. "You up for that rematch?"

"Not today, buddy." There was another man in a suit standing down on the walk. "We need to have a little chat."

"What is this?"

Lonnie pulled an ID from his pocket and showed it to Stuart. "My name is Agent Lorenzo Rodriguez with the FBI." He showed Stuart his identification. "This is my partner, Agent Noah Bradshaw. I need to ask you to come with us."

"Can I see that ID?" Stuart asked after a long hesitation. Lonnie handed it to him and Stuart examined it closely.

"You can spot fake FBI credentials?" Lonnie asked.

Stuart had never seen an FBI agent's credentials at all. Lonnie's was pretty official looking. "Not really," he answered honestly, "but if you printed this at Kinko's ten minutes ago, you wouldn't have let me see it." Noah laughed lightly, and something about his calm manner convinced Stuart they were telling the truth.

"It's legit," said Lonnie. "I'm FBI. I would rather you just come with us. Please don't make me insist."

"Where are we going? Am I under arrest?" asked Stuart.

"No, you aren't under arrest. Right now, we need to go someplace we can talk," said Lonnie. "And we sure as hell aren't going to do it in your house or out here on your stoop. You can get your keys and your phone, but you need to come with us now."

Stuart asked to see Agent Bradshaw's credentials, and the man produced the same. He did as they asked and went with them. Lonnie attempted to make conversation on the drive, but it was clear he was trying to fill the silence. In fifteen minutes, they came to a nondescript office building within a couple blocks of Baptist Hospital. They entered the office and walked through the space like they were there every day. They were definitely legitimate, unless they had set up an office with twenty actors for the sake of a ruse. Lonnie's workout clothes clashed with the white shirts and blouses of the people working there, but he looked as at home as he would have been at the gym. Noah and Lonnie led him into a small conference room with a table that sat six people. Noah shut the door behind them.

"First off," said Lonnie, "I need you to give Noah your phone. It's just a precaution, you'll get it back." Stuart handed his phone to Noah, who turned it off and slipped it into his suit pocket. "Now if Wiley would hurry up and get himself in here..." At that instant, the door opened and a heavyset man in his twenties entered carrying a laptop and several folders. He wore a button-down dress shirt, like many other men in the office, save that his shirt fit him like a paper grocery bag. "Finally!"

The man shut the door behind him and put the folders and laptop he carried on the conference room table. "Give me a second."

"This is Agent Percival Wiley," said Lonnie with a gesture to the man at the table. "You think you got some moves, Stuart? Wiley here is the deadliest man in the world with a fork."

"Go fuck yourself, Rodriguez," Wiley muttered, tapping at the laptop.

Stuart took in the three men in the room. Noah caught his eye and shrugged at the exchange. "That was mean. You guys are on the same team, you shouldn't mock one of your own," Stuart told them.

Noah looked at Lonnie. "Looks like Percy has an advocate."

Agent Wiley looked at Stuart over his glasses. "I can speak for myself, Leavenworth."

"And just that quick, I can see why you're so popular," said Stuart, to which Noah smiled, but Lonnie gave a genuine laugh. It did not strike Stuart as mean-spirited, though. Even as an FBI agent and no longer the gym rat boxer, Lonnie still had something sincere and likable about him. Stuart hit on what it was in that moment. His back-story might have been fabricated, like his being an electrician, but he was from the streets. No matter how much military discipline, academy training, and classroom education the man had, he was toughened by an upbringing of scarcity that would forever mark him with a grit and candor that made Stuart feel he could relate to him. His Latino way of talking was real; it was another thing he liked about Lonnie.

"FYI, we're recording this conversation," Lonnie started. Noah sat down at the table and Wiley mounted a tiny webcam to the top of the laptop monitor and nodded at Lonnie. "This is for use in our investigation." Lonnie didn't sit at the table, but pulled one of the chairs out and put a foot on the seat, giving himself a knee to lean on while he talked. "Stuart, I'm going to be straight with you right now and I need you to be straight with us. I brought you here because, for the last eleven months, we have been investigating Perry Tellerson and a number of others with the Tellerson Foundation."

"They're some bad people," said Stuart.

"We aren't investigating them because they're nice."

"I don't like Tellerson. I'd help you hang him, if I could."

"Then start by telling me how you're mixed up in this," said

Lonnie. "You're the puzzle piece we can't seem to make fit. You know those investigation cork boards you see on cop shows, the ones with all the pictures of persons of interest--how they play connect the dots with the push pins and colored string? We're too high tech these days for that, but I'd love to make myself one of those. You know who would be on there? You! And you'd have a string connecting your picture to every damn other person on that board. Even that gorgeous shrink you got." Lonnie put a photo of Ella on the table.

"Doctor Pendelton? What does she have to do with this?"

"A lot, apparently. Did you know your brother used to see her?" asked the agent.

"Yeah, she told me. It was part of the reason why she spoke to the judge and offered to take my case."

"No, I mean he used to *see* her, as in they used to fuck."

"What? No!"

"As far as we can tell, she never saw him after the death of her best friend at the end of last year. Woman murdered in her home on New Year's Eve. Strangled. No murder weapon, no suspects."

"What are you saying?"

"I'm not saying anything; he wasn't in the city at the time. As for their banging... he wasn't her patient anymore, so as fucked up as that is, nobody could prove anything. But a lot of late nights out on the town together is not keeping a professional distance. But now," Lonnie pulled a photo from the folder and put it on the table, "she's besties with this woman, Sophia Rubinstein, who used to be on the board of... take a guess."

"The Tellerson Foundation?" Stuart ventured.

"Bingo. And she owns a building that contains a BDSM dungeon space. Really nice one, too, if the website can be trusted. Who works there? Lori Mercer, a dominatrix." Lonnie flipped through another folder on the table and produced a photo of Lori. "We've been watching her for a little while. Rylen was going to the dungeon for months. She was the last person to see Rylen alive. She also owns a tea shop. Guess who she's been seen with?"

"Me," said Stuart dryly. "You going to slide a photo of me in front of me?"

"You. Again. And last week, she was almost abducted on the street."

"You knew about that?"

"I'm sorry I wasn't there to see it myself, but she's a big enough player that we had an agent keeping an eye on her. I heard you went running in there like Captain America. Beat up the bad guys, saved the hot girl, probably got laid after that too. To hear him tell it, you went straight up action movie, man. I wish he had gotten video; I would have broke out the popcorn for that shit. But see, if you hadn't done that, he could have followed them and had them for kidnapping."

"You had someone there? Why the fuck didn't he do anything?" Stuart's fist instinctively clenched under the table.

"He was about to when he heard one of them shout to abort," Lonnie answered. "He was on foot and some distance away. He couldn't follow you two in a car. So, as soon as he heard that, he ran back to his car so he could follow the van. He made the right call. They took the one guy you hurt to a clinic, and we knew who they were within the hour. I wish I could say it had a happy ending."

"They're in jail, right?" asked Stuart.

Lonnie looked at the other men in the room. "No, they are not in jail. We're after the whales, not the little fish."

"You just let them walk away?"

"Nobody just walked away from... do you know you killed a man that night?" Lonnie asked.

"What?" said Stuart, "I didn't kill anybody! Are you trying to pin me for murder?"

"Relax," said Lonnie. "You aren't being charged with anything and you're never going to be. We know the circumstances. It was unintentional, and it was self-defense, but yes, one of the men you fought with died from cerebral hemorrhaging due to blunt force trauma to the head. As far as the rest of the world knows, the guy fell off a ladder. That was the story they gave at the ER they took him to, and everybody bought it. The clinic is owned by the Foundation, so it's no surprise that nobody asked any questions. I'm telling you because I think you should know." Stuart had to process this. Had he hit the man that hard? He took a man's life. "I can tell by the look on your face that you didn't. I'm sorry, jefe. I wouldn't beat myself up about it. They would have done the same to you and probably worse to her."

Stuart sat in silence, and Lonnie gave him a moment. The agent put his foot down and turned the chair so that he could sit on it backwards, folding his arms over its back. "Is this payback for that beating I gave you at the gym, or do you just like dropping bombs like that?" Stuart asked, still stunned by the knowledge of having killed a man.

"A little of both, honestly," said Lonnie in a quiet voice. "Why didn't you report it?"

"I don't have anything to hide. I don't want to get mixed up in any more criminal charges."

"I understand that, but why were you there?"

"I asked her out on a date and we were going out that night. I left my truck at her shop and was walking to the restaurant on foot." Stuart explained.

"I told you we were watching tea shop dominatrix girl. I did say that, right?" Lonnie said, looking at the other men in the room who humored him with a nod. "So you see, the attack happened three blocks from the tea shop and you were parked across the street before she ever even closed the place. Our agent said she closed up the shop when you got out of your truck and were following her. Not catching up to her, but *following* her. You look like you could do a four-minute mile, but you couldn't catch up to your date in three city blocks. So am I crazy, or does it kind of look like you knew what was going to happen?"

"Fuck," Stuart mumbled. "I did know. And I couldn't warn her because I would have to tell her who I really am and I didn't want to b..."

"What? You didn't want to what? Dios mio, *please* tell me you were about to say that you didn't want to blow your cover!"

Lonnie let out a belly laugh that was mildly echoed by the other two agents. It irritated Stuart all the more because that was exactly what he was going to say, but knew how silly it sounded. "What are you, fucking James Bond?"

"I'm just a guy trying to find out what happened to his brother," said Stuart in annoyance. "His death wasn't an accident. I'll tell you everything, but I couldn't go to the police or anybody else because they would laugh at me. Sort of the way you did right there. And I couldn't take a chance on getting into any more legal trouble."

"On that note," said Lonnie, picking up one of the folders from the table and flipping through it, "you need to learn to keep those punches in the ring, man. Those guys you beat up in the bar this past summer: even if you get off on the criminal charges, and it looks like you will, that doesn't mean you'll get off on the civil suit. I don't blame you. If that pendejo slapped a girl around me, I would have met him out in the parking lot and beat his ass, but that's just me. I'm FBI, I think this shit through before I start swinging. They both have criminal histories. One of them has a record that makes you look like Mother Teresa. They're going to sue you and they have a real case. Even if they lose, you will still get tied up in litigation and legal expenses. We can make them drop the civil suit. You won't even have to hire a lawyer."

"You can do that?"

"We're the FBI. Of course we can do that. With records like they got, it'll be easy. Whatever charges they have pending, we can pick our favorite felony to drop in exchange."

"And in return?" asked Stuart.

"You give us something we can use on the Tellerson Foundation. You met with the man himself this week, that's the reason we brought you in here today."

"I'd like to help you put them away. Shit, I'd love it. They're some scumbags," Stuart told him.

"Music to my ears, buddy."

"The problem is, it's a long story and I don't know if you'll be able to use any bit of it."

"Well," said Lonnie, "I have all day. And if we can't use it, hell, I have a feeling this is going to be awesome. Let's get this man some coffee. Water? Juice?"

"Water is fine," said Stuart. "And I'm going to need my phone back."

CHAPTER FORTY-FOUR

DID IT WORK

"I'm alive, as you can see," Sophia told Marcus Harrier in the video chat.

"I was betting on you from the start," said Marcus.

Ella sat quietly on the couch while Sophia talked into the camera of her phone. She had warned Ella to keep as quiet as possible, lest he know someone else was involved. The less anyone knew about Ella, the safer she would be. Ella had nothing to fear from Marcus, that much was certain, but explaining who Ella was and how she was involved was more than Sophia wanted to grapple with. "How's it going with clearing me and proving Perry is the lying bastard that he is?"

"It isn't that simple. I'm only one person, I need to reach out to the other four who aren't in on this secret society of theirs."

"What the hell did he tell them?"

"Steve either couldn't or wouldn't say at the time, but he didn't go along with it."

"Why didn't he stand with me when they voted me off of the board?"

"I don't know, but he had no part in this assassination madness. Whatever it was that Perry used to convince them that you were going to expose and testify against them, it got them to agree that this was the only way to solve the problem. Perry's no fool, he has to know we're still in contact, so it wasn't easy for me to get as much information out of McGuire as I did."

"So there's nothing to be done. It's my word against his."

Marcus nodded in the video. "Not until I contact the others and we can get you someplace safe. I won't let anything happen to you. And I'm certainly not going to let Perry have you killed over this bollocks."

"You're a little late for the first round," Sophia told him.

His face grew serious. "What do you mean?"

"I already had a visit from the guy Perry hired."

"Shit! What happened?"

"I'm fine," she told him. "I got the better of him and persuaded him to see things my way."

"Now I really don't like the sound of that," said Marcus suspiciously.

"I can't explain now, but I'm about to find out what I can from him."

"Do I even want to know what that means?" he asked her.

"No. When do you land?"

"In two hours. And I'm bringing some security of my own. The cavalry is coming, darling. I'll contact you when I get there. Be safe."

Sophia disconnected the chat window and shut down the app before nodding to Ella. "Is that thing secure?"

Sophia nodded. "It's our own software and encryption. Now it's time for the moment of truth. Want to go see how Mr. Koenig is doing?"

"Are you sure this will work?" Ella asked, standing up from the couch.

"We'll find out shortly." Sophia stood and took up her Ruger 380 from the desk. She unloaded the clip of Christoph's gun and ejected the one in the chamber. "On second thought, it's best you stay up here. If things go sideways, call one of your friends at the precinct."

"What do you want me to do up here?" asked Ella.

"Enjoy the show," said Sophia, tucking the Ruger into the back waistband of her yoga pants and letting her oversized t-shirt fall over it.

Sophia returned to the dungeon as Ella watched on the monitors. Setting the knife and the unloaded gun on the table that held the laptop running the Tungsten headset, she shut down the computer and removed the gear from the man's head. His eyes were open. He was alert and lucid, but he said nothing as she packed the Tungsten away in its case and put her laptop back in the bag. "How are you feeling, Christoph?" Sophia asked.

"I'm fine, I think," he said.

Sophia took the knife and sat in the chair that Ella had placed there earlier. "Why did you come here today?"

"My orders were to abduct you, if at all possible. If I didn't have any chance of bringing you to him alive, I was to kill you."

"Why did he want me alive?"

"He believes you responsible for the missing data files last year."

This was unexpected, Sophia thought. "Perry knows about the files I took and wiped from the backups?"

"Yes, I was to acquire you and any electronic devices in your posession. I was to bring them and you to him directly. I am to communicate with no-one else but Tellerson."

That part made sense. She had stolen weapons designs with military applications that he was planning to sell himself and blame on espionage. When they went missing, he blamed it on a security breach and moved all critical R&D data files to The Church. The servers were kept in a vault with any hard copy logs. How he had figured out she was behind it more than a year after the fact was more than she could guess. "Are you working alone?"

"Yes."

"Why? They have people far better suited to this than you are."

Christoph nodded. "His primary extraction team has been delisted."

"We had more than one in our asset lists when I was there. Why not use a secondary one?"

"His actions are not free of oversight. If Perry had enlisted an extraction team, the other members of the group would have known he was looking to obtain information and it would have raised inquiries into his actions."

A single member of the group could not release one of the assets independently, since their actions could come back on all of them. A hit had to be agreed upon by more than one member of the group. So Perry fooled the others into signing off on a hit and then used the hit man to do the job of abduction and interrogation, all so he could retrieve the stolen files he was planning to sell for himself and cut the others out of the deal. Bastard, she thought. "How did Perry know I was the one who took the data files?"

"I do not know that," Christoph said, which was only to be expected, but it was worth asking. Perry would have given Christoph as much intel as he needed to carry out his job and nothing more.

The man was entirely awake and clear minded. The program had planted in him the perception that she was one whom he trusted and must protect at any cost to himself. He would do whatever she told him and was absolutely incapable of disobeying any order she gave. She had prepared this programming as a safety measure as soon as she had been forced out the Foundation. "What were you going to do if you did somehow manage to take me alive?"

"I was to make contact with Perry to get a drop location," the man replied.

This was not something Sophia had planned for. If Perry knew she had the project files, he would not stop until he got them. Could he have guessed that she was in possession of something like the Tungsten? If he knew she had something like that, he would have sent an army after her. She decided to try a different line of questions. "What will you do when I free you?"

Christoph reflected on that. "I will contact Perry and tell him that I killed you. That will give you a chance to run and start somewhere else."

Sophia sighed and ran her fingers through her hair in exasperation. The man was a complete paradox. How could so expert a killer be so inept a tactician? How had he thrived in his profession for so long? "You do not think that Perry would notice that there was no report of my murder, no funeral, and no body?" she asked.

Christoph nodded. "Of course. It would buy me time to get close enough to him to kill him. It is the only way to protect you," he said earnestly.

That made a lot more sense. "So you want to protect me?"

"Yes."

"You came here to kill or kidnap me for someone who will kill me."

Christoph looked at her with complete sincerity. "I know. I was wrong. I see that now. I don't know how I ever could have wanted to harm you."

This was something that Sophia had seen before. Once a suggestion was planted through the Tungsten, the subject would remember everything that had come before the transitional programming, but he would justify the new views as being his own. Even knowing what had been done to them, subjects always believed that the changes in their minds--no matter how profound--had nothing to do with a device they had been plugged into, but something that they had spontaneously realized on their own. "I am going to set you free now," she told him. Ella, who had been watching all of this from the office upstairs, gasped upon hearing this. "I will need your help. Are you willing to help me?"

"Of course. I will do anything you need. I owe you that much," Christoph replied.

Sophia cut the duct tape holding his upper arms through the now shredded sleeves of his sweatshirt. She then unlocked the cuffs and chain holding his neck, wrists, and ankles. Although she didn't show it, her heart beat quickly as she unlocked the last one. She was betting her life on the Tungsten having worked in his case. If Christoph turned on her, her only hope was the Ruger she had tucked into her waistband, which she made certain he had not seen. Christoph's arms fell and he pulled off the tattered shirt. Then, he moved to the ladder-back chair she had been sitting in and collapsed into it, rubbing the areas on his wrists where the cuffs had been. He was completely naked except for the running shoes he was wearing. "Thank you." he said, sounding as though he truly meant it.

Sophia deliberately left the gun and knife on the table a few feet away from him. He was an expert and would know the gun was not loaded the moment he picked it up. The knife was another story. He could get to that, but she had her hand behind her back, ready to pull out her gun and shoot him dead if he came for her. He did nothing of the kind, but sat rubbing his arms to help circulation. "Do you have a change of clothes?"

"Yes," he answered. "In my car. I have a bag in the trunk."

"Where's your car?"

"It's in the gravel lot behind the building. I wanted it close to the door if I was able to knock you out," he said. Then he actually looked embarrassed and added, "Sorry."

"Shit happens," the woman answered. From his expression, the dry sarcasm in her voice was not lost on him. "Go get them and come back in here. Your keys are on the table. Get your clothes from your car, come back in. Don't get dressed. Leave your bag or whatever by the door. Then sit back down in that chair and wait for me."

Christoph stood and went to the table. He did find all of his personal items there, which consisted of a set of keys, a wallet with false identification, a set of lock picks, the destroyed tracer she pulled from the heel of his sneaker, and his phone. His phone had been turned off, but was still intact. He took his keys and headed to the door. "Block the door with the half brick outside or it'll lock behind you." Christoph half turned, nodding to her in acknowledgment, and walked out of the room. "I'm coming up," Sophia said aloud to Ella, who sighed in relief.

CHAPTER FORTY-FIVE

GO GET PERRY

Sophia opened the door to the office, carrying the laptop bag and the Tungsten case. Ella was still standing in front of the monitors. "He's outside. He blocked the door with the brick as you told him to."

"I don't think we have anything to worry about from him," said Sophia, putting the case and laptop bag on the desk before pulling the Ruger from her back waistband and setting it down as well. She was glad Ella had not run, given all that she was witnessing.

"You sent him outside naked."

Sophia gave a dismissive wave. "There's no one around behind the building. He was willing to risk bringing an unconscious woman out to his car. The man may be an oaf, but he knows his business. Besides, if anyone happens to see him, consider the nature of the place we're in."

"Good point," Ella admitted.

"It was also another test of sorts."

"Look, he came back in." Ella pointed to one of the monitors. The two women watched as the man entered through the back door carrying a large gym bag, which was a rather peculiar sight for a man wearing nothing but a pair of running shoes. He entered the dungeon and put down the bag before going back to the chair and sitting down. "Why did you tell him not to get dressed?"

"He probably has a second gun in that bag," Sophia answered. "He has no way of hiding it like this. It's alright, though. He isn't going to hurt me or anyone else unless I tell him to."

Ella turned to Sophia with a look of awe on her face. "I can't believe this is all real."

"Oh, this is all very real," said Sophia, her arms folded in front of her. "But now comes the part you aren't going to like," she said, putting her hand on Ella's arm. "You have to go."

"What are you going to do?"

"I'm going to wait for Marcus to get here and we'll take my new bodyguard with us to confront Perry. Tonight."

"I don't want to leave you alone with him," said Ella.

"I don't want Marcus knowing you're mixed up in this," Sophia persuaded. "You have to leave before he gets here. Christoph won't say anything unless I tell him to. I'll tell Marcus I bribed Christoph over to our side, and Christoph will back up every word. He's still very much himself."

Ella raised her eyebrows and turned to look at the monitors showing the naked man sitting in the middle of the dungeon downstairs. "Really?"

Sophia rolled her eyes. "Yes, he is. Only his motivations toward me have changed. He could go back to whatever phony life he lives when he isn't busy being a contract killer. No one else would ever notice any difference because there is no difference, save that."

With some obvious difficulty, Ella relented. Sophia walked her downstairs to the back door where they embraced and kissed a final time. "I'll call you tonight and let you know what we're going to do," said Sophia.

"You'd better," Ella replied.

Sophia watched Ella as she walked to her SUV parked on the other side of the gravel lot. She wasn't sure if Ella had detected her lie and clung to it as a desperate hope, or if she truly believed what Sophia had told her. Sophia shut the door and leaned against the cold steel. "I'm so sorry, Ella," she said in a whisper that was barely audible to herself. "It would have killed you to know."

Sophia returned to the office to get her own pistol before returning to the dungeon where Christoph waited. She went to his bag and dumped everything onto the floor. It contained clothes, another knife, a plain jacket, and a concealed carry holster. "Get dressed," she said. The man did as he was told.

When he was done, he had on a pair of jeans, a pullover shirt, and a jacket. Sophia then took him upstairs to the office and explained in detail what they were going to do. Certain that he understood the plan exactly, she moved the desk chair to the center of the room and sat down. "Do it," she said, bracing herself against the arms of the chair. Christoph then drew his hand back and struck her across the face, nearly knocking her out of the chair.

"Are you okay?" he asked, which she found reassuring.

"Again," she said, bracing herself. This time, the strike came from the other direction, an open-handed slap across her lower jaw and mouth. Had Christoph made a fist she would have lost teeth, but as it was, it gave her a split lip that would swell in seconds. "Time to make a call," she said to him.

Christoph turned on his phone and made a call to Perry Tellerson, putting him on speakerphone. Perry answered on the first ring. "Yes?"

"Priority one is accomplished. I have her alive and need a drop off location."

"What?" said Perry, sounding shocked. "Confirm." Christoph took a picture of Sophia's battered face. "Outstanding! How the hell did you do that so fast? Witnesses?"

"None. Yet. But I need a location," Christoph urged.

There was a brief pause. Clearly Perry had not expected this. "Take her to The Church. It's the only site I can have ready in so short a time."

Christoph looked at Sophia, who nodded encouragingly. They had discussed this as the ideal contingency. She silently mouthed the word, "video."

"What about video monitoring?"

"I'll make sure we go black at seven. Be there at ten after," said Perry.

"Will you need any security?" Christoph asked.

"I'll have Chase with me, but I would like you to stay on as a backup."

"Understood," said Christoph.

"Great work," Perry said before disconnecting.

Sophia took up her phone and checked the time. They had two-and-a-half hours to get to The Church and carry out her plan. If she lived through it, she would have nothing to worry about from Perry Tellerson again. "We had better get going. We need you to buy a car."

Ella received a text message from Sophia at eleven PM which read, "I am fine. Everything is alright now. I have nothing more to fear from the snake. I love you and can't wait to see you again. I will call you in two days."

CHAPTER FORTY-SIX
I'M NOT BOND

For more than an hour, Stuart explained to the agents how he had become involved in finding out what happened to Rylen. He told them how it had all started with a phone call on Rylen's phone and the strange text message containing an image of a leaf. He told them how the caller had stayed on the phone until the police found it. Much to his relief, they took him seriously. Up until that point, they believed Rylen had died in an accident, but now Stuart was providing them with a doubt at the very least. He then explained about how the phone was stolen and how that led him to Lori, both because she was the last person Rylen ever saw and the image of a green leaf being the last thing that came across Rylen's phone. Wanting to leave Spider out of the story as much as he could, he had to tell them he had a programmer friend who had made a duplicate of the phone in order to see if he could find out where the messages came from. Then, when his friend found it had a spyware app that ran in the background, they used it to figure out who took the phone.

When he got to the part about Perry Tellerson and Steve McGuire planning to abduct and possibly murder Lori Mercer, Lonnie stopped him. "Are you telling me that you had a video of these two guys planning a kidnapping and you didn't call the police?" he asked, sounding incredulous.

"There wasn't time," said Stuart. "They planned it and

executed it on the same fucking day! If I warned her, how would I explain knowing that it was going to happen? Obviously, they were going to take her at the first given opportunity. I couldn't go to the police and expect them to take it seriously."

"So you gave them the opportunity to take her by asking her to meet you at a restaurant five blocks away, knowing she would probably walk?" asked Lonnie. "Holy shit, I don't know whether to be impressed or disgusted by that, homey."

"It was the best I could come up with at the time. I don't think she had anything to do with what happened to Rylen, but..."

"But you can't be sure?" Lonnie finished. "You got the hots for this girl, don't you?"

Stuart sighed. "Yeah, kind of."

"You been seeing her?"

"Not exactly."

"Did you know about the whole dungeon thing before I told you?"

"I knew. I've been there."

"Oh, so it's like that!"

"No!" Stuart answered. "She invited me to a hypnosis demonstration. You can understand why I was curious; I wanted to see if someone could be made to do something self-destructive."

"And what did you learn, mister PI? Can it be done?"

"Any expert will tell you it can't but after what I saw... I'm not so sure," Stuart finished.

"You have to get us a copy of that video."

"I can do that right now," said Stuart. "May I?"

"Please do." Stuart sent Spider a text message asking him to send the video of Tellerson and McGuire. As they waited, Stuart told them about the meeting he had with Perry Tellerson and Steve McGuire. "They admitted all that to you. Just like that?"

"He didn't seem too worried about me telling anybody," Stuart said.

"I'll tell you something most people don't know. It isn't

anything top secret, but we would rather it not become too widely known. A lot of people work there, so of course it would get out that they can do this, but most people wouldn't know exactly how. They have some tech that lets them disable wireless devices and transmissions."

"So what?" said Stuart. "I'm no tech wizard and I know stuff like that has been around forever."

"Not like what they have," Lonnie explained. "Like I said, we don't know exactly how they do it, but if you're around them--we don't know how close, but close enough to have a conversation--your shit quits working. Your phone shuts down. You could be wired up and the signal will be intercepted. Police radios won't work, it doesn't matter what frequency it is."

"Like a tiny EMP?" asked Stuart.

"No, nothing like that. It doesn't damage anything. Get far enough away from them, everything is back to normal. That's why it has been so damned hard to get anything concrete against them."

"Then how did I get the video?"

"That's what I would like to know. Maybe they fucked up and let their guard down at the wrong time. Hell, I saw a squirrel fall out of a tree once. Mistakes happen."

Stuart's phone buzzed on the table. It was a message from Spider that contained a download link. Stuart tapped it and downloaded the video to his phone. When it finished, Wiley took the phone and plugged it into the laptop on the conference room table. They watched the video and, when it finished, the agents in the room looked at each other in silence. Stuart asked, "So can you use it?"

"Fuck yes, we can use it," Noah answered. This man spoke so little, Stuart had started thinking of him as the quiet Yin to Lonnie's verbose Yang. "One way or another, we'll use it."

"Can I go home now?" Stuart asked.

"Do you even realize what you just did?" asked Lonnie.

"I'm starting to."

Lonnie drove Stuart back to his house. Stuart waited until they were parked behind his truck in his driveway to show Lonnie the text message that he received telling him that Rylen was a rapist in four known cases and not to trust Lori. "Did you send me this?" he asked.

Lonnie whistled after reading it. "No, it wasn't me, bro. You could have brought this up back at the office."

"I meant to."

"Well, no, it wasn't me."

"I thought it was Steve McGuire, but you became a better candidate today. Listen, you know the backgrounds of everyone associated with the Foundation. Rylen worked there for years. I guess what I'm asking is," Stuart paused to swallow, "is it true?"

"Ah, man," said Lonnie with a sigh, "your brother had a clean record, but he was under investigation too. There were accusations made over the years, but he was never charged with anything. That's all I can tell you for sure. I didn't see any need to bring it up back there; I know that wound is still fresh and there was no point."

"Thanks for your honesty, anyway," said Stuart as he got out of the car.

"You have my number," Lonnie said, "stay out of this mess. I have a feeling it's about to get ugly. If anything happens, you call me! Twenty-four hours a day."

"I will," said Stuart before he shut the car door and went inside.

CHAPTER FORTY-SEVEN

A GHOST FROM THE PAST

Krista entered the coffee shop and spotted Stuart waiting at the table. He stood and greeted her as she approached, but he could tell that she was not happy to see him. They did not hug or shake hands. She sat down on the other side of the table without ceremony. He followed her example. "Do you want some coffee?" he asked.

"Just ask me what you wanted to ask."

There were times in Stuart's life that he wished that he were an eloquent or persuasive speaker. This was one of those times. He decided to do what he did best and go with unfiltered honesty. "Thank you for coming. I couldn't ask this over the phone," he said, pausing to collect himself. "It's about Rylen."

"What about him?" she asked, looking guarded.

"There was something you said at the funeral... something about wanting to say goodbye to a part of your life. I just wanted to know what you meant by that," he told her, feeling as though he were in a kickboxing match and losing badly.

"Like I said, Rylen was a part of my past."

"So you came to show your respects?" Stuart asked, having prepared this question ahead of time.

The woman's green eyes peered at him suspiciously. "No, I was there to lay a part of my past to rest, not to say goodbye to Rylen."

This was what Stuart had feared the most. "Listen, please, Krista. I'm learning a lot about Rylen since he died. A lot of things I never knew about him, but wish I had. It's starting to seem like I didn't know him at all."

"Why am I here, Stuart?"

"Some people told me things about Rylen. Things that I'm hoping aren't true, but if they are, I have to know. I was hoping that you could help me."

"What things?" she asked in a whisper.

"They said that he... hurt women. The two of you dated for months in college. It was so long ago and yet you went to his funeral, not to say goodbye to the man, but to the part he played in your life. Why is that?" Stuart asked.

Krista looked down at her lap and when she turned her face back up, her eyes were full of tears. "It was senior year. We had been dating for a while, but we still didn't have sex," she said, taking a tissue from her purse to wipe her face. She took a deep breath and continued. "He always said that he wanted to wait and not rush into it. I thought it was nice because most guys aren't like that. Did you ever know Justine, my roommate?" Stuart just shook his head in answer. "She was so beautiful. All the guys wanted her. I was so proud that I could get a guy like Rylen being... well, not being the best-looking girl on campus. I came back to our room after class one day. She was lying on the floor... lying in her own vomit and blood. I called 911. She said someone broke into our room and attacked her when she came in the door. He beat her so badly she couldn't see."

Stuart couldn't wait anymore. "Was it Rylen?"

Krista nodded. "She knew his voice. He had been in our room so many times, talking to her, flirting with her. I used to get pissed when he came on to her right in front of me. He laughed it off and would always say he was trying to make me jealous. She told the police everything, but one of his frat brothers said Rylen had been in his room studying all day. When did you ever know Rylen to study anything? He could flip through a whole textbook and have it memorized in a few hours. He loved to show off for us all the time."

"What happened to Justine?"

"When I saw her in the hospital, she swore to me it was Rylen. She said the entire time he was raping her, he was talking to her. Calling her every disgusting thing imaginable. But she said he was calm, which was what frightened her even more. He wasn't angry or raging. He was just getting off on it. She quit school for the rest of the year."

"What did you do after she told you that? Did you confront him?"

"Of course! Do you know what he did?" she asked, the tears streaming down her face again. "He laughed at me. Yes, he laughed. He was completely indifferent to her pain or my fury."

"I'm sorry, Krista. Did he even admit to what he did?"

The woman nodded. "He said the reason he ever pretended to be interested in me was to get close to her. Since he got what he wanted, I could fuck off for all he cared."

Stuart leaned back in his chair, unable to believe what he was hearing. "I never knew. Any of it. I swear."

"I know," said Krista. "You always were a nice kid, but the only person who ever admired Rylen was you."

Stuart walked into his house, barely realizing that he had driven home. The time between his arrival home and his parting with Krista was a fog of pain and confusion. Could she be mistaken? Could she have been lying? No. He could choose not to accept that she had been telling the truth, but in his heart of hearts, he knew it was true, every word. Too many puzzle pieces fell into place with the knowledge of what Rylen was. Their mother had died from the beatings his father inflicted. Stuart had sworn for as long as he could remember that he would never hurt a woman or child. He promised himself that he would never stand by if another man did, either. He always believed that Rylen was the same. He still wanted to think so, but any denial he might have nurtured had been ripped away from him.

Stuart's eyes fell on the urn in the middle of the table, right where he had placed it so he might see it whenever he first walked in the door. He heard the scream of rage before even knowing that it was from his own mouth that it came. The room shrank as space distorted to bring the table before him. His hand was a blur as it swept the urn from the table and sent it shattering into a cloud of dust on the other side of the room before the scream finally died.

CHAPTER FORTY-EIGHT
THEY ARE BACK

Stuart was sitting on the floor with his back to the wall when his phone buzzed quietly. It was still on the floor where he had dropped it before dusting one side of the room with the remains of his brother. How long ago had that been? He heard the sound again, but left the phone on the floor where it lay. He pulled himself off of the floor and went to his bathroom, hoping the soap in his shower was strong enough to wash away anger, shame, human ashes, and disgust. When he finally returned to his living room, he picked up his phone and looked at the screen. He had four missed calls from Lori. She did not leave a voicemail, but there was a text message asking him to call her, which came in after all the missed calls.

What was he to do with this? The wisest thing he considered would be to block her number and forget he had ever met her. Not likely. He would never be the same person he was before her, as he had discovered a new form of release, but from what, the anxiety he no longer had, or from himself?

The message he received earlier that day warned him to stop looking for answers. Maybe he would have been better off if he had listened, but he knew that was not really the case. He wanted the truth, no matter how ugly it was, even if it forever changed the view he held of the brother he loved. An even uglier thought occurred to him. What if Lori had been one of Rylen's rape victims? Rylen met her that night and went home with her; he had plenty of chances, and it would explain why they never had any contact afterward. Even if that theory was true, it made his own position worse, as he was Rylen's brother and she still didn't know about it. What could be the urgency that she would call him four times? As he was wondering, another text message came through on his phone. Lori wrote, "Stuart, I keep seeing a white van drive past my house. I'm scared. Please call."

After a long hesitation, he pressed the callback button. The phone picked up on the first ring. "What's going on?" he asked.

"I saw them again. The white van. I saw it when I first pulled in, so I kept watch. I've seen it three times now."

"Call the police," he told her with a numb indifference that surprised him.

"You know I can't do that," she said.

"Lori, something bad has happened and I'm about the last person you want to be talking to right now," said Stuart. "A white van drove past your house a few times. What do you want me to do?"

"I want you to come over and be with me. You can tell me all about what happened," she replied.

"I'm not going anywhere," he said flatly.

"I need you here, Stuart. I'm so scared. Please, sweetheart. Come over," she said, sounding terrified.

Tellerson had lied, but that was only natural. Stuart had to admit that it was selfish of him to be so absorbed with his own issues, about which he could do nothing, that he would ignore her when she was in present danger. "I'll be there as soon as I can," he said.

"See you soon," she said and hung up.

When Lori opened the door, she didn't look as worried as Stuart expected. Her makeup was perfect, and she was wearing skinny jeans and a t-shirt. With the exception of her being barefoot, she looked exactly the same as she had on the day he met her. "Have you seen it again since you called?"

"No," she answered, shutting the door behind him. "But I'm so glad that you're here." She hugged him and led him to the dining room. One of the dining chairs had been placed near the bay windows that looked out to the street.

"Are you sure it was the same van?" he asked, sitting down at the end of the table after moving the chair by the window back into place.

Lori went to the kitchen and talked as she did something with cups and saucers. "The logo on the back was different, but it looked like the same one."

"If they come by again, they'll see my truck in the driveway," he told her. She returned holding two cups and saucers and placed one on the table in front of him.

"White tea with orange peel and hibiscus," she said.

Stuart had forgotten all about the tea he bought from her shop when they first met. He hadn't asked for any tea, though, and he really didn't want any. "Thank you," he said, still watching the street.

She sat at the opposite end of the table from him. "Chai tea for me." She carefully took a sip, watching as Stuart tasted the tea. "How is it?"

"It's fine," he said quietly.

"You want to tell me what happened today?"

"Honestly, I don't want to talk about it."

"That's fine. Be a sweetheart and finish your tea. You'll feel better."

The tea was good, and it reminded him that he had not eaten all day. When he finished the cup, he placed it on the saucer. The daylight was fading, but he still watched out the window. Lori peeked at her phone on the table and sipped her tea in silence. "There never was any van, was there?" he asked, turning to her.

"Nope," she answered, not bothering to look up from her cup, "sure wasn't." Stuart moved to stand up.

Lori's hand whipped out from where it rested in her lap, her snub nose revolver pointed directly at him. "Sit the fuck down!"

The surprise flashed through Stuart's mind. He considered his next move and looked her in the eye. "Fire away," he said, standing up and spreading his arms wide.

"So help me god, I will shoot you where you stand."

"You got a way to dispose of a body?"

"I don't need one. You came in here and attacked me with the knife they'll find right next to your body, your fingerprints all over it. With your record of violence, I have a feeling they'll buy it. Trust me, I can be very convincing."

"Sounds like you have it all planned out. Since you're going to shoot me anyway, I prefer to die on my feet."

"Sit down and answer my questions and you might not live. Refuse," she said, cocking the pistol, "and you definitely won't."

"I prefer the gun."

Lori glanced at her phone on the table, keeping him trained at gunpoint for several more seconds. "Be a sweetheart and sit down." Stuart lowered himself into the chair without hesitation, but not without a twinge of surprise that quickly faded. "Good, we'll give it a little longer. Don't worry, in a minute you'll be free to do anything I want."

"What was in that tea?" he asked, thinking that he would probably not leave the house alive.

"Be quiet and keep still," she answered, keeping the gun trained on him. After another minute passed, she un-cocked and lowered the gun. "Fold your hands together on the table." Stuart did so. Lori closed the drapes and turned on the lights before sitting at the other end of the table again. "Tell me the absolute truth. Will you do that?"

"Yes."

"Are you Rylen Hollister's brother?"

"Yes."

"Why didn't you tell me?"

Stuart had to think about it before answering. There were a number of reasons. "At first, I thought you might have killed him, but not after I met you. Spider thought so too, but all I had to go on was my gut."

"Spider? Who the hell is that?"

"He's a hacker I hired to help me find out who killed Rylen."

Lori paused. "Did you know him before Rylen was killed?"

"No, I found him by going through a chat buddy I know on the Dark Web. I hired him to help me unlock Rylen's phone to trace the last call he received."

"Do you know who my father is?"

This was an odd question. "No, I have no idea. Spider looked up what information he could, but there was almost nothing about your parents. It said that your mother is deceased and your father is presumed to be out of the country."

"Did anyone ever tell you or ask you anything about me?"

"Yes, Perry Tellerson. He was Rylen's employer. He was the one who hired the thugs who attacked you."

"Tell me what happened," said Lori. "All of it."

"He called me when one of the thugs described the man who attacked them. He showed them my picture and they identified me. He said Rylen's death was suspicious and they wanted to question you about it. They do shit like that, apparently. Some of the board members are into organized crime and Rylen was in on it. I told them you had nothing to do with it and they appeared to buy it, but I still think they would have killed you. Rylen was helping them conduct criminal business dealings. He was their money man and his death hit them hard. They said they were done looking into the matter and I said I was too."

"I had a visit from Tellerson today; that's why we are talking now. I managed to get him off of my back for the moment. Is the phone call and the text message the only reason you came to me?"

"Yes," Stuart answered. "It led me to hire Spider and the information he gave me led to you."

"No other reason? Nobody else put you up to it? Police?"

"No, that's the only reason."

She remained quiet for some time. Stuart's eyes were struggling to stay open. "Stand up and put the keys to your truck on the table." He did so. "We're going for a ride."

CHAPTER FORTY-NINE
A BLOCKED NUMBER

Stuart awoke to find he was lying cramped in the back seat of his own pickup. The sun was filtering in through the back windshield. "Lori!" she shouted as he sat up and recalled all that had happened to him the night before. He was still in his clothes and was stiff from being in the same position for... how long? He was parked in his own driveway and when he got out of his truck, he checked himself and found his keys, glasses, and phone in the pockets of his jacket. He looked at his phone. It was a few minutes to nine. No messages. Lori could wait; he knew where she lived. She owned a brick and mortar business that she went to every day. Unless she was going to fly like the wind, where could she go?

Cursing himself for his own foolishness, he went inside his house and showered before eating anything and everything he could find in the fridge. He collapsed on his bed and awoke to find it was already past noon. He went out to his living room, only to be reminded of the breakdown he went through the night before. Rylen's ashes and the shattered pieces of the urn that contained them were on the floor by the wall. The point of impact scarred the drywall and left a charcoal halo on the paint four feet across. The ashes had fallen in a cloud and dusted a side table on the way down.

What to do? Should he try to salvage his brother's remains and scatter them somewhere? Would he ever get them out of the carpet? He thought about this for several minutes before making up his mind. He went to his pantry and took up a roll of paper towels, a bottle of spray cleaner, and plastic trash bags. Leaving these items at the crash site, he took his vacuum from a closet and set to work. Ten minutes into his chore, his phone chimed.

It was a message from Spider that read, "Foundation showdown happened last night. I have it all on video. Call me! If I don't answer, will call you back."

What the hell did that mean? Stuart called Spider, but got no answer. He didn't leave a voicemail. There was another call that Stuart didn't want to make, but knew he must. He called Lonnie. "Agent Rodriguez," Lonnie answered.

"Did you forget who I am, or are we on such formal terms now?"

"Stuart! Sorry, man, I don't have you in my contacts on this phone yet. What's up?" he asked, distracted.

"My brother's accident. I think I know how it was done."

"What are you talking about?"

"I went to see Lori Mercer last night. She drugged me with something. I think it's how she made Rylen wreck his car."

"Shit, Stuart, are you okay?"

"Yeah, I'm fine. She gave me some tea... slipped something into it. I woke up in the back seat of my truck parked in my own driveway."

Stuart could not be sure, but could have sworn he heard Lonnie snicker. "You went to see this woman?" he asked. "I told you to stay out of this! You're lucky that's all that happened to you. I said this shit was about to get ugly and... well, it has. I'm in a world of shit right now, but whatever happened to your brother, I promise we'll get to the bottom of it. I have to go. I'll talk to you as soon as I can." The agent hung up.

Stuart tried twice more to reach Spider as the afternoon waned. He jumped at the phone when he heard a message chime. It was from a blocked number. The message read, "911. Stuart, this is Spider. I can't risk using my own phone. I met

Lori Mercer. I'm with her at the dungeon in Salem. Meet us here before five o'clock." Stuart read the message several times. He replied and asked for details, but as he suspected, no response came.

Stuart considered before sending a message that read, "What's the name of the English thug with the bad hair?"

A few minutes later, his phone rang with an incoming call from a blocked number. Stuart swallowed and answered. "Hello?"

"Mister Hollister. Well played. We've never met in person, but it's a pleasure to finally talk to you. Text messages are so impersonal." It was a woman's voice, dark and velvet.

The name came to Stuart in a flash. He thought of the photos that Lonnie had placed on the table when he was at the FBI office. Lonnie said that Stuart was linked to everyone in the case, but that wasn't true. Of the three women, there was only one person Stuart didn't know. "Sophia Rubinstein," he said.

"Well, well, aren't you the clever one," she chortled. "You're right; I am the one who extended the invitation just now. I will see you at the dungeon at five."

"Fuck you."

"And we were off to such a good start. Don't you want to know what happened to your brother? I can tell you. Be here by then if you want to see Lori Mercer alive again."

"Be sure to give her my regards."

"You and I both know you don't mean that, but I guess we'll know by five. I would tell you to come alone and tell no one, so on and so forth, but I'm sure you know what's expected of you."

Stuart sat at the desk of Detective Connelly. He told the detective everything that happened and Connelly listened patiently. When Stuart mentioned the name of Sophia Rubinstein, he could tell it caught the man's attention. Connelly pointed out that kidnapping was a federal issue. Stuart said he had been in contact with the FBI, but had reason to think his phone was tapped and he had been warned not to talk to anyone in law enforcement. There was no time for him to visit another office. Strangely, the detective left to make a phone call at another desk while Stuart waited. When he returned, he said that someone would be with him shortly. Stuart checked the time. It was closing on four o'clock when he rose to leave in irritation. Ella approached him.

"You're not here by chance, are you?" he said.

"No, I'm not. Let's talk outside." Stuart turned to Connelly, who returned his look with a shrug and a wave. Stuart and Ella left the building without saying anything to one another until they were out on the street. "Stuart, if you're going to help your case, you need to stop doing things like this."

"Like what?" he said in astonishment. "I went to the police to tell them someone I know has been kidnapped, and they called you!"

"He said you told him it was Sophia Rubinstein."

"That's because it is."

"Sophia is a close personal friend of mine, Stuart. Connelly knows that, which is why he called me. He did you a favor."

"A favor? Your friend threatened to kill Lori."

"Lori? That's the dominatrix you were telling me about? The one you were falling for?"

"She demanded I meet her by five o'clock, which is now less than an hour from now because I pissed my time away talking to Barney Miller in there."

"Who?"

Stuart ignored the question. Old television shows are the province of the insomniac, he thought. "I have to go." He turned and walked to his Truck and Ella followed.

"Where are you going?"

"To meet her at the dungeon in Salem."

This stopped Ella in her tracks. "The dungeon on the first floor of an office building?"

He stopped and looked at her. "You know it?"

"Yes," said Ella. "I've been there. That is where Lori works out of?"

Stuart paused to consider this. "Yes," he answered thoughtfully, "but our relationship has taken a step back since she drugged me and left me in the back seat of my truck last night. But I don't want her to die. If you're such good friends with this woman, why don't you come along and keep her from shooting me?"

"Exactly what I was going to suggest," Ella answered.

CHAPTER FIFTY

ROADTRIP TO SALEM

During the drive to Salem, Ella told Stuart about Sophia and explained everything she had been through with Sophia and Christoph the day before. Stuart found the story about the Tungsten almost impossible to believe, but he was personally acquainted with the drug she described. The two used in combination were the perfect nightmare.

He was not sure he was ready to tell Ella about his meeting with the FBI, especially since she was still sure of Sophia's innocence. He had to ask, "Why were you treating Rylen?"

Ella hesitated for a long time. "I'll tell you," she answered decisively. "But I don't want it to damage your memory of him." Stuart kept his eyes on the road, but came close to telling her that was extremely unlikely. "He came to see me for sex addiction. We only had a few sessions before he quit coming."

"Is that when you started screwing him?"

Ella's sharp intake told him he had hit a nerve. "How did you know about that?"

"I didn't, but now I do," he answered flatly, his eyes focused on the road.

Ella looked at him in silence for a long time before she finally sighed. "You should learn to play poker professionally. I think you'd be very good at it."

"What does that mean?"

"You are the second hardest person to read that I've ever

met, Stuart. Your depths are as hidden in the shadows as Rylen's were by his shimmering facade."

"I'm on the spectrum; it makes me hard to read."

"Autism Spectrum Disorder? Who told you that?" Ella asked.

"A former therapist."

"You should have fired that person immediately. You aren't on the spectrum. You don't have ASD; you aren't even close to having any form of autism."

"How can you be so sure? You've been seeing me to assess whether I need an anger management course."

Ella laughed. "Have you ever heard of someone calling a computer technician to fix a computer that wasn't plugged in? Psychologists, like any kind of doctor, can get so bogged down in the details that we miss the obvious. I know you don't have any form of autism because you turn it off whenever it suits you. I've seen you do it myself. People with ASD can't. So, you can stop using that mis-diagnosis as an excuse to hide behind because you don't want to put in the work to overcome some mild social anxiety."

"Why did my anxiety fade when Rylen died?"

"Do you want my personal or professional opinion?"

"Are they so different?"

"I'll give you both at once. Rylen was more than a brother to you. Whatever was causing your anxiety, Rylen was at the root of it. Maybe some part of you knew what he really was and kept it burried. Loss of a loved one is one kind of pain. The destruction of our illusions is something else entirely, and can be every bit as painful."

She was astute. Might she be able to provide some insight about Rylen? If she could, would he really want her to? "I found out some things about Rylen recently. Did you know what he was?"

Ella took her time in answering. "He started to demonstrate signs of an antisocial personality disorder. It was why I stopped seeing him personally, and seeing him professionally again after that was out of the question."

"A man comes to you for help in treating his sex addiction and you start sleeping with him yourself. I'm not judging, but do you see nothing inherently wrong in that? Can't you get into some kind of trouble?"

Stuart expected her to become defensive, but Ella accepted the question with equanimity. "He wasn't my patient anymore. And yes, sleeping with a client--even a former client--is not only unethical, it's illegal. I could lose my license if anyone had ever reported it."

"If anyone *had* ever reported it?" Stuart asked. "Meaning it isn't a problem now that he's dead?"

"It's certainly much less of one."

Stuart had to let that sit for a minute. "What do you think Sophia wants with me? What could be so important that she would kill somebody if I didn't show up?"

"She isn't a murderer. Not like that." said Ella.

"She killed Rylen just like that. You think she wouldn't do it again?"

"Did she actually *say* she killed your brother? Or did she just threaten your friend to get you to meet with her?"

"No, she didn't say it outright," he admitted. "She knew Rylen's accident wasn't an accident. What does that tell you?"

"She is not a killer!" Ella shouted.

There was something of fearful denial in her voice that made Stuart glance at her before asking, "Are you in love with her?" Ella did not answer quickly enough to keep Stuart from saying, "Oh, Jesus."

Ella collected herself. "Yes, I am. I thought our friendship was just that, but there was more to it for both of us. I'm bi-sexual. I live with my boyfriend, Paxton. He's a good man, but Sophia is... otherworldly."

Stuart sighed. "I'm starting to think psychopathy is your aphrodisiac. Now I know why you wanted to come with me."

"Why did you ask me to?"

"She would expect me to come alone, not bring a close

friend of hers with me. You were my backup plan to call for help if she decides to kill me."

"She isn't going to kill you."

"She threatened to kill Lori if I didn't show. What else could she want? She didn't ask for money, so this isn't ransom."

"She doesn't want money," said Ella. "She's richer than Croesus."

"If she feels the same way about you that you do about her, maybe you can make her think twice."

"What are you doing?" she asked as Stuart pulled the truck to the side of the street, still blocks away from the dungeon.

"You should get in the back seat. The back windows have a dark tint and nobody will see you back there if you keep low. If I'm not out in five minutes, call the police. Or come in and surprise your girlfriend. Improvise, but don't get killed."

"That's your plan?" asked Ella as she got out of the truck and reentered in the back. "I'll tell you this right now, you're way out of your depth."

CHAPTER FIFTY-ONE
THE GANG IS ALL HERE

After pulling into the gravel lot behind the building, Stuart parked the truck in a spot he believed was out of range of the back camera. He parked so the passenger side of the truck faced the building. He took his jacket from the back seat where Ella crouched and put it on over his hoodie, pulling the hood out from under the jacket and making what necessary preparations he could. He sent Sophia a text message saying that he was there. He received an immediate reply telling him to keep his phone on him and that she would meet him inside the dungeon.

Over the last few blocks of the trip, Ella had tried to convince him that it would be better if they entered together, but he felt sure that would be a mistake. He would enter first to find out what she wanted before Ella showed up unexpectedly. "Be careful," she said before he got out of the truck and made his way across the gravel lot to the alley.

He found the alley door unlocked and entered the building. As he made his way down the hall, careful to keep an eye on his back, he considered how different the mood and aspect of this place was from when he had seen it in Lori's company. He reached the double metal doors to the dungeon and found them closed. He entered.

Sophia sat on a wooden ladder-back chair in the center of the room, her arms folded and her legs crossed. She stared at him as he approached and stopped a short distance in front of her. She was wearing black yoga pants and white sneakers with a close-fitting gray shirt. She had on a thin, black leather jacket that somehow worked with the athletic wear. She was heavily made up, but Stuart could still tell that she had been struck in the face recently. Nevertheless, it galled him to admit, she was absolutely striking. He had only to look at her to know that she was the type of woman whom it would be dangerously easy for men--and apparently women--to fall in love with. She was also far too cool for Stuart's taste as she looked at him.

Lori was sitting in one of the metal chairs they used for the attendees during her demonstration. Her hands were cuffed behind her back.

"I brought company," Sophia said, looking to the changing room. Dothan stepped into the dungeon from the darkened doorway, a gun in his hand. He handed Sophia his mobile phone, and she examined it before putting it onto the table next to the rack.

"You can search me," Stuart told her, spreading his arms wide. "I don't have any weapons."

"That isn't your style," said Sophia. "You're far too hands on for that. Still, I wasn't taking any chances." She stood and moved her chair to the side of the room. "I would go into introductions, but it seems we're all quite well-acquainted already."

"What do you mean?" Stuart asked, thinking that there was something familiar about the big man in the tight sweater and loose khakis.

"Don't either of you recognize him?" asked Sophia. "This is Dothan. He and his friend, Ari, are the newest members of my full-time payroll, as they were recently removed from service to the Foundation. I was thrilled to find that out and hired them both into my exclusive employment without delay. The enemy of my enemy and all that."

"He's one of the men who attacked Lori," said Stuart.

"Excellent," said Sophia. "There was a third in their group, but unfortunately... you killed him."

Stuart paused, not wanting her to know he was aware of that fact. He was not an actor, but he didn't want Sophia to know that a federal agent had already shared that piece of news. He kept his mouth shut for a few beats before saying, "I never meant to kill anyone."

"His name was Yosef! He was my friend from the time we were children, and he is dead because of you!" spat Dothan angrily. His voice was husky and rough, probably from steroid use. He had a mild Israeli accent.

"He should have chosen a better occupation than kidnapping women," Stuart said.

Dothan raised his gun and pointed it at Stuart's face. "No!" shouted Sophia. He slowly lowered the gun, never taking his eyes from Stuart's. "Oh, yes," said Sophia. "Dothan here is dying to *get a piece of you,* as he says. But that isn't why we're here. Behave yourself and I promise he will do the same."

The doors opened behind Stuart and he turned, expecting to see Ella, but Ari entered, gun in hand.

Sophia looked at Ari. "Get it and search him."

Ari walked to Stuart with his gun trained on him. He made a gesture with the barrel. "Hands out to your sides," he said in the same subtly accented voice that Dothan had, though his was not as deep. He put his gun in a shoulder holster at the same instant that Dothan trained his weapon on Stuart. Ari frisked him, checking the inside of Stuart's jacket, waist, and pockets, before touching his sleeves and the legs of his pants. Ari took Stuart's phone and the stun gun Stuart had in the pockets of his jacket. He then went to Sophia and handed her Stuart's phone. Ari held up the stun gun for Sophia to see, pressing the button to make it spark before setting it on the table near her.

Sophia glanced at the stun gun before giving Stuart a half smile. "Liar," she said, turning her attention back to his phone.

"I was returning that to you," he said to Dothan, who glared at him.

"Password?" she asked him. Stuart hesitated. What was her interest in his phone? She looked up at him when he said nothing. "Seriously?" she asked in disbelief. She had a point. He gave her the unlock code.

Sophia looked at Ari and pointed to Lori. The man went to her as he took keys from his pocket. He unlocked the cuffs holding her hands. "Go," he told her. Lori stood and went to Stuart's side.

"Are you going to tell me what you want?" said Stuart.

Sophia looked up from his phone. "Oh, I have what I want." Sophia put the phone on the table and said, "Excellent. We're all good here." Ari took a handbag that belonged to Lori from a chair and handed it to her. "You should stop carrying that empty revolver around with you." Lori didn't answer as she took her handbag from Ari. Ari nodded to Sophia and left the room.

"Can I ask a question?" said Stuart.

"You can ask anything you want," Sophia told the pair that Dothan now held at gunpoint.

"Did you kill Rylen?" he asked. Sophia touched Dothan's arm, indicating that he could lower the gun. He did so.

Sophia's face grew dark and wicked. It gave Stuart a glimpse of the evil of which this woman was capable, but her voice remained passive. "You're only just figuring that out? I don't know how well you knew your brother, but he was a monster straight from hell. So that was where I sent him. I killed him because he raped my daughter, Candice. She took her own life because of it."

"She killed herself?"

"No, he killed her!" Sophia said before visibly reigning in her anger with a deep breath. "I was on the board of directors at the Tellerson Foundation and I used my influence to get her a position there after she graduated. That was where she met him. They went out only once when... when it happened.

"You really have no idea what your brother was, do you? The things he did and got away with? The night it happened, I found my daughter waiting for me downstairs in the garage. She had been beaten bloody and was in shock. And she was just sitting there in her car, waiting for me to get home and find her. It was a miracle that she managed to drive herself the mile or two from where it happened. She didn't even call me.

"I took her to the ER and police were called, but until she was ready to talk, there was nothing they could do. I knew Rylen was responsible before she ever told me. I told them who she was supposed to see that night, and the police did go and talk to him. He said they went out to dinner and he dropped her off at her car. He left out the part about driving into a back alley where he beat and raped the shit out of my little girl before dropping her off at her car and driving himself home.

"Two days after she was attacked, I was staying with her at her home. I didn't want her to be alone. She told me what happened that night. Every single detail. She seemed to be somewhat... better. Badly shaken still, but at least she would be able to talk to the police now. After that she said she wanted to be alone, but we could go to the police in the morning. I refused to leave, but she insisted I go home after being there for days. I hated to leave her, but I would see her the following morning, so... I went home and got some sleep." Stuart watched in silence as a single tear rolled down Sophia's cheek. "It was the last time I saw her alive. After I left her, she took the entire bottle of Temazepam, which the doctors had given her to help her sleep.

"What hope did I ever have of proving anything after that? After the funeral, I went to Perry Tellerson," she said, her eyes growing colder. "My associate, my friend, who was so supportive throughout. The man who came to my daughter's funeral. The one who told me to call him if I needed anything. I told him everything she told me the night she took her own life. What do you think he did?" she asked, seeming to expect him to answer.

"I don't know," said Stuart quietly.

"Nothing!" she answered. "He did nothing. Why? Because that fucking rapist was making too much money for them."

"So you killed Rylen yourself?"

Sophia looked incredulous. "Don't you see? Perry had

me removed from the board. And the rest of those bastards concurred. We could have had Rylen killed if we had wanted to, but he didn't even lose his job. By the time I knew that Perry was putting me off with false promises of actions he would never take against Rylen, he had already persuaded them to have me removed. How many do you think sided with me? One! One fucking member."

"How did you make him fall asleep behind the wheel of his car?"

"I didn't hypnotize him myself. He knew I blamed him and that fucker would certainly never have let me get close enough to him to shoot him, let alone anything else. I had him followed for months. He was heavily into BDSM and had a fascination with a dominatrix," said Sophia, pointing to Lori.

"Stuart, I swear I didn't know," Lori said in a whisper.

"No, she didn't know what I planned to do. She thought I was going to take Rylen for money. That's what she does, you know. She seduces wealthy men, hypnotizes them and takes them for cash. They give it to her willingly, they can't help themselves. Yet she's so unwilling to harm anyone, she carries around an empty gun. Stupid. An empty pistol is more of a danger to you than a loaded one. However, she's a very talented hypnotist, in addition to being a brilliant biochemist, and I do not dole out that kind of praise lightly. When my PI wasn't able to get in to see what Rylen was getting up to in here, I saw to it that the owner of this dungeon admitted him as a guest and installed a hidden camera system for my own personal use."

"What? How did you do that?" Lori asked.

"I bought the entire building," Sophia answered, focusing on her. "I don't work for the company that bought this building, I own the company that bought this building. As for the dungeon, I bought it and every last item in it from the previous owner and kept it exactly as it was, so both it and the building were now mine. Rylen was truly fascinated with you, but you were so indifferent to his wealth, intelligence, charm, and good looks. I thought of killing you just to spite him, but later I had a better idea. So I approached you with an offer." Sophia turned back to Stuart. "I paid her thirty thousand to seduce and hypnotize Rylen. And give me his trance trigger. I used it to make him fall into a trance behind the wheel. I had him undo his seatbelt and sleep his last."

CHAPTER FIFTY-TWO

WHO IS IRA

"So there you are," said Sophia to Stuart. "You think you know what pain is, you piece of filth? I saved every one of your brother's future victims, and every parent the pain of what would be done to their children. I was glad to wipe him from the face of the Earth. And if you think he deserved to live, you are just as loathsome and cruel as he was. If you want me to be sorry for taking your brother away from you, I'm not. I attended the funeral, you know. You saw me there, the veiled woman in black at the back of the church, listening to you talk--so pained, so bereft. Let me tell you something, you worthless fuck, there is no greater suffering than a mother's loss of a child."

Stuart met her eye and said, "If a man did that to my daughter, I don't know what I would do to him, but I think it would be something much worse than what you did." Sophia showed a hint of surprise at this and Stuart knew his statement had an impact. "The one thing that started all of this... why would you send Rylen that image of a leaf? Did you really think Perry would be misled by something so obvious as that?"

Sophia sighed. "Of course not," she answered. "It wasn't so obvious because it was meant to fool anyone. It was obvious so it would be easy to follow back to her," she said, pointing to Lori. "It was meant for you."

"For me?" Stuart asked, glancing at Lori, "What for?"

"You have rage issues and violent tendencies," explained

Sophia. "You nearly beat a man to death for slapping a woman you know only slightly. What, then, would you do to the woman who killed your beloved brother?"

Stuart could not believe the woman's ruthlessness. And she knew a lot more about him than he did about her, but she was mistaken if she thought him a killer. "You expected me to kill Lori?"

"It was a long shot, but it would have been so ideal if you had," Sophia answered. "Think of it: in one phone call I could have taken Rylen's life and destroyed those of the two people he cared about--one literally and one practically, but I certainly wasn't counting on it."

"We were friends!" shouted Lori. "What did I ever do to make you want me dead?"

"Because he cared about you! Both of you! You two are the only ones Rylen ever gave a shit about. I wanted him to suffer the way I suffered! To know what it is to have someone else take someone you love away from you! You were not just another victim for his rape journal. He saw something real in you. I could see it. And you..." Sophia said, looking to Stuart, "his beloved little brother. That technician who fell down a shaft, he was filling in for you. You were the only one scheduled to work that job at the construction site."

Stuart's blood ran cold. "That was you," he said, horrified. "You had the wrong man killed."

For an instant, Sophia looked saddened, but it passed away as fleetingly as it had come. "That was an unfortunate mistake and one I regretted, but there was nothing to be done. However, it caused me to change direction. Instead of making an accident befall Lori too, I decided to kill Rylen by using his infatuation with her against him. I sent that leaf image for you to follow back to Lori. I figured you would find her and do what you seem to do so well. She would be dead and you would be in a cage, which in my opinion, is where you belong. I had you on a timer, though you didn't know it. If you didn't blame her for his death as soon as you found her, the accident I had planned to befall her before Rylen died would have happened at that time, lest she tell anyone about our little arrangement. Of course, I never would have guessed you would end up fucking her instead of killing her."

Stuart shook his head. "I get it. You have her help you kill Rylen without her knowing what she was doing, frame her with a simple clue, then kill her before anyone has time to follow the trail. And you get away free and clear."

"You can be taught," Sophia said. "She thought I wanted to screw that louse for money."

"My god," Stuart breathed, "you are one crazy fucking woman."

"That doesn't make any sense," said Lori. "You came to me and offered to buy my formula after you framed me? The offers, the payoff and debt removal... all of that for someone you planned on killing?"

"My plan with Rylen worked perfectly well. In fact, it was too perfect," Sophia admitted. "It would take time for Stuart or Perry to get the phone, get into it, see the image and follow it back to you. In the meantime, I wanted to know how you did it. Even with all of my skill, I would have doubted it was possible, but you were so certain you could pull it off. When I found out about the S-24, that was a game changer. I had to have it no matter what it cost, and I could not let anything happen to you until I got it. Meanwhile, my own plan was backfiring because they were both closing in. I didn't have time to arrange an accidental death that would fool anyone. And my loyal Israeli friends here were not in my employ at the time, alas. By the time our deal was concluded and you gave me the formula, you had already turned Stuart here into your lap dog. And Perry, he got to you a mere twenty-four hours before I could do anything to you, by which time, I had my hands full. You didn't tell him about the S-24 you made, because if you had, you would be dead. So instead you told him about our agreement. Then you threw in that other little tidbit about a harmless comment I made to you. You almost got me killed without even knowing what you were telling him. Well played. I didn't think you had it in you."

Stuart and Lori looked at each other. "Why did you want my phone so badly?" he asked her.

"I am tying up loose ends. I have been all day. I had to make sure you didn't have any information that could compromise me. If I asked you for the phone, you would have known of its importance."

"Why tell us all of this?" Stuart asked. "Are you planning to kill us now?"

Sophia laughed and looked at Dothan, who returned her look with a questioning expression. "Kill you? What would be the point of that now? What did you think I was going to do, have you shot here and now in my own building?" she asked. "I have what I need. Ari and Dothan are here for my own protection. You can go."

"Why would you let us leave?" he asked.

Sophia's expression shifted from amusement to annoyance. "What will you do?" she hissed. "Nothing. You will do nothing and you will say nothing. Tell me right now how you might use everything I just told you! Maybe you will go to the police. And say what exactly?" She pointed to Lori. "Maybe you can tell them about the S-24, that amazing drug you developed in that drug lab in your basement. Or that you created it using Scopolamine and other controlled substances you smuggled into this country with the help of your Colombian drug lord father? Or how about telling them you tested that drug on unsuspecting massage clients and hypnotized them into giving you money? They ought to love that." She turned her stare to Stuart. "Wait, I know, you can tell them I arranged for one of your coworkers to have an accident and fall down a shaft. Or that I hypnotized your brother to make him fall asleep behind the wheel of his car. Your coming here today with my false promise of killing her told me that you would risk your own life for hers. Why else would you come here without even asking me what I wanted? It was a test, dumb ass! You will never make any move against me. If you do, guess what will happen to her? Get out of here! You are starting to bore me."

"You gave your word," said Dothan.

"Another time," Sophia replied firmly, "on your own time." Dothan moved aside and the pair walked to the door. "Sorry to hear about Ira Calovik," she said.

Lori and Stuart stopped and turned to look at her. "What?" asked Stuart.

"My condolences on the loss of your friend, Ira Calovik," Sophia answered. "You know him as Spider, but you should use a person's real name when paying respects to the dead."

CHAPTER FIFTY-THREE

WE FIGHT OUR WAY OUT

"What are you talking about?" Stuart asked, fear growing quickly.

"You haven't heard?" Sophia asked. "He was killed by a hit-and-run driver this morning. Boston traffic is out of control these days."

"You're lying," said Stuart calmly, though he was anything but calm. "I got a message from him this morning."

"Let's call him," Sophia said, taking up Stuart's phone from the table and entering his password. "Not a lot of contacts. You should get out more. Here we are," she said, touching the call button.

A phone started buzzing somewhere in the room. Stuart and Lori looked around. The vibrating phone was sitting on a table by the rack. It was the one Dothan handed to Sophia when he first entered the dungeon. A wave of fury washed over Stuart, and he took two steps in Sophia's direction before Dothan had his automatic pistol pointed at his head. He stopped mid-stride and stood frozen before he stepped back. Sophia tapped the screen and the phone on the table went silent.

One of the doors opened and Ari pushed Ella into the room, holding a gun to her back. "She was in your office upstairs," he said to Sophia. "I found her watching this room on the monitors."

Dothan waved his pistol at Stuart and Lori. The pair moved

away from the door to the side of the room. Sophia walked quickly to Ella, whose face was covered in tears. "Ella!" she said, moving as if she intended to embrace the woman, but as soon as Sophia neared, Ella swung a backhanded fist that caught Sophia across the jaw and caused her to stumble back. Ari raised the butt of his pistol.

"Stop!" Sophia shouted at Ari, his gun raised, ready to bring it down on the back of Ella's neck. Sophia held one hand on her jaw and the other motioned for Ari to lower his gun. "Why did you come here?"

Ella glared at her defiantly. "I came because I could not believe you could be a killer."

"You shouldn't have come. You've ruined everything!" Sophia cried, her voice breaking.

"Are we still free to leave?" asked Stuart. "I'm kind of thinking you two could use some privacy."

"No!" Sophia shouted, then growing still, as though listening to something. "It can't end like this. Not like this. I won't let it," she said quietly. "Watch them!" she said to Dothan as she hurried to a valise on the table by the door. Removing a case from within, she extracted a syringe before saying to Ari, "Hold her." Ari holstered his gun and seized Ella in a choke hold from behind. Ella screamed and struggled when she saw the needle, but Ari held her still. Stuart considered charging Dothan while Ari's gun was in its holster, but the man had them both in his sights and never took his eyes off of them.

"No!" Ella cried as Sophia moved to her, the needle prepped and ready. Ella struggled in vain.

"It's okay," Sophia said soothingly. "It's fine. I won't hurt you." She pushed the needle into Ella's neck and pressed the plunger. "It will be alright, my love. Everything will be fine, I promise. I will make you forget all about this." Sophia returned the needle and case to her valise and said to Ari, "I need you to get the helicopter. Marcus is expecting us. Ella will be coming with us, so Dothan needs to stay behind." Ella's eyes locked with Stuart's and she silently mouthed two words to him. A minute later, her expression softened, and she stood on her own, no longer struggling against Ari. "You can let her go," said Sophia, stepping close to Ella and talking to her quietly, saying something Stuart could not hear. Ella continually nodded in agreement.

"What about them?" Dothan asked.

Sophia paused and looked at Stuart and Lori, contemplating. Stuart wondered if Ella's presence would change her mind about allowing them to leave. "Let them go."

"You promised me an opportunity for revenge!" Dothan said angrily.

Sophia sighed in irritation. "As long as they can walk out of here on their own, do what you want," she said as she moved to the door and paused again. "Actually, give Ari your gun." Ari chuckled in approval and held out his hand for Dothan's weapon, which Dothan made a show of handing over.

Ari took the pistol and held out his hand again. "For Yosef," he said. Dothan pulled a folding knife from his pocket and handed it to Ari.

"She has a gun on her," said Ari, "but she has no bullets." He put Dothan's gun under his belt at his back.

"If you get any blood on this floor, you clean it up before you leave," Sophia said to Dothan. Ari held the door open and Sophia left the room, leading Ella by the hand. With a nod to his companion, Ari followed them out and shut the door behind him.

CHAPTER FIFTY-FOUR
UNFINISHED BUSINESS

Dothan took off his gun holster and rolled his shoulders. Stuart took off his jacket and pulled his sweatshirt off over his head. He rolled the sweatshirt it into a bundle before handing both it and his jacket to Lori. He leaned close to whisper in her ear. "As soon as we start fighting, get to the door and get out of here. Keep the hoodie rolled up. The keys to my truck are in the jacket pocket. If he comes out, you know what happened to me. Just get away."

"I'm not leaving you alone with this guy," she whispered.

"If he beats me to death, there's no saying what he will do to you."

"Then don't let him."

"If you two are finished," said Dothan.

"Let her leave," Stuart told him. "It's me you want."

Dothan made a gesture to the door. "She is free to go. My fight is with you."

Lori took up her handbag and tucked Stuart's jacket and hoodie under her arm. She made her way to the door, looking at Stuart a final time before she exited. Stuart took off his glasses and put them on the seat of the chair. A second later, the door opened again and Lori stepped back through it. The two men looked at her.

"What?" asked Lori. "Stuart, just hurry up and kick his ass so we can get out of here."

Dothan wasted not another second and lunged in Stuart's direction. Stuart planted himself, thinking the man meant to tackle him, which would have been a fool's move, but he was just closing the distance. When Dothan was within striking distance, he snapped into a classic Krav Maga fighting stance before launching a series of punches that Stuart blocked while backing up. Stuart side-stepped and threw a spinning back fist that Dothan blocked and tried to grab, but Stuart managed to land a low punch to the ribs that forced Dothan back. Dothan preferred grappling; he was counting on his superior weight and strength advantage to give him an easy victory. He would have to be kept at a distance.

Stuart circled and put the open space of the room at his back to leave himself a retreat. Dothan stepped in and threw two quick high punches that Stuart blocked easily. Too easily, he realized too late, as these were a false attack for a low kick that Dothan landed on Stuart's forward leg. Pain shot through Stuart's leg as the kick struck his thigh and he nearly crumpled to the floor. Seeing his opponent off balance, Dothan quickly moved in for a front kick to Stuart's unprotected face. Rash, thought Stuart, who ducked under it by lowering himself to the floor and throwing a crouched sidekick into the knee of Dothan's supporting leg while his kick was still in the air. Dothan huffed in pain as he fell onto his back. Stuart jumped to his feet. The pain in his leg already subsiding. He did not attack his downed opponent, but withdrew a few steps and resumed his fighting stance. He could have taken a chance and moved in for a finish, but if Dothan managed to sweep his legs out from under him, it would become a wrestling matter, which was exactly what the man wanted, and what Stuart did not.

Dothan rose to his feet, nursing his injured leg. It was a transparent ploy as he was hurt, but not badly. He was a skilled fighter, but a lousy actor. Stuart knew when he hurt someone and so was all the more ready when Dothan charged again, this time with a front kick. Stuart blocked the kick and countered with a right punch that Dothan ducked and hooked at his elbow. Stuart moved to yank his right arm free of the hold, but Dothan twisted and swung his left arm around Stuart's neck. Stuart slammed the elbow of his left arm down and back into Dothan's ribs, but the man's grip tightened and he rasped in Stuart's ear, "I hope that bitch over there puts up a better fight."

Stuart struck another elbow shot to his ribs. Then a third. Dothan would not be able to withstand too many of those, but Stuart's strength was starting to wane. He threw his arm down to feel Dothan flinch in anticipation of another elbow strike, but Stuart threw his fist up and back, landing a blind punch to Dothan's eye. The choke hold was loosened and Stuart dropped to a crouch, slipping free. He threw a reverse elbow with his newly recovered right arm into Dothan's groin and the man doubled over, stepping back. Stuart sprang upright and spun around to slam a full force kick to the side of Dothan's neck.

Dothan fell onto the floor. Stuart kicked the prostrate man in the abs hard enough to move his motionless form over several tiles. Then he swiftly moved into a fighting crouch over his fallen adversary and raised his fist. "Stuart!" Lori shouted. He froze, his fist still raised, everything in him screaming for him to crush the man's head between his fist and the tile floor. For the flicker of an instant, Dothan's unconscious face turned into that of Rylen. "Stuart, don't," said Lori gently. "Come on. Let's go." Her hand was on his shoulder. Stuart rose and looked down at the man on the floor. It was Dothan. Stuart caught his breath and retrieved his glasses from the chair before the two left the dungeon together.

Sophia pulled into the parking garage of the Tellerson Foundation building. Something deep within Ella told her that she should be terrified, but she could not bring any feelings to the surface to act upon. "Are you going to use the Tungsten device on me?" she asked calmly, as though asking something trivial.

"Tell me the truth," said Sophia, "do you really love Paxton enough to want to spend the rest of your life with him?"

Ella considered. "No, I don't want to spend the rest of my life with him."

"Do you love me?"

"I think I did."

"You did, but you don't anymore?" asked Sophia.

"I didn't know what you really were until today. I saw and heard everything you said to Stuart."

"Pretend today never happened. Did you want to be with me? Not as friends, but as lovers?"

Ella felt a tear fall over her cheek, though she felt no sadness. "Yes, I really did."

Sophia nodded. "That's what I wanted to hear. And that is why I'm not giving up on you."

"What are you going to do?" Ella asked.

"I'm going to make this all go away. It will be like it never happened," said Sophia. "I will use the Tungsten when we get out to my yacht. There's no time now, we will be flying out to it soon. I know how you feel about heights, but I promise you will not feel the slightest fear. But first, I need to make sure you want to go with me. I can't have you undermine that before I have a chance to fix everything." Sophia tuned Ella's face to hers. "So you need to let me take care of everything. Will you do that for me?"

Though something in her called for her to resist, Ella ignored it. "Yes," she agreed.

CHAPTER FIFTY-FIVE

TO THE TOWER

Lori and Stuart drove in silence for some time. She had asked to drive, offering assurances that she could drive an extended cab pickup with no problem, but Stuart had insisted that he was fine. Finally, Lori asked, "Were you going to kill him if I hadn't stopped you?"

Stuart had been dreading that question. "I wish I had a distinguished accent," he said.

"What?"

"His accent," said Stuart. "I wish I had an accent like that. That's the problem with cool accents, they're always wasted on people who can't hear it themselves."

"Yeah, okay," she replied quietly.

"Was all that shit true?" he asked. "What Sophia said about you? You have a lab in your basement and your father is a Colombian drug lord? That you used that drug you gave me on your massage clients?"

"Stuart, it would take forever to explain... but yes, it was all true," she said. "But please promise to let me explain everything when this is over."

"I promise."

She remained quiet for a moment before asking, "where are we going?"

"To get Ella away from that lunatic. This Tungsten device she has--Ella told me about it on the way here. That's what

Sophia plans to use on her. She isn't just going to make Ella forget what she learned."

"What do you mean?"

He explained what had happened between Ella and Sophia the day before, including the device that Sophia used to turn a trained killer against her enemy. "Think about it. It can permanently reprogram someone's whole thought process. Sophia is a psycho and she's in love with Ella. With that device, she can make Ella into anything she wants her to be. Why make her forget something when Ella can find out about it again later? It would have the same destructive result. It would make more sense to change Ella in such a way that she won't care about anything Sophia has done. Or not care about anything but Sophia herself."

"My god. So where are we going?"

"When Sophia injected her, Ella mouthed the two words, *foundation*, and *rooftop*. You heard Sophia tell Ari to get the helicopter? There's a helipad on the Foundation rooftop. I could see it from Perry's office the day I met with him." Stuart thought of calling Lonnie before remembering he no longer had his phone. Lonnie would be a lot harder to look up than the local precinct. "Maybe I should try Detective Connelly again. He's friends with Ella."

"Again?"

"I spoke to him earlier today to get some help when Sophia kidnapped you," said Stuart. "He called Ella because he thought I was nuts."

"Will he believe you this time?"

"We can try. If we tell him Sophia abducted Ella *at gunpoint* right in front of us, and clearly said that she was going to the Foundation rooftop, I think he'll listen. Play up the story about her leaving a guy to guard us and fighting our way out. Maybe he'll take it seriously now. I don't know if he'll do more than tell us to come in and fill out a report, but maybe they'll send some patrols to check out the Foundation building. What happened last night? How did Sophia get you there?"

"After I drove you home last night. I called for a ride and went home."

"Thanks for the night in the back seat of my truck. You couldn't have had me go inside and go to bed?"

"I was pissed off," she said, darting a glance at him. "I thought about taking all of your clothes, so count yourself lucky. Anyway, I went out to my car from the shop this afternoon and those fucking thugs grabbed me. They must have been waiting. This time, they hit me from behind and got me into the van. They took me there. But you came for me, even after what I did to you," she finished, looking ashamed.

"Did they...?"

"No! Thank god. Nothing like that. They tied my hands and brought me to the dungeon. After what we just heard, Sophia probably would have killed them both."

"He was going to."

"What?"

"Dothan. He was going to rape you, beat you to death, or hurt you somehow. He said it in my ear when he had me in a choke hold."

"Oh," said Lori thoughtfully. "Is that why you went all berserker on him?"

Stuart nodded. "Yeah. That's why." A phone rang inside the truck. Stuart looked at Lori and she shrugged. "We know it isn't mine."

Lori searched over the back of her seat and found Ella's purse on the floor of the truck. "Oh, boy," she said as she took Ella's purse and found her phone within. "Paxton," she said, looking at the caller.

"That's Ella's boyfriend."

"What should I do?" asked Lori, showing the phone to Stuart.

He sighed and shook his head. "Just ignore it."

Lori put Ella's phone back into her purse after it stopped ringing. "The woman he loves has been abducted. Wouldn't you want to know?"

"Yes, but we have enough to worry about right now, like how we're going to get to the top floor of the Tellerson Foundation building."

"We? Meaning the two of us?" Lori asked.

"No, by *we*, I mean *me*. If I can get up there the way I'm thinking, I'll have to go in alone."

"And there it is," said Lori. "Let me ask you something. Sophia is a murderer and she has thugs with guns. Which one of us here has a gun?"

Stuart spared a smirk in her direction. "Very funny."

"I would never hurt you, Stuart," she said, putting a hand on his leg. "I could never shoot anyone. That's why it isn't loaded now; I don't even own any bullets for it. But it sure as hell will make someone pay attention."

"I knew it was empty last night."

She looked at him skeptically. "No, you didn't."

"You stayed on the other side of the table. You know I have trouble seeing in low light and it was aimed low, like you were going to shoot me in the crotch. You didn't want me to get a good look at the gun. I tried, but it was like you angled it deliberately so I couldn't. After you put it down on the table, I could tell it wasn't loaded, but the drug had already gone to work."

"Touché. The point is, Ella is your therapist. You almost beat a man to death just now. We got away, thanks to you-- again. Why go and risk your life for her?"

"She has good rates?" Stuart ventured. Lori gave a weak, humorless laugh. "Cops and I don't get along. And going to Connelly today made him think I'm unhinged. He didn't take a statement. He called my shrink. What does that tell you? All I know is that the police aren't going to do anything and if they do, it won't be in time to help Ella. Sophia had time to make it to the Foundation by now. Ari is going to fly them to some unknown location. If Sophia gets Ella onto that helicopter, there's no helping her. I don't want to let that happen. I asked her to come with me and now I'm the only hope she has."

"Before you decide to go in guns blazing, let's hear if her

cop friend will help." Before Lori could call the detective, Ella's phone rang. "Paxton again," said Lori, looking at it. "I think he should know."

"Okay," said Stuart, holding out his hand for the phone, "I'll talk to him."

Stuart answered the phone and introduced himself as a patient and friend of Ella's. He then went on to tell Paxton as briefly as he could that Sophia Rubinstein was dangerous and holding Sophia against her will. He did not want to sugarcoat the actual events, but going into excessive detail was unwise. The man sounded to be an impressive balance of concern and calm, neither too much of one over the other. When Paxton asked if the police had been called, Stuart told him that his friend was calling the police as they spoke. "Where did she take her? Where are you now?" Paxton asked.

Stuart considered not answering that question, but quickly thought better of it. "She was at the Tellerson Foundation building. We're ten minutes away."

"I'm about the same. I'll meet you there!" said Paxton.

"Give us your number. We will text you from the phone we have and call you when we get there," Stuart told him. Lori took out her phone and entered the number that Stuart repeated back to Paxton aloud before they hung up. "I guess he's coming along. Not sure how I feel about that."

"Let's see what the detective has to say," said Lori. When Connelly answered, Lori put him on speaker and explained who she was and what had happened since Stuart met with him earlier that day.

When she told him where Ella had been taken, he asked, "Did you say the Tellerson Foundation building?"

"Yes!" Stuart and Lori answered in unison.

"Oh, hell, listen, stay away from there! Come to the station, we'll take care of this," said Connelly.

"We're already there," Stuart lied. "We'll wait for you to get here. Ella is a friend of yours, detective. What kind of danger is she in?"

Connelly hesitated and spoke in a lower tone. "Perry Tellerson was killed last night at one of their satellite offices outside the city. I can't tell you any more than that because the Feds took the case directly and told us locals to piss off. And we were warned that any relevant details were to go directly to the FBI."

"That sounds time consuming, detective," Stuart said, driving faster.

"You did the right thing calling me. I'll handle it from here. We can't enter the building and search it based on a snippet of conversation you overheard while being held captive by a gun wielding man in another city! Doctor Pendelton is a lovely woman and every officer here will want to help, but you have to come to the station and let us do this the right way. And you can't tell anyone what I told you about Perry Tellerson. Even that little leak could cost me my pension."

Stuart took the phone from Lori. "We're on our way to the station now, detective," he lied. "I'm sure Ella will feel better knowing your pension is safe," he said in disgust before disconnecting the call.

CHAPTER FIFTY-SIX

STORMING THE CASTLE

Stuart pulled his truck into the public parking garage of the Tellerson Foundation Tower, where they told Paxton to meet them. They drove up as many levels as they could until reaching the private access level. They called Paxton, who was just blocks away. When she hung up the phone, Lori asked, "How do you plan on getting to the top floor? You going to scale the side of the building?"

"No, but I do know a thing or two about elevators," Stuart said, tapping at his phone. "I've worked on a lot of high rises in the Boston area. I work with security and building maintenance when contracted on a job. The Tellerson Foundation has the top two floors and leases the rest of it. Shue Bryson and Associates is the management company. When I came in for my meeting with Perry, I stopped and talked to the guard at the front desk to check in. They use the same contract security company all the Shue Bryson buildings use. It's the management company that hires out the building security contract."

At that moment, an SUV pulled into the parking space next to them and Paxton stepped out. Stuart got out of the truck and introduced himself before the two men got into his truck, where he introduced Lori and outlined what his plan was. Stuart's immediate impression of Paxton was that he was quick and capable. He wasn't a fighter, but was solidly built and clear-headed. He was also ready to face armed men with two total strangers, which marked him as a man of action in Stuart's opinion. After a brief argument about whether Lori would be entering the building with the two men, Stuart relented. Paxton expressed a wish that he had one of his pistols with him, but he couldn't return home and meet his two callers in time. At that point, Stuart insisted that Lori leave her unloaded revolver in the truck. They had no idea whether the police would be arriving soon, as was the hope, and they did not want to be found in the building with a gun, whether it was unloaded not. He then handed her the key to his truck, saying that she may need to leave without him, but he would not be leaving without her.

After Lori walked the private access parking levels to make sure Sophia's Aston Martin was there, she returned to the truck and Stuart coached Lori on exactly what to say when she called the front security desk. Paxton went out to the sidewalk and called Stuart when he was able to see the security guard in the lobby. Lori called the number Stuart found and Paxton confirmed that it was the right number when the guard picked up the phone. Stuart gave Lori a thumbs up and she said sweetly, "Hi, Officer Fields, I don't think I've met you yet. This is Amy Lux with Shue Bryson & Associates. I was supposed to call Gene today, and I completely forgot. We've had complaints from tenants about the doors to elevator one taking a very long time to open when arriving at any of the higher floors. Has service been on site yet?" she asked. "Oh, thank goodness, that would have put me in some real trouble," she laughed flirtatiously. "If you can, would you please disable that elevator at the console until they arrive? They should be there before nine. Thank you so much. Bye."

Stuart got out and took a number of items from the storage box in the bed of his truck. He was especially glad he had never bothered to return the ID badge to the company he previously worked for, but the overalls with the company name would be as convincing to security as any ID badge they never bothered to look at. By the time Paxton returned to the truck, Stuart was fully prepared for his part. Stuart took the garage elevator down to the main lobby and introduced himself to the guard. After being shown which elevator required inspection, Stuart told the officer that he could activate the elevator at the front console, as he would tape off the door at the lobby and isolate it from the call system until he was done. He was sure to mention that he had two trainees with him and that they would be down to sign in as well. When Stuart had control of the elevator car, he called Lori and told her that she and Paxton could join him in the lobby. He had outfitted the pair with as much equipment and apparel as might be convincing, but still did his best to distract the guard when his two passengers signed in. He quickly ushered the two workers into the elevator before the guard could get too close a look at them.

"I disabled the cameras in here," said Stuart, inwardly laughing at the massively over-sized overalls and ball cap that Lori was wearing. She was a stark contrast to the spare vest and safety goggles he had given Paxton.

"I cannot believe that worked," said Lori as she pulled off the overalls and cap, having kept her jacket on under it to give herself bulk.

"Neither can I," said Stuart as he took off his own as well. He then rolled up their disguises and stuffed them into the large toolbox he carried. When the elevator doors opened, the trio found themselves standing in a dark office space. "Follow me. Keep quiet," he said as they moved through the dark cubicle spaces. Stuart took one turn and paused at metal double doors. He tested them to find them locked.

"What is this?" asked Lori in a hushed tone.

Stuart quickly checked the edges of the door before pulling a crowbar from his toolbox. "Freight elevator. It goes down to the garage; we'll need it since we can't go back through the lobby. We may have to carry Ella out, so this is our escape route," he said, giving the crowbar four sharp tugs before the lock snapped and they were in. After making sure this elevator was not locked off, Stuart left his toolbox in the landing area and the three of them cautiously made their way to the other side of the floor.

"Think anyone heard that?" asked Paxton.

"Tellerson was killed last night," said Stuart, annoyed at the man's timing of the question. "The offices were probably closed today."

After passing Tellerson's office, they turned into a corridor that led to a lounge. The only way out to the rooftop was by passing through the lounge at the end of the corridor. The rooftop deck was the area that Stuart could see from Perry's office windows, which was how he spotted the helipad at the far side. The three were halfway down the corridor to the lounge when a hushed voice said, "Don't go in there yet." They turned to see Steve McGuire approaching them. He held a tablet device. "Come this way," he said.

"We're here for our friend," said Stuart defiantly. "Sophia Rubinstein has drugged and abducted her. She's about to fly off somewhere and we're here to see that doesn't happen before the police get here. They're already on the way."

"The helicopter is coming, but we still have time," said Steve. "In here," he told them, entering the nearest office and leaving the light out. Stuart glanced at the others in confirmation. They nodded. They entered the office and shut the door. Steve turned the blinds on the window that looked out to the corridor so they could see out, but no one passing would see them. Then he said, "Sophia is in the lounge with your friend. Now that you mention it, something did seem off about her. But she's also in there with Marcus Harrier, another board member, and his private armed security. Sophia killed Perry Tellerson and three other men last night."

"She killed my friend this morning," said Stuart. "She boasted about it."

"Ira Calovik?" Steve asked. Stuart nodded. "I knew that was her doing. Your friend got killed because he saw the same video I did. When I ran his fingerprints off of my phone and found out who he really was, I also found that he was dead within hours of stealing the video from me. I decided to be a little more careful about who I told. I spent the rest of the day making absolutely certain that Sophia and Marcus were not in on it together. They are old friends, maybe even lovers, but I'm sure he doesn't know about what really happened to Perry. I was about to go in and tell him in front of her, but then you came. I've been watching the three of you since you entered the building."

"Why should we trust you?" Stuart asked.

"Perry and I were not always in agreement. Who do you think sent you the warning, Stuart?"

"What was the warning?" asked Stuart, testing him.

"To stop looking."

"And?" In reply, Steve merely turned his gaze to Lori. This satisfied Stuart, who then said, "Sophia was telling the truth? You knew what Rylen did to that woman's daughter?" Steve remained silent, but shame was evident on his face. "You knew what my brother was. You knew what he was doing!"

"Look, judge me all you want, but we don't have time for this," he said. "Do you want to get your friend out of here or not?"

"The police really are on the way," said Stuart. "We have to make sure Sophia doesn't leave with Ella before they get here."

"The police won't get here in time," Steve replied. "Take my word for that."

CHAPTER FIFTY-SEVEN

SHOWDOWN ON THE ROOFTOP

Marcus, Sophia, and Ella sat enjoying drinks in the comfort of the plush leather seats in the center of the lounge as they waited on the helicopter that would take them to Sophia's yacht. Ella sat quietly, occasionally contributing to the conversation. Sophia had told Marcus that Ella was nervous about flying in a helicopter, and so had too much to drink before they arrived. Marcus was disappointed that Sophia had surprised him with the addition of a friend, especially given all that she had been through in the last twenty-four hours. He was gentleman enough not to show it and trusted that Sophia had an excellent reason for bringing this woman along. Doctor Ella Pendelton was very beautiful, if a little odd, and it was Sophia's boat they were going to. Nonetheless, this was more of a protection excursion than a pleasure outing; he had private concerns about bringing an outsider with them.

The lounge they were in was a twenty-by-sixty-foot room that had a full glass wall on the long side opposite the entrance from the corridor. The glass wall looked out to a rooftop patio and had double glass doors at each end of the lounge. Beyond the patio was a long stretch of paving used to extend the patio for large gatherings. At the far end of that, the paved area ended at the raised helipad on the very edge of the building rooftop.

The trio talked about what happened to Perry Tellerson the night before and what would happen to the structure of the Foundation without him. Sophia told Marcus that she had turned the hit man with a bribe and sent him back to attack Perry himself. Marcus worried about discussing this in front of Ella, but Sophia's assurances that Ella could be trusted without question went far to gain his confidence. Marcus had received the message that Perry sent out before being shot by Christoph, though why the man then took his own life was a complete mystery. Marcus would get to the bottom of it in due time. However, in the immediate crisis, a cleanup had taken place before the FBI had been called in thanks to the quick actions of Steve McGuire. Doctor Anlo and Chase were eliminated altogether from the narrative given to the FBI, and their bodies were never found on the property. Neither man would ever be seen again. Marcus decided the best thing that he and Sophia could do was stay as far away from that mess as possible, since none of the other members of the board even knew that he was now in the US. Sophia was safe; that mattered more to him than anything else. An emergency meeting of the board was called for the following day and he would attend it virtually from Sophia's yacht.

Patrick, Marcus' personal security, sat at the mini bar at the end of the lounge, nearest the door, tapping at his phone. Having already surveyed the floor and found it secure, Patrick relaxed his guard as they awaited the helicopter. Ari, Sophia's new driver and pilot--though she was quite capable of piloting herself--had been sent to her yacht. He was bringing the helicopter to the Foundation rooftop where they all waited. As the helicopter was a four seater, Ella's unexpected presence was quickly accommodated and Marcus instructed Patrick to wait behind, as they would need less security on Sophia's yacht. After all, it was miles offshore and the pilot could make a second trip to return for him.

A man whom Marcus recognized from a photo entered the lounge. He was disheveled and looking haggard, but walked to them with determination. He was followed by Steve McGuire.

"What's going on here?" asked Marcus, standing. Sophia

stood as well.

"My name is Stuart Hollister," Stuart answered. He was immediately intercepted by Patrick.

"I know who you are. That's not what I asked," said Marcus, stepping in front of Sophia.

Stuart looked from one to the other of them, ignoring the bulky man in a suit right in front of him. "I'm here because your friend there drugged Doctor Ella Pendelton and is holding her here against her will."

"Marcus," said Steve, "listen to what he has to say. He's telling the truth."

Marcus looked at Ella, who sat quietly observing, entirely unperturbed by any of it. "I will do nothing of the kind," said Marcus.

"Patrick," Sophia said, "escort this man from the building."

"I have proof," Stuart said, holding up a device he held in his hand.

Marcus put his hand on Patrick's shoulder, and the man stepped aside. "What proof?"

Stuart played part of a recording of the conversation he had with Sophia in the dungeon. He played only the few seconds of the conversation where Sophia admitted to killing Rylen. Sophia was dumbstruck. "That's impossible," she said.

"Not with this," said Stuart, holding out the device he held. It was the microcassette recorder he had stolen from Detective Connelly's desk. "Your thug never checked my hood when he searched me. I heard you people can create dead zones for wireless devices, meaning you can disable any transmission device. This is a microcassette recorder. There was nothing for your jammer to disable. You can keep this, if you want. That was the only snippet I had time to copy," he lied. "I hope you don't mind if I keep the original, because, well... analog. Sometimes old school just fucking works."

Sophia looked at Marcus and then back to Stuart. "You poor idiot. Do you really suppose I can be convicted of murder on the basis of that?" she asked, pointing to the device in his hand.

"A little time studying the law might save you a lot of time and effort in the future."

"You're right, but I can let a lot of people know what it is that you did." Stuart told her. "But the murder of my friend by your men today won't certainly help your case. You killed him because you knew he found out what you did to Perry Tellerson. You probably thought he managed to hack into the Foundation security system, but he never could. That was why you wanted my phone. He sent me a message telling me about it, so you needed mine too."

"But Calovik got the video from me," said Steve.

Stuart gestured to Marcus. "Something I'm betting your friend here doesn't know."

At this, Sophia smiled. Marcus put his hand on Sophia's back. "Don't say another word, love," he said. "Mr. Hollister, I suggest you come back with the police if you have some evidence of a crime. Otherwise, you will be arrested for trespassing if you are seen in this building again." He turned to Patrick. "See Mr. Hollister out."

"I have something you should see before you leave here with Sophia," said Steve.

"What would that be?" Marcus asked, holding up his hand again and signaling Patrick to take a step back.

Steve continued, "When The Church went black for two hours last night, I used a back door I installed in the system to reactivate the video feed."

Marcus glared hard at Steve. "You deliberately violated blackout protocol?"

"I had excellent reason. Perry had gone so far out of bounds, he couldn't even see the field anymore. Just watch," he told the room, tapping a few buttons on a tablet he carried.

"Wait! Whatever you're going to show me, we need to get this man out of..."

"He can stay," Steve said. "He already knows. It's why he's here. Stuart has been working with a man named Ira Calovik, AKA Spider. He was a gray hat hacker Stuart hired to help him investigate his brother's death. He was not able to penetrate our protections, so he used a more direct approach and hacked my company phone."

Marcus' eyes widened. "Our phones cannot be..."

"Not remotely," Steve interrupted. "He ran into my car on the street this morning and pretended to be a drunk driver. While he was giving me all of his fake information, he picked my pocket and paired my phone with one of his own devices. I found my phone on the front seat of my car when I went to get in it after the exchange. I thought I'd dropped it. When I downloaded the video from The Church, it went to my phone. I was going to send it to you before I knew I had been breached and the phone was sending the video to an unknown location. I put it together and checked my phone for fingerprints that I ran through the police database. Still, he got a copy of the video. I don't know how Sophia found out that he acquired it, but she knew who he was because she had spy software on Rylen's phone--the one that Stuart had given to Calovik to help him find her. She sent Ari and Dothan after Calovik to stop him from sending it to the police, or to anyone else."

The video of everything that transpired at The Church played through.

CHAPTER FIFTY-EIGHT
SHOWDOWN IN CHURCH

The front gate to The Church opened as soon as the car approached, closing when it had passed through. The bollards had already been down, but they now raised back into place. The Lincoln pulled up to the front walkway. Perry stood framed in the doorway. As Christoph exited the car with the laptop bag in his hand, he opened the trunk where Sophia waited inside, gagged with her hands cuffed behind her back. He roughly pulled her out of the trunk to her feet. She had clearly been beaten, but was mostly unharmed. She wore plain black yoga pants and white sneakers with a t-shirt that was several sizes too large.

Perry turned and entered the building without a word. If Perry had more than one security person with him, her plan would fail spectacularly and she would never leave the building alive. If not... Christoph half walked, half dragged Sophia inside. Chase, Perry's personal security, closed and secured the door behind them when they entered. "This way," Perry said, already several steps ahead. Sophia was taken to an empty utility room off of the boardroom on the second floor. The space was being used for the storage of unused computer equipment racks, but had been prepared for another purpose.

A man Sophia had never seen waited inside. He was wearing a bowling shirt with khaki shorts and boating shoes. If this man was to be her interrogator, clearly he hadn't planned on it himself. He had a plain blue gym bag sitting on a long folding table at the side of the room. A metal folding chair had been placed in the middle of the room. The entire scene was one of hasty improvisation. Christoph sat Sophia down on the folding chair and reached behind her head to undo the gag, pausing to meet Perry's eye questioningly. Perry nodded and Christoph removed the gag. He dropped it onto the table, followed by the laptop bag he carried.

Sophia looked up at Perry with a look of resignation. "I am insulted. Only two men," she said wearily.

Perry smirked. "And I am disappointed that it was overkill. Doctor Anlo here is going to see that I get all the information I need. I don't suppose you would just save me the trouble and give me the files now?"

"There's nothing on that laptop, so go fuck yourself," Sophia spat.

"Those designs would have made us a fortune. I can't let that information die with you. I take no pleasure in this, Sophia," Perry said with a look of solemnity that would have convinced anyone who didn't know the man. "I truly don't."

"Even if you make me tell you where there are, you'll never be able to get them." Sophia laughed.

"We'll find out, then, won't we?"

"Tell me something," said Sophia, looking at the floor as she collected herself, then looking Perry in the eye, "how is the Foundation doing? I assume you got a suitable replacement for Rylen, hmm? How instrumental was that fucking rapist to your finances that his removal could not be accomplished within a year! What happened when he died? Did the Foundation go into a death spiral? Did your criminal dealings grind to a halt?"

"If you had waited a little longer..."

"What? You would have cut his pay? You refused to do anything because he was making you too much money on the side, with all those fucking land deals and selling weapons designs to the highest bidder?" Sophia was tense with rage and went to stand, but Christoph was standing behind her and forced her back down to the chair.

"How many millions did you make because of me and those deals?" said Perry. "I promised you everything and I delivered. Well, I couldn't have done any of it without Rylen."

"She was my daughter! He was responsible for..."

"Nothing!" Perry shouted back. "He was a man who took advantage of a young girl's attraction to him. He didn't kill your daughter, she took her own life! You were too blinded by your own rage to see it," Perry paused to calm his own irritation before continuing in a lower tone, "and those deals were good enough for you when you were getting a cut of the action. The real tragedy here is that you let this lead to your own death. It didn't have to come to this. You stole from the hand that fed you."

"You can't do anything to me here," said Sophia with a laugh. "The Church can be monitored by any one of the others. The board will know that you have gone rogue."

"You're right," Perry admitted, "they didn't agree to this. That's why I had to disable all monitoring systems in The Church. We went black two hours ago. One privilege of my position. Like I said, I'm not happy about this. I promise it will be painless."

Sophia's face transformed from a visage of rage to one of beatific calm. "Thank you," she said.

Christoph's gun came out of its holster and fired a single round past Perry's face and into the forehead of Chase, standing a few feet behind. Christoph then crossed his right hand over his chest and glanced left as he fired two rounds into the chest of Anlo, who had been waiting to begin his work. The interrogator fell back, knocking over the folding table as he dropped to the floor. Two men were dead, and the gun was pointing at Perry's face before three seconds had elapsed. Even if Perry carried a gun, and he did not, he would have been the third corpse in the room before he could have drawn it and fired against his own assassin.

Perry took a step back and raised his hands. "Christoph,

listen, whatever she offered you..."

"Oh, shut up, Perry." Sophia stood up, her hands free from the cuffs. "Sit down."

Perry made no move to comply, but Christoph stepped closer and Perry did as she said. "How did she turn you?" he asked Christoph, but the question was ignored.

Sophia stared at Perry and shook her head piteously as he turned from her to the gunman. "With a fool like you at the helm, it's a wonder our little secret society had managed to get away with it at all. You bring an enemy into your most secure location, you tell me how many men you have, and then tell me you have disabled all video monitoring both inside and out." Perry's eyes shifted. "Worst of all, you trust your hit man so completely that you don't even search me? You might have noticed that these aren't even real handcuffs!" she said, tossing the cuffs to the floor at his feet. Perry's eyes glanced down at the handcuffs as they landed in front of him. When he glanced back up, Christoph had handed her the second gun he had in the holster at his hip. Sophia took it and shot Perry in his leg.

Perry gasped and pulled the dart he found protruding from his thigh. "What was that! What did you do to me?"

"I promise it will be painless," she answered.

Sophia had prepared a dart loaded with S-24. They waited. Perry sat waiting to die, but he did not fall to the floor. Once she was satisfied that he was under its influence, she asked, "How did you know I was the one who took the data files for those weapons projects last year?"

"Lori Mercer," he replied. "She told me about your hiring her to hypnotize Rylen for you. When I told her that you used to work for me, she thought she could buy my good will with tip. You used her and set her up for Rylen's death, so she had no qualms about telling anything that might help her."

"What tip? I never told her anything about that."

"She said you once told her that you used to work on some interesting projects for your former employer and took some information with you when you left. She had no idea what that meant, but since I was your former employer, she thought I might. She was right. I knew exactly what it meant."

There it was. A seemingly innocuous comment made to someone to whom it would mean nothing had come back to haunt her. Perry had inadvertently gleaned the truth from the statement and thought Sophia had been behind the missing files. This, as it turned out, was entirely true. However, Sophia had been thinking of the Tungsten device when she had said that to Lori; the stolen data files were something else altogether. "What were you going to do with the project files once you got them?" asked Sophia, knowing the answer, but wanting to have the confirmation from his own lips.

"I was going to reach out to the potential buyers I had lined up last year to see if they were still interested," came his predicted response.

"For yourself?"

"Of course," he answered. "I wouldn't have to tell the others I recovered the designs. I did this all on my own."

Sophia took his company phone and instructed him to take her down to the vault and open it. He complied. She then entered the vault and had Perry provide her with an external hard drive containing all of their library's research data, prototype plans, and pharmaceutical formulas, both theoretical and completed. She then instructed Perry to wipe every local copy and cloud backup of the data research archives he had just given her. Any finished drug samples and prototypes small enough for her to easily carry were given to her as well. She instructed Christoph to load everything into the trunk of the car he brought her in. The twelve-year-old car was one which Christoph had purchased in cash at her instruction that very evening.

She had Perry open the gates and lower the security bollards before she led the two men back into the vault. She gave them each a set of specific instructions.

An emergency video call from Perry Tellerson went out to the eight other members of the board. "The rumors were true," he said, sounding frantic, as instructed. Sophia stood outside the room with Christoph. "The Foundation has been infiltrated and The Church has been compromised. I am on site now. I accused Sophia Rubinstein of working with the FBI. She had nothing to do with it, and I suspected her of corporate espionage. It is my own fault for not finding the real conspirator sooner."

Christoph entered the room and fired one round through the back of Perry's head. Perry slumped over the table. Christoph then picked up the phone and made sure his face was seen by the camera. Then he dropped the phone on the floor and fired a round through that as well. Lastly, he put the barrel of his gun inside his mouth and fired one final time.

The old Lincoln drove through the open front gates.

When the video finished, Marcus turned to Sophia, a horrified expression on his face. "My god, love, what have you done?" Steve McGuire had edited the video down for length, but included the most crucial parts in the few minutes he showed the room.

"Done?" Sophia spat. "He sent a fucking hit man after me, and for what? All so he could torture me for some fucking tech files?"

"She had the hacker who got a copy of the video killed this morning after he sent Stuart here a message telling him what he'd found."

"You what?" asked Marcus.

"It's true," Stuart confirmed. "I'll be happy to send you a copy of the tape, too."

"Marcus," said Sophia, "you know I was the victim here."

"I know! I'm on your side. That's why I came here, to help you! That," he said, pointing to the monitor, "was not self-defense! That was using his own plan against him so you could steal all the data files from the archives? You murdered this..."

"Spider," Stuart supplied.

"This computer hacker for finding out what you did?" A

thought occurred to him. "Bloody hell, is that what I think it is?" he asked, pointing to the laptop bag and the large duffel bag by her chair--the luggage that Sophia had been prepared to bring with her. "Did you really drug and abduct this woman?" Marcus asked, his head reeling.

"She drugged Doctor Pendelton here the same way she drugged Perry and Christoph," said Steve.

"So what now, Marcus?" asked Sophia, folding her arms defiantly, Patrick still standing behind her. "Are you going to side with them? Are you leaving with me, or are you going to turn me over to the police?"

Marcus sighed and gave her such a pained expression that he knew she would know what he had to do. There was no need for him to say it. "Even I cannot protect you from this, love," he told her.

"Meaning you're going to turn me in to the police," she said, twisting her upper body to look at Patrick behind her as he put his hand on her shoulder, "or are you going to have your man here do it for you?"

"Sophia, you haven't left me any..." Marcus began, but never finished. A gunshot exploded in the room and Patrick fell back to the floor, a hole in his chest.

Sophia had her hand on a gun the entire time her arms were folded. She was wearing a holster under her jacket and had just fired through the holster and the back of her jacket to kill Patrick standing behind her. With the speed of a viper that not even Stuart could react to, she pulled the pistol free and held the three men at gunpoint.

"Sophia, think it through," said Steve. "Where can you go?"

"Any fucking place I want," she answered, backing away a few steps to better keep the three men in her sights. "Ella!" said Sophia, "Pick up those bags and get behind me." Ella stood, but did not reply. "Ella, do it now." Ella slowly rose and, with visible reluctance, picked up the large duffel bag and laptop bag from the floor before she walked to stand behind Sophia. Then Sophia aimed and fired her gun a second time.

CHAPTER FIFTY-NINE
WHO ARE YOU PEOPLE

Steve McGuire's head snapped back as the bullet entered just under his left eye and exited out of the back of his skull. Stuart flinched, thinking for a split second that he might be able to tackle her, but she was too far, and that slight twitch caused her to point the gun at him.

"Sophia!" shouted Marcus. "What are you doing!"

"Waiting for my ride," she said, glancing out of the windows to the helicopter that was just landing on the pad.

"You just murdered two innocent people!" he exclaimed. The man had a gift for the obvious, thought Stuart. Marcus was apparently not used to seeing violence, but on reflection, Stuart had never seen someone murdered either.

Sophia gave a little shrug. "Your man was invading my personal space," she said. "And if Steve had just done his job and stayed out of it instead of violating blackout protocol, this wouldn't have happened."

"Are you going to kill *me* now?" said Marcus. "Are you really going to shoot me too?"

"Only if you try to stop me," she answered. "Please, Marcus, don't try to stop me."

"I won't, but Steve was right. There's no place that you can go."

"Obviously, you have no idea what I'm capable of," Sophia answered, glancing out to the helicopter. Ari was already making his way down the small flight of steps from the helipad to the main rooftop deck.

"And me?" Stuart asked.

Sophia turned a dead eye stare upon him. "If you miss your brother so fucking much..."

"Sophia!" cried Ella. "Don't! Please."

Stuart spotted Lori when she and Paxton peeked around the corner; he desperately hoped that Marcus would not to indicate he had seen anyone over Sophia's shoulder.

"Ella?" said Sophia, glancing back at her. "No! Not yet!" she shouted, her composure gone.

"Please don't hurt anyone else," said Ella. The drug was wearing off.

Stuart's left hand fell on Marcus' right shoulder and he shoved the man aside at the same time that his right hand threw the microcassette recorder at Sophia. The device struck her squarely in the forehead just as she turned back to the men she had in her sights. Stuart crouched as he lunged toward her, glad that her gun didn't fire when she got hit. She recovered fast, but he was already on her, knocking the gun to the floor and twisting one of her arms behind her back. Sophia struggled furiously to keep Stuart from securing her other arm, but he managed to grab her upper arm with his free hand, ending her struggle.

Paxton ran to Ella and embraced her, but Ella had not fully returned to herself. "They're with me!" said Stuart to Marcus. "They came to help me get Ella out of here." Paxton tried to lead Ella from the room, but she resisted. Ari was approaching.

"Get her out of the way!" Marcus yelled to Paxton, as Ella and Paxton were between him and the approaching pilot. Marcus picked up Sophia's gun as Paxton dragged the struggling Ella to the side of the room. He pushed her to the floor behind one of the leather sofas and lay atop her. Ari entered the lounge through the sliding glass doors to the patio. His eyes fell on Sophia and Stuart in the middle of the lounge. He immediately reached inside his jacket, drawing an automatic pistol.

"Drop it!" Marcus yelled, pointing Sophia's Ruger directly at him.

Ari froze until Sophia shouted, "Shoot him!"

Ari raised the gun and Marcus fired into the center of Ari's chest. The man fell face-first to the floor. Stuart felt Sophia's muscles slacken in his grip, but he held on all the tighter, not falling for that trick. Paxton stood and helped Ella to stand.

"Somebody, get his gun," said Marcus.

"I got it," said Paxton, taking up the automatic pistol from the floor and handing it to Marcus, who examined it and engaged the safety before tucking it under his belt.

Marcus told Stuart to make Sophia sit down on the floor with her back to the wall and her legs stretched out in front of her. Paxton took Ella aside as she was returning to normal. At that moment, Lori reentered the lounge from the hallway. Stuart went to her, glad to find her unhurt. Marcus continued to keep watch over Sophia with her own gun. He had such a look of despair that Stuart felt for the man. "I never would have believed you a murderer," Marcus said.

"There's still time," said Sophia. "You can shoot them and we can get away together."

The look of awe and misery that Marcus cast down at her was one Stuart knew well. It was a look one might have when he learned that someone he loved, respected, and admired turned out to be the most despicable of human beings. Marcus said, "You just ordered that man to shoot me. Me! I've known you the whole of my adult life."

"The men you just killed may have had wives, children, parents, siblings, friends... Somebody loved them. Every life you take destroys more than one," Stuart said. "You should have learned that by now."

"I'm sorry, who the hell are you people?" asked Marcus. "I recognize you," he said to Stuart. "You're Rylen's brother. But..." he trailed off, looking at the rest of them.

Stuart answered, "They're with me. That's Ella's boyfriend, Paxton," he said, pointing to the man at Ella's side. "Ella is my court-appointed therapist. And this is Lori, my dominatrix," he finished, choosing to ignore the look of incredulity on Marcus' face.

Lori sighed and shook her head. "Hi, lovely to meet you," she said dryly.

"I came here with the two of them to get Ella out of here," said Paxton. "Can we please move to another room while we wait for the police?" he asked, looking to Steve's body on the floor.

"Phones won't work anywhere on this floor. I can't call security and the police and watch her at the same time."

"I'll watch her," said Stuart. Marcus extended Sophia's gun to him. "I don't need a gun."

"Yes, you do," Marcus insisted.

"I'll do it," said Paxton, holding out his hand for the gun.

"I would rather you do it," said Marcus to Stuart. "My dearest friend just held me at gunpoint and ordered me shot. I don't know you from Adam and you pushed me out of the way before attacking her. I don't know him either, but I know whose side I'm on."

"I don't do guns," Stuart refused again.

Marcus handed Paxton Sophia's gun and went out to the patio with his phone in his hand.

"Ella," said Sophia. Ella looked at her, but said nothing. "I want you to know that I'm so sorry. It wasn't supposed to happen like this. Why did you have to come to the dungeon tonight?"

"Because I'm an idiot. I thought the friend I loved was in trouble," cried Ella, tears welling up in her eyes.

Sophia hung her head for a moment. "Friend? Just a friend? You risked your life for me. I want you to know that I planned on our having a future. A long and happy one."

"What?" said Paxton. "What the hell are you talking about?" he asked, keeping the gun expertly trained on the woman he was guarding. Sophia ignored him.

"I'll tell you later," Ella said to him quietly, though Stuart still heard it.

When Marcus returned a few minutes later, Sophia said, "Ari has the archives."

Marcus froze and looked at her. "What?"

"Careful," said Stuart to Marcus in a whisper.

"The files I took. The archives from the Foundation's database. I transferred the files to a thumb drive Ari has on his key ring," she told him.

Marcus moved to walk to Ari's body, but Stuart stopped him. "Watch her. I'll check his key ring."

Stuart walked to Ari's body cautiously. For all he knew, the man might have had a Kevlar vest. He crouched over the man. He was undoubtedly dead, as the blood was starting to pool out from under the body. Paxton turned to Sophia, the gun down at his side. "What did you mean? You planned on having a future with Ella?" he asked her again.

This time, Sophia looked him in the eye when she answered. "Paxton, I need you to remember who controls you."

CHAPTER SIXTY

JUMP

Paxton blinked twice and, in the interval between them, he regained his memory of recent events that had been locked behind a closed door in his mind--one he did not know was there.

Paxton met his new client, Brandon Holdshire, at his office. After going through the concept plans he had designed for the mixed-use property on Boston's south side for an hour, Brandon received a text message. The owner of the company of which Holdshire Realty was a subsidiary had arrived and was in her office. She asked Brandon to send Paxton to her office with the plans for the project as soon as the two of them were done. Paxton's heart beat faster, though he could not let it show.

He had met Carmen Reese on his last visit and, though the meeting started professionally enough, there was a visceral attraction between them that was not like anything he had ever experienced before. Their conversation continued to deviate from the project that they were there to discuss and move into personal topics. Finally, at one point, as they were leaning over the large glass table across which the drawings had been laid out, she drew close and kissed him. It was gentle and probing, as if she were overcoming a shyness and throwing herself into an overture that might explode in her face. He did not pull away. The kiss quickly turned passionate and progressed to a point that ended with the two of them having sex on the sofa in her office.

When it was over, she was quiet and embarrassed, confessing that she had never done anything of the kind before and did not want for this to be the last time they saw each other. It was odd that the woman who never did anything like that had condoms in the cabinet of her private office bathroom, but she was no doubt involved with someone else, same as he was.

Brandon pointed him to the office at the end of the hall as he put on his coat, but Paxton remembered its location well. The door was closed when he reached it, so he knocked. "Come in," replied Carmen's voice from the inside. Paxton entered to see Carmen standing in front of her desk, wearing a black lace bra and matching thong, with stockings, a garter belt, and stiletto pumps. She looked awkward and uncomfortable as she pointed to the door. "Best lock it behind you," she said in a hushed tone. Paxton smiled and locked the door.

"You look breathtaking," he told her honestly.

Carmen giggled, blushing as she walked toward him with a coquettish air. "I was hoping you'd like it," she said. She took the roll of drawings from his hand and dropped them to the floor. "I love the design. You're hired," she said, wrapping her arms around his neck and kissing him, gently at first. Then harder. Her hands probed for his belt buckle. She pushed him back against the door and pulled his pants down to his ankles.

He was fully hard already, and she dropped to her knees, taking him into her mouth. Paxton gasped and braced against the door as she tried to swallow the whole of his length. After a minute, she removed a condom hidden in the cup of her bra and sheathed him. Then she stood and tugged him by his proud cock, leading him to the sofa, nearly tripping him as he clumsily stepped out of his pants on the floor. He fumbled with the top few buttons on his shirt, but gave it up and pulled it off over his head. The couch leather was cold against his skin as she pushed him onto it and straddled his hips. She guided him into position before thrusting him inside of her.

She rode him hard for a few minutes before thrashing into the throes of orgasm. She kept her hands wrapped around his neck, grabbing his hair and forcing him to look into her eyes as she came. She never blinked, but laughed in a way that chilled the marrow in his bones. The woman was insatiable and multi-orgasmic. She came twice more before he finally released himself, locking his arms around her as she pressed his face into her chest.

They held each other, sweaty, locked, and panting, until she slowly peeled herself from him and rose up, pulling herself off of him and drawing him out of her before she collapsed to the couch.

Paxton felt the mini water balloon at the tip of the condom. "Uh, I'll be right back," he said, and she favored him with a limp-handed gesture toward the bathroom on the other side of the office, still breathless.

When Paxton returned from the bathroom, Carmen was holding two glasses and brought one to him. "A toast to our newfound relationship," she said. He took it tentatively and raised it before throwing it back. She put their glasses away, and they both sat on the couch, an awkward silence lingering in the air. She sat close to him with her head against his shoulder, stroking her hand over his chest, remaining in that attitude for some minutes.

"Listen," he began, "I need to tell you, I'm with someone. We live together."

She looked at him with a horror-stricken expression for a moment. Then she laughed and leaned her head back against his shoulder. "I figured as much."

"Just now, when you said, *our newfound relationship*, I realized we never talked about that," he told her. "Are you married?"

Carmen looked up into his face with an expression that was a mixture of pity and disbelief before she shifted, putting a slight space between them. "I like your watch. Let me see it."

Paxton, feeling a sense of post-orgasmic grogginess, held out his hand to her so she could see the timepiece on his wrist. Carmen took his hand with both of hers, "Thanks, it was a gift from..."

"Do you wear it at night when you're sleepy and completely relaxed, when you're so comfortable and drifting off, with your eyes closing and falling so deep that all thoughts are drifting, *sleep*." Carmen's hand touched his forehead and his eyes closed. Her voice continued talking to him, but it sounded like she was somewhere far away. Her voice faded until silence drowned it out altogether.

His eyes snapped open and he looked about in confusion. Carmen was still next to him on the couch, looking at him. "Did I start dozing off?"

She stood and went to where her clothes lay on the desk, ignoring his question. She slid on a short, black skirt and a blouse of red silk. Paxton stood and pulled on his pants. He reached for his shirt on the floor, but Carmen said, "Leave it. Sit down on the couch and don't move," she told him. He did so. She then went behind the desk and produced a black case, from which she removed what looked like a silver virtual reality headset.

"What's that?" Paxton asked as Carmen walked over and put the laptop on the couch next to him.

"Be quiet and let me put this on you. Keep your eyes open and follow all the instructions," she said, putting it down over his eyes and adjusting the headphones.

Sometime later--how much later Paxton could not discern--Carmen lifted the device from his head and placed it next to the laptop on the couch beside him. "Tell me about this woman of yours," she said. It felt to him like some time had passed. The daylight in the room had changed. He was sitting up on the couch, still shirtless. "I want to know about her," Carmen told him as she went to a side table and poured herself a glass of wine.

"She's a doctor, a psychologist," he replied, unsure of how to answer.

"Do you love her?"

What was happening? Had he fallen asleep? "She's nice enough. She's very smart and doesn't like to let me forget it."

"That isn't what I asked. Tell me the complete truth."

"Not really," he admitted after pausing to reflect. "She... well, she isn't like you."

"Ella doesn't deserve you," said the woman, leaning against her desk and sipping her wine as she eyed him critically.

Something twinged at the back of his memory. "I never told you her name," he said. His guard was up by this time, but there was something else he was missing. Why had he been wearing that VR headset?

"No, you never did," Carmen answered. "But I know her name because Ella is very dear to me. She doesn't know my middle name, Carmen, she only knows me by my first name, Sophia." Paxton felt his heart sink into his stomach. However, that feeling, like several before it, vanished quickly. She was one of Ella's closest personal friends, the one he had heard so much about. "Did you tell her about meeting me?"

"No," the man answered, misery trying to rise, but being suppressed every time by a resignation he could not account for.

"Of course you didn't," she said with a sardonic grin. "And just so you do not confuse my meaning," she said as she put her wineglass on the desk and walked toward him, "when I say that Ella doesn't deserve you, I mean that a magnificent, powerful, kind, marvelously intelligent goddess of a woman like Ella Pendelton deserves so much better than an untalented, unlettered, unfaithful, unappreciative fucker like you!" Paxton felt the heat of anger well up within him, but then it too dissipated. "Yes?" said Sophia, standing before him. "Something wrong?"

"No," he answered, feeling a look of confusion pass across his face. It was true; he had been unfaithful to a woman who loved him, and he had lied to her. "You're right, she deserves better."

"Of course," Sophia said, walking back to the desk and sitting on it after taking up her glass of wine again. She crossed her legs. "But that isn't your concern right now. Come here." Paxton stood and took one step in her direction. "Stop!" Sophia shouted. "Get down on your hands and knees and crawl over here." Paxton winced, but after a second of hesitation, he got down on all fours and crawled across the office floor to her. He reached her, and when he moved to stand, Sophia said, "Stay!" She stood such that he was on his hands and knees in front of her. "Get into a kneeling position." He dutifully rose up onto his knees. She ran her fingers through his thick, ash-brown hair. "Just so you know, Ella is mine. She and I will be together very soon and there is absolutely nothing you can do about it. What do you think of that? Is that fine with you?"

"Y-yes. It's fine with me," he stammered.

"I'm not ready to take her away from you yet, so you get to play house with her a little while longer. However, you're going to treat her like a queen until I'm ready. You will not ever be able to cheat on her--again--or do anything else that might hurt her. I am going to see to it that you do everything in your power to make her happy until the day comes that I am ready for her. And then, *you* will be tossed out on the street like the fucking garbage that you are." Sophia stared into his eyes, Paxton knowing she could see the turmoil taking place behind them. "Anything to say?"

"What did you do to me?"

"Not as much as I'm going to do, which is still far less than you deserve," she said, walking around him as he knelt on the floor. "Not to worry, though. You won't remember any of this. I stopped you at half of what it will take to condition you fully. We aren't done with that yet. I wanted you to be able to feel some modicum of remorse while a measure of your shit character was still intact. If you had been loyal to Ella instead of being so ready and willing to fuck me, this would have worked out a lot better for you. Also, I'm still somewhat new to this, so any feedback you have for me now would be highly appreciated. Come now, be honest, what are you feeling right now? Anger, fear, confusion?"

Paxton furrowed his brow. What was he feeling? Any of those things? "A little confused, but just a little."

Sophia continued to pace a circle around him. "You still have a touch of resistance left in you, but not enough to act on. I told you to crawl across the floor and you hesitated, but you obeyed. Now you are kneeling here because I told you to. Why?"

He struggled to put his thoughts and emotions into words. "Because I want," he began, but paused to select another word, "because I *need* to do what you tell me."

"Any why is that?" she asked.

"Because you control me," he answered, giving her the answer that had been embedded into his sub-conscience by the Tungsten program.

"How does that make you feel?" she asked.

"Good," he answered. "It feels good. It makes me whole. It's why I exist."

"You've been very helpful. You need another 30 minutes, but we'll make it an hour to be on the safe side. You won't remember me or ever having met me before. You will forget all of this and your afternoon will be replaced with a memory of an excellent meeting with your new client, Brandon Holdshire. You will forget who controls you. You will forget until I tell you to remember."

Paxton returned to the present as Stuart stood up from searching Ari's body for the key ring Sophia claimed held a memory stick. "He doesn't have any keys."

"Paxton," Sophia said, "shoot anyone you need to shoot to help me escape."

Without a second of hesitation, Paxton pointed his gun at Marcus and fired. Marcus tried to dodge and simultaneously raise his weapon at this new attacker, but the bullet from Paxton's gun ripped through his side and he fell to the floor, pressing a hand over his ribs. Paxton swung his empty hand in a back fist as Ella cried out his name. His blow caught her across the cheekbone and she fell backwards into the stools in front of the bar. Sophia sprang to her feet and ran to the sliding glass door to the rooftop as Lori ran from the lounge and into the hall. Stuart had ducked behind one of the easy chairs as Paxton fired at him. Seeing the open door to the roof, Stuart sprang from behind his cover in an effort to reach it. Paxton aimed and fired as Stuart bolted in a crouched run before the sliding door had a chance to close. The shot missed his head by inches and struck the wall beyond.

The instant Stuart stepped into the night air, he knew he would soon be dead. The main deck was wide, long, and well-lit with nothing but some spindly patio furnishings for cover. So he ran harder, chasing Sophia down before she could reach the steps to the raised helipad at the far end of the deck. If he could reach her before Paxton put a bullet in his back, maybe the man would think twice about taking the shot at all. He reached her halfway to the helipad and grabbed one of her arms. He planted his feet and yanked her to a stop. Stuart had heard stories about the strength of the insane, but had never given them any credence until he had to use Sophia as a body shield. Unfortunately, if he knocked her unconscious, she could not tell Paxton to stand down.

She fought him with the strength of a man far larger than she, and when he managed to wrap his arms around her, pinning her arms to her sides, she reverse head-butted him. His glasses were knocked from his face, but out of the corner of his eye, he caught a glimpse of Paxton approaching quickly, gun raised. It was like wrestling a tiger. He squeezed tighter and lifted her off of the ground, managing to keep her between himself and the approaching gunman.

Oddly, Sophia stopped struggling. "Enough," she rasped. Stuart was crushing her rib cage and she could not breathe. She did not resist as Stuart put her down and gripped one wrist. He pinned one of her arms behind her back as he had before, but this time holding a fist full of her thick hair with his other hand. He held her at arm's length to prevent her from clawing at his face or kicking a heel to his groin. Paxton would surely shoot him dead if he lost hold of her. "I give up!" she said.

"Tell that to him!" shouted Stuart, shaking her in a way that he knew was painful enough to make his point.

"Paxton," she said, "put the gun down on the ground." Paxon lowered the weapon and set it on the pavement at his feet, showing his other hand empty as he did so.

Paxton was about fifteen feet away as near as Stuart could tell, but the man knew how to shoot and Stuart wasn't taking any chances. "Tell him to step away from it! Now!" he growled, shaking her and tightening his grip on her wrist, not caring if he broke it.

"Paxton," Sophia said, "I need you to walk over there to the edge of the rooftop and jump off."

Paxton walked swiftly toward the low parapet wall at the edge of the rooftop deck. Stuart heard Ella scream from somewhere out of his range of sight. Paxton reached the parapet and, stepping atop it, was tackled by Stuart, who ran in from the side, placing one foot on the parapet to propel himself forward as he caught the suicidal man around the waist and fell with him back onto the rooftop. Paxton moved to scramble to his feet, but Stuart grappled with him. Stuart was no wrestler, but he knew enough to deal with an untrained fighter, even one so much larger than himself. He twisted and wrapped his legs around Paxton's torso, locking an arm around the man's neck. He squeezed as he rolled onto his back, keeping the struggling man on top of him. Paxton pulled at his arm, but Stuart tightened the hold, cutting off Paxton's breathing and the blood flow to his brain for the several seconds it took for the man to go slack in his grasp.

Stuart loosened his grip and rolled the unconscious Paxton face-down onto the paving. He expected to hear the sound of a helicopter starting up, but it never came. He put a hand on the parapet to help himself stand, but found he was staring into the barrel of a gun. Sophia had picked up the gun and, instead of escaping, she stood by and waited to look him in the eye as she ended his life with a clear shot.

A gunshot cracked out over the deck and Sophia's body jerked weirdly as her arm flew outward. She fell back, stumbling over the parapet. Stuart would later try to understand what impulse made him throw his hand out to catch her from going over. Maybe he did not want a falling body to kill an innocent person on the street below. He could not have known there was a second rooftop corner patio four floors down. Was she already dead from the gunshot? He could not tell where the bullet hit her and he would never find out. Perhaps it was reflex, the way one might catch a dinner plate that is sliding off of a countertop. He did not want to see someone die in that way, and that was enough. Regardless of whatever it was that made him reach out to grab her as she was falling, his fingertips merely grazed the sleeve of her jacket. He leaned over the parapet as she fell out of his reach, and then out of his range of vision. He could only vaguely make out the illuminated patio four stories below to which she fell.

A figure approached Stuart. When it got close, he saw that it was Marcus. He was holding his hand against his side and his yellow shirt was dark on that side of his body, but he was walking unassisted. He would live. In Marcus' other hand, he held a gun. It was Ari's gun that Paxton had handed him.

CHAPTER SIXTY-ONE

THE WILL

Ella's office phone rang as she was showing a patient out. She did not have time to answer before it went to voicemail. Back at her desk, she played the message on speaker phone and listened intently as the man's voice said, "Hello, Doctor Pendelton. My name is Simon Aires. I'm the attorney of the late Doctor Sophia Rubinstein. I don't know if you remember me, but we met in passing at her penthouse this month. I'm calling because you have been named as one of the beneficiaries in her will. If you would, please give me a call back as I would like to arrange a meeting..."

Ella had stopped listening and missed the callback number he had given her at the end of it.

Ella entered the office of Attorney Simon Aires on the 19th floor of the Boston skyscraper. She walked into a cushion of silence as she crossed the waiting area to the receptionist's desk. The red-haired girl smiled brightly, exuding an easy confidence that spoke of a shrewd professional. Ella gave her name and was told that Mr. Aires would be with her momentarily. She seated herself in one of the plush chairs in the waiting area she had passed through. The dark woods and soft lighting gave the office a warm atmosphere, which smelled of new carpeting and furniture polish.

The receptionist returned a minute later and invited Ella into a corner conference room with a magnificent view of downtown Boston. She asked Ella if she could bring her a cup of coffee or tea, which Ella declined. When she departed, Ella waited and took in the view of the city from her seat at the conference room table. It seemed a lifetime ago that such a view would have terrified her. Simon Aires entered, carrying folders tucked under his arm.

After a few words of preliminary greeting, they sat at the table as the attorney said, "I know this must come as something of a surprise, given the circumstances of Doctor Rubinstein's death."

"To say the least," Ella told him.

"If I may, doctor," he began.

"Please, call me Ella."

"Thank you. Simon, if you will," he said with a gracious smile that Ella felt suited the older gentleman. "The day that we met at her penthouse was the day that she included you in her will. I realize now the significance of the timing and urgency for the change. If I had any idea that she was in any way unbalanced..." he trailed off.

"There was far more to her story than most people know. She was not entirely to be blamed for the path she went down," Ella said, unsure how much the man knew of what his client had done. The story never made it into any news outlets; Marcus and the FBI saw to that. Whatever Simon had heard must have come from unofficial channels.

"I'm very glad to hear that much," he said. "I considered her a dear friend and always found her to be such a lovely woman." He opened one of the folders in front of him. "Well, this will not take long. There are three things she wanted to bequeath to you. First, a portion of her liquid assets in the sum of one hundred thirty million dollars," he said, remaining stoic, but still not able to hide the fact that he expected some kind of reaction.

Ella's eyes widened. "What?" was all she could say.

The attorney nodded with a twinkle in his eye. He repeated the sum as he opened another folder. "The second item is one of her properties, a two story building located in the historic district of Salem. There is a stipulation that not only the building, but all of its contents become your exclusive property at the time that you assume possession. Are you familiar with the property in question?"

"Yes," Ella answered, wondering if he knew that building contained a BDSM dungeon. Aires opened a third and final folder, taking his time in doing so to give her a moment to absorb the news.

"There is one last thing," said the attorney, pulling a small yellow envelope from inside the folder. "This is the key to a safe deposit box, the contents of which are also yours."

Ella stood alone in the vault, hesitant about opening the large safe deposit box that now rested on the table in front of her. With everything that Sophia had left her, what could this one box contain that could have been of any importance? She slowly opened the lid as if it might be wired to explode.

Inside the box she found four items. The first was a felt bag that contained another Tungsten headset and cables. The dark, silver plastic object filled Ella with revulsion when she thought of what it had done to Paxton. How much trouble would she be in if the Tellerson Foundation found out that she possessed this?

The second item was a metal case that contained four glass cylinders nested in protective foam rubber. The labels on the glass told her they were all samples of S-24, but two were a clear liquid while the other two were a dark, crystalline substance like burned rock salt. She closed the case and put it with the Tungsten in the backpack she had brought with her.

She then removed the third item, an external USB hard drive. This, Ella supposed, contained the software drivers to run the Tungsten from a laptop. Then a thought occurred to her. Could it possibly contain all the data archives that Sophia had stolen from the Foundation? Sophia had the whole of the following day to make a copy and get into the bank. She could check when the box was last accessed, but what did it matter? She would know soon enough.

The last and most singular item she took from the box was a brown leather book, which was in fact a three-ring binder. Opening the soft leather cover, Ella found herself looking at the title page of a printed manuscript without a byline.

ON THE MEHODS
AND PRACTICAL APPLICATION
OF HYPNOSIS, MIND CONTROL,
AND MANIPULATION

There was a hand-written passage on the bottom half of the page that read, "I have outlined herein the tools and techniques to which I have found the brain to be most responsive, and therefore the mind most susceptible. Usage of these in combination facilitate various means of achieving acute permanence of suggestion."

CHAPTER SIXTY-TWO

ELLA AND MARCUS

Ella received the text message as she was preparing to leave her office for the final time. Pausing long enough to reply to the text and give her former work space a last look, she turned off the light and walked the short distance down the hall to the building entrance. When she opened the door, there was a stretch limousine parked at the curb. The window rolled down as she approached. Marcus Harrier sat at the window.

"Will you ride with me, doctor?" he asked. "I haven't had the chance to talk with you as soon as I would have liked. I can take you wherever you're headed." The smooth English accent of his was as polished and classy as the car he rode in.

"I'm going to the police station to talk with Detective Connelly. It's only a few blocks away. We won't get many more days like this for a while; will you walk with me?"

Why she expected the man to balk at leaving the comfort of his limo to walk a few blocks of the city streets in her company, she was not sure, but was inwardly pleased when he gave her a smile and said, "Oh, lovely! Even better," hurriedly taking up his long coat and scarf. After some quick instructions to his driver, he stepped out onto the sidewalk, and donned his coat after tying his scarf. She smiled at his little shiver at the temperature that was, to her, unusually mild for a sunny Halloween in Boston.

"I'm not sure how you did it, but the FBI is satisfied with

the much simpler version of the story you gave them of what happened on the rooftop that night. Connelly has been dying to know the details."

"Ah, that," said Marcus. "I met the detective. He seems like a good man, but the complete truth is far above his pay grade, I'm afraid."

"Can I ask you a very impertinent question?"

Marcus peered at her. "Given what we've been through, I think we might consider ourselves intimately acquainted, don't you?"

"Candice, Sophia's daughter, were you her father?" Ella asked delicately.

"I wanted to be," he answered after a long hesitation.

"That isn't really an answer," she told him.

Marcus sighed, looking grieved. "It's the only answer I have to give you, doctor."

"Please, call me Ella."

"Ella it is. Call me Marcus." They walked in silence for several more steps when he asked, "How's Paxton?"

Ella considered telling him that they were no longer together, but decided to stick to answering his question. "He's shaken, but not afraid to talk about it. I used conventional hypnosis therapy to restore his memory and to help him distinguish between his own memories and the imprinting she imposed with that Tungsten. He's fine. Please, if you do nothing else, destroy that evil thing."

"I cannot do that. However, it was the software program Sophia created to drive it that made the device work. How and why the software driving the retinal imaging lasers had the impact on the brain that they did is a secret Sophia never shared. Without that, the device is nothing more than a modified VR device. Now that we know it works, we are reopening the program and trying to convince her former team of developers to return and try to re-engineer her program. If we are successful, I will make it available to you if you would like to undo the damage that she did to Paxton."

"The last thing I want is to use that thing on him again."
The offer pained her because he was genuinely trying to help.
As for Paxton, he had moved out the same week, claiming that
he could not live with her knowing what he had done to her. It
was a lie. She did not call him on it, but accepted his excuses. As
far as she was concerned, trying to move forward and rebuild
their relationship was more of an effort than she was willing to
invest. She never felt the need to tell him the truth that Sophia
had extracted from her while she was under the influence of the
S-24.

"It may come as no surprise that how she made it work
has some of the brightest minds in the country scratching their
heads. She was far ahead of her time, it seems. You are the
only living person ever to see it used outside of a lab. Even its
two remaining developers have not had that experience. Vile
as what she did to Paxton was, that device has far too many
beneficial uses for us to abandon it. Surely you realize that."

"I do. It can't be un-invented and we've seen what it can do
in the hands of the wrong person," she told him, wondering
what he would say if he knew she had a working model in her
possession. Based on what he was telling her, she was the only
person in the world with a working copy of the device. She
would do what she could to see that it was never used.

"I'm happy you realize that. How did Paxton react to the
news of your newfound situation?"

Ella winced at the question. "I haven't told him," she
answered. Marcus said nothing, but looked at her expectantly.
"I should tell you, we're no longer together. He moved out.
Some things happened that were a little too much for us to get
past."

"Oh, I see," said Marcus, looking embarrassed. "Forgive
me."

"It's fine. It was inevitable."

He gave the conversation a pause before changing the
subject. "It sounds callous of me to observe, but with so much
wealth, it rather makes one wonder why Sophia didn't simply

hire a killer instead of going about it in the way that she did."

"If any man had done something like that to my daughter, I wouldn't settle for letting somebody else pull the trigger. Would you?"

Marcus looked surprised at her answer, but then laughed lightly in appreciation of her candor. He shook his head. "No, I don't imagine I would," he admitted. "May I ask you an impertinent question of my own?"

"Maybe my answer will not be as cryptic."

"Did she leave you anything else of interest? Anything of a personal nature?"

Ella recalled the day she visited the bank. "Nothing other than the property in Salem. I am the new proud owner of a BDSM dungeon."

Marcus looked embarrassed a second time. "No laptop or hard drive, by any chance?" he asked hopefully.

"No. I promise I'll give it to you if I find it. I've only been to the building once since and I didn't find anything like that,"

"You were not quite yourself at the time, so you may not recall this from the video, but when Sophia killed Perry Tellerson at The Church, she first had him download all the archives to an external hard drive."

"What was on it?"

"Everything," said Marcus anxiously. "Everything the Foundation has ever worked on. Her laptop must have held her working copy of the Tungsten software. The software and prototypes we had were hopelessly sabotaged, but the rest of it is on an external drive. The one that none of us can find."

"You had her laptop bag on the rooftop that night. She had it with her."

Marcus shook his head grimly. "That laptop bag contained only project logs. Something important enough in themselves, but not the electronic files she took. The information in our archives contained some technological marvels. Experimental drugs that have not been submitted for FDA approval. Those are only the things we don't want to bury. There were some things even worse than the Tungsten that were never meant to see the light of day."

"Worse?" said Ella in disbelief.

"I'm afraid so. We have searched everywhere--the yacht, the helicopter, and the penthouse. Nothing."

Ella stopped walking and Marcus took a few steps before he stopped and turned to her. "Oh, my god," she said.

"What is it?"

"Lori," said Ella. "She disappeared when the shooting started. But you traced the position of every person who had been there when we reconstructed our story for the FBI. You did that for every person but one!"

Marcus considered that. "She said she ran and hid at the freight elevator. Stuart told her that was the only way down."

"Yes!" said Ella. "But that doesn't mean she couldn't have come back into the room when we were all out on the rooftop. She could have been in there when we were outside."

"But everything was there."

"You're assuming someone would grab the laptop bag and make off with it. That would be noticed. But you never opened the bags before that. If she opened it and found a laptop and hard drive, she could take the computer and drive, leave the books, and close the bag again. You would think the books were all it ever contained. Do you recall what you said after you watched the video? You looked at the bags and asked Sophia if those were what you thought they were, meaning everything she had taken. So Lori then knew what was in them."

"That would have to mean she ran into a room with three dead men on the floor, took a laptop and/or a hard drive from the bag, closed it again, and hid the items somewhere so she could take them with her when she left." Marcus rubbed his chin, failing to hide his shock. "Oh, good god alive," he muttered. "What sort of person has the wits and gall to do something like that? I never would have even guessed."

"The same way I didn't," said Ella. "We were a little overwhelmed by everything else. I was so blinded by my love for Sophia that even I, a psychologist, couldn't see the signs of a dissociative disorder."

Marcus peered at her sideways. "You really loved her?" he asked. Ella opened her mouth to answer, but closed it again and nodded. "For what it's worth, so did I. God, that woman was stone-cold brilliant. Of course I loved her. It was losing Candice that changed her, you know. She was never the same after that, but even I would never have guessed she was barking. Please forgive the layman's term." Ella smiled cordially.

The pair arrived at the police station and stopped before the door. "Give my regards to the detective. Thank you, Ella. I will be paying Miss Mercer a visit," he said.

"You aren't going to hurt her, are you?" Ella asked.

"I am not my predecessor," said Marcus with a laugh. "The Tellerson Foundation is soon to become the Harrier Foundation. It will be a noble institution on my watch, which brings me to the reason I wanted to talk with you. I want to sponsor you for membership to the board."

"Membership? You want me to join the Foundation?"

"You can do a lot of good, and the Foundation needs all the good people it can have on the board, especially right now. I have appointed a new head of technology already."

"I don't know anything about..."

"That's alright," he interrupted. "Of course you would have to know what you're signing on for. I will call you in two weeks when I get back to Boston. I can introduce you to the other new board members and show you all you would need to know to make a decision then. I promise you will not regret it."

"Thank you," said Ella, amiably, "I will be honored."

CHAPTER SIXTY-THREE

STUART AND LORI

Stuart entered The Green Leaf. It was Halloween night, and they had chosen to attend a party in Salem as Phantom of the Opera and Christine. Stuart wore a white tuxedo shirt with a black bow tie and black vest. Black slacks with polished dress shoes and a wide-brimmed hat of black felt completed the bulk of his costume. As these items were real and fitted for him; the only costume elements he needed were white gloves, an opera cape, and, of course, the white plastic mask of Phantom.

Lori gave him a round of applause when he entered the shop. "That's perfect!" she complimented, touching the fabric of his cape. "What about your glasses?"

Stuart had been saving that piece of information. "I finally got contacts."

"Better late than never, huh?"

"The jury's still out on that." Lori locked the front door and turned off the illuminated sign in front of the shop before going to the back to change into her costume. After some time, she returned from the back room in her costume of Christine. She wore an ankle length white gown with a black bodice and velvet sleeves. She swung a long hooded cloak of black velvet around her and tied it at her neck. "Wow. You look stunning."

"Thank you," she said with a curtsy. "I'll do my makeup on the drive."

"I have to admit, I expected..."

Lori looked at herself. "What?" she asked, a look of concern on her face.

"I thought you might decide to do a kinky Christine."

Lori smirked, "I'm a dominatrix; I don't need Halloween to slut it up. Besides, Christine is Victorian, polyamorous, and goth. I say that's Kinky enough."

They drove to the party venue in Salem. Lori applied her makeup while Stuart thought about the discussion the two of them had the day before. True to her word, she explained everything, and the day left him with no small amount of things to think about.

They sat at the table in her dining room and talked over tea as Lori explained what had happened between her and Rylen.

"Stuart, I never even knew Rylen was dead until Perry came to see me. I trusted Sophia. We knew each other for a better part of this year. She taught me a lot about hypnosis that, as good as I was, I would never have learned on my own. You think I'm good? She was a lot better than I am, and I had the S-24, but she didn't know about that at first. She and Rylen knew and hated each other, but I never knew why. I'm so sorry, Stuart, I had no idea what she really meant to do. I would never kill anybody! You must know that by now," Lori said, tears coming to her eyes that she forced back.

Stuart buried his face in his hands over the table and after some seconds, leaned back in his chair with his eyes still closed. "The night I was last here, I had just found out what kind of man my brother really was."

"Sophia never warned me that he could be dangerous. He invited me to this black tie function at an art gallery and I accepted. Afterward, I invited him to come home with me. This is where I did it. I slipped some S-24 in his drink and hypnotized him with the trigger that she would use later. My god. I actually had him in my home and..."

"Fucked him?"

"I didn't have to. I drugged him, like I said." She stood up. "I said I would explain everything, so I'll start at the beginning."

Lori led Stuart into her kitchen. She went to a door on the far side and punched a number into a keypad beside it. It looked like a regular wooden door, but when Lori went down the stairs and asked him to pull it shut behind him, he found it was made of steel that was scored and painted to match every other door in the house. When it shut, automatic bolts locked it in place.

At the bottom of the stairs, Stuart stopped and gaped when Lori flipped a light switch. He found himself in a first-rate modern chemical lab. There was a large central counter that stretched nearly the length of the basement and wrapped around the edge of the room, broken occasionally by a glass-door freezer or refrigerator. One wall had a rack holding several aquarium tanks with live plants growing inside them. The lab was loaded with every piece of equipment one could imagine. The center counter was overburdened and cluttered with a computer, microscope, and countless other implements. It was white and pristine, especially compared to any basement he had ever seen. Only the wheeled desk chair at the center counter and the black large screen monitor provided some contrast against the white of the tile floor and painted block walls.

"Welcome to my lab," she said, a tone of pride in her voice as Stuart took it all in. "I'm a chemist; this is where I developed S-24, the drug you drank in your tea that night."

"I forgot you have a degree in biochemistry."

"You really did some homework, huh?"

"Actually, Spider did the homework. I just read the information he found about you." The memory of Spider saddened him. Even though he only knew the man briefly, he could not help but feel they surely would have become friends.

"Yes, I do." Lori went to one of the tanks and opened it as she took up a pair of pruning shears from the shelf. She snipped a single leaf from the plant growing in the tank and using the shears like tweezers, she held it out the leaf for Stuart to see.

"Look familiar?" she asked.

He looked at it closely. "It's the same as the one in the photo."

"It's a stinging nettle. This is the plant leaf I based my tea shop's logo on, though no one has guessed it yet."

"A stinging nettle? That's a weed."

"So are dandelions, but they both make an excellent tea," she said. "It's a nice-looking leaf, but you wouldn't want to get it on you. It's poisonous. Tea is brewed from the leaves before the plant is mature and dangerous to the touch." She threw the leaf away and returned the sheers to the shelf. "Have you ever heard of Devil's Breath?" She went to a safe under one of the counters and rotated the dial. A safe was a queer feature to have in a chem lab, but made sense in an illegal one.

"No, I haven't," he replied, putting his eyes to the microscope, but seeing nothing.

She showed him a capped glass cylinder that held a few ounces of a clear liquid. "This is S-24 in liquid form." She handed him a plastic container of what looked like chunks of crushed smoky quartz. "I created a new chemical compound based on the psychotropic properties of Devil's Breath, which is a drug called Scopolamine or Hyoscine. It's normally used to treat motion sickness in small doses. In higher doses, it can be used as a date rape drug. Under its influence, someone can be made to do anything they're told and will have no memory of it after. But it's highly toxic. This," she said, showing him a third plastic canister containing about two cups of a white powder that looked like baking soda, "is Scopolamine in its pure form. I don't know what the street value of this much would be, but well over three hundred thousand."

"Jesus," said Stuart, looking at the powder in the container.

"It's easy to overdose on it. People die using this in the wrong way."

"Please tell me you didn't slip that in my tea."

"No, it was the S-24. It's a completely different chemical formula. I called it that because I went through twenty-four variations before finding one that was both effective and completely safe. You never asked why I chose the name *Crystal Dark* as my alter ego."

Stuart looked at the container holding the cloudy S-24 crystals. "Oh, very cute," he said sarcastically, though the name sounded much less laughable in that light.

"Yeah, anyway, it isn't toxic, it doesn't last very long, and there's no memory loss. You could drink that entire vial and it wouldn't do much more than the dose I put in your tea that day, except last a while longer. There are people who would kill to get that formula."

"Sophia?"

Lori nodded. "I sold her the formula."

"Why would you do that? You could have made a fortune."

Lori looked at him as though he were a dim-witted child. She returned the S-24 sample and Scopolamine to the safe. "You really think so? Damn, why didn't I think of that?"

"Sophia was right."

"Yes, she was," she said, shutting the safe. "I can't exactly apply for a patent on a drug I developed in my illegal drug lab. The lab isn't illegal, but what I do with it is. Just smuggling Scopolamine in that quantity into this country is a felony. Not to mention that I used it on my massage clients without their knowing it."

"You really did that?"

She went to the end of the counter and took up a plastic bottle and handed it to Stuart. "The massage oil I use is infused with S-24."

Stuart looked at the bottle in his hand. "You used a drug that you made yourself on your massage clients?"

Lori folded her arms. "Only a couple of them died and it looked like natural causes." Stuart stared at her in revulsion. "I'm kidding!"

"This isn't funny."

"I know, but the look on your face... I said it's safe and it is. I tested it on myself many times long before I ever used it on anyone else. It takes time to be absorbed cutaneously, and then takes time to wear off, but a little over an hour is just enough time to use it that way. Think about it, I have it on my hands all day. You can't give a massage with gloves on."

"Why aren't you affected by it?"

"They have it covering their entire bodies. It's only on my hands. That isn't enough of a surface area for it to have any effect. I line up four or five clients a day on Fridays."

"And nobody ever caught on?"

"Not yet," she said. "There are no side effects, grogginess, or memory loss. A little dehydration, but I have bottles of water handy. They get an excellent massage and feel compelled to leave me an absurdly large tip afterward, which they can all afford. They feel better and so I. And I keep coming back."

"You offered to take me on as a client."

"Yes, I did." There was a long pause between them. "What can I say, that you were the real thing from the start? Look, you called and asked me out to dinner and I decided that I liked you. I wasn't going to do anything to you after that. Before you get on your high horse, try to remember that you only asked me out to investigate me."

Stuart did not know what to think. "I'm no moral exemplar," he said, putting the bottle on the counter, "and I'm not about to judge you. Why did you ask me if I knew who your father is?"

"I'm half Colombian and my father is a major player in the drug trade there."

"Your father really is a Colombian drug lord?" Stuart asked in disbelief.

"I never heard that term growing up, but yes, he's one of the largest producers. He's powerful enough that his rivals would love to know about me. I have only met with him in person twice in the last three years, but we stay in touch though Skype. He almost lost his mind when I told him I was nearly taken on the street. For my own sake, he doesn't want me to get too close to him, but he would love nothing better than for us to have a normal relationship. He wants to retire altogether, and he will.

In two more years, his protege will take over. But I digress."

"What happened with Sophia and Rylen?"

"Rylen started coming to the dungeon before that. He was a regular and I took him on as a client. We had a couple sessions together, but he started wanting more. He wanted to date or be a couple. He was a pain, but it was never to the point of my banning him from my demonstrations.

"She supposedly worked for the company that bought the building the dungeon is in. It would be renovating the upper floor. She was into BDSM and loved the dungeon in the building. She said she would personally see to it that it stayed open and that the work would not interfere with its ordinary operation. She even got the rent cut in half for the duration of the work. That was how we met, but she never came for demos or open nights. Sophia and I used it for private sessions, and when she found I had an interest in hypnosis, she offered to teach me everything she knew. We came to be solid friends, or so I thought. She eventually worked out a deal to buy the dungeon from Carol, the previous owner. I didn't tell her about the drug I was working on. I kept that to myself at first, but I did confide in her about some of my less ethical uses for hypnosis.

"That was when she came to me and presented me with the idea of hypnotizing Rylen for her. She wanted me to install a trance trigger that would drop him into a trance without fail, no matter what. Her plan was to make him forget the enmity between them. It was supposed to be so that she could take him for a lot of money. She paid me thirty thousand to pull it off. I didn't know it at the time, but money was the last thing she cared about. She still didn't know about the S-24. I got Rylen to ask me out and accepted his invitation to go out one night. He had been trying to get me to go out with him for months, but I refused. I just had no interest in him."

"You weren't even a little tempted?" Stuart felt he had to ask.

Lori smiled. "You really find that so hard to believe?"

"To be honest, yeah, I kind of do."

"You can believe it or not, that's up to you. But when it comes to personal relationships," she gave him a knowing smile, "I only go for the nice ones. When it comes to hustling, Rylen fit my target profile, but he gave me the creeps. After the first couple play sessions, I wouldn't have him as a client anymore. Not as a BDSM client, or anything else. The sessions we had were enough for me to know I didn't want him around at all." Stuart nodded, though he remained skeptical. "Anyway, he came back here with me and I gave him a drink with a dose of S-24. I hypnotized him and installed a trance trigger phrase that would put him into trance. When hypnosis is used in conjunction with the drug, hypnotic suggestions become far more powerful in effect and duration. I then had him unlock his phone so that I could install a spyware program she gave me. When that was done, I made him forget all about me and everything that happened to him that night. He had become annoyed at my refusing him all the time, and he was the kind of guy who didn't brook rejection by a woman very well."

"If you only knew."

"It worked perfectly. We did all of it here in the living room and he awoke right there on the couch. He was confused and didn't know where he was, but thought he'd just had too much to drink. He pretended to know me, but it was obvious he didn't. I offered him some tea before he left, but he refused and made his excuses before he walked out. After he was gone, I called Sophia and told her it had worked. I forgot to delete my phone number from his phone, but she said she would take care of it. I never heard from him again, so assumed it was a complete success.

"I saw Sophia a couple days later and she said she had not tried to call him yet, but would soon. The only thing was, she knew I had a secret I hadn't told her about. She was too good a hypnotist to think it was a simple suggestion that I used on my massage clients. I didn't know it at the time, but in a way, she was admitting to killing him. You cannot hypnotize someone into harming themselves. They will not knowingly injure themselves while in trance; making someone fall asleep behind the wheel of a moving car is the equivalent of suicide. She found the potency of my method a little too potent. Also, I was a little too confident that I could pull it off. She was a better hypnotist and she knew its limitations. That was when I told her about the S-24; I showed her everything I just showed you.

"She wanted it in a really bad way. Wanted to buy it from me. She wanted to buy the formula, not the drug alone. I refused. It was only then that I learned how rich she really was, which explained why she never had me at her home. She offered me six figures, but I still refused. Finally, she said she could pay off my mortgage and this house would be mine, free and clear. It was then that I accepted."

"She bought you this house?"

"No, I bought the house and was living here, but she did a debt removal in exchange," said Lori.

"Debt removal?"

"Yes. There are a lot of ways of transferring value. If I want to buy something of yours for a lot of money and we don't want it to be so obvious for tax purposes, I don't write a check or just show up with a suitcase full of cash and hand it to you. That would work, but you don't want to deposit either in your bank account. One way is to remove debt that someone already has. She set up a finance subsidiary of an LLC she already had. I refinanced my house through it for a lower interest rate so it looked legit. It was legit, to a point. That made her the legal holder of my mortgage. Then, she declared the mortgage paid and reported it to all the credit bureaus and gave me the deed. And the crazy thing is, it's legal, it just can't be traced back to her and I don't look like I came into a ton of cash I have to explain to the IRS. Better yet, I don't actually have cash that I need to stash away somewhere. The whole thing was done in less than two weeks. I got the deed to the house and turned over the formula just a day or two before Perry showed up at my shop. That was when I learned that Rylen was dead and who you really were.

"I gave her the formula, the process, my research notes, samples... everything. The company that she used to do all of this was the same one that she claimed to be working for. The same company that's renovating the building that our dungeon is in. She was telling the truth. All of this was to get to him. She knew he frequented the dungeon, and she wanted him so badly that she bought the whole fucking building. I feel ridiculous saying this, but for my part in this, I really am sorry, Stuart. She manipulated me like she did everyone else."

The two returned to her living room and sat on the couch, finding there was increasingly little else to say. A question occurred to Stuart. "You found out how rich she was when she bought the formula. Didn't it seem odd that she would want to scam a guy who had less money than she did?"

"Yes, and I even asked her that," Lori answered, "and she asked me how I thought she made all of her money to begin with. How could I argue with that?" He leaned back and sighed before Lori said, "Stuart, I want you to listen to what I am about to tell you and think about it before you answer."

"I'm listening."

"If you wished you didn't know any of this, and you wanted to start fresh," she said with a hint of guilty sheepishness, "I could... make you forget all about it."

"Forget about what?"

She pointed to herself. "Everything I just told you about me. What I am. Ignorance really can be bliss. I promised I would tell you everything and I have. But if you wanted to, we could start all over."

"That sounds like something Sophia would do."

"Ouch. It isn't. You have a choice. She would never give someone a choice. Try to keep an open mind, here. I am just saying that the option is there if you ever want it."

"No," he answered. "There is something you should know about me. I always want the truth, no matter how ugly it might turn out to be. That was why I kept going, trying to find out what happened to Rylen. Even though it almost got me killed,

I would do it again."

It was after one o'clock in the morning when Stuart and Lori left the party. They walked through the Salem streets as wind tugged at their costumes. "It's so great that Halloween fell on a Saturday this year," she observed, taking his arm as they turned a corner and made their way along Essex Street. "Are you okay to drive?"

"No, that punch snuck up on me like a mugger. You couldn't taste the alcohol in it."

"I had too much wine to even think about driving."

Stuart took off his phantom mask and deposited it in a trash can on the street before returning his black felt hat to his head. "It's okay. I got us a room at Hawthorne, where we parked."

She took his arm as they continued walking. "We should have this conversation when we're both sober, but I'm dying to know," said Lori as she pulled the hood of her cloak up to guard against the chill breeze at their backs. "I'm not a great person, but I'm not all bad either."

"Are you going to keep hypnotizing your massage clients?"

"No, I'm done with it," she said. "I never planned on doing it forever. I could go to jail."

"I'm relieved to hear it."

"Between massage, the dungeon, and the tea shop, I'm spreading myself too thin. Money won't be any problem for me soon, anyway."

"What does that mean?"

"We'll talk about it tomorrow. My question is, do you think you could be with someone like me?"

"Long term?"

"Yes."

"Exclusive?"

"Not necessarily. That's not really my style," she admitted. "Is that what you want?"

Stuart considered. "I would like to say that I do, but I would need to think about that clear-headed."

"I'm asking because you never gave me an answer to my proposal."

"Your proposal?"

"I asked you to be my submissive. I still want you to be."

Stuart stopped walking and turned to face her. "Honestly, I don't know what that really means in practice."

She leaned forward and kissed him lightly on the lips, her breath tasting of wine and mint. As she withdrew, she slowly lifted the felt hat from his head and donned it over her hood. "It's only in practice that you can know what it really means."

Stuart smiled and put his arm around her as they continued walking down the brick-paved sidewalk.

THE END

www.ingramcontent.com/pod-product-compliance
Lightning Source LLC
Chambersburg PA
CBHW031506210626
46816CB00019B/1553